General from the Jungle

B. Traven

General from
the Jungle

Translated by Desmond Vesey

American Century Series

 HILL ᴀɴᴅ WANG 〰️ Nᴇᴡ Yᴏʀᴋ
A division of Farrar, Straus and Giroux

Published in the United States
by Hill and Wang, a division of
Farrar, Straus and Giroux, Inc.

Library of Congress catalog card number: 72–81292

ISBN (cloth): 0–8090–4904–X

ISBN (paperback): 0–8090–0113–6

First American Century Series edition, 1974

Printed in the United States of America

1 2 3 4 5 6 7 8 9 0

General from the Jungle

1

 "Tierra y Libertad!" With this war cry an army of
Indians marched out of the jungles in the south of
the Republic, in order to overthrow the dictator and secure
land and freedom for themselves.

Simple and short though this slogan was, it rang like a paean
of triumph to the marching men.

Whatever, in their miserable oppression and their pitiful ig-
norance, they sensed of poetry, of a desire for beauty, of love
for mankind and living creatures, of natural faith in some abso-
lute justice that must be found somewhere, as well as deeply
felt sorrow for their comrades who had been horribly murdered or bestially tortured to death—all this, and much
more that, unknown to them, slumbering within them, found
its expression in that single war cry. Even when, one united
mass, impelled by one and the same urge, they raised their
clenched fists in unison as if exhorting God not to forget them,
and with one voice yelled out their solemn slogan to the universe until it echoed like a mighty wave thundering against the
rocks, nevertheless every man in that throng sensed clearly his
own individual cry mingling with the others, for in the depths
of his being he felt it as his very own, his deeply personal
prayer.

Folk songs, jingles, political and patriotic phrases immediately lose their sense and meaning the moment they are soberly
considered and logically thought out. And it could well be

that even this war cry of the Indians, if examined in cold blood, would evaporate into meaningless words.

When their sufferings, their tortures, their deprivations under their masters in the jungles—the mahogany concessionaires and their underlings—grew so intolerable that they and, extraordinarily enough, almost all the others working at that time in the remotest regions of the tropical forests simultaneously came to the realization that it was better and more worthy of their human dignity to perish in a revolution than to live longer under such humiliations and torments, then they took action. They took action firmly and decisively in order to make an end at last—either an end to their own lives, or an end to the lives of their tyrants.

In spite of their sufferings and humiliations, they nevertheless had within themselves a glimmering of an understanding as to their bitter situation. Seeing the birds of the jungle, and even the millions of insects which all, in freedom and joy of living, came and went at will, they never lost the sense of a longing for freedom.

Timid, fainthearted, uncertain at first, then strong and single-minded, they had at last decided on rebellion.

Once begun, things developed far faster than they had ever believed possible.

The owners, managers, and overseers in the *monterías*,* who as a result of their power and their brutality were more feared than Almighty God Himself, shrank in the first two hours of the insurrection, as soon as they saw that every vestige of their authority had collapsed, into helpless, pitiful puppets who suddenly seemed to have forgotten how to speak, how to move, and how to take with dignity their long-earned, well-merited deserts.

In a short fight, all who did not side with the rebelling Indians were destroyed.

By this means the revolutionaries were able to secure some weapons. Not many. About fifty revolvers, not all in good order. About twelve sporting rifles, some of them undepend-

---

* Tropical mahogany forests.

able and hopelessly rusted from the humid-hot climate of the jungle. In addition there were a few light shotguns and ten ancient Spanish muzzle loaders. The plunder in ammunition, not much in itself, was as varied in caliber as were the weapons themselves.

Nonetheless, all the muchachos were excellently armed with machetes, bush knives, axes, and hatchets. With these weapons, with these machetes and axes with which they had daily been compelled to fight the jungles, they were better able to fend for themselves than with automatic rifles.

Of course, in contrast to the modernly equipped federal troops and forces of the *Rurales*, it was absurd to speak of the revolutionary mahogany workers of the jungle as being armed. In the face of the regular troops, their courage, their hatred, their frenzied rage against their oppressors must make up for what they lacked in weapons. Each one of them knew that. And each one of them considered this hatred and rage to be of greater worth to them in battle than a superfluity of ammunition.

Under the dictatorship, no one, apart from the dictator, El Caudillo, was more feared and also more hated than the *Rurales*.

The *Rurales* were a mounted police force, the special weapon of the dictator, who at times was none too sure of the officers of the Federal Army. The *Rurales*, particularly feared by mutinying and striking workers, were an elite troop of men and youths, excellently equipped, superbly drilled, well looked after and well paid. Hundreds of young men had been specially enrolled in the corps on account of their sadistic instincts. For their activities and actions, arrests and executions, their officers were responsible to no judge, only to El Caudillo himself. They were the instrument of terror, by which El Caudillo mercilessly and ruthlessly repressed the slightest resistance or criticism of his authority. When, as happened in several of the textile workers' strikes, the officers of the army refused to undertake—after the suppression of the strike— a bestial slaughter of the now humbled and conquered men and women workers, as ordered by El Caudillo, a troop of *Rurales* was marched at top speed to the region. And there what the army officers had refused to do the *Rurales* carried out with such brutality that in the general massacre no one was spared who had the misfortune to find himself in that quarter of the workers' town which had been cordoned off by the *Rurales*. Workers and non-workers, women, children, old people, the sick—no distinction was made between them. And that happened, not during a strike, but days, often weeks, after the strike had ended, when the workers had returned to the factories and the whole district was entirely quiet. It was the law of retribution and vengeance which the dictator invoked as a warning to all those who disagreed with him as to the benefits of the glorious, golden age which he, El Caudillo, had brought to his people.

An encounter with half a battalion of these *Rurales* while on the march must, according to the honest judgment of any sensible man, mean the certain defeat of the rabble of rebellious jungle workers, and with their annihilation the swift end of the revolution in the jungle regions.

Even though the war cry of the muchachos who had taken upon themselves to overthrow the dictator seemed clear and simple when it was yelled out with full enthusiasm, all of them would have fallen silent had anyone asked them what they really understood by the "Land" and "Liberty" for which they had determined to fight.

Every single one of them bore within himself a different, entirely individual conception of *Tierra y Libertad;* because to each of them "Land" and "Liberty" meant something different, according to his desires, sorrows, circumstances, and hopes.

Many, who had been sold as contract workers in the *monterías*—because of their own debts, or for their fathers' debts, or for non-payment of police fines, or as surety for relatives who had been unable to pay and had died—many of these owned in their native villages a tiny plot of land they loved and would exchange for no other piece of conquered land, even had it been better and richer. For these people the battle cry had apparently no meaning because they already possessed land. But the freedom to exploit it and to enjoy the fruits of their labor in peace and quiet was denied them.

And they were denied freedom from the thousands of corrupt officials of all kinds, great and small, who flourished under the dictatorship in order to guard it and maintain it, and who had to be fattened up so as not to be dangerous to El Caudillo. If it happened that the activities of these officials stank too grossly, they were promptly excused for having acted thus out of overzealousness in the interest of the welfare of the State and in devotion to their beloved El Caudillo.

Whoever was relieved of these parasites could say with justice that he now knew what freedom meant.

For others, *Tierra y Libertad* meant unrestricted freedom to be able to return to their parents, to their wives, their children, their betrothed, their friends and relations, their native villages.

Others again saw in *Tierra y Libertad* the simple right to be allowed to work where they pleased and for whoever treated them well and for a wage which they considered fair.

To the majority of these Indian mahogany workers, who were ninety percent agriculturalists, the conception of *Libertad* was nothing more than the clear, simple wish to be left in peace from everything connected with government, State welfare, increased production, economic development, capture of markets, obedience, duties without rights, docile submission to the national destiny, and whatever other such senseless and idiotic virtues as were pumped into them by the dictatorship in order to bewilder the brains of the common people and prevent them from looking where the roots of all evil flourished.

When they shouted for *Libertad*, the muchachos hoped that after they had won their battle for freedom they would be allowed to lead their lives in their own ways, untroubled by men in whom they could put no trust because they could not understand their needs and sorrows and took no pains to try to understand them, but simply came again and again with forms that had to be filled in for money to be paid. The liberated wanted to be allowed to enjoy alone the results of their heavy labors; and they had no desire to be robbed from a hundred directions of all or a considerable proportion of these products of their labors, for purposes which they could not understand and did not appreciate and which solely served to provide El Caudillo with further opportunities and means to bolster the supremacy of his golden age.

But however unclear in detail the conceptions of land and freedom might be to the rebels, they nevertheless felt instinctively and rightly what they wanted. And what they wanted was: no longer to be dominated, no longer to be commanded. Any wish to share in the great wealth and culture of modern civilization—such as the program of the industrial proletariat in civilized nations always demands—was alien to them. They could not have understood such a desire, even had one attempted to explain it to them for days and weeks. They knew nothing of democracy, socialism, organization. And had anyone suggested that they should demand a seat in Parliament or in the nation's Congress, they would have regarded him who suggested this as a traitor who only wanted to confuse them, and they would doubtless have replied, "What has Parliament and Congress to do with us? We want to be left in peace, damn you; that's all we want. And now get out, you swindlers!"

The vile, disgraceful, and cruel treatment which they and all their class had been compelled to suffer throughout the long years of the dictatorship had fundamentally and thoroughly changed the characters of the rebels.

From peace-loving farmers, woodcutters, charcoal burners, potters, hut weavers, basket-makers, leatherworkers, mat weavers, who wanted nothing else in life than to be allowed to work unhindered, to cultivate their land, to raise their cattle, to bring their wares freely to market, to found families, to have children, to celebrate a feast now and then, and once or twice in the year to make a pilgrimage to the great *ferias* in the state, and then, grown old, to be able to die in peace and quiet surrounded by their good friends and neighbors—from such as these the dictatorship had succeeded in turning them into savage creatures of vengeance, obstinate, eternally mistrustful, quarrelsome, hypocritical, addicted to strong drink. For this reason, and this reason only, these savages thought of nothing else, once the rebellion had begun, than of destroying everything in their path and of mercilessly annihilating all and everyone who wore a uniform or even had a uniform cap on his head, and all those who from position or profession were regarded by them as their tormentors and oppressors.

They had been treated like childish slaves, who might open their mouths only when spoken to. And in the manner of such slaves, whose chains had suddenly broken, they were now behaving.

They had been tortured, beaten, humiliated, struck on the mouth by beasts with human faces. And like beasts they now set forth to ravage the country and to kill everyone who did not belong to their own kind.

When they had one day destroyed and desolated everything that El Caudillo had created from their blood, their sweat, their want, their cares, their tears—the golden age of the Republic—then they would return home, sated with vengeance, back to their houses, villages, settlements, and huts, and from that time on lead a peaceful life.

It was only to be foreseen that the Scribes and Pharisees of all countries would, in their accounts and histories, ascribe such bestialities as were practiced to the savage natures of the perpetrators who had no understanding of the great age in which they lived.

And it was equally to be foreseen that the dethroned and the tyrants and their sycophants here and everywhere upon earth would announce to the listening world, when all was over, that now anyone could see and understand why the dictatorship had been right in treating these savages as they had been treated under the dictatorship, and why dictatorship, an iron and merciless dictatorship, was the only form of government that could rule to their own benefit a people consisting of slaves and having only the mentality of slaves. Down with the demoralizing democracy! *Viva* the vital and rejuvenating dictatorship!

The rebel horde numbered almost six hundred men. No one had counted them exactly. It would indeed have been difficult to arrive at a precise number.

Every day during the march through the jungle they were joined on the paths by small groups or by escaped individuals who, long before the general insurrection in the *monterías* had begun, had deserted from the remotest corners of the jungles where they had worked. Even peons, who had fled from their *fincas* and then remained hidden in areas close to the jungle, took the opportunity of permanently freeing themselves from their debt-slavery and joined up contentedly with the army, happy to have met the revolution about which only vague and unclear rumors had reached those regions.

On the terrible march through the great jungles many were lost. Some were drowned crossing rivers; some sank in swamps and morasses; others were carried off in twenty-four hours by violent fevers; several were bitten by snakes and stung by poisonous insects; and others again were kicked by terrified horses or mules when following narrow mountain tracks, and these fell into the ravines. There were also many who died of wounds that they still bore on their bodies from work or torture and that could not be healed by their comrades. Thus the numbers of the people fluctuated from day to day.

With the troop marched a considerable number of women and girls and probably a dozen or more children, family dependents of the laborers who had been sold into the *monterías*. These women and children had been unwilling to leave their husbands, fathers, brothers, and nephews, and had gone with them voluntarily into the jungle.

The army was led by a young fellow, twenty-one years old, called Juan Mendez—or, rather, *he* called himself that, for to all the other muchachos he was simply "General."

He had belonged to the little group of workers who had started the rebellion. Since he had had some military training, it was quite natural that to him should be entrusted the supreme command of the army.

By race he was a Huasteca Indian, with an admixture, to

judge by his appearance, of some Spanish blood. At the age of sixteen he had joined the army as a volunteer. He progressed rapidly until, at nineteen, he was promoted to sergeant.

He had persuaded his favorite brother, some years younger than himself, also to become a soldier and to join the same battalion. In the course of his duties the younger boy committed some act of negligence of no great importance. In normal circumstances his offense would have been punished with two days' arrest or a few unpleasant hours of extra guard duty. A friendly disposed lieutenant would have given the boy a sharp dressing-down, and the matter would then have been forgotten. Under the dictatorship, however, superior officers in the Federal Army, and still more in the *Rurales*, had been gradually exalted to the status of infallible saints who represented God on earth. The inferior soldier vis-à-vis his betters possessed no other right than that of blind obedience and silent acceptance of whatever was demanded of him. So it happened that an officer, who was probably still drunk, punished the boy for his remissness by ducking his head in a pail of water and keeping him under water with his boot until he was drowned. The murderer was not punished, but instead he was commended in the orders of the day for having acted in the interests of discipline, as was his duty—for discipline was the highest sacrament.

The sergeant had not yet been wholly indoctrinated with the ways of the dictatorship, probably because he was more an Indian than an obedient soldier. Therefore he forgot for an hour the godlike nature of the officer and stabbed him to death, without being able to feel the least regret for his deed. This made it necessary for him to desert and to leave the army.

His closest friend in the regiment, Lucio Ortiz, was a corporal, also of Indian origin. He was the only man in whom he confided what he had done and where he had hidden the body of the demigod, in order to gain time for flight. True friendship meant more to the corporal than patriotism and far more than the solemnly sworn oath of loyalty that was as much a matter of indifference to him as a divorce in Tlaxcala would have been to a funambulating ape. "You know, Juanito," he said simply to his friend, "I'm going with you, and to hell and damnation with the whole accursed army and all the stinking crap about patriotism and love of one's country. What's it to do with me?" So the two of them went off together.

They thought of escaping to Honduras or San Salvador. Anywhere away from their sacred fatherland.

On the way they met a recruited gang of Indian workers who were being driven to the *monterías* as contract laborers. They enlisted in this gang. In the *monterías* nobody looked for them, and anyway no one would have gotten them out, whoever was being looked for or whatever the crime that had been committed; for a contract worker in the *monterías* was ten times worse off than in a prison or even in *El Valle de la Muerte*, the dreaded concentration camp for political prisoners from which seldom anyone returned, and, if he did return, remained a broken man for the rest of his life.

Now, the corporal, Lucio Ortiz, had been appointed by General to the rank of colonel in the army.

As chief of staff, General nominated Celso Flores, a Tsotsil Indian. Celso had worked for several years in the *monterías* as a feller. Although he was unable to read or write, he possessed an acute natural intelligence. Also, he was endowed with the rare talent of being able to inspire people to extreme exertions, mostly in the Indian manner. He never demanded anything that he would not himself do first—and do better than anyone else—if it was suggested that it was impossible to carry out his command.

As general in charge of the commissary, the muchachos chose Andreu, a Tseltal Indian who had worked in the *monterías* as an ox driver dragging away the felled tree trunks. He could read and write, and had acquired experience and a certain knowledge of logistics as overseer of oxen on the *carreta* caravans, which brought trade goods and passengers from the railway station on the coast far into the interior of the state —a distance of more than four hundred miles.

The spiritual chief, the brains of the army, was Professor, as the muchachos called him. Professor had been a secondary-school teacher. Gradually he had begun to understand the true position of the people who lived under the dictatorship. So it happened that he became more and more unwilling to beat into his pupils by way of their behinds—as had become customary in all schools—an admiration and idolization of the system. The further he progressed in his political awakening, the less was he spiritually enslaved. Therefore, whenever he had the opportunity, in school, on the street, in cafés, he began shamefully to abuse the dictator and his supremacy; and although he knew what would happen to him, he did not come, as his colleagues put it, to his senses. Once he had properly understood the situation, he could no longer hold his tongue. From a well-paid position in the better schools and in the big towns, he was continually transferred to lesser posts. Each fresh transfer was preceded by several months in prison or a concentration camp.

Finally, he found himself in a little mining town, where he was employed in a louse-ridden elementary school of the lowest grade, which was attended by the children of the poorest and worst-paid mine workers. He had been at his post scarcely three weeks when every evening, in one or another of the miserable adobe huts of the workers, there took place a meeting of the fathers, mothers, and elder brothers of his pupils. Six weeks later there were explosions, now here, now there, in the galleries and even in whole sections of the mines. God was on the side of the *mineros;* for it so happened that after none of the explosions and floodings in the mines was there a single dead proletarian to be found, although there perished a great many military personnel and agents of the secret police who had been introduced into the mines, dressed as laborers, in order to discover why the output was falling off and who stuck the dynamite into the false boreholes. When it finally came to strikes and open mutiny, the buildings of the mines administration were bombarded with stones and the police troops started to pepper the crowds of recalcitrant *mineros.* Then Professor was arrested again. This time the government seemed to have withdrawn him from public life once and for all. This time even the fathers and brothers of his former secondary-school pupils could no longer obtain clemency for him, as they had hitherto always been able to do successfully, since they held influential positions. This time Professor was included in a transport of incorrigibles and recidivists, a transport that took them to *El Inferno*, a concentration camp that was only called "Hell" because even the brightest wit had been unable to discover a stronger word to describe the hell that reigned there. Even here, Professor could not keep his impertinent mouth shut. From time to time he was gagged for twenty-four hours on end, was allowed neither water nor shade from the tropical sun. But scarcely was the gag removed and scarcely had the cramp left his tortured lips than the first words he always shouted were: "*Abajo El Caudillo!* (Down with the dictator!) *Que muera la dictadura! Viva la revolución social! Sufragio efectivo! No reelección! Viva la revolución del pueblo!*" And immediately he was gagged again, and he was carried out into the burning sun, tied up like a parcel, and laid on the sand. Finally, he succeeded in escaping with several companions in suffering, but most of these either perished or were recaptured and then slowly tortured to death. In the course of his flight Professor encountered the sergeant and the corporal dressed in rags and indistinguishable from wandering Indian peasants. And in company with these two he also allowed himself to be recruited as a mahogany worker in the *monterías*, in the hope of waiting in the depths of the jungle for the outbreak of the rebellion, which was already flickering throughout the country, and then opening the attack from there and winning the south of the Republic for the cause of the revolution.

The rebel army was divided into eight companies, each commanded by a captain and a lieutenant, with corporals as platoon leaders.

On the journey through the jungle, each company marched at a day's interval from the next, partly on account of the more than 150 horses, mules, donkeys, oxen, cows, and goats which accompanied them, and partly also in order to allow the swamplike trail through the jungle, saturated by heavy tropical downpours, time to dry out somewhat after a company had marched over it, and thus lighten the passage of those following. When a company and its animals had marched over one of these narrow jungle paths, they left behind them a trail compounded of deep, porridgelike slime in which men sank to their knees and beasts even to their stomachs.

After weeks of marching, terrible and exhausting as only a march can be through tropical jungle, where the ground is never dry, the army at length reached a settlement on the very edge of the jungle.

The hardships of this march, wading through swamps, crossing streams and rivers, struggling over numerous mountain ranges, gave the rebels rich opportunity to show what they were capable of.

No academically trained and experienced general could have brought a regular army on this march through the jungle and accomplished it with so few losses and so little sickness as General and the rebel officers had managed to do. It was excellent training for them and for all belonging to the army. An army that had succeeded in conquering the jungle so triumphantly had the right to hope that it might overcome any other forces. And these other forces that had to be fought and conquered were drawing nearer every day as the horde advanced farther into open country where the great estates, the *fincas*, lay, with their feudal overlords, the *finqueros*, and where were also villages, towns, army posts, military patrols, and roving squadrons of *Rurales*.

The army marched ahead without having any particular objective. "The objective will appear when once the march has begun," said Professor and General.

The muchachos would have had as little use for a narrowly circumscribed objective as they would have had for a program or a statute of some sort or other. They were guided solely by their one desire to acquire land and freedom. Once they had found both these things and were certain that they could keep them, then they would settle down, just as the Nahuas after a march lasting more than a hundred years had settled in a region that attracted them and that guaranteed them land and freedom.

Now, of course, *Tierra y Libertad* could be gained only

when those who owned and defended these estates had been vanquished. Therefore the first task was to fight them, to conquer them, to overwhelm them utterly, and to destroy them. The next task after that was to smash all who hindered or might hinder the achievement of *Tierra y Libertad*. So it might even be necessary to march on the capital, to occupy the government buildings, to slaughter the governor and all his bureaucrats, and then to direct from the government buildings everything further that had to be done, and from that day forward to keep a sharp watch that everything done was carried out in the interest of and for the well-being of the victors.

That, in the broadest possible outlines, was the idea of the cleverer brains in the army. On this matter Professor generally uttered only brief pronouncements: "Let's win the revolution first and destroy our enemies. Then will be the time to discuss what's to be done. Much talk beforehand is wasted time and energy which we have greater need of for our more immediate tasks."

Of the immediate tasks, nothing was more important or more urgent than the procuring of arms. And the rebels could obtain these arms only by taking them from those who at present possessed them. And their present possessors were the soldiers and the *Rurales*.

After reaching this first settlement, the individual companies no longer advanced with a whole day's march separating each from the one following. Henceforward, the companies marched in closer formation so that each was about two hours' marching time behind the next. Since it was possible that soon the first battle would have to be fought, it would have been a tactical error to have allowed the companies to march at too great an interval.

On the second day after departure from the settlement the army reached the Rancho Santa Margarita.

It was afternoon when the first company arrived there.

Santa Margarita consisted of the owner's house built of adobe—unburned clay bricks. It was flanked by two barn-like bodegas, also of adobe. Here were stored the harvested corn, beans, and henequen fiber for making ropes and mats.

Here also were to be found the pack and riding saddles and the few agricultural implements that the ranch possessed.

Four miserable huts huddled around the bodegas.

All these buildings formed a large courtyard, or patio, for they were built to form a quadrangle. One side was, however, open. Here a rough fence separated the patio from the corral where the horses and cattle were kept. On one side next to the owner's house was a space, also separated from the outer world by a thorn fence. In the fence was a gate leading from the patio onto the trail followed by all travelers and caravans passing the ranch.

The ranch itself lay on a hill that was just large enough to allow space for the buildings, the patio, and the surrounding fence. On the slopes of the hill lay the primitive palm huts of the peons who belonged to the ranch. There were fourteen such huts.

In three extremely wretched huts, which, like the owner's house, were situated around the patio, lived the major-domo, the rope-maker, and the chief *vaquero*, the man who was responsible for the cattle. These three families were half *ladinos*, whereas the peons and their families, who lived in the huts scattered on the hill, were Indians.

The mansion was, indeed, only a mansion, because all the other buildings were miserable *chozas* and palm huts of the most primitive type. It possessed no window apertures, only heavy, rough doors of solid mahogany. The floors were made of ill-baked clay bricks, the roof of rough, weathered wooden shingles. The house consisted of two rooms only. The sole object in the mansion suggesting that the occupants were not living in the fourteenth century, and in fact the only object that could be described as modern, was an American sewing machine that had begun to rust badly.

Table and chairs were of mahogany, roughly carpentered with a machete. The beds were simple frames of ebony over which were stretched strips of raw cowhide, crisscross, on which lay thick fiber mats woven from the leaves of palm trees. Dirty pillows were stuffed with Louisiana moss containing an abundant proportion of the adjacent bush.

This mansion was regarded as elegant and the owner as

well-to-do. Everything that the family needed, apart from silk, cotton, and ironware, was manufactured on the ranch. Here spirits were distilled, woolen blankets woven, saddles and sandals made, ropes and stout henequen fibers spun, from which were knotted nets, bags, and hammocks.

The mistress of the house led the prayers and the singing in the chapel belonging to the ranch. This chapel was a small hall, without partitions and covered with a palm roof. At one end of the hall was a rough table on which stood a picture of the Holy Virgin of Guadalupe. There were always fresh flowers before the picture. They were gathered in the bush by the wives and daughters of the peons and placed there daily every morning. Each Sunday morning the floor of the chapel was thickly strewn with green branches so that the worshippers could kneel on them.

The mistress was also doctor and midwife to the people who belonged to the ranch.

As to hard cash, there was seldom a hundred pesos, and often only five pesos, to be found in the whole ranch, owners and peons included. Everything was borrowed. Each borrowed from the next. And all borrowed from the masters. The "masters" felt it a moral no less than a shrewd economic duty to keep their peons alive and healthy.

Here and under these circumstances, which existed at the time of the arrival of the rebels and which had existed thus for four hundred years, what a revolution could achieve, or even what it could change, would have defeated even the most radical European thinker, had he been commanded to liberate the peons from their servitude and to give them, through the revolution, something more than they already possessed.

There was nothing there. And liberty—for which they would have had to thank a revolution—would have left these peons twice as poor and helpless as they now were.

There was plenty of land available. The ranch ranked as a large estate. But four fifths of the land was bush and jungle, stony and mountainous. Of the remaining fifth, one part was prairie land, suitable grazing for cattle, horses, and mules. Only one tenth was cultivated, hard as cement in the dry season and a slimy morass during the rains. If the dry season lasted too long, all the inhabitants of the ranch, including the almighty ranchero and his family, were near starvation. His only wealth consisted in his cattle, horses, and mules, which he bred. In order to breed these animals, he had required capital, for he had to buy breeding beasts and then wait years until the offspring were big enough to be sold. If a drought lasted too long, the animals died.

What could the rebellion, which had some sense in the *monterías*, do here to improve the lot of the peons? Even if it brought them freedom from their master, Heaven would soon rob them of that liberty; for their liberty was worthless if they had nothing to eat because nothing grew, and because the peons, once they were free, would use their freedom to work even less than before. No one had taught them self-discipline, how to work without being told and supervised. No one gave them seed, because others who were nearer the distribution points—insofar as these existed—required the seed more urgently. No one had taught them how to organize their work, in order to be able to form themselves into a cooperative society. Their community sense was so weak, if it ever had existed, that a cooperative organization would have been of little help to them; for envy, jealousy, and eternal quarrels over leadership would have gradually disintegrated any such organization. People who have lived in such servitude for four hundred years, or possibly four thousand, and all that time have been compelled to surrender to their masters and the authorities all thinking, all responsibility, all organizing, all consultation and discussion, all direction—such people cannot within a year of a rebellion be made into free peasants, capable of independent thought, action, and productivity, and requiring no one to tell them to be up and about at four o'clock in the morning to plow the fields.

The rebels who now arrived at this ranch certainly did not regard it as their task to ponder that a revolution alone does not alter a system, that it only changes ownership, that only the name of the owner is altered, and that the nation or the State in its role as capitalist may be more brutal, relentless, and tyrannical than ever the former masters were. What did systems, new or old, matter to the rebels?

They had been so long whipped and hanged, so long humiliated and robbed of free speech, that their community sense, which bound them to all their other compatriots from purely natural causes, had been killed. They knew only vengeance and retribution. Destruction was the sole thing they understood. The more they destroyed, the more they slaughtered of those whom they regarded as their enemies, the freer they felt themselves to be. For everything that existed and everything that lived and did not belong to them was the cause of their slavery. If they desired to be released from their slavery, then they must destroy. They no longer worried about the morrow; they worried only about the yesterday, when they had been tormented.

The tragedy is not that there can be and are dictators; no, the tragedy is that each and every dictatorship, even the most flourishing and apparently benevolent, must end in destruction, desolation, and chaos, according to the iron law of Nature that no man is able to change or influence: that is the true tragedy, because mankind thereby is hurled back hundreds of years in its irrepressible drive toward ultimate liberation from animality and anarchy.

When the advance guard reached the ranch, the muchachos found all the huts deserted. The patron and his family had retired deep into the bush. All the families of the peons had followed him.

"There we have proof that someone has betrayed our arrival and our march," said General. "They've had news here, and fear has driven them all away."

"To know that is worth a great deal," replied Professor. "Now we can be certain that we shall come up against *Rurales* at one of the two next *fincas*."

Two men threw off their packs and listened to what General and Professor were saying to one another. One of them said, "General, we can easily find the patron in the bush.

You've only to say the word, and we'll be off and drag him back to you with all his brood."

"What's the point of that?" answered General. "Kill all the cattle you find, and have a good meal for once. What's left over, we'll take with us on the march. And the last company fires the place. Then there won't be a stronghold at our backs. You, Nicasio, take the order to every company following that we're camping here for the night. It's going to rain again and we can use the huts for the night. I'll go with Professor and Celso, and as many others as can find room, into the master's house. Tomorrow morning at four o'clock we march off."

The next day, when the first troop packed up, they were well lighted on their way: all houses and huts were blazing. There was scarcely a glowing cinder left when the last company left the ranch. All pigs and cows had been slaughtered, and all horses and donkeys were taken away as booty of war.

Toward midday the troop arrived at the Rancho Santa Isabel. As at Santa Margarita, the huts there were also deserted. Cattle and swine had obviously been driven by the occupants into the bush. Only a half-dozen cats were licking themselves sleepily outside the empty huts. Two or three hounds, which had probably been knocked about and had arrived too late to take part in the general flight of the inhabitants, gaped at the muchachos, then crept behind the huts when the hounds of the troop took up the hunt against them.

Scarcely half the troop had passed through, and all the huts, the owner's house, the bodega, and gates and fences were in flames. Before the ranch had been put to the torch, the muchachos had searched for saddles and machetes—and found none. The general impression was that the inhabitants had left their dwellings the day previously, if not perhaps some days before that. All the hearths were cold and damp. A few iron water pots were all that was left in the huts.

On the subsequent march the muchachos discovered that even the tiny settlements of the independent Indian farmers were deserted. Idle hounds and cats lay around, or stole secretly and mistrustfully away at the approach of the troop.

"The reputation that precedes us," said Professor to General, as he commented on the solitary and ghostlike appearance of the deserted huts, "is a bad one. I'd like to know who has decried us as murderers, arsonists, and bandits."

"Well, we don't give a damn for what's said about us." Celso had joined them, taken off his pack, and squatted on the ground to rest. "We're rebels. Or perhaps we're not rebels? We haven't come here with sugar bonbons. And anyone who doesn't like it can just get out."

"Celso's right," said General. "What do we care whether the Inditos are afraid or not? One day they'll realize that we're not bandits. If they won't help us now to clear out the tyrants, then they'll have to put up with the patrones and the whips for a few years longer. But *we* won't put up with them. What do you say to that, muchachos?" He turned to a group of lads who had marched up and just arrived at the hard-trodden square of the little village. Like Celso, they threw their packs off and squatted down to gain fresh breath and new strength. There was still two or three hours' marching to the place where their next camp was to be pitched.

This little village consisted of only ten huts, each containing one room. Here the revolution could bring nothing to the small Indian peasants. The revolution would have to bring a more fruitful soil, cattle, and grass for the cattle, and also a few sacks full of rags before these miserable peasants and their wives and children would have even the most essential clothing. Out of the inhabitants of this tiny pueblito, only three families possessed a machete, while each man had a rusty, half-broken knife. Each family had a single communal spoon. There were no beds, no chairs, no tables to be found in the whole village; no axes, no nails. After searching all the huts, about twenty yards of wire had been collected. It was wire that the men on their long marches into the countryside had found and gleaned piece by piece, or had cut down from hanging telephone cables, or had torn off wire fences which they had passed. All they possessed to cultivate the meager, stony ground was a stout, pointed stake that they stabbed into the earth when sowing the corn.

Even these men and their families had abandoned their miserable habitations and fled deep into the bush from terror of being killed by the rebels who marched to their war cry, "*Tierra y Libertad!*"

They could have listened for a whole day to Professor expatiating on dictatorship, tyranny, and the bondage of the proletariat, and they would not have understood him. They possessed here land and freedom, and they asked nothing more of life and their tyrants than that they should not be murdered, that no one should steal from them, and that they should be left in peace to their own ruination when the arid ground became yet more arid owing to lack of rain or due to an excess of rain washing away the shallow surface of the soil, and when their wretched crop of corn and beans was one third consumed by rats and another third by corn borers and bean maggots. They would have been grateful to a revolution, could that revolution have protected them from the eagles, hawks, martens, and coyotes that stole their chickens, and from the jaguars and alligators that preyed on their pigs and calves. Their problems were so simple that even the grandest revolution and the most inspiring rebellion, which liberated the country from its dictatorship, passed them and their lives by without their even noticing it. Their only awareness of the revolution was that in the marketplace at the nearest small town it was no longer Don Damaso who collected their market dues, but Don Dionisio now; and that whereas before the revolution they had had to pay two centavos tax when they wished to sell twenty-five centavos worth of wool, now they had to pay five centavos tax, of which one centavo was reckoned as an extra tax for a country school that was never built.

The rebels could easily have been made content with land, which was abundantly available and could have been distributed to them out of the hundreds of thousands of acres of land which belonged to the *fincas*, but had never been cultivated, and which the owners never would cultivate. It would have been cheaper for the *finqueros*, for the owners of great estates, to have given away these uncultivated tracts. It would have been cheaper to abolish debt-slavery. And for the whole nation and for the good repute of the dictator, it would have been a thousand times better if genuinely free elections had been instituted, if the autocratic rights of the dictator had been curtailed, if he had been made answerable to a parliament, even though that parliament consisted of men who talked for hours without saying anything and argued for days without deciding anything. It would have been better and cheaper and, for the people, more useful, if the dictator had allowed all his compatriots, friends or foes, the unrestricted right to gabble themselves silly. But like all dictators whose names have been recorded in history, he permitted no opposition. What he commanded was law, without the man who had to obey and observe the law having been given the right of any say in the making of that law. He knew only one answer against the wishes and demands of the citizens, and that was the answer of his uniformed henchmen with their truncheons and revolvers.

It would have been so simple, had the chief of police of the district sent a few sensible and peaceful men to meet the troop when he received news of their approach. Such men would certainly have achieved more—far more of value for the State—than the *Rurales*, whom the police chief dispatched with the order to enter into no kind of negotiations, but simply to start shooting as soon as the bandits and murderers came into sight.

2

  The troop was now marching along a broad road. The road was not a constructed one, but was broad and open only because it led across the plain. This plain belonged to the Santo Domingo *finca*, the whitewashed church of which could already be seen from a hilltop. As far as the eye could see, into the distance ahead and to left and right, all the land belonged to the *finca*.

Forty families of peons lived in their huts close beside the main house. Fifty more families lived in four small settlements that lay strewn at the four corners of the vast area of the *finca*. Placing these further settlements at such a distance from the ranch house had the advantage that the peons, who were cowherds, could better watch and gather their herds, which strayed far over the grasslands.

General, Professor, and Celso were resting on the hilltop whence they could see the church of the *finca*. Rather more than halfway from the hill to the *finca* there was a deep depression in the ground, which, so far as could be estimated from their vantage point, must be at least two miles in length. The plain was undulating and broken by numerous little hills. These hills were seldom more than fifty feet high, most of them being lower. However, to the south in the gray-blue distance rose a range of mountains that stretched across the whole of the visible horizon. Over the countryside were scattered a few trees, solitary ones and some in clumps of ten or twenty combining to make a copse. In between, similarly strewn about the countryside, were wild bushes, singly and in clumps.

From the hill, at the foot of which the first company had just arrived, the route to the courtyard of the *finca* was clearly visible. This route consisted of four or five well-beaten tracks, running beside one another, sometimes joining up into three or only two, then again dividing into five or even eight and nine. These tracks looked as though they had been made by the wheels of wagons. But no wagons were in use here. The tracks had been trodden out of the green grassland by the cattle ambling back to the farmyard at evening and returning to pasture in the morning. Here, too, came the mule caravans, which traveled from Hucutsin to the *fincas* and to the *monterías*. Last and least, the Indians tramped along them when they went to market.

These tracks had been so trodden down that no grass grew upon them. Thus they were plainly visible for many miles.

The grass itself did not stand very high, scarcely three feet. It was not dense, but stood more in thickets. However, it was very green following the rainy season.

The road from the jungle had been broad and open for the last two hours of the march, even though there had been bush on both sides. Now, however, the bush opened out farther and farther to both sides, which made the plain seem far greater and more extensive than it was in reality. The harsh sun, hanging over the flat land enveloped the plain far into the distance in a shimmering, thin haze, so that the little white church and the courtyard of the *finca* sometimes vanished or seemed to reappear in a different place from where one had believed it formerly. At moments cattle looked like dogs in this shimmering, flickering light, and great stones appeared like houses; charred tree trunks, which stood upright, and burned palms resembled now the standing columns of ruined temples, now the brown figures of motionless Indians.

Normally the traveling caravans encountered here whole herds of cattle and half-wild horses, the property of the *finca*. Now and again, nearby or in the distance, two or three peons or *vaqueros* riding away on horseback would be seen, searching for these herds to seek out calves that had been born in the night or sick cows or horses, and then to lasso them and take them back to the ranch to be looked after and cured.

But on this day there was not a herd to be seen on the whole wide plain, only here and there a few solitary, stray cattle. Not a *vaquero*, not a peon was visible. Some ten or twelve vultures were circling high in the air. And in the distant courtyard of the *finca* could now and then be seen a swirling plume of smoke rising—sometimes from the kitchen of the *finca*, sometimes from one of the huts of the peons.

"That Santo Domingo is a damned great and fine *finca*," said Celso, squatting down and rolling a cigarette. "I know it. It belongs to Don Patricio. I know it well. Spent the night there several times with the peons. It's a grand, rich *finca*."

"I know it well, too, and so do you." General turned to Professor. "We spent a day and two nights here when we were marching to the *monterías*."

Several more muchachos now came up the hill and sat down beside them.

Professor stood up and looked back down the way along which, at this very instant, the second company was coming into view and preparing to make camp when they saw the first company already resting.

"Yes, we've been here before," said Professor suddenly in a changed voice. "What do we do now? We've reached the first large *finca*. Something's got to be done. We could march around it and go on as if we hadn't seen it. But what's the point of being rebels if we choose to go on our way without snapping up the first good morsel we find in our path? And if we're really serious about making a revolution and giving all the peons *Tierra y Libertad*, then we'd better make a beginning. An important axiom of revolution runs: 'Never leave an enemy in your rear!' If we just go through here peacefully like a herd of sheep, we shall have a powerful enemy at our backs! So what do you say?"

"The same as you," answered General.

Celso blew out a thick cloud of smoke and said dryly, "Right. Why should the *finquero* and his brood reign here any longer? It's time the others had their turn, who've been ruled over so long and haven't dared open their mouths."

Professor laughed. "Then we're all agreed. Agreed in thought. Agreed in action. Agreed on battle. What do you say, muchachos?" he called in a loud voice across to the men nearby.

"*Tierra y Libertad!*" they all yelled together in reply. And then they shouted: "*Viva, Professor! Arriba General! La muerte a los tiranos y todos los patrones y dictadores! Libertad para todos!*"

When Professor had sat down again, Celso said, "The *finca* isn't deserted. Otherwise there'd be no smoke."

"That's just what I've been thinking." Professor gazed over in the direction of the ranch. "Why is there smoke coming from the house and from the huts? Because none of them has run away, although they know that we are many and have revolvers and rifles. And why has none of them run away?" He looked questioningly at Celso and General.

"Because they believe we'll only slaughter a few cattle and then go on our way," answered General, ironically winking an eye.

"And you, Celso, what do you think?"

"They've got *Rurales* in the *finca*," replied Celso.

"Celso, I promote you to colonel," said Professor, laughing. "Do you confirm that, General?"

"Confirmed."

"Well done, Celso," exclaimed Professor. "You're a damned clever lad. What you said is right. They've got the *finca* full of *Rurales*. They must have received news of our approach some days ago in Balun Canan or Achlumal, otherwise the *Rurales* couldn't be here already."

"But it's possible the *Rurales* were on a tour of inspection, to make sure that all's quiet and there aren't any insurrections or cattle-robbing by the Bachajon Indians."

"Celso, you're right again. It's far more likely that there's only an inspection patrol there the *finca*, twenty or

twenty-four men, a captain, a sergeant, and three or four
N.C.O.'s. They have rifles and usually carry a machine gun
with them."

When the muchachos who were squatting about the hill
heard this, they grew excited. "Rifles and revolvers! *Viva las
armas!* Hurrah for weapons!" they shouted, jumping up and
dancing around as though they had already won the battle.

"A report could hardly have gotten to Balun Canan," continued Professor. "And in Achlumal and Hucutsin there are
only occasional small guard commandos. But without doubt
the news is already on its way to Jovel, and that will bring
half a battalion out against us. Where do you think those *Rurales* would be at this moment, General?"

"When we were on commando raids, we didn't wait at a
finca—we waited in open country, or went after the rebels."

"Why didn't you wait in the yard, which is walled and of-
fers good cover?"

"Simply because, first of all, too much damage would be
done to the *finca*, and, second, we might easily find ourselves
caught in a trap, particularly if the insurgents were five
hundred strong and we only five and twenty. In open country, with our machine guns, rifles, and well-disciplined soldiers, we had a superiority even if we were only twenty and
the rebels five hundred."

"Then you think they'll come after us here, out in the
open?"

"I don't think. I'm certain of it. I wasn't a sergeant for nothing. I know how it's done—having done it myself."

"Against peons and workers?"

"You can't do much about it when you're caught up in the
army. It works like a machine: whether you like it or not, you
have to conform, and you can change things only by stabbing
a few officers or bashing their skulls in and then taking to
your heels. But if you know you've got a few dozen in the
battalion on your side, and if you have the nerve for it and
strike at the right moment, then you can win the whole battalion to your side. After all, they're all ill-treated hirelings like
yourself."

While General talked, Celso had been squatting there, quiet and relaxed, smoking his cigarette and blinking as he stared across at the courtyard of the *finca*.

Now he gave vent to a half-choked, excited cry. He changed from his crouching position into a kneeling one, placing both fists on the ground, ducked down, and stretched his head as far forward as possible.

"What in God's name has gotten into you?" asked Professor.

Several muchachos, who had gathered on the hill, took up the same attitude as Celso. It was their natural posture when they wanted to observe in the distance something which they wished to see clearly and to judge before it came closer.

"General's right," muttered Celso to the muchachos nearest to him.

General and Professor crawled closer. "What did you say, Celso?" asked General.

"They're in that hollow," answered Celso, as quietly as if he feared the *Rurales* might hear him. It was more than three miles to the depression.

"I've seen things flashing at several points in that hollow. It might be their cap badges or the barrels of their rifles or their buttons. They're *Rurales*."

"By God, Celso, I've just seen those flashes, too, and at three different places at the same moment," said General.

Olegario, one of the muchachos who had crept up the hill to them, asked, "How many do you think there are, General, waiting for us?"

"A commando troop, probably. Perhaps twenty-five men."

Another muchacho, Herminio, who heard that, called out, "Would to God they were two regiments. Think how many good revolvers, rifles, machine guns, and cartridges we would have if they were two regiments."

General laughed. "Just keep calm, muchacho. We'll have our hands full dealing with that one machine gun which those wageslaves have. But we shall get it all right. Don't worry. And once we've gobbled up the commando sniveling and driveling in that hole over there, then we can comfortably take on a battalion. Don't expect everything at once, muchachos. Little by little. Make no mistake. I tell you in advance that when we've dealt with those over there, half of our first company will no longer be alive."

Then Olegario said, "Whether we live or not doesn't matter a damn, not a dog's damn. But those who do remain alive will at least know why they are living and what for. I want to have a rifle, by God, and the cartridges for it. I'll go after them alone, if you won't."

"You'll stay here," said General sternly. "You'll go when I say so, and when we all go. Perhaps you may get your rifle, but rammed into your belly if you try to wage war on your own."

"General's right, Olegario," said Celso soothingly to the muchacho. "We can't all be in command here, everyone doing what he likes. That way, one after the other will be slaughtered, and none will be left. We'll all go at it together, and not alone; and we'll go when General says it's time to go."

The muchachos crawled down from the hilltop. The two companies that had camped around the base of the hill could not be seen by the *Rurales*, though whether the few muchachos who had been on the hill could have been seen was not certain. General, however, said that he believed the *Rurales* had seen them, because their captain must certainly have had field glasses.

Meanwhile, a further company arrived, which General ordered to make camp also, and if the fellows wanted to move about they must do so doubled up. He wanted to keep the *Rurales* from learning the extent of the force that was temporarily encamped there.

He proved, by what he now propounded and arranged, that, although he was only the son of a poor Indian peasant, he deserved to be a general. No experienced officer of the *Rurales* could have managed things better. It might be said with certainty that out of a hundred trained federal officers, not two probably could have improved on or even equaled what he planned and the way in which he then carried out his plans.

He called Professor, Celso, Santiago, and the captains of the companies that had arrived, to confer and to outline his schemes.

"If we just march against them like sheep, they'll let fly with their machine gun, and not one of us will remain alive, and the rebellion in this state, and most certainly in this district, will be at an end for this year. We must entice them out of that hollow."

"A dozen muchachos could have a go at them. Then they'd come out. And we'd all rush forward against them," advised the captain of the third company.

"No, they won't come out of their holes like that. They'd let our dozen men come on, without firing a shot, and only when the muchachos marched right into the hollow would the hirelings attack them and cut them down so that the following muchachos would hear nothing and know nothing of what had occurred."

"All right. Then let's all charge forward and storm them," suggested a muchacho who was sitting nearby and was not one of the council of war.

"That would be even worse," said Celso. "Even you can grasp that, although you only fed the oxen in the *monterías*."

"Correct. That would be the worst thing we could do." General took up the word. "We could establish a large, fortified camp here and let a lot of smoke rise from it. The *Rurales* could respond to that in various ways. One way would be for them to retire to the *finca;* then they wouldn't have to lie out in the wet day and night, for they're too lazy, too pampered, and too overfed to do that. Once back in the *finca*, they'd wait for half a battalion of federals to reinforce them."

"Perhaps they don't know how many we are and think we're only sixty or so muchachos, just from one *montería*," said Professor.

"That seems to me likely, Professor. For even if we have been betrayed, no traitor could know how many we are, since we haven't been marching as one group. Only in that little ranchito where the peons settled the hash of their Don Chucho, could the peons living there know how many we are. But not one of them has run on ahead of us. I took care to find out how many of them there were when we arrived, and how many were still there when we marched on. They were all there. But someone from one of the other small estates must have ridden to the *finca*—either the owner or a major-domo. But it's all the same who carried the news to the *finca* or even to Hucutsin or Achlumal; he knew only the approximate number of the muchachos in the first company, our shock troops. And the *Rurales* believe they've only this one company to deal with."

"How can you know that?" asked Celso.

"It's very simple. If the *Rurales* knew we were approaching about six hundred men strong, and with twenty revolvers and ten or twelve shotguns, and six hundred machetes besides, then, as I know these slaves of the dictator, they wouldn't be waiting here for us with one commando and only one machine gun. Not those uniformed mercenaries. Those torturers and floggers are brave only when they're a dozen together, each with a bludgeon and a revolver, and faced with a single defenseless prisoner. But here, in the open country, twenty-five of them, each with one revolver and a solitary machine gun, while we are several hundred with a number of revolvers and all with machetes—no, they wouldn't wait ten minutes, they'd be running like hares, not even taking time to dismantle the machine gun and unload because they might otherwise lose their precious skins. And just because they're still squatting over there in that depression, I know that they don't believe we're more than sixty or seventy half-starved muchachos. They think they'll be able to defeat us easily. They've certainly arranged a banquet in the *finca* to celebrate their victory with the *finquero* and his neighbors."

Another company arrived.

Celso had been gazing around and had noted the dark clouds that were gathering in the west. The thicker the clouds grew, the faster the storm approached. The sun, which was now nearing the zenith, was still brilliant and burning. "There's the Indian god coming to our aid," said Celso. "If they don't want to get wet, they'll have to come creeping out of their holes; and they're more scared of getting wet than old cats. Don't you agree, General?"

"Yes, but it doesn't change my plan. It only hastens it. You, Olegario, climb up the hill again. But keep your head under cover. And then watch—watch well. They'll soon begin popping their heads up. And just because of the approaching rain, they'll try to bring the encounter to a rapid conclusion, so that they can get back to the *finca* to remain dry."

"But it's possible," objected Professor, "that they won't go for us at all, but just behave as if they hadn't seen us. They may simply move off and leave us to attack the *finca*."

"That's part of my plan." General's gaze followed Olegario, and he waited to receive a sign from him as to what the *Rurales* would do. "That's what the scoundrels would dearly like, Professor: simply to retreat to the *finca*, and there to drink, guzzle, and play about with the women. But that's not so easy for them. In that *finca*, and assuredly in all the *fincas* in the neighborhood, everybody knows that we're on the march. They must wait for us, if only to preserve their reputation as brave soldiers. They can't make themselves laughingstocks, on account of the women and somewhat less on account of the *finqueros*."

"You've forgotten the most important thing, General," said Celso, laughing. "They can't run away from Indians, and certainly not from peons. They'd never dare show their faces again in front of a *ladino*. People would spit at them if they, the *Rurales*, armed to the teeth with rifles and automatics, were to be scuttled by us lousy, filthy lumberjacks. And, what's more, they'd find themselves before a special tribunal of the Chief of the Secret Political Police. *And* they'd be shot."

"You're a good pupil, Celso." Professor laughed loudly. "Three months ago you knew nothing of automatics and hadn't an idea about the secret State police, who are responsible only to the old cacique himself. Now you talk about it and toss it off as if you'd done nothing all your life but read prohibited newspapers."

"Nothing wonderful about it," said Celso, growing red in

the face with embarrassment. "I've had a good teacher. Besides, I'm a colonel. Don't forget that."

"Hunh!" called Olegario from the little hilltop at that very moment. "There are signs of life. Three have stood up, are looking over here and gazing around in all directions. One has something in front of his eyes that he's looking through."

"That's a pair of field glasses." General now became busy. But he displayed no excitement. He behaved as calmly and as coolly as if he were making preparations for a hare hunt, such as he used to organize with the other boys in his village.

"Stay up there and continue to watch them carefully." To the muchachos of his staff squatting around him he said, "We must draw them to the attack. We can't attack them so long as they remain in that hollow. We wouldn't get a man of theirs, and it would just be a futile slaughter. They know now that we're somewhere near. They even know from what direction to expect us. That's why they've popped up, to study the battlefield. If we can once get them out, they won't be able to get back to the hollow. Away behind them, on the roof of the *finca* building, are standing the *finquero* and his major-domo, and maybe even the other *finqueros* from the district; and they'll have their field glasses with them and see everything that goes on here. And now for it. We'll entice them out of their hole."

It began to rain, slowly, in long thin streaks.

General called Santiago to him. Then he beckoned to Fidel. "From now on you're both sergeants. You, Santiago, take twenty men, all with packs on their backs, and march off. But not straight ahead, not toward the depression where those uniformed slaves are squatting and waiting for us to hurl ourselves on their machine gun so that they can have the pleasure of mowing us down. You must march farther to the right, always to the right, diagonally, you understand? At first your line of march will keep your men close to the bush. There in the distance, do you see that pointed mountain peak?"

"Of course I see it."

"Good. That's your direction. To the watchers in the hollow it must look as if you and your men are trying to keep out of the way of the *Rurales*. They're to know that you know that they are hiding in that fold of the ground. They're to believe that you want to avoid them. If they should start shooting at you, throw yourselves on the ground, take your hats off, and tie the hats on to your packs. The packs will be higher than your backs, and the swine will think you have your heads under your hats. They can't see as clearly as all that. They're too far away. Then go on crawling along the ground, so that your hats move along with the packs. Always aim at that mountain in the distance. When you've marched about three miles in that direction, turn, and then proceed left, toward the *finca*. If they haven't crept out of their hollow already, they'll come out then because they want to protect the *finca*. As soon as they come out and prepare to attack you, turn and run, bent double, back to the bush. It must appear exactly as if your trousers were glued to your asses from fright. Just when they are properly out of the depression and mounted on their nags and storming after you, then we'll come out and entice them toward us. Then they'll leave *you* in peace. Then you go into the bush. As soon as you're well in, come straight back to the place where we are now. We'll lure them farther into the bush, and thus you'll be able to attack them from the rear and we from the front. You, Fidel, you take twenty men, too. If anyone doesn't want to go with you, give him a few hefty cracks on the snout."

"I shan't need to crack anyone on the snout, General." Fidel laughed confidently. "They're tearing to be off and have a go at the *Rurales*. We need their rifles and cartridges, and they've got good shirts and trousers, too."

"You know this: every rifle that's captured belongs to the man that took it. Also the cartridges and whatever else the stinking hound may have. Watch or rings. But money will be handed in. We need the money at headquarters. If we don't get any, it won't matter much. I'll get everything we need— if not with money, then without money. Now you, Fidel, must not go out of the bush. Go to the side here, just deep enough in so that you and your muchachos won't be seen, and attack them from there when we have gotten them farther along, taking them from the rear also, like Santiago. Have you both understood what you're to do? If not, I'll find other sergeants who can understand."

"Don't worry, General," answered Santiago. "Understood or not understood, we'll get them all right."

"Off then, both of you, to your posts."

In less than half a minute, the two new sergeants had collected their troops. It was only necessary to say that the order had been given to attack the *Rurales*, and a hundred muchachos sprang up to take part. The fact that these two troops were to attack the *Rurales* in the rear and thus have an excellent opportunity of taking their weapons made participation in this maneuver particularly desirable. And not one of the muchachos gave a thought to the danger of being killed or captured. Rebels have to attack and to conquer. If rebels do not conquer, then, by the nature of things, it is in any case better not to survive. None of the muchachos needed to be told or reminded what failure of the rebellion would mean. The full brutality, bestiality, cruelty, and repressed perversity of a hypocritical and morally stunted washtub bourgeoisie, who temporarily could regard themselves as bosses and as policemen, always broke out in its most revolting form whenever the Indian proletarians, daring to rise against tyranny and dictatorship, were crushed. For every snotty youth who had fallen, a hundred, sometimes even three hundred Indian proletarians were tortured, flogged, and then slaughtered like hogs, or else hanged like thieves, twenty on one and the same tree. The horror stories that sometimes appeared in American newspapers did not tell a tenth of what really happened.

But what did the muchachos care about defeat? They cared only about victory. Their immediate anxiety was not to win in order to gain freedom and land, but simply to win in order to get their weapons from those uniformed slaves and to leave the swine, who had hitherto carried the weapons, to make a meal for the vultures.

3

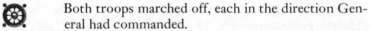 Both troops marched off, each in the direction General had commanded.

The troops had scarcely gone a hundred paces when General ordered all the muchachos in his vicinity to prepare to march. The great mass, who were encamped farther off, received instructions to pack up and set forth, not forward however, but back, along the way the companies had come earlier that day.

It was raining, not heavily but in thin, dreary strings. Visibility fell off, but it was sufficient to permit observations of the terrain as far as the depression.

Meanwhile, Santiago's troop had marched about a mile and was now almost level with the depression.

At this moment the *Rurales* lying in wait in the hollow seemed to notice that they were in danger of being outflanked. That they must avoid, the more so since any envelopment might result in the muchachos coming between the *Rurales* and the *finca*. Once within the perimeter walls of the *finca* the muchachos would have an uncommonly strong position, further strengthened by the fact that the *finquero* and his family could be used as hostages.

A shrill whistle rang out from the hollow, and then immediately the *Rurales* emerged. Some were already mounted. Others, and they were the majority, were dragging their horses behind them up onto the edge of the hollow in order to reach the crest faster. Once at the top, they swung themselves into their saddles and waited for their major's command. The horses were restive, plainly made nervous by their riders, who, so it seemed, could not bring the skirmish to an end quickly enough. The cause of this zeal was, admittedly, less rooted in bravery or military ardor to join battle than in the fact that the soft, penetrating rain, which now drizzled down wearily and gently, just *chipichipi*, as the Indians say, was threatening to develop in half an hour into a heavy, drenching, tropical *aguacero*. The sooner the encounter was over, the quicker the *Rurales* would be back in the *finca* again. With half a hundred louse-ridden Indians, the *Rurales* would be finished in ten minutes. They had fought Indians before.

As soon as they were all mounted, they began to advance toward Santiago's troop at a gentle trot. The uneven, yielding ground, into which the horses' hoofs sank if they trod heavily, did not permit a fast gallop.

At first only about ten of them were visible. General believed that these ten men were half the squad of *Rurales* which had been lying in wait here for the approaching rebels. But it was not long before more and more riders emerged from the depression. At last General saw, to his great astonishment, that the *Rurales* were about sixty men strong; and, as he could infer from the accompanying mules, they carried two machine guns with them.

"My God!" he said. "There's almost half a company coming crawling out of there. Now there's going to be some fun around here."

"Hope it'll be good fun," called someone. "Two machine guns are better than one, and we can use forty rifles better than twenty. What do you say, muchachos?" he asked those who were lying near him.

Before they could answer, General gave the order that sixty men should be ready to march within five minutes.

General called to Professor; "You take the main troop and start to march back along the same way we came."

The men obeyed reluctantly. There was no time for Professor to explain the plans that General had made.

General kept sixty men close to him and said to them, "As soon as I fire a shot from my revolver, stand up and march after me toward the *finca*. I'll tell you when to attack. If you attack before I say, then I'll shoot each one of you to hell, by God!"

The *Rurales* had by now advanced so far toward Santiago's troop that they were only about five hundred yards from them. Thus this troop's way to the *finca* was cut off.

Now, correctly and faithfully following General's plan, Santiago ordered his men to pretend to be frightened and to make with all speed for the bush in order to seek cover there.

When the Indians began to run thus in terror, the major commanding the *Rurales* regarded this as a sign of victory. He said, grinning to his lieutenant, "Now you see what I've always told you. These Indians are only full of bravado, deep in the jungle. But when once the swine see a uniform cap, they run like startled hares. Get after them and finish 'em off! If any of 'em is carrying a weapon, even a machete or a knife, he's to be shot down immediately without mercy. Anyone unarmed is to be taken with a lasso and brought to the *finca*, where we'll put them up for tonight. The womenfolk at the *finca* will enjoy seeing what we do with prisoners. Off! Forward march! Machine guns remain in the rear for the time being, but ready for action. *Marcha adelante!*"

A bugle blew the signal. The troops went into faster trot. But the horses stumbled and their hoofs caught and stuck in the thick undergrowth. So the attack did not develop in the militarily elegant style the major and the lieutenant would have wished. Both knew very well that they were being observed with field glasses from the roof of the *finca*.

General, lying stretched at full length on the ground, raised himself on his elbows. Now he drew his revolver. There followed several seconds of tense waiting for the muchachos, who kept their eyes riveted on General's every movement.

Santiago's troop, running away, had now reached the edge of the bush. The *Rurales* were only some two hundred yards behind the troop. In spite of the bad terrain, they were determined at all costs to get into a full gallop in order to stop Santiago's troop from gaining cover, because in the bush it would be more difficult to catch the muchachos than in open country.

The signal to gallop was given. The horses tensed and sprang forward.

But simultaneously, from the hill, two revolver shots rang out, one from General's gun and one from a muchacho to whom General had given the signal. Immediately they began to move straight toward the *finca*. They ran, in accordance with General's order, not in one solid mass, but in little groups of five or six men, to avoid offering too good a target.

The strategy that General had worked out was worthy of an experienced and brilliant field marshal. To lure the hidden *Rurales* from their secure hollow where, because of their superior armament, they were as good as unassailable, was in itself a masterpiece. In the open country the *Rurales*, in spite of their horses, were not only assailable but conquerable. The horses were more of a hindrance than an asset, the more so as the downpour grew heavier and the ground, already saturated from long rains, was turning once more into a swamp. The major of the *Rurales* had realized too late how heavy the going was over this terrain. It had been much firmer between the *finca* and the depression, and he had assumed that it would be similarly so between the depression and the bush. He had overlooked the fact that any stretch of country, the nearer it got to a large jungle or an extensive tract of bush, takes on more and more the characteristics of the bush, holding moisture much longer than open ground, where, under the tropical sun, the land dries out in a few days even after the heaviest rains.

General had taken this into consideration in his plan. The closer the *Rurales* could be enticed to the bush, the less use could they make of their horses. Apart from which, it is much harder for those wearing boots to march in swampy bush ground than for the Indians, who went barefoot. The unshod Indians can run across this slimy surface, whereas the man with boots has a bitter struggle to progress at all.

The rain had come opportunely for General, although this downpour was more an unexpected—though welcome— ally than a reinforcement that had already been taken into his calculations.

But what made General a field marshal far superior to the major of the *Rurales* was his gift of being able to think and work with his opponent's brain. He had estimated correctly, to the last and minutest detail, what an officer of the *Rurales* would do under the circumstances, and how he would react.

It was natural that the officers of the *Rurales* should regard as their highest duty the protection of the inhabitants of the *finca*, whose guests they were, and as caballeros they felt it their pleasantest task to save the female members of the *finquero's* family from the brutal and unwashed hands of the Indian rebels.

That was why Santiago's troop must not reach the rear of the *Rurales*. Furthermore, the commanding officer had had good military reasons for preventing the rebels from possibly outflanking the *finca* and advancing toward Hucutsin, which was temporarily denuded of soldiers. Thus Santiago's troop compelled the major, against his plans and against his will, to abandon his safe cover and commit himself to the open country.

Now it was only necessary to lure the *Rurales* toward the main troop. This was somewhat more difficult. But General solved this tactical problem in just as brilliant a fashion as he had solved the other one of bringing his opponents out into open country.

His plan was to draw the *Rurales* into the broad clearing, which, like a highway, formed a deep indentation into the bush.

While the *Rurales*, in order to achieve victory, pursued Santiago's troop, who were apparently fleeing in terror, Fidel's troop was moving to the left, keeping to the verge of the bush, close to the exit from the clearing. At the same time General packed both sides of the clearing with men in such a manner that these hidden assailants could not be seen by the *Rurales* when they entered the clearing.

After everything had been prepared for the battle, only one thing remained for General—to lure the *Rurales* into the clearing. He did this so cleverly that no experienced commander-in-chief could have done it better.

When the two shots were fired, one by himself and the other by his assistant, the mounted *Rurales* all without exception halted, without even waiting for a command, so unexpected were these two shots, and coming from a direction where they had never expected rebels could be.

At the same moment they saw the troop, led by General and about sixty strong, running wildly toward the *finca*. As the Indians ran, three of them, obeying General's command, fired their shotguns at the *Rurales*.

"By all that's holy!" shouted the major to the lieutenant, who was riding on the left wing. "We're on a goddamned false trail!"

The lieutenant came galloping up.

"Over there are the swine that we ought to be after," said the major in explanation. "Those muchachos we were hunting like hares are wretched escapees, nothing more. Probably they're running away from those rebellious hounds who are trying to steal their hard-earned pittances. Come on! Bugler, blow the signal. Right wheel. Attack with all weapons!"

The bugler blew, and the charging ranks of the *Rurales* changed direction and galloped toward the clearing from which the storming rebels had broken forth. About two miles separated them.

Scarcely had the *Rurales* turned in this new direction than Santiago's troop withdrew into the bush, a maneuver that the major believed to be one of fright, the fellows desiring only to avoid the fight they saw impending and not wishing to be hit by stray bullets. Had Santiago's troop not behaved thus and instead marched in their original direction, the major would certainly have sent off an N.C.O. with six men to follow them.

This would have been contrary to General's plan. He had to avoid Santiago's troop being involved in a fight in which the commander of the *Rurales* would have learned that Santiago and his men belonged to the rebel army and that this side march was only a tactical maneuver.

As soon as General saw all the *Rurales* riding toward his own shock troop, he allowed every man who carried a gun to fire one round at the *Rurales*. Two of the *Rurales'* horses fell. Whether they had been hit or had only stumbled over one of the high thickets of wiry grass could not be determined. But two *Rurales*, whose horses had not fallen, were hit, as the muchachos realized from the erratic movements that each of the wounded made.

Without these hits, which were essential for the plans General had worked out, the major might have been able to recall his men to the hollow in order to await the rebels there, or to attack in some other manner, or even to withdraw right back to the *finca* buildings and then to swarm out fanlike over the terrain.

But once again General had reckoned rightly with the mentality—or rather, in this peculiar case, with the particular psychology—of an officer. Whether they are commanding helots or grenadiers or snot-nosed recruits in brown, green, or black caps, they are all the same. Their honor is injured if they are bespattered with muck or paving stones by the proletariat. And in this case the honor of an officer in the *Rurales* had been mortally wounded, since filthy, louse-ridden Indians had dared to shoot at them. Indians had to stand at attention when an officer passed—rigidly at attention, their arms crossed over their chests, and bowing deeply when he addressed them; for to look in his face was a greater crime for an Indian peon than to seek to scrutinize the face of God Himself.

The rain, which was now beating down in whipping streams, made the major thoroughly irritable. Why couldn't the sun shine when an honorable warrior wished to fight a battle! To hell with this accursed rain! Soaking wet down to their clammy shirts, and now having to chase after lousy Indians! Why in the devil's name hadn't all Indians been simply slaughtered off in the first century after the discovery of America? Then there would have been some peace and quiet, then one could have lounged comfortably and cozily in a *finca*, playing with girls under their skirts and taking pesos by the hundred off the *finqueros* at *vingt-et-un*.

"Advance! Attack the swine! We'll teach them to shoot at honest soldiers. Not one to be left alive that carries as much as a hint of anything like a gun or a knife! That's the order! Understood?"

Stumbling and blundering, the *Rurales* rode toward the clearing. All, without exception, were depressed by the drenching rain. They stuck to their horses, crouched low as if they hoped thereby the better to protect themselves from the rain. They could not use their rubber capes, for these would have hindered them in battle.

The shock platoon of the muchachos continued to march on toward the *finca*. When General had advanced so far into the open country that, in retreating, he would reach the entry to the clearing at roughly the same time as the *Rurales*, he formed ranks against the *Rurales* and gave the order to fire. Two or three men seemed to have been hit, but they remained on their horses and rode onward toward the clearing.

A bugle blew the signal, and the *Rurales* attempted to charge in a glorious attack. But because of the ground and the rain, the attack did not get very far. The major called a halt and ordered covering fire on the shock platoon for some minutes.

The muchachos replied with scattered shots and then, true to General's command, ran, as if overcome with terror, in a chaotic mob, into the roadlike clearing in the bush.

Now the major thought the time had arrived for wiping out the rebels. He pursued the disorganized troop into the clearing. This clearing was overgrown with stiff, short, bristling grass. the soil was therefore less soggy than the open country, and thus the *Rurales* were able to gallop somewhat faster. The muchachos ran like hunted hares, and it was a pleasure to the *Rurales* to chase after them. The pleasure was all the more pleasant when the heavy rain lightened and the clouds started to clear.

"Don't fire," ordered the major, "until I give the signal." He turned to his lieutenant. "D'you see, Lieutenant, down there in the clearing is an even bigger crowd of them. When we've got them all huddled together, then I'll have both our machine guns pepper them. Caramba, you'll see then how our sweet automatics can avenge us. It'll be good for you to learn how effective they are. Bit of the art of war."

The shock troop, in their retreat, had now joined up with the other companies that long before had been ordered to withdraw into the bush. The racing mob, reinforced by these companies, now amounted to some two hundred men. They seemed confused enough, and it was only natural that the *Rurales* should rejoice in pursuing these fleeing herds. It was more pleasurable than rounding up cattle. For beneath the fleeing muchachos were also numerous horses, mules, and donkeys that had been stolen from the *monterías*. These terrified animals, which were being beaten to incite them to greater speed, brought the fleeing crowd to such a state of confusion that it appeared to the well-drilled, smartly riding *Rurales* that nothing could bring order out of this panic-stricken mob.

But the major, so certain of victory, never noticed—and none of his officers seemed to notice either—that this indescribable confusion only served to conceal a subtle strategy that General had worked out.

The fleeing mass took up the whole width of the broad clearing. They spread out to either side until both wings were forced into the verge of the bush to left and right of the clearing. The excited muchachos were so confused that, in order to escape quicker, they pressed their flanks into the bush in order to force a passage that was denied to them in the center.

The prospect seemed uncommonly favorable to the *Rurales* when the muchachos, like scared ants, scrabbled and stumbled away. But the *Rurales* still did not realize that the muchachos whom they pressed and squeezed against the edge of the bush sifted farther and farther into the undergrowth, ran deeper and deeper into the bush, and stood waiting until the *Rurales* should once again come level with them. As soon as the *Ru-rales* had passed them, pursuing the retreating mob, the muchachos, still remaining in the bush, crept back once more in the direction of the *finca*. When they had gone a few hundred yards in this direction, they then turned and approached the edge of the clearing. Now they were at the rear of the *Ru-rales*.

Had the major had to deal with experienced soldiers as opponents, or with trained revolutionaries led by knowledgeable officers, he would certainly have exercised more caution. Probably he would never even have ridden into that clearing, but would simply have awaited the rebels, who, sooner or later, would have had to show themselves in open country. But these louse-infested, filthy Indians could not think for themselves, and that was why they needed dictators and tyrants to relieve them of the burden of thinking. And because these Indians could not think for themselves, they certainly couldn't make any plans. Therefore, at them! Charge ahead!

Only the men of the first two companies understood what General was intending, for they had listened while he had explained his plan to the captains. Thus the companies farther behind knew nothing of the plan. They saw only those fleeing, and were swept up in the fight themselves. They resisted, but in face of the stronger leading companies which bore down upon them, they could do nothing and were swept away by the surging tide. Every few minutes they screamed: "We're no cowards! We don't run away! Turn on the *soldados!* We need their rifles!"

Unfortunately for the complete success of the scheme, the fleeing mob burst upon the two rear companies of the line of march, those very companies that formed the powerful reserve force. It was these companies that numbered among them Andreu and Lucio Ortiz, called Colonel, and several others of the more intelligent muchachos.

Neither General nor Professor nor the initiated captains had either time or opportunity to acquaint the rear guard with the plan. Thus, scarcely had the first groups of fleeing muchachos surged against the two approaching rear-guard companies than these two companies broke out into a wild yell: "You miserable sons of bitches, would you run away from police and soldiers? We're rebels! *Tierra y Libertad!* Up at the hirelings of the tyrants! At them and kill them! They've revolvers and rifles! The bloody swine! Attack them!"

Like maddened steers, the muchachos broke through the fleeing herd, and in a few minutes they found themselves at the front, scarcely fifty yards away from the *Rurales*.

The battle began some ten minutes too early.

The two enveloping wings had not been able to spread out completely along the sides of the clearing. The several dozen muchachos who had been able to slink into the bush had not yet reassembled and were not strong enough to cut off the retreating *Rurales*, who were mounted, and thus encircle them. If the rear guard had arrived just a quarter of an hour later, not one man of the *Rurales* would have escaped.

The muchachos of the two last companies, caring nothing for bullets, ran, machetes in their hands, screaming and howling, at the *Rurales*. Even those muchachos who possessed revolvers or shotguns could not waste the time to use these weapons. It would have taken too long and was too troublesome. Besides, any young fool could shoot with a pistol. There was no bravery in that! It was better and bloodier with machetes! Thus excited, inflamed, embattled, the muchachos threw away not only their packs but also their guns. Anything like that was cumbersome in a real battle such as now confronted them.

The *Rurales*, as they rode to the attack, had brought their rifles to the ready, resting upright on their right thighs. They needed only to raise the butts—and fire. This they tried to do, but the majority of the shots whistled away over the tops of the trees. For the shrieking and screaming of the oncoming horde of raging muchachos threw the horses out of the control of their riders. It had come too suddenly and unexpectedly. The horses reared, struck out, whirled around, tried to take the bits in their teeth and to gallop wildly to the rear. A dozen riders were thrown. The unhorsed *Rurales* pulled themselves together and began to shoot their rifles. Not one of them succeeded in firing a full magazine. Long before that, three or four of the enemy were at their throats. And three seconds later each man had been hacked to pieces.

If the ground had been really hard, the *Rurales* could probably have fled and escaped in greater numbers. But now when one merely attempted to wheel his horse and spur it into retreat, five muchachos immediately hung on to the horse's tail and three clung to the reins and three more dragged the man from the saddle.

An attempt to set up the machine guns got no further than unbuckling the straps. The crew was immediately torn to ribbons.

The major and the lieutenant both tried to bellow orders. But no one attended to them. The bugler lay headless in the mud. Horses were trampling on his body.

"Save himself who can," shouted the major, to provide himself with an excuse and reason for riding off. His lieutenant was dead.

The major had fled barely fifty paces and believed himself already hidden, when there burst from the side of the bush five muchachos—some of those who had crept in there on their retreat. It took no more than two seconds for a shot from his elegant gold-chased revolver to miss its aim, and five seconds later his best friend would not have been able to identify his corpse.

Four managed to escape. They owed it to their horses, which were so scared that they forgot the mud and the holes in the ground and scampered away for dear life.

The two flanking troops reached the clearing half a minute too late. Otherwise not even the boldest horse could have succeeded in saving its rider.

Yet in fact the successful escape of the four *Rurales* was no loss to the muchachos. For the *Rurales* had thrown away their rifles and ammunition in order to make sure their escape.

These four fleeing *Rurales*, in their headlong gallop, met their two comrades who had been thrown off their wounded horses before the advance on the clearing. These two were marching on foot back to the *finca*. Fortunately for them, several riderless horses were also careering in that direction. The four mounted *Rurales* were able to catch two of these horses and mount their hobbling comrades, so that these six returned to the sheltering walls of the *finca*, defeated and humiliated, the only survivors of the troop that had ridden out so proud and elegant.

The *Rurales* who had been thrown had not even their weapons left. Their rifles had remained hanging at the pommels when the horses tumbled and flung off their riders. The horses themselves, however, had gotten to their feet after a few moments and, in spite of their wounds, had cantered after the main troop and followed them into the clearing, where later they collapsed from loss of blood, and the muchachos were able to appropriate the saddles and rifles.

When the booty was counted, the rebels found themselves the richer by six new rifles, eight revolvers, and three pairs of field glasses. In addition, they were now in possession of two new machine guns complete with ammunition. The magazines of the rifles were, admittedly, with very few exceptions all empty, but every one of the fallen mounted *Rurales* carried forty to sixty additional rounds in his cartridge belt and pockets.

Among the booty were watches, rings, pocket knives, and other belongings of the *Rurales*. These objects belonged to those who had overcome and killed the owners, and when this could not be clearly decided, the muchachos did not quarrel over it. Most of them laid no value on getting any of the plunder. All money found was handed over to Professor for the military treasury. There were about 320 pesos, of which more than 250 had belonged to the major and forty to the lieutenant. The rank and file had, in many cases, less than a peso in their pockets, several of them not even ten centavos, for it was six weeks since they had last undertaken house searches in the premises of citizens who had been denounced.

Colonel, who had arrived with the rear troop, had had experience with machine guns, for he had received training in these weapons in his battalion. His heart rejoiced when he saw these two beautiful, brightly polished *ametralladoras*. He embraced them and kissed them like sweethearts. "Oh, won't I tickle you up beautifully, *chamacas tan dulces*. I'll make you hop!" he said, stroking and caressing them. "And you'll sprinkle all those mangy mercenaries until God in Heaven will have to laugh. These are what we've been wanting, muchachos."

"General," he shouted, "who are you going to put in charge of these two humble squirts? Their polished brass looks like sparkling gold. Hey, *mi general*, you must have someone in command of them. What do you say to that excellent suggestion?"

General walked up and laughed. "You, Colonel. You're in command of the machine guns. I can't take care of everything. You're appointed."

"*Gracias, mi general*. I'll form a machine-gun company right away and start instructing the muchachos. *Que chinguen todas las madres*, curse it, now we're over the hump. I'd take on two of the Cacique's regiments with these. Hope he sends us two regiments. Or, better still, a division. The more the merrier. We could do with two light field guns as well. What do you think, General, about us acting in such a way that the bloody hangman, sitting on his throne plastered with eagles, has to send out two divisions against us? Perhaps with six field guns? He'd only need to send them out, and we'd soon take them. Then we could march against Tullum and visit the governor."

He saw Andreu standing near, and called out good-humoredly, "Hey, Andrucho, what do you think? Do you know enough reading and writing to make a new governor? We need a governor from among our people."

Andreu laughed. Then he winked at Colonel, General, Professor, and Celso in turn, laughed again, and said, "We'll discuss the state of the bridge when we get to the riverbank. It's a damned long way to Tullum. And between here and the *zócalo* of Tullum, where the governor's palace is, there are three battalions of infantry, four cavalry regiments, and probably twenty companies of mounted *Rurales*."

General made a long face, then a wry one, and then eyed from foot to head the officer in charge of the machine-gun section. "Did you hear that, Colonel?" he asked. "There are twenty companies of *Rurales* between here and Tullum." He smiled ironically.

Colonel glanced around to see what sort of faces the muchachos were making. They were impassive. They did not worry about their future. Regiments and battalions might stand in the way, or they might not. They would be attacked when they were met. So long as they were not met, it was all the same whether there were eight regiments or eight hundred to be conquered.

The fight, as rapidly as it had developed, and as successfully as it had ended for the muchachos, had nevertheless taken its toll. If General's plan had succeeded in its entirety, it might have been possible to overwhelm the *Rurales* before they were able to fire off even ten rounds.

Although the majority of the shots fired by the surprised troops had gone off into the air, without doing any harm apart from a few tattered treetops, enough of the soldiers, all trained men, had found an opportunity to blaze off their full magazines into the close-packed throng of muchachos before they were torn down. But even if the machine guns had been set up and ready for action at the moment of the attack by the rear guard, the defeat of the *Rurales* would still have been inevitable, for the muchachos had occupied the bush on either side in sufficient strength, and in the bush the best machine gun is useless. But the losses on the rebel side would probably have been of such a magnitude that perhaps half of all the muchachos would have been left on the battlefield.

When the men had collected their dead, they found that nineteen had fallen. More than thirty were wounded, the greater number by bullets and a minority from saber cuts and the hoof blows of terrified horses. Before evening eight of the wounded died, so that the number of dead mounted to twenty-seven.

They were buried without much ado. When they had all been interred and a few muchachos had gabbled one or two remembered prayers over them, the dead were forgotten.

Professor said to the men standing around the little mounds of earth, in which crude crosses were stuck, "We're rebels, aren't we, muchachos?"

"*Tierra y Libertad!*" they shouted in reply.

"Right, *camaradas, tierra libre para todos. Tierra sin capataces y sin amos.* And because we're rebels, we haven't any time now to mourn our fallen brothers. We'll remember them when we've won the revolution. And then we'll remember them with honor, with devotion, and with gratitude, because they fell in the cause of the revolution. But now we have no time for that. Now we must think of the living and of victory. The fallen can celebrate no victory. To the victors belong the celebration. Only the living can enjoy the results of a victory for our revolution. The muchachos, our true comrades, who now lie buried here, must fall in order that we may conquer. They were not the first to die for land and freedom against the Cacique, and they will not be the last to die so. One thing I can promise you, muchachos, and what I promise you here will one day come true. Of all of us who stand here today at the graves of our dead brothers, not two dozen will be left alive when the revolution is finally won. But that is no matter, brothers. We are not the first men on earth, and we are not the last. After us there will come hundreds, thousands of generations, and these generations that will come after us will live in freedom from tyrants, oppressors, and dictators, and they will give us thanks and honor, we who died for their freedom. That, too, is worth something, to be honored by future generations. But these—these *Rurales* who are now lying about in shreds and pieces—fallen as mercenaries of the dictator for the sake of keeping him in power so that he can feed the people with lies, they will soon be more forgotten than that broken branch lying over there. The coming generations will remember them not as fighters, not as faithful soldiers, but as tools of the executioner, as torturers, as uniformed slaves, whose wisdom consisted of being the obedient lackeys of El Caudillo and his aristocrats and scientificos. The tyrants and dictators and oppressors of men occupy but a brief part of the history of mankind, even though that part is ever the richest in terror and fear. But to us, as to all fighters for freedom, for human justice, for democracy, to us belongs the whole history of man. We are the helpers, while these menials are the hinderers of time; they are the enemies of peaceful progress. And thus, *camaradas*, we take leave of our fallen brothers. Let us all remove our hats in honor to our brothers who have fallen for our revolution. Let us each take up a handful of earth, and then let us lay this earth upon the graves in which our brothers now sleep. And after that we will shout: *Tierra y Libertad! Viva la revolución proletaria! Abajo los dictadores y los tiranos! Tierra y Libertad!*"

When the muchachos had shouted this invocation which Professor had declaimed before them, and kept a second's silence, Professor raised his hand and said, now in a quietened voice, "*Adiós, muchachos. Que duerman bien. Adiós, muchachos. Dulce es morir por la revolución de los pobres.* Sleep well, children. It is sweet to die for the revolution of the poor. Sleep in peace."

He put on his hat and walked over to General. In a completely changed voice he said, "Now—to the *finca!*"

General leaped onto a horse in order to be better seen and called across the crowd, "*A la finca, muchachos! Adelante!*"

As the last man in the mob heaved up his pack and set out on the march, following the advancing muchachos, the mangled remains of the *Rurales* were already swarming thickly with red ants.

High above the bush one could see a troop of vultures wheeling around, gradually nearer and nearer, until at last they formed a narrow circle over that part of the clearing where the battle had taken place.

Far ahead, leading the troop, marched General, who had dismounted from the horse, together with Professor and Celso.

Around General's neck were slung the major's field glasses. He stopped, peered through them toward the *finca*, focused them, looked again, and then let them fall to the extent of their strap.

Professor, too, had glasses, while the third pair was carried by Colonel, who once more was leading the rear troop, supported by Andreu as commissary and quartermaster.

"It's a fine thing having such good glasses," said Professor, affectionately tapping his binoculars, which, like General's, were hanging on his chest at strap's length.

"I suppose so," replied General indifferently and thoroughly uninterested. "I suppose such a piece of tin's a fine thing. But it's not worth a lot. When one can only see the swine through the things one's too far away to manhandle them. When they're near enough to be given a hot reception, there's no need for any glasses. And when they're so near that you can run a machete into their stomachs, the lousy things only dangle around your waist and get in the way. What would I do with such muck? It may be all right for those hirelings, but not for a rebel."

He removed the glasses from around his neck and handed them to Celso. "Here, take them. You're a colonel and can use them properly."

"Hell," answered Celso. "I don't need any glasses. I can see well enough with my own eyes. And at five hundred paces I can see a little bird sitting on a twig, and I can tell you what sort of bird it is."

General laughed. "There, you see, Professor, no one will have the things as a gift."

"All right. Give them to me. The glasses I have are so full of bubbles and flecks, I'll be glad to have yours. I can use a good pair. My eyes aren't as sharp as yours. Give them to me."

"With pleasure," said General.

Professor removed his binoculars, took those offered him, hung them around his neck, and called to the marching muchachos, "Here, who'd like some field glasses?"

Nobody said a word.

Professor stopped for a moment and looked about him. Then he saw little Pedrito striding determinedly toward him. The lad had his small pack slung on his back.

Beside him marched his young aunt, Modesta, also carrying her pack. She was a Tsotsil girl, about seventeen years old, and it did the eyes of a man good to look at her.

"Hey—*chamaco!*" Professor called him over. "Here's a present for you—two little tubes nailed together. If you look through them, you can see the men in the moon canoeing on their rivers."

The lad turned to his aunt. "Is it true, *verídico, tía*, that with these little black cotton-reels one can see the people of the moon in their canoes?"

"I don't know about that, *m'jito*," answered Modesta, smiling at him. "But take it, when Professor gives it to you. Professor's a very clever and educated man. If he says you can see the people in the moon through those tiny *tubitos*, then it's so."

Professor hung the glasses around the boy's neck. The lad felt as if his teacher had decorated him with a medal. Beaming, he beckoned to another somewhat older boy who was marching in their troop and showed him his new toy.

The older boy examined it from all sides and then said contemptuously, "You couldn't even shoot a broken-legged hare with that. I want a rifle. And that's what I'll get for myself in the next battle. You just watch how I win it. With my pocketknife here I'll get myself a rifle. All through this march I've prayed morning and evening to the sacred Virgin that we'll come quick upon some *Rurales*. What you've got there is just a toy for little boys like you, not for men like me. *Soy un rebelde*, and I'll get myself a rifle."

This lad was ten years old, but he carried a pack that must have weighed sixty pounds.

But Pedrito wasn't going to have Professor's present despised. He nudged Modesta's arm furtively. "Is there a moon tonight, Aunt Modesta?"

"No *mi vidita*. I don't think so. It won't shine till next week. You'll have to wait till then before you can see the men in the moon paddling their canoes."

"Aunt," he said after a moment of silence, "then perhaps I can see the departed who live on the stars?"

"Perhaps, my son. We'll have a good look tonight to see if the stars come out. And then we'll find the biggest of them, which has the most lanterns burning, and maybe we'll be able to see the people who make the clouds for us, and paint the flowers and birds so brightly."

4

The rain, after the brief battle, had gradually eased. It had not lasted as long as the muchachos had expected. But it had come very opportunely for them and had stopped as they were burying their fallen comrades.

Great tatters of dark clouds scurried above them and dispersed. And as the troop now marched toward the big *finca*, the sun stood rejoicing in a blue sky.

The *finca* was, like a fortress, surrounded by a high wall. Outside, at a distance of about 150 yards from the wall, and, from the viewpoint of the *finca*, to the north, lay the peons' village.

The troop came marching toward the *finca* from the east. General, Professor, Celso, Andreu, and some ten other muchachos had sought out horses for themselves and were now mounted on them. They were horses that had been captured from the *Rurales*. The great majority of the remaining horses, mules, and donkeys of the troop were saddle-sore from the packs and famished and exhausted from the long march through the jungle swamps and over the rocky heights. Many had collapsed on the way and had had to be unloaded in order to be able to progress at all. Many more had been lost by plunging from the narrow mountain paths, while others had sunk into swamps or been drowned at river crossings because they had been too exhausted to swim through the swirling currents.

The muchachos who were farthest forward in the troop and were in a position to have a good view of the *finca*, particularly those who were on horseback, found the *finca* buildings remarkably quiet. Not a soul was visible.

"The *finquero* has fled, with all his brood," said General. "Those accursed mercenaries who escaped us must have brought the news to him, telling him of how many survived from that proud gang of cavaliers, telling him that there's none left today for the *fiesta* where they'd hoped to display their glittering uniforms like well-groomed apes upon a hurdy-gurdy. But I tell you it's a good thing the *finquero* and his company now realize at last that we're serious and that we know how to attack and don't care a damn whether we die or whether we live."

"Well spoken, General," said Professor. "That's what these festering sons of bitches must learn sooner or later. They'll have to find out that in the end they'll lose, whether we win or whether we're thrashed like hounds. Even if we don't win, they won't any longer have peons or slaves that they can beat and drive around."

One of the muchachos who had captured the *Rurales'* bugle and had been appointed trumpeter of the troop and now rode at General's side, said, "It's good for us if the *finca* is deserted. We'll have it for the night, and tomorrow we shall be able to have a day's rest."

"We shall have two days' rest there," replied General.

"But then the Federals will arrive," said another fellow.

"Let us hope so." General took that for granted. "It's all the same to us whether we deal here at the *finca* with the battalion that'll be sent against us—or on the way to Hucutsin or Achlumal or anywhere else before we reach Jovel or Balun Canan. The sooner we meet them, the more weapons we'll get and the sooner we'll get them. As long as the dictator squats on his throne and hopes he can throttle the revolution with machine guns, they will go on sending Federals against us. Whether it's here or there is unimportant.

"*Ay, caramba!*" he interrupted himself suddenly. "*Caray, que chinguen todas las madres, cabrones, y mulas.* What in hell is happening there?" He stood up in his stirrups, then shouted to all the muchachos who were mounted: "Advance! Attack! Get at those peons!"

A large group of peons from the *finca*, men, women, and children, about half a hundred in number, had burst out from their miserable mud huts and, panic-stricken, were attempting to flee toward the west where the bush was closest. Their dogs barked, and several of the peons were making an effort to drive their goats, sheep, and donkeys with them. When they perceived that this livestock was holding them up, they left the animals to fend for themselves and raced after the families leading the flight.

The mounted muchachos took less than ten minutes to round up all the families and cut off their line of escape to the edge of the bush.

A despairing cry of fear rose from the peons. Men, women, and children fell to their knees, raised their hands in entreaty, and begged the muchachos to spare their miserable lives, for they were only poor—wretchedly poor—Indian peons who had done no harm to anyone and had never betrayed to the patron a word about the rebellion in the *monterías*.

"Stand up, you! All of you!" shouted General. "There's no need to kneel to anyone. Get that into your heads. No one any longer is superior or inferior."

Not comprehending this assurance, plain and forthright as it was, but simply obeying the command, all the men and women stood up. Submissively the men held their hats in their hands, bowed forward, and fixed their eyes respectfully on the ground until such time as one of the victors might be pleased to call a peon by his name and thus grant him permission to raise his eyes to his master.

The women covered their heads completely and only peeped with one eye through a fold in their cheap and tattered *rebozos*, without even daring to look higher than the horses' hoofs. Several of the women sobbed and sniffled into their kerchiefs, while the children, whimpering and howling, crept behind the grownups. Several babes in arms, woken from their sleep, wailed and tried to stick their little heads out of the tightly corded bundles on their mothers' backs, feeling they were going to suffocate. Other babies cooed happily and beat their little fists on their mothers' necks. One mother, to avoid assuming an immodest position before the mounted men, attempted with her head to squash her baby down into the wrappings on her back, as if she hoped thereby to deny the existence of the child. The dogs began once more to snarl, and some particularly bold ones made attempts to snap at the legs of the horses. As soon as the peons perceived such impertinence in their dogs, the owners gave them such hefty kicks that the animals flew several yards through the air.

The fact that the muchachos on the horses were more ragged, filthy, and vermin-infested than the peons seemed to have escaped the notice of the overawed people from the *finca*. No more did they seem to perceive that the muchachos who had arrived here as conquerors were Indians like themselves, that they were of their own class and, like them, regarded all patrones as tyrants.

But the muchachos were mounted on proud horses, and they carried weapons. And whoever came riding on such fine horses, and had revolvers and rifles, and fought with *Rurales* and conquered *Rurales* must be a new master, probably a crueler, more relentless and unjust master than the former one. What happened at this *finca* now was exactly the same as occurred later throughout the whole Republic: the peons, accustomed for years to masters, tyrants, oppressors, and dictators, were not in truth liberated by the revolution, not even where the feudal estates were divided among the families of peons in little holdings, in *ejidos*. They remained slaves, with the single difference that their masters had changed, that mounted revolutionary leaders were now the wealthy, and that the politicians now used small-holding, ostensibly liberated peons to enrich themselves immeasurably, to increase their political influence, and, with the help of the now independent peons, whom murder and bestialities kept in a constant state of fear and terror, were able to commit every conceivable crime in order to become deputy or governor, and that with no other intention than to fill their chests and coffers with gold to over-flowing.

He who has the rifle and the revolver is the master of him who has no revolver. The muchachos carried revolvers and were therefore looked upon as the new masters and patrones. The fact that they were ragged Indians was pure coincidence. Tomorrow they would be smartly clothed, like *ladinos*.

The peons had reason enough to flee and be in mortal terror when they saw the rebels approaching. They knew their country, their poor, beautiful, pitiful country. They had been born in this country and grown up in it. Revolvers were not worn for decoration. They were worn for the purpose of shooting when the opportunity offered; and, as in war, when no opportunity offered, it was created. Here was a battle between *Rurales* and rebels. The victors were now the rebels, but a number of them had fallen in the fight. The fallen must be avenged, and vengeance had to be taken on those who were unable to defend themselves. There would be no inquiry as to whether they had had anything to do with the fight. Dictatorship distinguishes itself from other forms of government chiefly by its impatience toward other men and by the relentless wreaking of vengeance upon the humble and the weak. The peons belonged to the *finca*, where the *Rurales* had lain in wait, where they had been tended, and from the master of which they had received all possible support. The *finquero*, together with his family and house servants, had fled. No vengeance could be taken upon them. But the peons, who had not fled because they had perceived their master's flight too late, were here, and from them the victors could just as well exact vengeance and satisfaction as from the guilty. The prisoner is always guilty.

After more than thirty years of dictatorship, the peons knew that they were always the losers, always the punished, always the whipped, and always the hanged. Rebels fell in battle. The surviving proletariat, who had not so much as lifted a finger on behalf of the revolution, were always the ones who paid for that revolution—with their few hard-earned and buried savings, with their skins, and with their lives.

"Why were you running away, *hombres?*" asked Professor. He dismounted from his horse and went up to the men standing nearest. He clapped them on the shoulders and backs to show them that he regarded them as friends.

But it was not out of friendliness—for peons never relinquished their mistrust—it was only out of politeness and in order not to anger the victors that they now looked up and strove to behave as if they accepted the genuineness of this offer of friendship. Some of the women came forward and kissed Professor's hand. The men and the majority of the women ran over to the remaining muchachos, who had gradually dismounted from their horses, and bowed deeply to them, kissing their hands, too.

Professor asked again, "Why were you running away? We don't bite the heads off poor Indian peons."

The men tried to form a sad smile with their lips. It was not entirely successful.

"Well, tell me why." Professor put his arm about the shoulders of one man. "The patron told you we were bandits. Didn't he say that, the filthy son of a whore?"

Fearfully the people shook their heads. That was exactly what the *finquero* had said to the peons who were working in the patio at the moment of his flight. But not even the rack would have extorted such an admission from the peons; for had they repeated what the patron had said to them, the rebels would have assumed this was what they themselves thought. That was how it had always been in questionings by the *finquero* and by the police. If a man admitted to something that he had heard, he was then immediately accused of having said that himself. Dictators teach one to see nothing, hear nothing, know nothing, think nothing, and only to open one's mouth to shout *Viva!*

"There's no cause for you to run away from us, *amigos,*" said Andreu now. "We're your friends."

"*Con su permiso, jefe,*" replied a man, "we were not running away. We knew very well that you were our friends. We all just wanted to go into the bush there."

"Then why were you taking your pots and your goats and pigs?" asked Colonel.

"We wanted to have a very, very small *fiesta* there this evening. Just a very tiny feast, for a saint, a little saint, a saint of the Indians, and we didn't want the patron to know that we still prayed, though only occasionally, to our Indian saints."

Andreu saw Celso standing up and went over to him. "They're not so stupid," he said, laughing. "I'd never have thought of such a good excuse on our *finca*. If they want to celebrate their own old saints, they can't do it near the *finca*, where the patron could see them and accuse them of being godless heathens. Therefore they go into the bush. And, of course, they do that only when the patron is not at home, having taken his whole family to the city or on a visit to another *finca*."

"*Donde está tu patron?* Where is your master?" Professor asked one man.

"Ah, *patroncito*, forgive me. I don't know. He didn't tell us. I think he has gone off with all his family to a wedding. He said something about it last week."

"Where is the wedding?"

"I don't know exactly, but I think it's in Tumbala."

That was about six days' journey distant.

Now that the advance troop had approached quite close, General shouted to them all to march on into the patio, the great courtyard of the *finca*. The buildings there were large enough for all the muchachos to sleep under a roof for the first time in nearly six weeks, protected from rain, thunder, and storms and against prowling animals and creeping snakes.

"And all of you," Professor turned to the peons, "you're coming with us now into the patio."

At this the wives of the peons began wailing and screaming and threw themselves on their knees and begged for mercy. They were certain that they had been ordered into the patio only to witness their men being murdered. The men themselves showed no sign of fear. They marched, as commanded, into the patio. What was the use of whimpering? They marched ahead like obedient soldiers who know precisely that if they are fated to be murdered they can do nothing about it, either by weeping and whining or by abjectly begging for mercy. The only positive course would be to resist, not to obey, and to take their weapons and shoot down those issuing the orders, and this they will not do simply because they are obedient soldiers whose brains and powers of resistance have been numbed in the first few weeks of their military training. Besides, they have their honor; and for the sake of their honor they must accept everything. For only the dishonorable rebel, and only the godforsaken will look askance at his country's flag, shrug his shoulders, and say, "Red, white, black, or green, flowers throughout the world are seen." Of course the peons knew nothing about a soldier's honor, but once given an order, they marched as willingly as other sheep.

Within a few minutes campfires were burning in the patio. Like ants, the muchachos swarmed through the rooms in the buildings. Everything that was found and considered useful was looted: blankets, saddles, clothes, shoes, suits, chests, and boxes. A typewriter flew in a wide arc into the patio and burst into fragments. Three sewing machines followed. Everything made of wood was hacked up. Tables, chairs, bedsteads, cupboards simultaneously fell victim. Wood for the campfires was more important to the muchachos than a piano, which was flung piecemeal into the flames. Next came the doors. For years the muchachos had been accustomed to having no tables or chairs, and no doors in their miserable sleeping huts. And they had never learned that a piano was anything more than a wooden box with wires. Why should they respect objects that had never been intended for them, that had no meaning for them other than as the property of their masters; which might not be touched, not because such things could be useful, but because they were the property of those who had learned and been taught to enjoy these objects?

"Who's that in that picture? The man with the medals and

crosses on his chest?" asked one of the muchachos, pointing to a great portrait on the wall.

"That's the cursed swine of a Cacique, the dictator, the noble leader of the country," shouted Colonel, and spat a huge gob of phlegm in the middle of the portrait's face.

The slime ran down over the beautifully painted decorations on the breast. But before it reached the broad leather uniform belt, and soiled and sullied the handsome gold eagle on the buckle, one of the muchachos leaped up, tore the picture down from the wall, stamped on it, and said, "I should shit right on his nose. But I'm not so vulgar as to do it here in this fine room, where we're going to sleep well tonight for once. I'll do better to hang it against my behind." He tore it from its frame, pushed the top of the canvas under the back of his belt, and let the rest dangle down like an apron over his buttocks.

In the rooms there were a number of paintings, finely executed portraits of the patron, his wife, his father, and heaven knows who else. There were pictures of scenes from operas and from Greek tragedies. Not one picture was left intact. They were all flung into the fire. The rooms soon took on a desolate aspect, but the emptier they became, the more the muchachos felt themselves at home. Not one of them, not even Andreu or Celso—Professor only excepted—had ever seen furniture in a house in which they or their parents had lived. And if they had ever known pictures, then it was those yellowed, faded reproductions surviving from out-of-date advertising calendars sent out by cigarette firms and breweries, and here and there perhaps a representation of a saint in which not a feature was anatomically correct.

In nooks and corners and on the tiled floor were spread out the mats and bundles and packs of the muchachos. Only two rooms in the whole *finca* had wooden floors. They were certainly the bedrooms of the master and mistress or else rooms for guests. In these rooms the women and children of the troop camped.

In the wide patio things had become lively, noisy, and gay. Dead friends and comrades were now wholly forgotten. There were more important things to think of. Who will and must live cannot worry about the dead. Let each estate take care of itself.

The muchachos were luxuriating in good drinking water. At twenty places baths were being taken and articles of clothing washed. Crackling and roaring, ten or twelve fires burned merrily in the patio. For as long as the muchachos could remember, they had never had such wonderful fires as these. In the past it had always been damp, green wood which they had had to burn, the smoke biting their eyes. But these pictures and beautiful furniture and the thick-gilded frames of the great mirrors were as dry as old bones and made a fire that sometimes stank of varnish and paint, but which burned joyfully and openly and not sadly with thick, blinding, stinging smoke.

There was yowling, dancing, singing, music from mouth organs and guitars, whistling, joking, and horseplay. It was as if this was no gathering of grown men, now warriors and rebels, but a happy, exuberant throng of adolescent boys and girls setting out on a short holiday.

The peons, with their women and children, stood in the middle of the patio, nervously huddled together like timid animals. They were close to the stone altar on which a huge fire used to blaze each night, kept burning till almost midnight, to make the patio and the many extensive *finca* buildings appear less somber and gloomy. Even in the largest and richest *fincas* of that far region there was no electricity. A gasoline lamp was an unheard-of luxury which the *finqueros* and their families from the neighboring estates would willingly undertake a hard two or three days' journey to see. The gentry themselves used only candles, generally made on the premises. Even paraffin lamps of the simplest kind were seldom to be found in the *fincas*, and anyone owning one was regarded as very modern. The peons had no other light in their huts than that emanating from a cooking fire on the ground or a fire burning in a low clay hearth. When no fire was burning, pine slivers served for illumination. The peons burned candles in their huts only at a death watch or in honor of a saint. Everything today was as it had been for years. Everything, for master and peon alike, up to this very day.

It was still too early for the pile of wood to be lit on the altar, for it was yet three hours to sunset.

For a good while the *finca* peons who had been ordered here were left to themselves. None dared to run away, although they were well acquainted with the buildings and could easily have escaped, for the sentries at the two gates were as negligent as only sentries with rebel forces and revolutionary armies can be and are.

Now, however, Professor came up to the peons, followed by General, Celso, Andreu, Santiago, and about twenty other muchachos who took more interest in the rebellion than the hundreds of their fellows who were content to be allowed to fight but otherwise had no responsibility and were not required to use their heads or to wrestle with those ideas about which Professor talked so much. They were always ready to have their bodies mangled and to sacrifice their lives in battle with the *Rurales;* but apart from that they wished to be left in peace and only to have their share in the fruits of a successful revolution. Their idea of the rebellion was limited to the simple thoughts: "Down with the dictatorship!" "Down with tyrants and oppressors!" For, so long as the dictatorship was not overthrown, there could be no *Tierra y Libertad.* That was clear to all. Everything else that was discussed by the more intelligent men—the rights of man, profits, capitalism, democracy, or even socialism and cooperation—made them sleepy. That is why so many rebellions and insurrections by the proletariat go awry, because the workers are literally fed up with ideas and problems for the discussion of which there will be plenty of time when the rebels have enjoyed five years of undisputed victory.

Professor jumped up onto the stone altar. Then he shouted to the peons to come closer. When he began to speak, more and more of the muchachos in the patio came to listen to him. But they did not press to the front when they realized that Professor was only addressing himself to the peons of the *finca.*

"Don't be afraid to crowd around, *hermanitos*," he said to the peons. He said it with a laugh. And the people gathered a little confidence and pressed closer.

"How big is the *finca* here?" he asked.

"Maybe a thousand *caballerias*," called out one.

"You don't know what you're talking about," interrupted a neighbor. "It's at least three times bigger."

"Of course it is," shouted someone boldly from the back. "Of course it is. It's ten times bigger."

Then one of the older peons began reflectively to describe the boundaries of the *finca*. Professor and General, from the elevation of the stone altar, could estimate the extent, the more easily since the ranch house had been built on a hill situated approximately in the center of the vast feudal estate.

"It must cover between twenty and fifty thousand acres," said Professor to General.

"Apparently."

"How many families are you here?" asked Professor now.

"About ninety," answered the man Professor was looking at.

"It's not ninety. There are more than a hundred," interposed another.

"You're both asses, that's what you are," shouted a third. "How do you make out we're ninety families? If you count in the major-domo and the carpenter and the rope-maker, even then we're not ninety. And they're not peons like us. They all went off with the patron. And you've forgotten, too, that five families were given by the patron to his son-in-law, and he sold four families to Don Claudio for his two best horses which Don Claudio gave him for them."

"Who is this Don Claudio?" asked Professor.

"Don Claudio is the patron of the Las Delicias *finca*, about twenty leagues from here."

"Then all told you're about ninety families working here for your patron?" said Professor.

"That may be right. Quite a number of families are farther out, watching the herds. They have their own little *aldea*, all for themselves, with a *capataz*. We seldom go there. How can we know how many they are? And another watch is down there by the river."

"Good. Let's leave it at ninety families." Professor saw that he would never achieve his object, however long he discussed the number of acres and peon families.

His voice took on another tone: "Do you know what we are and why we have come here? Your patron lied to you. We are not bandits. We are your *amigos*, your friends. From now on there are no more peons. You are now *campesinos indepen-dientes*, free and independent peasants. Understand? It is true that we have come here to kill your patron if he doesn't give you freely all the land that you have been cultivating. He who tills the soil and is not honestly and properly paid for his work, to him belongs the fruits of the earth. Do you under-stand that?"

The peasants were unable to work their brains fast enough to comprehend this new ordinance. But they all said, "*Sí, mi jefe!*"

"I'm not your chief! I'm your friend and comrade. We are all comrades. There are no more bosses, no patrons, no major-domos, no *capataces*. You are now the masters of this *finca*. First thing tomorrow morning go out into the land and divide it among all your families, each family getting twenty acres. You seem to be the leader here." Professor turned to one of the older peons.

"No, *mi jefe, perdóneme, mi jefe,* I mean *mi amigo,* and I mean to say I'm not the leader here. It's Braulio. He is the old-est, and he is the *compadre* of almost all the families here."

"All right, Braulio, come here."

Judging from his appearance, Braulio was not the oldest of the peons. But all the peons said he was the oldest and must certainly have had good reasons for recognizing him as their leader. The causes might lie five hundred years back. Professor did not worry about it.

Braulio came up close. All the peons now crowded around in order not to lose a word from Professor. Plainly they had forgotten all their fear. The women, less interested in what their husbands were now discussing with the rebels, began to approach the wives of the rebels and to chat with them. The children had already scampered off and made friends with the children of the rebel troop. They were in haste to seal the friendships, and they set about it by taking the children into every possible hidden corner of the patio and there revealing secrets such as bring to all children, of whatever race, cruel and shocking experiences.

There were holes, the depths of which no one could guess, but which, the children asserted, were the breathing holes of a subterranean passage which led from a vault of the *finca* to Hucutsin and came out again in the crypt of a cathedral. In there were crabs, as big as a boy's head, and the children of the *finca* said they were not real crabs at all but the old wives of long dead peons, and some of them were the grandmothers of the last *finquero*, whom the *brujo*, the magician of the Indians, had transformed into crabs and who turned back again into women for three hours during the night of San Juan. Four of the children had seen, on the last San Juan's night, these women creep out of that old stone altar, and then they had watched how the women had gone to the river, but what they did there they didn't know, because they had been too frightened to go after them.

Thus the friendship of the children was sealed, and the women of the rebels lamented with the women of the peons about the trouble they had with their children, and how the mothers of the husbands always had to interfere in things that had nothing to do with them, leaving behind them nothing but trouble and discontent.

Meanwhile, also, the peons in front of the stone altar had begun to talk to the muchachos from the *monterías* who were standing nearby, exchanging tobacco and inviting them to come to their huts for the evening, where they had a half bottle well buried so it shouldn't be found by the old people.

Thus it was that, long before Professor had reached the high point of the evening with the distribution of the land, the peons had lost the last spark of fear and mistrust. Indeed, the peons assured each other that the rebels were thoroughly friendly and respectable muchachos; while the men from the *monterías* for their part asserted that the peons were in no way such stupid mules as had been thought. They could open their mouths and talk quite sensibly, when for ages one had imagined they were simply idiots, and since they were idiots, that was why they were peons and stupider than their goats.

Now came Braulio's turn to speak. He did not climb onto the stone altar, but spoke from where he stood, close to the feet of Professor, who was perched aloft and to whom he had to stare up obliquely in order to see his face. "This is a wonderful happening, *amigo*, that you've now given us the *finca*."

"Yes, it's your property, from now to all eternity. You tilled it, and everything that it contains belongs to you," confirmed Professor.

"The cattle as well?" called one of the peons.

"The cattle as well, and all the buildings here."

With both hands Braulio scratched his thick black hair, which showed a few gray streaks. It was the uncertain gesture of a peasant who of necessity must buy young piglets, but finds the price too high and can discover no other piglets on the market at a lower price.

"That's fine, that we now have the *finca*, *amigo*. But what shall we do when the patron comes back?"

"We'll take care that he never comes back."

"But if the Federals catch you, what then?"

"They won't catch us. Don't worry."

"You're not going to stay here on our *finca*?"

"Of course not. We're marching away, to give other peons their land."

"Then who'll protect us against the patron when you've marched away?"

"You'll have to protect yourselves. You're now the patrones and everything belongs to you."

"But if the patron comes back again and brings *Rurales* with him, what can we do then?"

"What we do with the *Rurales*. Kill them like mangy hounds."

"*Bueno, muy bueno, camarada,*" said Braulio. Pensively he turned away and vanished among the peons.

"*Tierra y Libertad!*" shouted Professor from the stone altar.

"*Tierra y Libertad!*" answered the muchachos. This time some of the peons also joined in the cry.

"*Viva la revolución!*" called General.

"*Viva la revolución de los índios y de los peones!*" came echoing from the patio.

On the second day, at a very early hour, when thick mists were still hanging heavily over the *finca* and morning was creeping up sleepily and slow, the troop had already left.

And it was toward eight o'clock that General called a halt on a hilltop and turned around to see how the troop was coming along. A hundred yards ahead there was a river crossing in their way. On the opposite bank two canoes lay in the sand. These were the property of the *finca*. The river was deep and its waters fast and turbulent, swollen by the rains that had filled the upper reaches of the river. Some of the muchachos would have to swim the roaring stream in order to bring the boats back. They were the very canoes the *finquero* and his family had used in their flight.

While General was still surveying the situation, he said suddenly to Professor, "They're having fun back there."

Professor raised his field glasses. "You're right, General. They're certainly having fun. The whole muck heap's on fire. There are only a few buildings still standing. *Dios mío*, that's what I'd call a bonfire. Now the chapel's burning, too. The dictatorship takes its farewell; the country begins to fill with ruins. With blazing martyrdoms it began; with burnings and ruins it will end. A perfectly natural cycle."

General was no longer listening. He was looking down at the wide river. "A perfectly natural cycle. And for God's sake how shall we get our army across there? That's what I'd like to know. It'll cost us at least two, possibly even three damned hot days. But cross we must!"

5

    The rebel army was on its way toward Achlumal. The staff had long debated which important center should first be visited, Achlumal or Hucutsin. Both places were small towns, and in both a chief of police had his seat, since these towns were the centers of their districts. Also, in both places were a company of *Rurales* as well as an important garrison of Federal troops.

Once again General anticipated the thinking of his opponents' officers when he suggested marching toward Achlumal instead of Hucutsin. He said rightly that the *Rurales* and Federals who were stationed in Hucutsin must be convinced that the rebels would advance against Hucutsin in order to reach Jovel via Teultepec, Oshchuc, and Vitztan. In Hucutsin were assembled the majority of the *finqueros* of the region, all armed and all accompanied by their armed major-domos and sons and cousins and such of their employees as were devoted to them.

The only natural way for the muchachos was through Hucutsin, for it led to those regions where most of the muchachos came from and where they had been recruited. It was the way they knew best, and one where they would always be sure of meeting friends and relations of their own race who in some form or other would assist them, either by espionage or by offering good concealment and showing them the best ways by which the rebels could fall on the uniformed troops from the rear.

The council of war was influenced by the capture of numerous peons who were making their way home from Hucutsin to their various *fincas*. These individuals, returning from market, confirmed General's conclusions as to what course the soldiers intended to take against the rebels. According to the reports of these captured peons, there was in fact a large concentration of State police and Federals in Hucutsin, as well as a considerable number of *finqueros*, who were so plentifully present that the peons thought some sort of *fiesta* or holiday must be taking place. Several peons, once having regained confidence, declared that everyone there knew that the rebels were on the march toward Hucutsin in order to encircle the city and to slaughter every living creature found therein.

When this report became known to the rebel staff, the captains of the individual companies were scarcely to be restrained. They would have rushed immediately upon Hucutsin. It was the quantity of weapons there that attracted them. Ordinary booty took second place, so far as booty was thought of at all.

General had a difficult stand to take against this blood lust. It was possible that the muchachos might accuse him of overgreat caution and even of cowardice.

But he, like Professor, Colonel, Celso, Santiago, Andreu, and Pedro, was clever enough to see that under these conditions the encirclement of the city could only be carried through with the loss of half their army.

General said, "Don't be fools. The *Rurales* and *finqueros* aren't such asses as to wait for us in Hucutsin. There, we'd be superior to them, with our adaptability, our knives, and our machetes. They know that. They'll wait well away from the town—three or four miles outside the place. I can even tell you where they'll wait for us. It will be at a fast-flowing river some distance out. We can't get around that river. We will have to cross it. Immediately after the crossing is a ravine, thickly surrounded with bush. That's where they'll sit and wait for us. And that's where we'll outwit them now."

Some peons were coming along the road on their way to market in Hucutsin. General called several of the muchachos to him, who, as a result of what he said to them, rapidly made friends with the traveling peons. These muchachos, knowing no better and in case of hesitation particularly urged on by Fidel, told the peons, with excited gestures, that in three days the troop would be in Hucutsin and would light such a blaze there that not even the walls of the patios would remain standing and not a soul would be left alive after they had finished with Hucutsin, for all the muchachos had a mighty reckoning to settle with the mayor and the chief of police there.

Scarcely had the peons arrived in Hucutsin than they hastened to repeat throughout the town what they had learned; and because they feared that they, too, might be slaughtered in error, they made haste to leave Huctusin again that same evening, which naturally confirmed in the minds of all the people, soldiers, and *finqueros* the belief that the rebels were in fact on the march toward that city.

"If we advance to attack Hucutsin," explained General further, "then we shall certainly have the garrison of Achlumal at our backs, and they have probably already received the information that we are marching against Hucutsin and have been ordered to attack us in the rear. Apart from that, the *Rurales* and Federals will attack us from the places that lie on the way from Hucutsin to Jovel. And they'd have overwhelmingly superior forces. They would wait for us on the plain or in some ambush and fall upon us unawares."

"What you say is right, General," interrupted Colonel.

"And that is why, since the people in Hucutsin are so damned certain we shall march against them, we shall now head toward Achlumal and attack the posts of the *Rurales* and Federals there. In that way we shall probably get another fifty to a hundred rifles more, perhaps even another machine gun, and so much ammunition that we couldn't shoot it off in a month. At the same time our rear will be free. Now for the purpose of this change in plans. Once we've taken Achlumal, we won't take the direct road to Hucutsin, but instead we'll march by San Miguel and San Jeronimo on Teultepec. There we won't encounter many *Rurales*. In Teultepec, as you will remember well from your march to the *monterías*, we shall be more than eighteen hundrcd feet above Hucutsin. There we shall be sitting as in a rocky fort, and from those heights we can swoop down upon Hucutsin like eagles on their prey. We shall then have the heights, the bush, and the passes—and let them then try to get at us! Not even the lice they have on their *bolsitas* will remain alive. In good time we shall occupy the road to Sibacya. When we then attack, only one way will lie open to them—the way back, along which we came, back to the jungle. And then the fun will start, then we shall have them where we want them. That's the way we'll do it, and not otherwise. Those in favor, raise their hands; those against will get a crack in the chops from me, and if you can tell me a better plan, and if it's really better, I'll accept it. But you'll find it damned hard to make a better plan."

So they marched toward Achlumal, while in Hucutsin *Rurales*, Federals, and heavily armed *finqueros* assembled in ever-increasing numbers to celebrate the impending victory.

The *finqueros*, in fact, had been celebrating this victory every day since they had been there. Flags waved over the Town Hall, proclaiming in advance the great day of victory.

In the bars there was endless and enthusiastic merriment.

"We'll soon teach these cursed, lousy swine of rebellious Indians who is master in this country and who's in command of Chiilum District."

"We'll drink again to that!"

"Spoken like a good man. *Salud, compadre!*"

"Of course we'll have another, Don Clementino."

"Of course, Don Cesar."

"*Viva El Caudillo!*"

"Long live the great leader of our glorious people!"

"*Salud, compadre!*"

"*Viva la patria!*"

The day's march had been a terribly hard one. The route the army followed was no more than a miserable, ill-trodden mule track. It rose and fell over rocky, stony heights. There were swamps, morasses, and boggy stretches where man and beast could no longer march or walk, but only crawl, dragging one leg after another out of the slime, to sink again with the next step into the muck and filth.

Toward noon, after a river had been crossed, the way broadened. Once more the flat country began.

The day before, another *finca*, the Santa Brigida, had been visited. Here, too, the master's family, so the remaining peons averred, had ridden off somewhere to a wedding. That the gentry had left a *finca* for fear of Indian rebels would never have been admitted by a *finquero*, his wife or daughter, not even on their deathbeds. In the eyes of his neighbors and friends, and especially of his peons, a *finquero* would have lost the last vestige of respect had he let a living soul—even his horse or favorite hound—believe that he and his whole family had ridden off to a wedding or a betrothal because Indian rebels were marching on the *finca*. Should it prove impossible to celebrate a marriage at such short notice, because the happy couple wanted a say in the matter and had not yet had time to make up their minds, then there was always a saint available whose name day provided one of the neighboring *finqueros*, or his wife, or his daughters or sons, or his mother, with the opportunity for a celebration at which all the *finqueros* and their families were expected.

At the *Finca* Santa Brigida, too, only the peons had been left behind, and just as at the other *fincas* that had hitherto been visited by the rebels, here also Professor granted all the *finca* lands to the peons and declared all debts due to the *finquero* canceled, null and void.

Here, too, the *finca* buildings went up in flames before the rebels were two hours on the march. Whether it was the last company of rebels who had had the pleasure of igniting the buildings, or whether it was the first independent action of the peons themselves, was never established. Nor did anyone care. Whatever the case, each *finca* destroyed meant one stronghold less in their rear.

When the troop emerged from the bush and the high country, and once more regained the open terrain, the leading muchachos saw before them, at a distance of some ten miles, the great *finca* of Santa Cecilia. The *finca* estates covered an area of about fifty thousand acres. Most of it was grazing land for herds of cattle, which were raised rather for their hides than for their meat. Other important sources of income to the *finca* were sugar, alcohol, aguardiente, and henequen fiber. In addition, considerable tracts of the *finca* were under corn and beans, while in the lower-lying fields grew sugar cane and pineapples. Naturally, the *finca* also raised considerable numbers of pigs, horses, and mules. If the *finca* had had roads fit for wheeled vehicles to connect it with a railway station, its yearly productivity would have been capable of realizing about a quarter of a million pesos. But like all other *fincas* in the region, this one's means of communication with the nearest towns were but miserable mule tracks, virtually impassable for three or four months of the year. Santa Cecilia ranked, undoubtedly, as one of the wealthiest and most beautiful estates in the district of Chiilum.

It, too, was built like a great fortress, its patio surrounded by high strong walls inside of which all buildings of importance lay. While the majority of other *fincas* considered themselves rich to possess a chapel, Santa Cecilia could boast a cathedral, having a bell tower visible from four miles away. The majority of paths in this region led past Santa Cecilia, and it was regarded as an important halting place for all caravans, where mule trains could rest for the night and replenish their provisions for the journey. This yielded a substantial additional income to the *finca*.

The estate, at a conservative reckoning, possessed 130 peon families, who were housed in a good-sized village not far outside the walls of the *finca*.

"We could easily reach Santa Cecilia today," said Colonel, as he observed the position of the sun.

"We could, easily," agreed General. "But the muchachos are damned tired, and it will be nearly sundown by the time we have marched to the *finca*. I don't want that. We don't know what's up there, and we might easily slip into a trap. In any event, we'd do better to spend the night here and start off very early, while it's still dark, so that we shall have the whole day before us by the time we get near the *finca*. What do you say, *compañeros?*"

"All right. We'll stay here. Whether we reach Santa Cecilia today, tomorrow, or in two days' time won't matter much to the rebellion," said Andreu. "And besides, I don't think this revolution is likely to be over in four weeks; in fact, we'll be lucky if it lasts only four years."

"That's what I think, too." Professor nodded in agreement. "A dictatorship that has existed for more than thirty years has suckled too many good-for-nothings ready to defend not only the dictatorship but their bellies as well. And when it's a question of defending bellies, the going is a good deal tougher than when only a superannuated dictator is trying to stick to his throne."

"In other words," General interrupted the political harangue, "we camp for the night here." He gave the bugler the order to blow "Halt." *El corneta* did it as well and as badly as was within his power. But the weary army understood the signal far better than it would have any other.

It turned out that considerable stretches of the terrain were unsuitable for camping because there had been heavy rain and large pools had formed.

"That suits me well," said General. "I never intended to have the whole army camp in one place. It would be too dangerous."

He divided the rebels into three sections. The first and best he ordered to camp on the spot, because here the ground was higher and thus afforded a better strategic position. The second division he sent off two-and-a-half miles to the southwest, to find a dry spot. The third portion of the army he dispatched about three miles to the northwest.

The *finca* lay to the west, as viewed from the central part of the army.

The plan was good. It took into consideration the possibility that the *finca* might be occupied by *Rurales*. General decided that the two troops on either side should march off long before sunrise, in order that one troop could attack the *finca* from the south and the other from the north, while he and his forces would spend the night eastward of the *finca*. The two wings of his forces were instructed that as soon as they had marched off, while it was still dark, twenty of their best infantry, together with a few mounted men, should proceed far ahead in line so that the extreme flanks of the two flanking armies would meet to the west of the *finca* and thus encircle the place completely. This western group, composed of about forty men from the two wing armies, would be, admittedly, very thin and in no event strong enough to prevent a westward breakout of the *Rurales* as soon as they saw that the battle was lost. General knew well enough that these positions to the west of the *finca* were the most dangerous of all, yet at the same time they were the most coveted, and the muchachos fought one another to be assigned to these perilous posts. For *there* would be the best booty in weapons, should the *Rurales* and Federals flee in confusion. It was by design that General allowed the enemy that escape route. To invest the *finca* sufficiently strongly on all sides would have been a mistake, because such a disposition would have had to be made during that very day, and the troops were too exhausted to stand a protracted fight should the *Rurales* attempt to avoid encirclement. Moreover, had General tried to surround the *finca* in equal strength at all points, he would have made another mistake, since the individual troops would all have been too weak in depth. For less than a fifth of the muchachos were armed, and, furthermore, the muchachos, being all inexperienced in military matters, would scarcely be able to prevent breakthroughs if these occurred simultaneously at several points, and the fronts where these breakthroughs and attacks were to be expected could not be sufficiently strongly manned to ensure numerical superiority.

Should the *Rurales* attempt to break out and escape to the west, the troops in that dangerous sector would have little or no hope of survival. Yet not one of the muchachos assigned to this duty gave a thought to himself. All they worried about was capturing rifles with their full complement of ammunition, and perhaps fine horses with handsome saddles. The capture of a rifle was the highest reward that General, who was unarmed, could promise. But none expected a higher reward, and not one of the rebels hoped for one while the revolution lasted.

Whether Santa Cecilia was occupied at all by soldiers or mounted State police was admittedly known to no one in the army. The muchachos had not encountered a single peon from the *finca*. For one thing, they were still too far away to be likely to meet any who might be going to work in the bush; for another, they were marching along a path that was never used by the peons on their way to market.

But that morning General had had a remarkable feeling, and he had thought to himself that it was very strange that not a single *Rurales* patrol had shown itself for days, although probably half a battalion must have been dispatched against the rebels. He estimated correctly when he told himself that, skillfully as he might try to entice the Federals to fall into a trap or to allow themselves to be caught in a pincer movement, these *Rurales* and Federals were by no means so stupid. It was certainly to be expected that they had the same or similar plans. No commander can work out a plan that the other side is not equally likely to have thought of; it all depends on who first formulates a particular plan, first uses it and exploits it most adroitly, and so acts that his opponents do not guess his plan prematurely. It was more than probable that a troop of *Rurales* or Federals had been sent southward from Hucutsin in order that the rebels, who, the authorities in Hucutsin assumed, would first attack that town, could be attacked in the flank or the rear, thus cutting off their road to Achlumal in case they should decide to move in that direction. Santa Cecilia was the only stronghold where such a force could be concealed and take up a powerful strategic position unperceived by the approaching rebels.

The leadership of the north army—so vitally important to his plan—was entrusted by General to his most experienced officer, Colonel. Colonel took with him one machine gun for his troop; the second machine gun remained with the central army.

The assembly point of the three armies was to be Santa Cecilia itself, irrespective of whether the place was occupied or not.

The central army camped behind a low chain of hills and could not be seen from Santa Cecilia.

The south army was given a route that took it partly through bush country and partly behind hills that covered their movement. The camping place assigned to it was behind hills covered with low scrub, so that it could pass the night unperceived from the *finca*, awaiting the order to attack at early dawn.

General had expressly ordered that campfires were not to be lit during the day because the columns of smoke would betray their position. At night the fires were to be so situated that they remained hidden behind the hills or burned in newly dug fire trenches. They were not to be allowed to blaze, in order to avoid any reflection in the overcast sky.

The north army, under the leadership of Colonel, had the most difficult task to fulfill. It could not march to its camping place through the bush. Covering hills were equally lacking on its route. It had to march across open ground. Thus, throughout the whole course of its march until its final destination, it would be under observation from the *finca*.

The north army marched off.

Professor followed it with his glasses, to see whether it would be attacked. But nothing happened. Finally, it reached the place General had appointed for it to spend the night. But it did not halt there. Professor offered as an explanation that there the land lay too low and was probably too swampy to offer a suitable camping place. The army marched farther, much farther than was good for defending it from the center in the event of its falling into a trap. It marched so far that it finally had gone far past the *finca* and now must have been due west of it, so that now the *finca* was surrounded from west, south, and east, leaving only the road north, toward Hucutsin, open.

"Hell!" said General when Professor reported this to him. "Colonel has thought out a damned good plan. He certainly hasn't done what I thought best. He should have stayed nearer to us. But what he has done is excellent. In the event of the Federals advancing from Hucutsin to Santa Cecilia, we shall have them in our clutches."

"Perhaps Colonel marched so far around the *finca* because he'd seen soldiers approaching from the direction of Hucutsin, and he, clever as he is, did not wish to retreat here, thereby betraying the position of our army and so letting the enemy get between our forces; whereas now they believe they have only to deal with a troop on their western flank." It was Andreu who expressed this opinion.

General and Professor admitted that this interpretation was probably the correct one. Anyhow, they couldn't alter what Colonel was doing or had already done, and each said, with justification, that Colonel knew what he was doing, and if he was carrying out the plan of campaign otherwise than he had been instructed, he must certainly have very good reasons for this.

In fact, Colonel had the very best of reasons for changing his troop's plan of movement. He would have been behaving stupidly and irresponsibly had he not altered that plan as soon as he saw that the conditions determining that plan had also changed. The master scheme of the attack was not affected by his deviation from the prearranged plan, for this master scheme was based on having the *finca* completely surrounded by daybreak and thus assailable from all sides simultaneously.

The north army had, as Professor correctly guessed, encountered such wet ground that Colonel could say, "If we were to camp here from this afternoon and until next dawn, none of us would be able to move an arm or leg before tomorrow noon."

So in spite of the weariness of the muchachos, they marched on in search of a dry place. During this march, one of the muchachos saw that a Federal patrol was approaching Santa Cecilia along the road from Hucutsin.

The muchachos wanted to attack this patrol, but Colonel forbade it. He said that if these Federals spent the night in Santa Cecilia, then next morning all who were in Santa Cecilia would fall into the hands of the muchachos, and it would be foolish to betray the presence of the rebel army before the *finca* was attacked.

He immediately ordered all his men to lie down and hide in the tall grass, in order not to be seen by the patrol, which was riding carelessly along. The muchachos who were mounted, like Colonel, remained on their horses and rode lazily onward in the same direction, without taking any notice of the patrol. The patrol plainly saw these riders, but they were too far away to be discerned clearly, and because they rode quietly and without any sign of haste, the men of the patrol could assume that these were *vaqueros* from the *finca* going to look for lost cattle. Soon the patrol had vanished from the sight of the troop, and the advance continued.

After another half hour's march, Colonel noticed a broad gully across the landscape, in which there were densely packed trees and bushes, differing from the solitary trees and bushes of the rest of the countryside.

"Down there, in that hollow, is a stream," said Colonel to the two captains riding beside him. "That's the place for our camp. We shall have good water, and if anything should happen during the night, we'll have the undergrowth for cover."

However, the patrol had been by no means so unobservant as Colonel believed. They had indeed seen the little army led by Colonel, even before the muchachos had seen the patrol. But the patrol intentionally behaved as if they had noticed nothing of interest in the landscape.

The patrol reached the *finca* and there reported that they had discovered the camping place of those stinking swine.

Santa Cecilia was, as General had guessed from instinct without being certain of the fact, strongly manned, being occupied by about fifty *Rurales*, seventy Federal soldiers, and about twenty *finqueros* who had gathered there, together with their sons, sons-in-law, major-domos, and *capataces*—making an armed force of more than two hundred men.

The garrison of the *finca* had received news of the approach of the rebel army from peons who had been out hunting or working in the bush. But they could obtain no more certain or definite information as to whether the rebels were making for Hucutsin or Achlumal, for the peons, as soon as they had seen the muchachos advancing in the distance, had fled in terror to the *finca* with their news without waiting to discover the precise direction of the army's march. That was the last thing the terrified peons worried about.

The soldiers were in no hurry to send out scouts, because they knew that in all events the muchachos would attack Santa Cecilia, and there was no better place than the *finca* for welcoming the rebel army with a devastating fire from a secure position.

The garrison of the *finca* possessed, all told, two machine guns, 110 rifles, sixty sporting guns of all sorts, including two dozen repeaters of heavy caliber, and in addition about 120 revolvers. Against such superiority of armament, it was unthinkable that the rebels could advance to within three hundred paces of the walls of the *finca* without losing three quarters of their force. And were they to come a hundred paces closer, it was certain that not a man of them would survive. Under these circumstances, the garrison could well afford to let the rebels march against the *finca* and to desist from attacking them in the open field.

General was a much greater commander than even his closest comrades would have believed. It would have been hard to make sufficiently clear to them how brilliant he was in his leadership. He had been, without knowing it himself, born with the gifts and talents of a great general.

On this occasion he sacrificed his north army in order to win the battle. Without that sacrifice, which, judged superficially, might appear merely ruthless, his whole army would have been destroyed at Santa Cecilia. He had sent Colonel ahead with the north army because he knew that Colonel was the one most capable of keeping the sacrifice as low as possible.

General had not been able to obtain precise information. Nevertheless, he knew from peons returning from market that the authorities in Hucutsin were fully informed of the approach of the rebel army. The remarkable tranquillity that lay over Santa Cecilia gave him the certainty that in that *finca* something decisive was in preparation. Should he be mistaken, should there be no soldiers in Santa Cecilia or its environs or lying in wait, nothing would be lost. The muchachos would take the *finca*, divide it up among the peons, equip themselves with fresh provisions, and the advance would continue. General was sure of one thing: that within the next three days a decisive battle must take place, because the Federals and *Rurales* dared not permit the rebels to capture a whole town. And within the next three days the rebel army would reach one of the two nearest towns of importance. The occupation of a town in which a chief of police had his seat would create such a demoralizing impression on the country that a general revolution could with certainty be expected. The fire of unrest was smoldering everywhere. That was why General had no doubt that a vital battle was impending. Much would be gained if he succeeded by strategic means in forcing the Federals and *Rurales* sent against him to give battle at a time and place most favorable to his plans.

In an uncommonly clever manner, he had managed to keep secret the actual number of the rebels. Only the more intelligent muchachos belonging to his staff knew approximately how many they were. The others cared nothing about it and had merely the vaguest idea of the strength of the army.

At least thirty peons and wandering Indian peasants must have seen the army, and these would probably have reported their observations here and there. But anyone who had encountered or seen the rebels had had no opportunity of seeing more than two companies together at a time. The man who met one troop seldom or never saw a second troop. And if he did meet a second troop, he could not be certain it was not the same troop that he had seen before.

So it was not only because of the difficult nature of the terrain that General had lately kept his army always marching in three or four groups, it was also in order to conceal their actual numbers.

Whenever news of the rebels reached the *fincas* or Hucutsin or Achlumal, mention was made of a hundred or 120 men. Even when the whole army was camped together in one spot, it would have been impossible for a peon chancing to pass near to establish the precise number, for peons and wandering Indians did not walk in and out of the camp. They slunk shyly by the outermost lines of the encampment and were happy if no one did anything to them and they were allowed to go their ways in peace. Besides, it is difficult for peons and Indians to estimate correctly large numbers of people or cattle. As soon as there are more than eighty, their guess becomes extremely inaccurate, and they very quickly begin to talk of many thousands.

The north army had been sent on such a route that it must inevitably be seen from the *finca* and remain within sight until it camped. General expected that on the way between Hucutsin and Santa Cecilia patrols would be out quartering the countryside, and these would certainly see the north army.

The north army was two companies strong and comprised about 160 men.

General could have made the north army comprise only one company. But that would have been a tactical error. He had to awaken the belief in the patrols and the garrison of the *finca* that that north army represented the whole rebel strength. He could never have created this impression with sixty or seventy men. In that event, the *Rurales* would have let the little troop march on and even camp in peace. They would have waited for the main body of the rebels to arrive, and only then would they have attacked, and not a man would have escaped.

Therefore, General hazarded one quarter of his army and reserved three quarters intact for battle when he considered the juncture favorable for loosing the main attack against the *Rurales* and Federals. This juncture would come when the enemy believed that they were the unopposed victors of the whole region and had nothing else to do but wait for a representative of the dictator to arrive and hang them with medals and promote all the officers a rank or two higher.

It is always a good thing for rebels and their leaders to know in advance what will happen to them if they lose a fight.

The less mercy they have to expect, the less they have to lose; and since they have nothing to lose, they are therefore better fighters than the uniformed sycophants of the dictatorship. These creatures have the posts and petty positions that best correspond to their mercenary souls. Of higher ambition they possess none. Their ideas are realized. What more can a victorious fight offer them? Nothing that they do not already possess.

Nevertheless, there was a real, hard fight. Three Federals, four *Rurales*, and three *finqueros* had lost their lives, and nine men had been wounded, before the garrison with twenty prisoners at the ends of their lassos marched back in triumph between the wide-open gate of the *finca*. About a hundred muchachos of the north army lay dead, strewn over the field of battle.

The night was already far advanced when Colonel, with the tiny group that survived, reached the camp of the central army and reported to General.

He and the muchachos whom he brought back with him were bleeding from numerous wounds. One man lacked a hand, another a forearm. There was not one among these muchachos who could show less than four wounds from shots or sabers on his body. Six of the muchachos were carried in on the shoulders of their wounded comrades. Five had died on the way back because they had been so badly wounded that they either bled to death or their lungs ceased to work.

Not one had a shirt left. Their brown-and-white cotton trousers were tattered. Every rag of material they were wearing had been used to bind or stanch the wounds of themselves and their companions.

Willing muchachos hurried to refresh the survivors with coffee and beans, to wash their wounds and bandage them.

"That was a charming little party," panted Colonel, squatting on the ground. "I'm damned thin, and I have the feeling that in ten minutes I'll vanish, I've lost so much juice. I'd never have believed I could have made it here. We were sitting quite happy and cozy in our camp. All tired as dogs after a tiger hunt. Hell and damnation, I knew that something was in the air, for I'd seen the patrol, but I thought, mule that I was, that they hadn't seen us."

"As a soldier, and particularly as a colonel, never believe anything, but assume that your opponent is at least as clever and probably cleverer than you are." General laughed as he interjected this.

"And because I suspected something, and because I know you, General, and had a pretty good idea of why you sent me with the army to that particular spot, I was damned careful. I had four sentries out. But before they could report, there was the goddamned gang already on top of us. And what a shame you didn't see it! You'd all of you have learned something from that. They were at least 250 strong. All mounted on fresh horses. Two bullet sprayers were on the ground. I don't know how they managed that so quickly. They must already have had the machine guns in their arms as they rode against us. The disgraceful thing was that they rushed us in daytime, in broad afternoon. That we've been able to get back here with even thirty men, how we've done that, I simply don't know. And that we actually managed to slaughter ten or twelve or whatever number of them, well—for all I know Saint Peter did it himself. There was no escaping in any direction. In a flash they were all around us like a wall, and three men deep behind the wall. And then they let loose at us. With sabers, with rifles, and with the hoofs of their horses. And the *balazos!* The bullets! Oh, dear Virgin of Guadalupe, they buzzed among us as if we'd stirred up a swarm of bees. And then they started to yell: 'Now we've got you at last, you damned, stinking, lousy swine. You want to have a revolution! Shout *Tierra y Libertad!* We'll give you revolution and *Tierra y Libertad! Hijos de putas, chingados por puercos*, you'll soon learn what it's like to start a rebellion! You'll be quartered, you *cabrones*, and flogged at the horse's tail, you filthy, stinking, lousy sons of bitches.' And then it was just all hell—crick, crack, plunk, plonk, smash, left and right, up and down, and the muchachos falling all over the place, skulls split down to the nose, whole arms mown off with the shoulder, sabers rammed through and through, and added to all that each man getting thirty or forty splatters of dum-dum bullets at once in his guts. I tell you, *hombres*, if you hadn't seen it, you wouldn't believe it. We managed to loose off a few machine-gun bursts and get in two or three dozen machete cuts, and where they fell they're still lying, I can tell you. But what can you do when you're squatting on your backsides with your men and thinking all's right with the world, and in the same second 250 men on horseback hurl themselves at you?"

"What have you done with the machine gun, Colonel?" asked General.

"Don't ask me, *hombre*. I'm happy still to have my head."

"That wouldn't have been a great loss, for it's not worth much if you let yourself be trounced like that."

"You can talk. I'd like to see whether you could have got away with thirty men even."

"And how many rifles and revolvers have you brought with you?"

"Two rifles and one revolver—mine, which I have here, but the bullets have all been fired."

"Well, muchachos, in the next few days we've at least got plenty to do," said General, and grinned contentedly. "The machine gun, the rifles, and the revolvers must be taken back again, or our friendship won't last long."

"The machine gun and the rifles?" Colonel smiled. And his broad grin may have caused the blood running down from his skull in two thick streams to flow over his cheeks and into his mouth. He spat it out, drank a hefty draught of hot coffee to change the taste, and then said, "You're thinking of the machine gun and the rifles, *compañero*? Leave them where they are. You can't use them any more. But I've seen two damned beautiful new machine guns and more than a hundred dazzling new repeating rifles with magazines, and the other things I've seen, about a hundred steel-blue Colts and automatics. Oh! They're something like revolvers! I only got the two cuts on my head because I was watching those things so lovingly instead of firing off my own bullets quickly enough. And I swear to you that if you don't do something about getting those things, we thirty, those of us remaining, will go out and get them alone. I must have those machine guns, rifles, and revolvers, and if I can't have them, my mucking life isn't worth a damn."

"Don't get so excited, Colonel," said Celso. "We'll get them all right. They've cost us 120 of our brothers, but the fun will be paid for. We're no longer in the *monterías* where *they* gave us fun and we were never able to repay them. Now we'll pay and pay, and we won't be any longer indebted for what they've given us."

"*Santos en ciel!*" shouted Matias. "When I think of what they've got for us in their shop there, the juice runs out of my nose and mouth like pure, smooth noodle soup. We must have that hardware store, and then we shall be able to equip half our army, and then we'll clear up the country once and for all. Life's wonderful. But if only it lasts until we've lit a fire under the asses of the whole tribe of tyrants and tickled them up so they won't rest in peace again for a hundred years."

"Shut your trap," shouted Fidel at him. "We've got campaign plans to make here."

"I'm allowed to say what I think," Matias defended himself.

"Of course, *muy cierto*," said General. "Anyone can speak here. But Colonel still has first turn." He now turned again to Lucio: "What way did you take back with your bleeding horde? I mean back here? Not the direct route?"

"Do you think I'm such a mule? That would have been fine, if we'd betrayed where our army was squatting. Those miserable *cabrones* don't even know that thirty of us are still surviving. They think they mowed us all down, and that all of us who remain alive are now their prisoners and have been marched back to the patio of the *finca* to provide a jolly evening for those uniformed crawlers."

"*Los prisioneros, los pobres!* The poor prisoners!" said Andreu, with a deep sigh.

"Yes, the poor prisoners will be wishing now they were lying dead and mangled on the field," added General. "They'll make them dance now. Hell, those who escaped being captured can thank all their saints. And there's nothing we can do. We must wait till we're ready and those swine have had their fling. Damned hard as it is, we mustn't think of that now. Well, Colonel, how did you get back here?"

"Those of us who escaped being cut into mincemeat weren't all together in one mob. Of course not. While we were on the march there, I told everyone that if we were attacked and had to retreat, no one was to take the direct route back to head-quarters, in order not to betray its whereabouts. And not one did. Not even in the worst danger. When we saw that we'd fought enough and couldn't do any more, then those who were in the middle of it all and couldn't escape otherwise flopped down among the fallen. They all had enough blood on their hides to make them look ten times more dead than normal. Others crept away into the thick bush to the west, in the opposite direction from this camp. The grass on the plain around here is high now. Then, once at a sufficient distance from the dust-up, it was difficult for the soldiers to see where we were hiding. I can tell you we crawled lower and stealthier than the best snake could. Besides, they had their hands full with the lassoing of those they wanted to capture alive. So at last we were able to squeeze ourselves out like maggots. In the beginning, of course, we were far more than thirty trying to make a getaway. And the prisoners they were able to take they caught from among those who were still alive and trying to crawl off but who couldn't transform themselves quickly enough into worms, as we were able to do. Meanwhile, darkness soon fell. Thank God for still allowing the world to grow dark now and again. And so, when it was night, the *cabrones*, howling with pleasure, departed with their prisoners. We then made a wide detour, twice crossing the river down below, right to the north—and here we are."

"Yes, here we are," said General. "But not here to stay. Back into the bush." He immediately gave orders to break camp and march back until all were at least two miles inside the bush and sufficiently hidden by the hills to be invisible to any watchers from the *finca*. He sent a messenger to the south army, instructing them also to retreat into the bush, but to remain sufficiently far to the south to be able to command the southern flank.

The victors, now reassembled in the *finca*, were fully convinced that they had destroyed all the rebels who had emerged from the jungle. It was just possible, so they said to one another, that perhaps ten or fifteen might have escaped, but these would be quite harmless and in a few days would be rounded up by the patrols and shot. In any case, the rebellion, at least in this state and region where the masters of estates ruled like kings of olden times, had been crushed, and undoubtedly for good, in view of that mass slaughter of the Indian mutineers. Others, particularly the peons, were now unlikely to entertain any further ideas of striking or rebelling for several decades. And in order to make sure that this actually was the case, they had had the good fortune to bring in alive enough of those stinking Indian swine to demonstrate in the presence of the assembled peon families what happens to rebels and such as dare to open their mouths against their masters.

The dictatorship and the feudal lords sat once more securely in their old saddle.

"Firm action is all that's needed, caballeros," said the colonel commanding the Federals. Although the Federals and the *Rurales* combined were only 120 strong, nevertheless a colonel with experience of rebellions had been put in charge. Since all the *finqueros* of the region, together with their major-domos and other vassals, were under the command of the colonel, this officer had no cause for complaining about the size of the force he led.

"Firm action, gentlemen. That is the only effective means for dealing with rebellions, strikes, mutinies, and other such madness," the colonel continued in his exposition to the *finqueros*. "I promise you, caballeros, that as long as I'm here and have any say, this state will remain free from every form of insubordination against our Caudillo. If unrest is showing its face in the north and west of the Republic, as well as in the sugar regions, that means little as long as we hold the south securely in our hands, so as to be able to push forward from here should the necessity arise. In confidence, gentlemen, I can tell you that at the moment things don't look too good in those parts of the country. But that is between ourselves. However, we'll overcome it and destroy these gangs; and then we'll show them who are the real masters in the land. Fine old tradition, law, order, tranquillity, and decency, that's what we're defending. *Salud*, caballeros, let us raise our glasses to our beloved Chief of State, El Caudillo, the irreplaceable leader and ruler of our glorious Republic! *Viva El Caudillo!*"

The *finqueros* and the officers of the Federals and *Rurales* were all sitting around a long, rough table that had been set up on the veranda of the mansion. This veranda, supported by pillars, ran the length of the building and was open on the side facing the great patio of the *finca*. Indeed, it was more of a portico and, as in all houses in the American tropics, was used as a living room by day, where meals were taken, where leisure hours were passed in hammocks, and where the women and girls pursued their sewing and other domestic occupations.

The long wooden table now erected here was covered with cheap, brightly colored cotton tablecloths. The board was richly set with dishes of reddish-black beans, roasted turkeys and chickens, fresh salad, great masses of onions, tins of sardines and Alaska salmon, and huge baskets piled to the brim with pineapples, bananas, melons, mangoes, custard apples, and other tropical fruits of the region. About five bottles of Spanish vermouth and muscatel stood on the table. There was not much wine. The *finquero* apologized for the scanty number of bottles. No one took offense, for each knew it was not easy to stock large quantities of wines in such remote regions. Of course, the *finquero* knew very well that good wine, and particularly large quantities of good wine, would be wasted on the officers whom he had to entertain here as uninvited guests. They did not understand how to appreciate fine wine. Besides, the *finquero* was clever enough to reserve the greater part of his really fine wine for himself, for real celebrations given in style and pomp for his landowning friends and their families.

They appreciated good wine. He could no more behave meanly to them than they would to him when they gave *fiestas*.

But at one end of the table was a five-gallon barrel of excellent old *comiteco*, and there was no one sitting at the table who did not prefer the *comiteco;* for the *comiteco* of the owner of Santa Cecilia had a great reputation in the country. It was distilled on the *finca* and never drunk until it was five years old.

In the patio and along the foot of the veranda the men of the *Rurales* and Federals and the major-domos and *capataces* of the victorious *finqueros* sat feasting. Two pigs and a calf had been slaughtered to feed the unexpected number of warriors. This crowd of valiant trenchermen consumed vast quantities at a meal, and the *finquero's* wife, Doña Guillerma, thought with concern of what she would do if the army should settle in for a week. It was not a shortage of meat or corn that she feared. It was the salt, the sugar, the coffee, and the disappearance of plates, cups, napkins, knives, forks, and spoons that frightened her. Of course the soldiers and major-domos all ate with their fingers. But they had to have spoons. And it was not only in the patio but also at the tables where the officers were fed that after every meal the implements, including saucers and coffee cups, grew fewer and fewer. It was not that these things were simply stolen. One of the guests would throw a cup at his servant's head to encourage him when he was called for and did not come quickly enough. Another wished to scare off the dogs, which crept between the legs of the eater, scrounging bones, and he threw knives and spoons at them. Yet a third felt impelled to display his skill as a juggler at the table, and he persevered with his balancing of cups, plates, and dishes until the whole pyramid collapsed and not a thing remained unbroken. Others knew tricks with forks, spoons, and knives in the course of which the cutlery had to become so bent and broken that at last the conjurer could make it vanish into his mouth or behind his ear. The success of these performances was overwhelming, but the knives and spoons were useless ever after. On top of all this, a third of the cutlery disappeared in the usual way, and Doña Guillerma saw coffee spoons and knives in pockets, a number of which belonged to officers' uniforms.

The *Rurales* and the Federals—that is, their commanding officers—charged the government, through the commissary account, for the cost of subsistence at the *finca*. And the government paid it. But the *finquero* who quartered all these men never received a centavo for his expenses. Of course not. For he lived under the blessings of a dictatorship. He did not even dare to raise the question with the officers. First, it would have been unworthy of the dignity of a caballero to concern himself with such trivial matters; second, the commanding officer would have said, "*Querido amigo mío*, you should be satisfied that we've beaten the rebels. If we hadn't arrived when we did, not even the walls of your *finca* would be left standing now, and it's by no means certain that you yourself would still be alive." Since the *finquero* knew very well that he would receive this answer, his pride forbade his inviting such a retort.

The patio was full of people. There were not only the soldiers, squatting on the ground and stuffing their bellies, there were also the peons, with their wives, daughters, and sons, who were either serving here or else lounging around and watching the soldiers enjoying a meal such as the peons were never offered even though they were the producers of everything there.

The soldiers, major-domos, and *capataces*, too, were enjoying their *comiteco*. For them the *finquero* had placed in the patio a gigantic stone jug that held fifty gallons. Of course it wasn't the same excellent vintage as in the miniature barrel standing on the table. It was the lees of the best *comiteco*, very young and fiery, and clear as water.

As a result of the good food and plenty of *comiteco*, things soon became extremely merry. The peons' wives and daughters and the Indian maids were seized upon and made to dance whether they wanted to or not. It was useless for Doña Guillerma to call the maids and wives away from the soldiers, to protect them from harm. The soldiers were the masters here and did not hesitate to laugh rudely in the face of the wife of the *finquero*.

Less than two hours had passed when about fifty revolver bullets whistled back and forth through the air, now thick with smoke from the huge bonfire that blazed in the patio. A few peons received wounds and crept away to their huts. Two soldiers and a major-domo were killed, and a half-dozen soldiers and *capataces* retired to the great harness room, where they had to be treated by helpful comrades. After that, all was once more peace and amity.

The prisoners were confined in a corral, a fenced-in area for keeping horses and cattle. No one had bothered to untie them. So they remained trussed and corded, just as they had been when they were dragged in behind their captors' horses. Like parcels they lay on the bare earth of the corral, which was slimy with horse manure and cow dung.

Four soldiers with rifles on their knees sat on the top rails of the encircling fence to keep watch over the prisoners. They were annoyed that they had to do duty here while their comrades were able to enjoy themselves in the patio. Later they were relieved, so that they, too, could eat. The new guard was even more annoyed than the first, because they had had to leave the feast to keep watch on the lousy Indian pigs here.

Peons from the *finca* had timidly approached and given the prisoners some water to drink and a few handfuls of boiled beans. They were in constant terror that the soldiers on guard would ram their rifles into their stomachs because they were doing an act of mercy for the prisoners. However, the soldiers were so disgruntled that they paid no attention to what the peons did, so long as they did not loosen the lassos with which the muchachos were bound.

A Federal lieutenant got up and walked over to a dark corner of the patio, close to the corral, feeling an uncomfortable pressure of liquid within him. He went up close to the fence and sought out a place where several of the prisoners were lying against the rails.

"Just stay where you are, you swine," said the lieutenant, as the muchachos attempted to creep away from the warm stream of urine. The muchachos moved no farther.

"Filthy, lousy swine, you ought to feel honored that a Federal officer condescends to piss on you. Do you understand? Answer!"

"*Sí, jefecito,*" said the muchachos submissively and did not move from the spot.

The lieutenant returned to the table. When he saw that, for the moment, the wife and daughters of the *finquero* were not near enough to overhear, he related his latest adventure.

A roar of laughter followed this, and all, officers and *finqueros* for want of better entertainment and more edifying conversation, got up in turn, went over to the corral, and summoned the muchachos to come close to the rails.

And during the succeeding hours when one or another of them felt the necessity, he went "to water the pigs."

The soldiers, major-domos, and *capataces*, as soon as one of them happened to discover the game, copied their officers' joke, until finally one of the captains of the *Rurales* forbade this, not out of pity for the humiliated muchachos, but from the feeling that the men had no right to use for their needs the same place as had been selected by the officers and caballeros, because such a state of affairs could easily lead to a blurring of the important distinctions of rank.

The next morning, as soon as officers and caballeros had wiped their eyes with wet fingers and the maids had offered each a morning cup of hot black coffee boiled with coarse brown sugar, the major commanded that the examination of the captured rebels should commence.

The major composed the trial. He was simultaneously prosecutor, judge, and the final court of appeal. The remaining officers and the *finqueros* stood or sat around as supernumerary judges. Their activity, however, was restricted solely to suggesting particularly effective forms of punishment that would leave an impression not to be forgotten in a hundred years.

To engage in rebellion was the prerogative only of the officers, *finqueros*, and industrial magnates when the dictator was not to their liking. Indeed, every person in the country, even an enlightened schoolchild, knew that the dictator only remained El Cacique so long as he did what these individuals ordered him to do, for they were able to keep the government under control because they held the cudgels in their money bags.

Each case was dealt with in a very brisk and military fashion. The prisoners stepped forward, or, to be more accurate, they were hurtled forward by hard fists and boots; each said his name and stood motionless, arms crossed over his breast.

The major, who had undertaken his duties voluntarily, asked each prisoner whether he had been a laborer in the *monterías*. Every one of them confirmed this. Not a muchacho fell on his knees and begged for mercy or prayed for forgiveness. Even in face of the agony that awaited them during the next few hours, they showed themselves greater and better men than their executioners, who later, when the dictatorship began to collapse, behaved just as would be expected of minions and toadies of any dictatorship the world over.

The colonel took no interest in the matter of the trial or in what happened to the prisoners. He had enjoyed a long and healthy sleep, then breakfasted alone in order to ensure a better meal, in which expectation he was not, to his pleasure, disappointed. Then he sat down at a little table in the farthest corner of the veranda, pensively smoked a powerful cigar, and dictated to his clerk an account of the battle for the benefit of the chief of military operations, who had his quarters in Jovel.

After the taking of their names, which no one troubled to record, the trial was at an end and the major's heaviest duties for the day satisfactorily concluded.

Meantime, he, the other officers, and the *finqueros* had acquired a fierce hunger as a result of the ardors of this tribunal. Since they had noticed with smiles in their eyes that the Indian maids had bedecked the long tables with steaming suckling pigs and vast brown mounds of roasted veal and chops, haste was necessary in order not to disappoint the wife of the *finquero* who had taken so much trouble to entertain them well. The delicious dishes must not be allowed to grow cold, and it was therefore essential that the contents of each platter should vanish just as rapidly as jaws could masticate.

"Sergeant Paniagua!" shouted the major.

"*A sus órdenes, mi comandante!*" answered the sergeant, standing before the railing of the veranda on which the major sat with a cigarette dangling from his mouth.

"Take away the prisoners, outside the walls of the *finca*, and execute them. But first you can have your breakfasts."

"*A sus órdenes, mi comandante.*"

In pious consciousness of having done his duty as soldier and guardian of the dictator, who gave him his daily bread, the major slipped down from the railing, went over to the washstand, washed his hands, beckoned to the other officers, and walked across to the table. A dozen *finqueros* were already sitting before their plates and waiting only for the colonel, the senior person there, to sit down also before they could at last begin their delayed meal.

"God," said the major, sitting down after the colonel and cleaning his nails with a toothpick, "I must say this is a damned good meal, enough to make the heart of an old soldier and fighter leap with joy within his breast. Well, up and at 'em, caballeros, and into battle with all the courage you have!"

The caballeros at the table were not halfway through their battle when Sergeant Paniagua reported to the major: "*Listo, mi comandante.*"

"*Muy bien!* You know what you have to do with the prisoners, sergeant?"

"*Sí, mi comandante.*"

"Good. Get on with it."

"Just a moment, Major!" interrupted the proprietor of Santa Cecilia, who as host occupied the center seat at the table, between the colonel and the major. "I would make the suggestion, Major, that we summon all the peons on my *finca* so that they can witness the punishment of these rebels. It will benefit all us *finqueros* for the peons to see it. It'll drive out of them once and forever, we hope, all that chatter about tyranny and injustice."

"*Bravo! Bravísimo!*" shouted the rest of the *finqueros* at the table. "That's a fine idea of yours, Don Delfino. Pity we can't get our own peons here quickly enough to join in the spectacle. Such an excellent. education can't be given them every day."

Several of the peons were already in the patio, where they were serving or standing around out of curiosity. On days like these, when great celebrations were held in the *finca*, there was rarely much work done, because the major-domos and the *capataces* wished to miss nothing of the banquets. Only the most important work was attended to.

Nevertheless, the *finquero* sent his major-domo across to the peons' village to summon all men, women, and children to witness the execution of the rebels.

To have the free and unrestricted disposal of such a large number of ragged, verminous, cowed, and totally defenseless prisoners would have rejoiced the heart of the sexually degenerate, spiritually defiled, uniformed invertebrates such as Central Europe produces so cheaply and in such great quantities. Dictators who feel safe and happy only when surrounded solely by slaves are content—for entirely understandable reasons—to rely for acclaim and support on abject minions. With free men capable of feeling even a glimmer of dignity, they wouldn't remain sitting on their thrones a week. It was not so in olden days, but in modern times protection comes from the meanest and most miserable henchmen and guard-room parasites, those human dregs, immature and snot-nosed, who, because they have no individuality, no spark of personality, can feel themselves alive only because they are permitted to don a uniform cap. These uniform caps transform a human cipher into a semi-being, but as soon as this semi-being is without his uniform cap, he immediately reveals himself for what he really is: an idiotically distorted, crookedly conceived cipher.

Sergeant Paniagua, who had received the major's order for the punishment and execution of the rebels, had, like the rest of the N.C.O.'s and policemen, no thought of satisfying any sadistic mental streak by beating defenseless prisoners for days and weeks on end or making them spit on one another or box each other's ears. Such a thing would have seemed to them so laughable, so idiotic, that they would have doubted their own sanity.

Usually, captured rebels were hanged on a nearby tree. That was done with such speed that ten men were hanged in ten minutes.

Sergeant Paniagua called out a squad and gave the order to take out the prisoners three hundred yards away from the *finca*, and there to hang them in turn from the trees, after having cut off their ears.

But no sooner had they reached the trees than there came up a major-domo of one of the *finqueros* who was still sitting at his meal, with an order to the sergeant to delay the hangings for a while, since the *finqueros* wished to be present.

The sergeant sent a corporal to the major to inquire whether such a delay was in order. The major gave his permission and commanded that the hangings should wait until the caballeros had finished their meal and had time to reach the scene of the executions.

After half an hour the *finqueros* strolled up leisurely, together with the major and a few bored officers.

"We can't have a celebration like this every day," observed Don Crisostomo, the owner of the Santa Julia *finca*.

"Too true," Don Abundio, the master of La Nueva Granda, nodded in agreement. "But that's not all. It's far better that we should see justice done and everything carried out to the letter of the law. What does a filthy swine of a peon care when he's hanged?"

This evoked a burst of healthy laughter from the caballeros.

"All the peons here?" asked Don Delfino.

"*Sí, patrón*," answered his major-domo.

"Why should we all have to stand around?" asked Don Faustino, the master of *finca* Rio Verde. He summoned one of the major-domos and gave him the order to saddle horses and bring them there in order that all could be mounted and not have to stand on their scrawny, bandy legs.

"*Oiga*, Major!" Don Eleuterio of *finca* La Providencia came up to the major. "I imagine it's all the same to you who deals with these rebel dogs."

"*Es cierto*," replied the major. "It doesn't matter to me. I've only got to report that the captured rebels are dead, either shot or hanged. I don't care. I'm a soldier. And my men are soldiers. And since we're soldiers we would be ashamed to beat or torture defenseless prisoners. We hang or we shoot. What the police do, we soldiers are not responsible for."

The major shrugged his shoulders and turned away.

"Look, Major," interposed Don Tirso of La Camelia. "In the next day or two you'll march away. Then once more we'll all be left here alone and completely defenseless. I know very well our peons are no longer what they were. They're restless. They're waiting for an opportunity, and then they'll be at our throats. We'll be slaughtered like sheep. All in one night. If we don't give them a thorough lesson on how we deal with rebels, here and now, which they won't forget for the next two or three years, we'll have no security."

"*Muy bien, caballeros!* Do what you wish. I'm going to have a quiet drink, get into my hammock, and spend a pleasant sunny afternoon. Sergeant Paniagua!"

"*A sus órdenes, mi comandante!*"

"You and all your men get back into the *finca*. *Los prisioneros para los caballeros*. Leave the prisoners for the gentlemen."

"*A sus órdenes, mi comandante!*"

The commanding officer of the police troop shouted to his men, "You remain here on guard." When he had given this order, he followed the major and the other officers who strolled back to the *finca*.

Don Delfino summoned some of his peons. "Run, get spades and pickaxes from the stores."

The spades were brought, and the *finquero* ordered the captured muchachos to dig holes, each about four and a half feet deep.

After these holes had been dug, the muchachos were forced to stand at the edges.

"You'll enjoy this, you lousy *cabrones!*" shouted the *fin-quero*. "One shot and it's over. But not so quick! Now, jump into the holes! Each into his own!"

The muchachos tumbled in. But as the *finquero* had antici-pated, the holes were not long enough for the men to lie in. They half stood, half lay, their heads projecting above the edge of each hole.

The *finquero* called up some of the *capataces*. "Cut off the ears of the swine."

"Hey, you, where have you got your stinking ears?" asked the *finquero*, walking over to one of the muchachos in his hole.

"*Patroncito mío*, they were cut off in the *monterías*."

"Ah, I see, because of mutiny."

"With your kind permission, *patroncito*, not because of mu-tiny. My little boy was drowned in the river. Then I was so sad that I went down the stream."

"A deserter, then. It's all the same." With a movement of his head he beckoned to a nearby *capataz*. "The dog's no longer got any ears to cut off. Chop away his nose. Hey, you, don't squirm so; if your cheek goes with it, so much the better. Then the devils in Hell will know who you are when you get there."

The peons who were present as witnesses said nothing. Not with an expression did they betray what was going on inside them. They looked as humble and obedient as ever. The *fin-queros* were convinced now that they had nothing to fear from them.

Then the peons received the order to fill in the holes.

When that had been done, and only the heads of the mu-chachos streaming with blood showed above the ground, a *fin-quero* shouted to the heads; "*Tierra y Libertad* is what you want? Now we're going to give you land and liberty. More than you can swallow. You lousy swine."

He jabbed a *capataz* in the ribs and said to him, "Stuff the *tierra* in their traps until it comes out of their tails."

He himself took up a shovelful of earth, flung it in the face of the nearest head, walked up to it, and kicked the soil into the mouth with his boots. "There's your *tierra* and your *libertad*. Now are you satisfied? Hey? And you too, we'll stuff you full of *Tierra y Libertad*. Fetch some water, José," he called to another *capataz*. "Get water for them all and pour it into their mouths, so they swallow *tierra* till they burst. *Libertad*. Freedom. Now at last you've got all the *libertad* there is on earth, and in Hell, too."

He called up all the major-domos and *capataces* and ordered them to treat all the heads in the manner he had shown them.

The *capataces*, fired by the *finqueros*, booted all the loose earth heaped up around the holes into the mouths of those heads, ramming it home with their fists, and when the mouths, noses, eyes, and bleeding earholes were so full of earth that not a grain more could have gone in and not even the cascades of water helped in cramming any more into the orifices, they stamped with their boots on the heads, stamping them deeper and deeper into the loose soil until the faces, wholly masked with blood and earth, had become unrecognizable and were composed only of a mass uncertainly held together by the thick black thatch of hair on the skull.

At the beginning of this distribution of *tierra*, the muchachos had spat, sneezed, coughed, moaned, and choked. But not one had complained. Nor had one spoken a single word that could be taken as a plea for pity or mercy. So long as they could still see with their eyes, neither fear nor reproach was in their looks. Only hate, and nothing but hate, glowed in the last flicker of their black and dark-brown eyes. And it was that boundless hate in them that made them forget all pain, that made them numb as if their heads were stones. It was the inextinguishable hate of the oppressed, who, downtrodden and tormented though he might be, knows only one emotion— hatred of the oppressor. It was the hatred of the proletarian who has never known justice—only commands and curses. A hate more bitter and remorseless than the hate of Satan for God, this was their hate that permitted no wavering of their courage, not even to beg for a last merciful kick that would extinguish life and that would certainly have made their tyrants rejoice at thus havng broken down the rebels.

Four of the muchachos, when they felt that the next kick in the face would stop them from ever uttering another word, screamed as loud and powerfully as the earth in their throats allowed, *"Tierra y Libertad! Viva la revolución de los peones!"* It came out far from clear and strong. But to all those muchachos who, with the last flicker of their lives, caught the stifled, choking sounds, though not the separate words, and yet instinctively grasped their actual meaning, these muffled, grunted noises were a hymn of praise such as all the heavenly host could not have sung for the muchachos at the birth of their Savior. It was a hymn that heralded no savior. It was a hymn of praise announcing the arrival of a new mankind. It was a hymn in praise of heroes such as only a dictatorship, an autocracy, could have produced, not in support of that autocracy but heralding its destruction.

The *finqueros* had not merely heard these last cries, the only cries uttered by the dying muchachos; they had also understood them.

And they were thrown into such a rage that they completely forgot themselves. They now no longer left it to their *capataces* to stamp the rebels off the earth; after those cries, they now leaped themselves upon the heads and trampled and danced about on them as if they had gone mad.

"Where are the horses, you filthy lazy dogs of *mozos?*" shouted several of the *finqueros*, beating their *capataces* with their fists. The horses had not yet been rounded up; they were grazing on the open pastures and had first to be found and driven in.

"Horses! Bring in the horses! We want to gallop these swines' damned heads into Hell!"

Not only the *finqueros* but also the peons had heard the cries of the four or five muchachos. And although they spoke Indian more easily than Spanish, they nevertheless understood immediately these rebel cries. And they understood rightly, for the first time in their lives, what these revolutionary words really meant.

The *finqueros* had made the greatest mistake they possibly could have made: they had invited the peons to the exhibition in order to terrorize them. And for the first time the peons had the sensation of being a part of humanity, bound one to another and all together, not just because they were peons, but because they had a common enemy, because their enemies were the masters who had always posed to them as benevolent fathers. Now they began to understand, for the first time in their existence, that these professing fathers had suddenly been transformed into monsters as soon as their paternal domination and the authority that went with it were threatened.

At this instant the peons, who had been invited as witnesses, realized that their oppressed and tormented class could bring forth heroes who in point of courage, of upright decency, of strength of character, of hate and pride were not a whit behind those who hitherto had regarded these human qualities as the inalienable inheritance of their class—the feudal master class—proclaiming to all the world at every opportunity that peons and proletarians were indeed peons and proletarians because they had no pride and no courage.

But now the peons felt pride swelling up within themselves as they heard the gurgling screams of victory from the muchachos. Their hitherto nebulous and undifferentiated individualities flowered to a comprehension of their own possibilities as human beings when they became aware that these rebels, who even under the most terrible pain could still fling their hatred into the faces of the dictator's lackeys, belonged in fact to their race, their class, and not to the class of their masters. Not one of them had ever seen a *finquero* die with such a great, glorious gesture as these rebels had achieved.

The *finqueros* had hoped to flood the peons with fear and terror when they commanded them to be present at the executions. Now, without the *finqueros* even yet suspecting it, their plan had gone awry and achieved the very opposite.

Filled in their hearts with a deep religious adoration for the rebels, the peons now slunk back to their huts and there told their wives and children of what they had seen and experienced. And they told this with a reverence and awe, as if they had seen in the bush the Holy of Holies appearing to them in person and commanding them to build a chapel.

Men and women knelt before the tiny, smoky, smeared pictures of the Holy Virgin, propped on little chests that served as altars in their huts, and prayed for the souls of the dead rebels with as much fervor as if they had been their own fathers. When they had ended their prayers, and the men had once more left their miserable huts in order to follow the majordomo to their places of work, they were no longer the same peons that they had been.

6

General, after he had withdrawn his main army and the west army about five miles back into the bush, now prepared for a decisive counterattack. The bush gave covering not only to his two armies but also to his preparations. He now held a wide field of approach and had sufficient room to attack his opponents from either flank, whichever suited him best. Guided by his healthy Indian instinct against being taken by surprise so long as this could be avoided, he placed his outposts and forward patrols so skillfully that he would be able to capture any peon or bush worker or hunting *finquero* promptly enough to prevent Santa Cecilia receiving news that might disturb his plans. The fundamental point of his plan was to make his opponents believe that the army of rebels from the *monterías* had been totally destroyed in that murderous battle he had offered the enemy, and that only around a dozen wounded and fleeing muchachos were wandering about in the bush and the plain, filled with terror and desperation. The one anxiety he had was that the Federals, the *Rurales*, and the *finqueros*, together with their major-domos and *capataces*, might leave Santa Cecilia on the day after that fight.

Early in the morning on which the prisoners at Santa Cecilia had been buried alive according to the rules by which mutinous Indian peasants were normally punished under the dictatorship, he summoned two muchachos whom he knew to be well acquainted with the neighborhood because they had been born and had grown up on one of the *fincas* in that region and had later been sold by their masters into the *monterías*.

"You two, Pablo and Mario, can you understand the idiom the peons speak hereabouts?"

"*Sí*, General. It's Tseltal."

"All right. Take your pack nets and cut a mighty pile of grass over there in that clearing. Masses of grass. Then stuff it into your nets, and stuff them so full that they look like huge balls. Then the two of you make straight for Santa Cecilia. Go into the peons' village there. Put on the stupidest expressions you can, and say to the peons that you are on your way to Balun Canan and from there you want to go to the coffee plantations as contract laborers, and that you want to sell the grass in Balun Canan for a good price in order to buy yourselves tobacco for the journey."

"We can do that all right and easily enough. I worked in a coffee place once in San Geronimo," answered Pablo.

"Stop there about half a day, as if you wanted a rest. Here's thirty centavos for each of you so that you can buy something from the peons—tortillas for the journey, beans, chilies, a few tobacco leaves. Then wander around, near the buildings, and keep your eyes open for anything you can learn. You know enough Spanish to understand what they'll be talking and shouting about. If you can, count how many men are there, whether they intend to stay one or two days or to go straight off again. Have a good look to see where the gates are, whether they're bolted at night or just pushed to; where the rifles are kept, and the machine guns; which rooms the officers sleep in, whether they drink a lot. Can you find out all that?"

"Of course, General. We have heads and good stomachs to give us plenty of sense."

"And when you leave the village, say casually that, on your way there, you met a few exhausted, dirty muchachos, carrying rifles and with wounds on their heads and bodies, and that these muchachos had been in great terror and had disappeared into the bush in a hurry. As soon as you have said this as if it were something quite unimportant, set out in the direction of

Balun Canan. Of course, when you arrive at the *finca*, no one must be able to guess that you've come from here; and when you leave there go at first half a league or more toward Balun Canan, and then turn off and double back on your tracks. It's important that no one in the *finca*, not even the peons, should guess that you have come from here and are returning here. Well—everything understood?"

"Everything, General. And don't worry about us. We'll find out all you want to know, General."

"Then be off. And should one of the soldiers or *finqueros* question you, tell them that you've seen two men with rifles running into the bush, and that they were so frightened they didn't even exchange a word with you. But most of all, avoid the Federals. Just keep your eyes open, and talk to the peons."

Later these two scouts returned and delivered their reports to General. From them the muchachos learned the fate of their captured comrades. But instead of being thrown into terror and shattered at the prospect of a similar or even worse fate, this news aroused in them an indescribable rage and evoked such hatred that, had not General, Colonel, Professor, Andreu, Celso, and a few other muchachos been calm and intelligent enough to persuade the inflamed muchachos to follow their carefully prepared plan, they would have started off immediately to attack Santa Cecilia by day without regard for the consequences.

Modesta, who was squatting beside Celso and combing the hair of her little nephew Pedrito, had heard the news. Little Pedrito had had both ears cut off, like his father. This hideous punishment had been inflicted on the father for an unsuccessful attempt at escape, whereas the little boy, in the presence of his father, had had to endure the same mutilation in order to add to the father's punishment and to mark the child for the rest of his life as the son of a deserter. If, as a consequence of his attempted flight, the father had been flogged half to death, as happened in similar cases, he would have been unable to work for several days, and this loss of his valuable working power would have annoyed the owner of the *monteria*. Whereas the cutting off of his ears did not prevent him from resuming work immediately, and production did not fall off as a result of his punishment.

When Modesta, who hitherto had believed that her own brother had fallen in the attack on the north army and thus suffered a rapid death, now realized from the mention of the prisoner with the missing ears that among those so brutally executed had been her beloved brother, she paled, and burning tears swelled into her eyes. But she gave no vent to these tears. She only pressed her lips tightly together, parted them again quickly and as if involuntarily, and then expelled her breath vehemently. Then she drew the little Pedrito close to her and kissed him. "Your father is one of the heroes of the fighters for *Tierra y Libertad,*" she said, and kissed him again.

"Isn't my father ever coming back, *tía mía?*"

"No, little one, from now on he lives with all the other Indian heroes on the stars, where all great men live whose wonderful deeds will never be forgotten by people."

"Then I will be able to see him with my field glasses, won't I?"

"Yes. I'm sure you will," she answered, with a sad smile.

Meanwhile, the scouts' report had ended. She had paid no further attention to it.

Now, however, when all around her were silent under the impact of the news, she looked for a long time at Celso, who was standing with his head bowed forward, staring at the ground. She touched him gently and said softly, "You're in charge of the second machine gun, aren't you, Celso?"

"You know well enough that I am, Modesta. And now that Colonel's so unfortunately gone and lost his own gun, I'm the only machine gunner in the whole army. And I needn't tell you how proud I am to be in command of such a beautiful, shining, fine-firing machine gun."

"Of course not, Celso. You're right to be proud of it."

She was silent for a while, and with her big toe drew a pattern in the earth.

Suddenly she said, "You like me, don't you, Celso?"

"Wha-a-at?" he answered in a long-drawn-out, astonished

voice. "Of course I like you. Why not? You're a pretty girl, and you can cook. Really, I like you very much, very much indeed. I didn't think there was any need to tell you that. Any sensible young girl could see that for herself."

"Then if you want me to like you, to like you very, very much, you must do something for me, too, Celso."

"Anything, Modesta, anything you ask. You've only to say it, and it's already done. But with one exception. I must say that right away. If you're wanting to have my machine gun, I can't give it you. At least not until we've won the revolution. Then I'll make a sewing machine for you out of it."

"No, Celso, I don't want your machine gun. What I want you to do for me is just to teach me to shoot so well with your machine gun that I can shoot down a mango from its branch at two hundred paces."

"But why a mango, girl?"

"So that I can cut to ribbons the cruel hearts of all who are not for us, who do not shout *Tierra y Libertad* with us, and who stamped on our brothers' heads, my brother's among them. The ears of little Pedrito will be paid for. Paid for dearly. And now his father's trampled head must be paid for, too. And very dearly. Very, very dearly, Celso."

"Well spoken, Modesta. I will teach you to shoot with my machine gun better even than Colonel taught me. What indeed does Colonel know about machine guns? He just shoots away without seeing whether he hits, because he likes the rat-tat-tat. I don't like the bangs, only the hits, and if I could score hits without the bangs, I'd be a hundred times more pleased."

"When will you begin to teach me the machine gun, Celso?" asked Modesta, becoming impatient.

"Not tomorrow, Modesta, but now, right away."

"Of course, without the bangs and without firing any bullets," a voice interrupted. It was General, who had caught the last words.

Celso laughed loudly. "The firing is the last thing to be learned. Assembling, loading, aiming, those are the most difficult things to learn, and it's even harder to learn to repair it when the gun suddenly jams. You've got endless things to learn, Modesta, before you can fire a shot. And that will be neither today, nor tomorrow, nor in the next ten days. That's why, General, you needn't worry that we'll go shooting off and betraying our position."

General squatted down, lit a raggedy, rolled cigarette at the campfire, and said to Modesta, "So you want to become a machine gunner, muchacha?"

"Yes, General, that's what I want, and that's what I will be."

"Good," replied General. "I love muchachas like you. A pity you've already chosen your husband." He squinted at Celso, who grew red-brown in the face and sank his head so deeply that only the thick, black, stringy, uncombed thatch on his pate was visible.

"I'd be very contented with a wife like you, muchacha. But I have a pretty, fresh, sturdy young widow whose tears I've got to dry. And she'll certainly make me a good wife. Of course, she isn't as wild about a machine gun as you are, muchacha. She prefers to cook something good for me and to fish the lice out of my dirty hair. Sometimes a wife like that is better for a soldier than one who wants to fight, too. What do you think, Celso?"

"I'm not a general, and so I've got fewer worries than you," answered Celso, now raising his head and looking at General with a smile. "And as I have only to look after my machine gun and the boys who help me with it, I'd really just as soon have a wife who'll look after the machine gun."

"Well, you can decide that between you: what suits each of you two best so that you can be happy and still attack the *uniformados* with all the more fury," said General, drawing deeply on his newly lit cigarette and standing up at the same time.

He now went close to Modesta, who had also stood up, clapped her on the shoulder, took her by the chin, raising it a little, and said, "*Oiga*, muchacha, listen! When you can hit a mango at a hundred paces, I'll make you the first female lieutenant in the revolutionary army. And you're a *soldadera* from now on. *Tierra y Libertad!*"

Modesta, raising her head, saluted in the manner she had just seen General do and replied, "*Estoy a sus órdenes, mi general. Tierra y Libertad!*"

"What have you got there in your packs?" asked General, pointing at the carrying nets of the two returned scouts.

The nets were still stuffed to bursting with high grass.

"In God's name, they're bobbing about in all directions, what have you got in them? Pigs, calves, goats, or what?"

"Trophies of war, General," answered Pablo.

Pablo and Mario now untied their nets, pulled out the grass from the tops and sides, and in each net there appeared a head.

"Just in passing I caught a mangy *capataz* and brought him along," said Pablo, dragging out his prisoner, whom he had wound up in a rope and whose mouth he had plugged so full of grass that not a sound could come out.

"And I found a major-domo." Mario prodded his prisoner in the ribs so that he rolled out of the net.

"Each of them had such a lovely shiny revolver," explained Pablo, "that we could never have forgiven ourselves to all eternity if we hadn't taken the pretty things away from them. And as it was all in the day's work, we thought we might as well bring the boys along here so that you can question them yourself, General. They know more than the poor peons who don't dare open their mouths for fear the *finqueros* will bury them up to their waists and then ride their horses over them. They wouldn't even sell us tortillas lest the *finqueros* might see it and accuse them of consorting with unknown *campesinos* who might perhaps know something about the rebels."

The peons of whom the two scouts had spoken were certainly at this time in a state of indescribable fear. But whether their fear was greater than that of the two prisoners who now stood half-cowering before General was a matter open to doubt.

To be carried on the backs of Indians, when tied up tightly and compactly like parcels, wholly enclosed in grass, with mouths stuffed full, and then to be delivered under the tropical sun at noonday is no pleasure, even if this were done out of friendship. But to know that they had been bound helpless and dragged here by Indian rebels whose comrades had only a few hours before been savagely martyred to death was enough to bring fear to the bravest soldier's heart.

There stood now in front of General two specimens who revealed more than any words could to what an unbelievable extent a dictatorship can destroy the characters of human beings. The miserable attitude of these two, just on this very morning when they had felt themselves so absolutely secure and had vied in being second to none in cruelty toward defenseless prisoners, would have aroused in any intelligent being the conviction that the dictatorship had reached a pitch where it could have been slapped down with a wet rag.

The two prisoners fell to their knees, begged for mercy, and even before being questioned, told all they knew about the plans and intentions of the officers and *finqueros*.

"This morning you helped to bury our comrades, and you beat them and spat on them," said General.

"*Por Madre Santísima, mi jefe*, we didn't even touch one of those poor muchachos."

General summoned Colonel and some of the other muchachos. They took the two prisoners away. After half an hour they came back.

"Was that all they knew?" asked General. "Well, it's enough. Now we can get ready to move."

Colonel asked, "What shall we do with the two of them? Shoot them?"

"And waste our ammunition like that!" said General. "You should learn, *hermanito*, to be economical. Where is your machine gun?"

"You know that, General."

"You're one of my colonels and a commanding officer, and you let your machine gun be taken away from you."

"So that's how you feel, brother? All right, I let it be taken away from me. But today I'll get it back again. And tomorrow I'll have another as well. Besides ours, they've got two brand-new ones down there in Santa Cecilia."

"Let the others do something as well. Don't always be wanting to be doing everything by yourself. Call up a few of the muchachos and tell them to stone those two swine until they stop twitching. Waste bullets on them? Or foul a respectable machete with their stinking juice? Even stones are too good."

A muchacho came running up. "They're coming! They're coming!" he shouted while he was still a little way off.

"Who's coming, you ass?" asked General.

"The Federals!"

"I don't believe it," replied General and sprang toward a tree, which he clambered up.

"Five men," he called down from the tree after a while. "They are *finqueros* after those frightened muchachos who, as we told them, slunk away into the bush. Colonel, take along twelve muchachos and capture those sons of whores. They're already well into the bush. Don't shoot. Catch them with lassos. I want the information they've got. Only if they start coming this way, then fire. But you'll get them all right without a shot. And if they manage to see our army here *and* beat a retreat *and* get back to the *finca*, then I tell you, Colonel, good friends as we are, I'll have your head cut off—or, rather, I'll cut it off myself. For certain."

"I'll get 'em with two fingers, and one of those sprained."

"Your head, Colonel, or those swine. You know that now." General laughed. "I mean that seriously, although I may laugh. I've appointed you colonel, and I know very well why. But just because I have made you colonel, I require of you twenty times more than from an ordinary muchacho."

"Well, you don't have bellyache over it, General. And I'll get back my machine gun tonight. Entirely alone. With just a machete and one muchacho to help me carry it. And I shan't even take my pistol with me."

"You'll do tonight what *I* order, not you. I'm General here, and you'll do what the General orders."

Colonel turned away and picked out his men. "Are you coming?" he asked Celso, who joined him at this moment.

"You insult me by asking. Of course I'm coming. I can catch cattle and half-wild horses, so I'll certainly be able to round up a mere half-dozen miserable sons of whores."

Two hours later the five *finqueros* lay bound hand and foot in the camp. Three major-domos had also been captured with them. These three men had not previously been seen by the outposts because they had separated from the *finqueros* and had headed into the bush in order to search for traces of the allegedly escaped muchachos.

At the interrogation dozens of the Indians crowded around the place. As soon as one of the *finqueros* attempted to lie, and one of the muchachos who knew the region well heard the lie, he would immediately yell out, "*Mentira!* Stinking liar!"

Then the *finquero* got one on the mouth from the muchacho standing nearest to him. The *finquero*, feeling humiliated at being struck by a verminous Indian, then refused, despite encouragement from machete and fists, to say any more, or uttered only a few unimportant sentences.

The major-domos were much more willing to tell everything they knew. And during the last hours of their lives the *finqueros* learned what sort of men they had honored with their trust. Without even being asked, the major-domos betrayed where their masters had buried their money and other treasures, or in which corner of the buildings they had been hidden or buried.

At last General was weary of the questioning and the lying. He summoned half a dozen muchachos to him and said, "This morning these caballeros and their hangman's assistants martyred our comrades to death. What shall we do with them? You may decide."

"Just the same. *Lo mismo*." Every mouth shouted in unison.

"No. Not the same," retorted General. "Hang them over there on that tree. All on the same tree. And let them hang there until they rot or until the vultures have eaten them away. And when I say hang, I don't mean in the way we were hanged in the *monterías*. Short and quick, with their own lassos that they've got on their saddles."

One of the muchachos called out, "And who gets their revolvers and rifles?"

"The muchachos who captured them."

"And if any of them has a pistol or carbine, who gets that then?"

"The one who hangs the swine quickest."

The *finqueros* did not utter a word. They crossed themselves and murmured Ave Marias.

The three major-domos, however, wasted no time with that. They fell to their knees, embraced the leather leggings which General had won in battle with the *Rurales*, and wailed, "Mercy, spare us, *mi general, mi jefe*. Have pity on us and our wives and children. Have mercy, not on us, but on our children."

General dragged his legs out of their clutches and kicked these whining lumps of misery so hard in their faces that they tumbled together in a heap. "Which of you goddamned sons of whores ever showed any mercy toward the muchachos? Well, which of you? Come on, come on. Which of you? Whoever of you had any pity will not be hanged—only shot. This morning you were fine and fat, glistening in the sunshine of those accursed executioners and torturers. Now you're groveling here."

"We've only always done what our *patroncitos* ordered us," whimpered one, half-raising himself.

"That's why. That's why it is right that you three shall not be hanged, but first flayed and then hanged."

He walked a few paces over to the *finqueros*, who stood upright and crossed themselves again as he approached. "You, caballeros, I ought also to have flayed before I have you hanged. Scoundrels, pitiful, stinking scoundrels in your hearts and souls, that's what you are, although you put on such haughty expressions here because you have to be shamed before Chamulas and Bachajones. I've thought of something better for you, to keep you company on your march to Hell. It will cause you more pain than a threefold skinning. It wouldn't mean anything to your filthy henchmen. Flaying is the only thing that worries them. But you'll worry when I tell you what, today and tomorrow and in the days to come, we'll do to your wives and daughters and nieces and granddaughters and mothers. *We*, the lousy, filthy, beaten Chamulas—yes, *we*, the stinking swine and mangy hounds—we shall amuse ourselves with your women. Not for pleasure, but for justice. And in order that justice may for once reign in this state, *that* is why I am General and this one here is Colonel and that one there Major, even though he can't read and write. But one thing we can all do. Slaughter you all, and pull down the dictator from his throne in the Palacio Nacional, so that at last we may be permitted to open our mouths and say what we please and not merely rattle off like parrots just what is rattled off to us every day. And now, caballeros, *adiós y buen viaje al infierno*, farewell to Hell. Come on, muchachos. Take them away," he shouted to the men he had appointed for the last execution.

"*Viva General! Tierra y Libertad!*" screamed more than a hundred muchachos, who, while General had been speaking, had gathered around in greater and greater numbers to hear what he had to say. "*Tierra y Libertad! Que muera la dictadura! Abajo los caciques! Abajo los patrones y capataces! Viva la revolución! Libertad para los indios!*"

In the course of the afternoon four more *finqueros* were brought into the camp by the outposts. They were landed gentry who were riding home, with their major-domos and *capataces*, back to their *fincas* after having celebrated in Santa Cecilia their victory over the rebels and after having received an assurance from the officers that the region was free from any scattered gangs of the defeated rebels.

When the *finqueros* came into the camp and found that the rebels had such a mighty army at their disposal, they were so astonished, shocked, and bewildered that for a full quarter of an hour they seemed to be totally oblivious of their own predicament. They realized what was in store for the garrison at Santa Cecilia, and they would have willingly scarificed ten years of salvation for a chance to warn Santa Cecilia of the approach of this army.

Two the caballeros, Don Fernando and Don Anselmo, still possessed enough caustic humor and brotherly love for one of them to say to the other as the lasso nooses were drawn around their necks, "It is neither pleasant nor Christian to dangle so humiliatingly from a branch without benefit of clergy, but what's ahead for our good neighbors now carousing so heartily in Santa Cecilia is not much better. Eh, Don Anselmo?"

Don Anselmo, twisting his neck in the noose, replied, "As always, Don Fernando, you have once again spoken to the point. I, too, prefer to depart thus quietly and unobtrusively from this—when one comes to think of it—very sad world, rather than to share in the confusion and distress that those in Santa Cecilia will suffer before, like us here, they peacefully—"

But Don Anselmo was unable to conclude his philosophical discourse. The world will never know what words of wisdom he would have dispensed at his last moment. The word "peacefully" turned to a choking gurgle as two muchachos hoisted him into the air at that moment. In the face of such decisive and unambiguous behavior, there is an end to all human wisdom. Even that of the greatest philosophers.

7

 There still remained three hours to sunset.

General had ordered every man to hold himself in readiness to march off at twenty minutes' notice, should the command be given.

The staff was squatting together, but not one of them spoke a word of the coming attack. The muchachos chatted about everyday matters. General squatted and scratched grass roots out of the earth with a little stick. As soon as he had dug out two or three, he scratched with the same stick another hole not far from the first place and planted the rootlets again. It was easy to see that he was doing this because his thoughts were far away.

Suddenly, however, he became active. Hurriedly he scraped the earth carefully over the last planted roots, sprang to his feet, went almost at a run around the circle of his squatting staff, and shouted out, repeating it again and again, "I'd give half my left arm to know whether at night or at first light of dawn. I'd give half my left arm to know . . ."

"Hell and damnation, General!" called out Matias. "Be thankful you've got your left arm and stop complaining. Even an old wife couldn't listen to any more of this eternal moan about your left arm. *Muy bien*, if it's in your way, come here and I'll chop it off at one stroke, just as we hacked off that muchacho's leg when it was bitten by a cascabel." *

* A Spanish muzzle-loading cannon.

"Come on, General. What's gone wrong again now? Out with it. Left arms are precious. Matias is right. We need every arm we have, and yours is no worse than ours." Celso spoke in a calm, soothing tone.

"All right, if not my left arm, then I'd give my left little toe to know which plan, which of the two that I've thought of, I should choose." He stood still and scratched his thick hair.

"If they're both good, it doesn't matter which you choose," said Andreu.

"It's not as simple as that. Each has its advantages, and each a disadvantage."

"Then pick the one that has the least disadvantage," advised Andreu.

"The difficulty is to know, or rather to guess, which of the two disadvantages is the lesser."

Colonel plucked at his tattered shirtsleeve as he stopped near him for a second. "Sit down here quietly for a change and cease hopping around like a green spring chicken. You can't even think with all that running about."

"I've tried it sitting down, too, but it's just as difficult." Nevertheless, he squatted down and took a cigar out of his shirt pocket. "The plan came to me this morning when I was sitting up in the tree for a while, watching the *finqueros* creeping about as they hunted wounded and escaped muchachos. I believe you sometimes get much better ideas by sitting up in a tree for a bit and looking down at the world from above instead of always looking at it from below. What do the ants know of our existence? To the ants we're only clouds or wandering mountains. One plan is to take Santa Cecilia tonight; the other is to attack the *finca* just before sunrise. We must attack it. But if we simply march on them, we'll be mown down like grass by their machine guns. We must attack them in such a way that they have no time to set up a single gun, not even to unpile their rifles."

"All right, then. Why not before sunrise?" asked Celso.

"There are a lot of early risers there. *Finqueros* riding home who have a long day's journey before them and want to take advantage of the cool of the morning. They will be awake and might hear us before we are near enough. It's possible, too, that the Federals and *Rurales* may move off at two in the morning. That's just what I couldn't find out from the damned clods that fell into our hands. But, curse it all, those troops mustn't be allowed to escape without our getting their rifles. We need the guns and every bullet those foul swine have. And Colonel wants to recover his machine gun—his Emma, as he calls it—otherwise he'll never be happy again. If we can catch those swine here at Santa Cecilia, then we won't have to chase after them and run the soles off our feet."

"Then up and at them!" advised Celso.

"At them? At them? You can talk, but I have the responsibility if I lose too many men. But now all of you listen closely and keep your ears open. If we set on them at two or three in the morning, then they may all be up and about, the *finqueros* to ride home and the troops to return to their garrisons in Hucutsin or Balun Canan. Before we're properly over the walls, they'll have everything ready in the patio to give us a hot reception. But the advantage is that we'll be attacking toward daylight and it will be light enough for us to see whose throats we're cutting. But in another respect it would be far better in the middle of the night. Then they'll all be half-drunk, lying about snoring in their first sleep. But it will be pitch dark and half of them could escape us and then attack us from outside."

"Yes, you fool of a general. And why don't we bring lanterns with us, as we put on our carts when there's no moon?" said Matias, grinning.

"Matias is right," opined Andreu. "Why don't we use lanterns? Not cart lanterns, of course. We could use our own lanterns and so save paraffin."

"I don't really know, although I'm general, what you mean and how you mean it," said General, looking at Andreu questioningly.

"It's not exactly my idea; I got it from the peons on the *fincas* that we visited on our march and to whom we gave the whole *finca* whether they wanted it or not. What I'm thinking of is very simple. As soon as we've completely surrounded the whole wall, some of us squatting on the wall and some of us already over it, we'll deliver the paraffin to the *finquero* of the Santa Cecilia. And if you still don't understand, what I mean is that we set light to all the palm roofs and all the outbuildings which are made of wood, and in two minutes the whole thing will be roaring up in the night wind. Then we'll have light enough. Of course, we will have to be in the *finca* in a flash, and muchachos must be standing simultaneously at all doors so that no one escapes."

"Perhaps I may yet promote you to brigadier one day, when I become a field marshal, Andrucho. You're cursed clever, and yet you've never been a soldier anywhere. If only there weren't those damned dogs who'll start barking wildly as soon as we get near and start climbing the walls."

"I'll take care of the dogs, General," said Emilio, who was squatting nearby. "I know a good trick to entice the dogs easily half a league away from the *finca* and the village. When the people in the *finca* hear the dogs barking, but running toward the bush, no one will give them a second thought, because they'll think a wild boar or jaguar has slunk up to the corral. But I'll have to start right away and get hunting. I'll be responsible for the dogs being quiet, General. And I'll need three muchachos with me."

"Good," agreed General. "And I'll talk to you later if the dogs muck up my plans and if we're still alive."

"You can shoot me, General, if I don't get the dogs away. Of course, there are always a few that are too lazy or too old and are afraid of going out at night. But those few can bark as much as they want. They'll give the swine inside a greater feeling of safety than if not a cur barked, because all night through there's always something to bark at, even if they only see a rat running past or a cat courting."

The commanding officer of the troops stationed at Santa Cecilia had issued orders for departure at eight o'clock the next morning. The certain knowledge that his estate would be freed of these expensive visitors by next day induced the *finquero* to give a farewell banquet, since it would be for the last time. So there was no stinting of suckling pigs, turkeys, and calves at this feast; and there was plenty of *aguardiente*, fine, old, and brown, for the officers and *finqueros*, and paler, but therefore all the stronger, for the men.

Such monumental suppers at the *fincas* in that remote region never last long into the night—chiefly because there is a lack of good illumination, which renders a long session, even at a richly laden banquet table, a matter of no pleasure. Candles droop in the heat, while open lanterns smoke intolerably and every puff of wind drives gusts of thick, black, sooty smoke over the guests and onto their white shirts. Paraffin lamps go out a hundred times and must be lit a hundred and one times, with the additional danger of explosion because of inferior fuel. The fire on the great stone altar in the patio gives a far-reaching light, but that, too, pours sooty smoke among the feasters.

And at eight or nine o'clock, generally before the fall of darkness, myriads of mosquitoes, midges, and other unattractive insects begin to get lively. They go, naturally, for the illuminated tables and faces. At this time of year the insects are particularly numerous and even more bloodthirsty. Quite apart from the discomfort of their stings, they fall in swarms into the soups and sauces of the diners and swim lustily in every wine or water glass. So, for even the most hardened toper, a lengthy session at table is generally more of a torment than a pleasure.

There was yet another reason why such banquets at remote *fincas* do not last far into the night. At nine in the morning the tropical heat begins to bear down on man and beast, on blade and earth. This compels people to rise very early, partly to make fullest use of the light of the sun and partly to accomplish such work as is necessary, of whatever sort, in the cool hours of the morning. The tolerable and useful working day ends for all who are not peons or laborers at eleven o'clock in the morning, and then, if anything remains to be done, it is resumed for another two hours after four o'clock. Thus it happens that everyone, including the soldiers, are so dog-tired by eight o'clock in the evening that they fall asleep at the tables. From all these considerations it happens that banquets begin at about five o'clock in the afternoon and finish at eight, but certainly not later than nine, with yawns and snoring.

Such customs must naturally be known to a commander-in-chief in order to enable him to evaluate his strategic plans. And General had learned that a mighty banquet was to be held, not only from the two spies he had sent forth but also, as a confirmation, from the questioning of the captured major-domos and *finqueros*. The *finqueros*, although they had been uncommonly cautious in all that they had said, had found the question about the banquet innocuous and had answered it truthfully.

General ordered the attack for about eleven o'clock that night. He needed time to get his army, unobserved, close to the *finca*. During daylight he marched only as far as the verge of the bush. As soon as it was dark, the advance continued.

All packs, all rifles, all horses, mules, donkeys, and dogs were left behind in the bush under guard of the women and a few muchachos who had been too heavily wounded in the last fight to take part in the coming battle.

Only those muchachos who possessed revolvers were allowed to bring their weapons with them. Nevertheless, many of these fellows left their revolvers behind. But every man, whether or not he had a revolver, carried his machete with him, and those who had no machete carried daggers in their woolen belts or stuck into a slit in their trousers.

General summoned the muchachos into a circle. "Those lads who up to now haven't had a revolver or a rifle will have preference. Machine guns must be looked for and immediately taken either out through the gate or into a corner of the building." He summoned twelve muchachos to whom he entrusted the task of searching for machine guns, getting them away, and guarding them, so that they could neither be used nor recovered by the soldiers. "You, Celso, as commanding officer of a machine gun, are responsible, together with Matias, that they are not used against us and that, once they are outside the patio, they are properly guarded. You, Colonel, will rescue your Emma, and when you've got her will take her to Fidel, who'll have the other, and will then yourself take part in the battle."

After this General detailed twenty muchachos to capture, secure, and guard all rifles piled or hanging up. Then he organized the four main troops for the four walls and two further troops for the two gates, which were not to be opened, but only to be guarded in order that no one should escape.

Finally, he picked out some resourceful lads whom he entrusted with the illumination of the battlefield.

His two scouts, outstanding observers, had given him a plan of the layout of the buildings, and how and where the soldiers, the police, and the *finqueros* and their henchmen were distributed. The scouts had also reported that in front of the main gate there was a guard of three men and a corporal, but that this detachment served more for ornament than for security. The ornament consisted in the fact that the commanding officer acquired greater regard in the eyes of the women of the *finca* if he entered this gate and the guard had to stand to attention and present arms. The guard slept at night, they, too, being amply entertained with the dishes, and especially the drinks, of this gigantic farewell feast. Even had this not been the case, they would nevertheless have fallen asleep, for they were tired, no one came to check on their wakefulness, and besides, all the rebels had been destroyed.

General, however, left nothing to luck or chance. He detailed three muchachos to go ahead of the main troop and make sure that the guard at the gate, consisting of four men, would never stand guard again.

"And now the moment for the attack, the signal," said General. "Not a shot will be fired, not a whistle given, not a command. All commands will be issued by me, here and now. Not one of you is to open his mouth until it is all over. Leave the shouting to the others when they see our knives in front of them. Like jaguars in the night slipping into a corral—that's how you must work, muchachos. The less noise, the better. The whole thing mustn't last longer than fifteen minutes. Thereon depends our success. As soon as the first roof is in flames and the patio is illuminated, you must be up on the wall and over in a flash. Each group must deal with the guards that I have assigned to that group. One group for each room, and four groups for the patio. Four small groups to be outside the four walls in case any of them attempt to escape. Not one must leave the *finca!* Incendiary group here!"

"Here we are, General." The men of the designated group stepped forward.

"Go ahead. Creep softer and warier than an old coyote. Once you get to the *finca*, search out some heaps of corn husks and spread these heaps everywhere where sheds and buildings with palm roofs and wood walls are. Don't forget to take enough kindling with you and plenty of matches. As soon as we are all assembled, I'll send Eladio to you, and he will bring you the signal when the illuminations are to begin. Take care it doesn't start too soon, for that could ruin our plan. Then, when you have had the signal and the thing has begun, make sure that there's a blaze and that it doesn't go out before we've got the whole gang under our control. God help you if you let anything go wrong. Then you'll really get to know me. You're the most important group for the success of the whole plan. Understand?"

"Don't worry about us, General. We'll light up the place till it can be seen even in Hell." The men laughed and gathered all the kindling in the camp, each one provided himself with three matches, and to be quite certain, every man took a great lantern filled with paraffin. Thus equipped, they started on their way. With them went the muchachos whose job it was to pay a call on the gate sentries and inquire after their well-being.

Since it was not yet quite night, the muchachos crept cautiously through the long grass in order not to be observed from the *finca*. Admittedly there was no reason to expect that anyone in the *finca*, while the great farewell banquet was in full swing, would bother to train his binoculars on the surrounding area in the hope of seeing a stray antelope. Nevertheless, General took every possibility into account.

Professor, who had been listening to all these dispositions of

General's, since he had been standing continuously at his side for the last half hour, said, "In my opinion, and after what we've seen and heard here, we were quite right to make you general. We could scarcely find a better."

"Oh, hell," grinned General, "I'm not nearly so important as you think, Professor. Tomorrow or the day after, I may be shot, or hanged, or buried alive up to the neck and have horses galloped over me, or be smeared with sugar syrup and tied to a tree in the bush. What would that matter? The revolution would go on, and it must go on. Generals die and new generals will appear—far better generals than I am. For the longer the revolution lasts, the more practice the revolutionaries get in the waging of war, and in a few months any one of you standing around here will be able to do much better than I can today because he will have had more practice and experience than I have had till now."

"That's all spoken so well, General," replied Andreu, "and it's really a pity you can't write it down so that all revolutionaries who are unable to hear you can at least read your words."

General burst out in a guffaw of laughter. "Me write? Write down my own words? I must tell you, Andrucho, that it always cost me a whole week's headache to write a letter to my mother when I was still a sergeant. I could just about fill one side of the paper. But when I came to the second side, the difficulties began because I had no words left by then, and even if I'd had any I didn't know how to write them. And it's quite a time now since I was a sergeant. Probably today I couldn't write more than my own name. And that, I think, is enough for a general. What do you think about it, muchachos?"

"Why does a general need to write more than his name, I'd like to know?" said Celso, glancing questioningly at all the muchachos around. "Look at me. I can't even write my name; a very wobbly, crooked C is all I can write with difficulty, and yet I'm colonel and, what's far more, in charge of a machine gun. Whether you can write or not doesn't worry a machine gun. All it bothers about is whether it's well oiled and whether you handle it properly so that it hits the target."

Professor smiled at General. "I'd be very much interested to know, General, what was on the first page of that letter that you wrote to your mother."

"It's very simple and quite clear. I wrote 'My dearly beloved, noble, and respected mother,' and then I put a period."

"And what else was there on that first side?"

"There couldn't be any more because the page was full and there wasn't room for another word."

"And on the second side? What was there?" inquired Professor, grinning all the time.

"That's just as simple and just as clear," said General, as though he were talking about the most ordinary thing in the world. "What else could I write but just 'I am well, Your grateful son who kisses your hands and feet, Juan Mendez.' And then both pages were full. I put the letter in an envelope, bought a stamp, licked it, and shoved the letter in a mailbox."

"And what did your mother write to you in reply?"

"Nothing at all. She couldn't write. But she could read my letters all right. And what more do you want of a letter than that it can be read by the person you send it to? But let's not think any more about that. We've other things to do, and besides, I believe my mother is dead. Much better for her if she is dead. Her life was perpetual work, eternal hardship, a lot of love, always worry about our food, and only once did I see her laugh." General frowned and made an extraordinarily comic face. The muchachos who were sitting around looked up at him and were just about to burst into laughter when he sprang to his feet and shouted, "Where are my superintendents of the illuminations?"

"They're already half an hour on their way, General," answered a man.

"And the charmers of the gate sentries?"

"Long gone, too."

"Then get ready to march off. Come on! Jump to it! Shake your bones and be damned to you! You lazy, lousy lot, sitting around here and gossiping like old wives instead of doing a bit of drill and oiling your weapons and sharpening your knives and machetes. A fine lot of soldiers! Bandy-legged, unwashed tramps, that's what you are, not worthy of making a revolution. Get on with it, and a bit quicker than usual. Make everything ready for the march. The moment the sun disappears behind those mountaintops, we move off. And I'll smash to porridge the brains of any man of you who takes up another position than the one I've designated for his group. I'll watch damned closely, even if I have got my own hands full. And you'll regret it, I promise you, if I find anyone bending over a throat that doesn't belong to him or squatting in a corner where another's supposed to hide."

He unstrapped his revolver holster, threw the revolver to a woman nearby, and said, "I don't need a revolver for work. Hey, you, muchacho!" he shouted to one of the men, "give me your machete and get yourself another. You've got enough bloody rags on you from yesterday's fight, so you can stay here and guard the camp with a rusty machete."

He felt the edge of the machete the man had given him and said, "Not very sharp, is it? But all the better. Those goddamned swine will at least feel it when they're being sawn apart, and they'll have an extra couple of miserable seconds to consider how quickly one can get to Hell without falling out the window."

At about the same time, an hour before sundown, the banquet at Santa Cecilia was beginning. As at all festivities at which a victory is being celebrated, and where all the brave combatants are relaxed comfortably in the exhilarating knowledge that the enemy has not only been defeated but also rendered permanently harmless, things waxed noisy and hilarious.

Why should the corporal and his three men forming the guard of honor for the night at the main gate be excluded from this victory feast? They had fought valiantly in the skirmish yesterday in which the rebel gang had been destroyed, and they regarded it as a well-earned right that they should attend the victory celebrations in person, like all the rest. They were certainly no defaulters, and certainly not deserters who had attempted to hide when for a few minutes things seemed too hot and the rebels loosed off all they had to shoot with. Besides, since there was no reason for an officer to come near the gate, it would be nothing short of idiocy for a corporal in the Federal Army to keep hanging about outside with his men, watching from afar how the other soldiers, police, *capataces*, and N.C.O.'s clutched at the breasts of the Indian girls carrying food past, and sometimes slapped them on the thighs in order to feel whether, later in the evening, they could try a little higher up without having their faces scratched.

The officers, who sat at the table on chairs that, although very roughly carpentered, were nevertheless chairs, and who, in contrast to the soldiers and N.C.O.'s, ate with knives and forks, would have considered it a gross discourtesy to their hostess if they had gotten up, summoned the corporal, and given him a good dressing-down in front of everyone for having left his post. That could be dealt with next day, and the dressing-down would be emphatically reinforced with half a dozen slaps on the corporal's face and a few well-placed slashes from a riding crop across the shoulders of the men. The colonel was not only an officer but also a gentleman. That he must never forget, and least of all when the wife of the *finquero*, her three grown daughters, two grown nieces, and the wives and daughters of neighboring landowners were also seated at the table.

Besides, the main gate was of no great importance, since there were three machine guns in the patio. They were all packed up for departure and in no way ready for firing, but they were still machine guns, which fulfilled their purpose as a fearsome threat, even though they were entirely dismantled and lay in a corner, tightly corded up. Where each soldier's rifle was not one of them knew after the banquet had been in progress for about an hour and a half. If one couldn't relax as a human being now and again and yield to human pleasures, then the soldiering game held no attraction. The uniform itself provided this only by day; at night the buttons didn't shine, and the gold-and-silver galloons looked like any other common braiding.

In the course of the conversation at the table, the talk turned to the rebels who had escaped. One or two made guesses as to how many there might be who had not been caught. The smallest number, suggested by two *finqueros*, was three. The highest was put forward by a lieutenant who asserted that no fewer than eleven had succeeded in getting away, but he was convinced that all eleven were so severely wounded that they couldn't have gotten far, and since they could hope for no assistance they would certainly hide in the bush and there perish miserably, for their terror was assuredly so great that they would never dare to come out. So they must still be hiding in the bush.

"It's remarkable," interjected a captain of the *Rurales*, "that the caballeros who rode out with their major-domos to catch those escaping swine haven't come back yet. Nothing can have happened to them."

"Don't worry, Captain," the *finquero* of Santa Cecilia reassured him. "It was not the intention of my neighbors to return here. Anyhow they had to take that way along the bush in order to reach their homes. And since they had the whole long day before them, it was their idea to rout out the muchachos and hang them there in the bush. They'll have done that and then ridden on toward their *fincas*. They'll spend the night at Santa Rosita. That's where they are now, and they're probably sorry they didn't stay another day here to enjoy this banquet. But they came from Jovel, where they had business, and since they've been away from their *fincas* for more than three weeks, they were anxious to get home quickly. There's nothing remarkable about that, Captain."

The meal was finally ended, and then began the process of swilling it down so the *frijoles* wouldn't stick in one's throat and also in order to wash away the green chilies from gums and tongues and thus stop the eyes from weeping.

The gramophone was rusty, but it rattled around sufficiently to scratch out some twenty squeaky dance tunes from records that had already begun to grow moldy from the rains. In the *finca* there were two American accordions, a few guitars, and two equally mildewed violins. Half-a-dozen soldiers were able to perform on these. Even though they produced no recognizable melody, it sufficed to persuade people they were dancing as they leaped about in response to these musical efforts, and wriggled and swayed backward and forward as an excuse for pressing against the thighs of the señoras and señoritas until the limit was reached where it ceased to be dancing and had quite openly become barefaced, unmitigated indecency, in which soldiers are permitted to indulge, but not caballeros, whether they are officers or *finqueros*.

But after half an hour of dancing on the hard, gritty paving stones, with heavy revolvers dangling and banging against posteriors, flesh began to melt away from bones and the beautiful uniform trousers were in danger of being split through; whereupon the officers and *finqueros* found it more comfortable to unstrap their revolvers and belts and hang them over the balcony rails.

The ladies certainly did not enjoy dancing with caballeros who had firearms buckled around them; indeed, they considered it all the more impolite when the serpentine, sideways movements of the pleasure-seeking dancers caused the revolvers to produce blue bruises on feminine legs, thus mercilessly destroying the sweet dreams induced by dancing and turning them to an all-too-hard reality.

The colonel, in order not to let his dignity seem impaired, had longest resisted the desire for greater comfort and had delayed removing his artillery. When, however, the señorita with whom he happened to be dancing said suddenly, "*Perdóneme,* Colonel, but your pistol is rather too hard against my ribs, and I would prefer to sit out," what could the colonel do? Only his duty as a gentleman.

Thus, toward eight o'clock, all revolvers were hanging over the balcony rails or on nails on posts, or lying peacefully across saddles in the patio or under the camp beds on which the guests were sleeping.

Revolutionaries who take things seriously should not rely on luck or favorable chances, or upon a growing understanding or awakening sense of justice on the side of their opponents. Regular soldiers may better count on the stupidity of the enemy and persuade themselves that fortune is always on the side of the brave fighter. Revolutionaries must never depend on dreams, and in no circumstances may they believe in news which has no support but their desire that the news be really true.

When the muchachos were discussing the plans of attack, Gabino had said, "Perhaps they're all so drunk they're sleeping like dead dogs."

To which General had replied, "Perhaps! Perhaps doesn't help us in the least. Depend on nothing. That's my advice to you all. Assume for certain that not a soul is sleeping, not one drunk, that every man has his rifle or revolver in his hand, that they're all alert and lying in wait, and that somehow our plans have been betrayed to them. Don't rely on luck. Never. Always assume that the enemy can do more, knows more, and is stronger than you; is more on the alert than you hope, and has learned or guessed all your plans. For what we've thought out on our side can be just as easily thought out by others. The only real advantage that we have is that they don't know that we have more than four hundred men squatting here in the bush. And even that may somehow have become known to them. If I were to rely on good luck and on their being drunk, we wouldn't even need a plan or to be divided into groups. But because I'm not counting on luck, there's only one thing that can defeat our attack, and that is if there is a full regiment in the neighborhood of Santa Cecilia, unknown to us, which can attack us in the rear as soon as we have reached the outside of the walls. But that's what we have our superintendents of illuminations for. If nothing goes up in flames, then something is wrong; but once the place is lit up, we shall be upon them, irrespective of who and what may be at our backs."

General, accompanied by Celso, had crept up close to the *finca* while his army lay scarcely a mile away, hidden in the grass. The *finca* was already completely surrounded, so that each of the four attacking groups was roughly equidistant from the walls. The one gap in the encirclement was caused by the peons' village. The plan of the two groups, which here formed an angle to each other, was to cut off the village from the *finca* in the course of the attack, a small party being detailed to guard the village so that the peons could not reach the *finca* in case, driven by fear, they attempted to flee there.

Naturally, those muchachos who had been entrusted with the task were not able to lure away all the hounds in the *finca* and the village. Several still barked here and there. Even these were all quickly silenced by each man whom they approached too closely, or at least they were reduced to a miserable whimpering by cracking a stone on their skulls.

In the darkest corner of the wide courtyard, where not even the faintest glimmer from the patio bonfire shone, General clambered up onto the wall. When he noted to what extent all the men were engrossed in either drinking or dancing, and that not one had his revolver strapped on, he thought for a moment of giving his incendiaries, whom he had visited at their posts only a few moments before, the order to ignite and thus flash the signal for attack.

Celso, too, had climbed onto the wall in order to survey the battlefield. When they were both down again on the ground, General said, "It wouldn't be at all bad just to sweep into them right away. But I don't think it's decent to attack people when they're dancing and laughing."

"Maybe," whispered Celso. "But perhaps it will be no more decent and polite to disturb them later. Don't imagine that after this evening, with all that good eating, drinking, dancing, and thigh-squeezing, they'll settle down to praying."

"Well said. And what you say convinces me all the more that the signal mustn't be given prematurely; we mustn't change the plan; we must still attack about an hour after the last candle has gone out, as I've fixed. Then it'll be quicker, and it may even be that we won't lose a single man."

General now once again visited the incendiaries, who were lying flat on the ground about fifty yards from the roofs with piles of straw which they had to ignite, not even permitting themselves the luxury of smoking a cigar.

"When I howl four times, like a coyote, set fire," he ordered each gang. Then both of them, General and Celso, returned to their own army groups.

Not one sound, apart from the occasional baying of a hound, who, as soon as he had opened his mouth a few times, quickly slunk away intimidated to the buildings of the *finca* or the huts of the village, betrayed the nearness of the armies. Cicadas, crickets, and grasshoppers chirped and shrilled in their millions of tiny voices, drowning even the suppressed coughs or sneezes of the muchachos, who lay so cleverly hidden in the grass that even a powerful searchlight, had there been one on the *finca*, would not have discovered them. In fact, a *finquero* could have ridden back and forth over the prone muchachos and a sudden shy from his horse, who, then recognizing a man, trotted on peacefully, would have been all he would have noticed as being out of the ordinary in his progress. And even then he would have thought it was a wild beast his horse had scented, perceptible to the animal but not to its rider. And had he, in fact, seen two or three of these almost naked bodies, he would have attributed no particular significance to the encounter, because he would have been certain that they were drunken peons from the *finca* who had reeled out here and simply fallen where they lay because their legs could carry them no farther.

But not a *finquero* rode home before the gray of dawn, not a soldier left the safety of the walls during the night, and the peons of the *finca*, as soon as they were released from their duties, hurried to their huts and lay down to sleep, for at four o'clock in the morning the bells of the *finca* would ring to wake them for another day of work.

When General saw that the great bonfire on the hearth in the center of the patio had not been replenished for more than an hour, and that only here and there the glimmer of a candle was visible in one of the rooms of the *finca*, he let out a terrified howl, and the four armies began, like so many snakes, to creep forward over the ground.

Although they made no sound, the dogs remaining in the *finca* began to bark once more, and a dozen of the peons' hounds felt obliged to join in the chorus.

In the patio were to be heard a few curses from the soldiers lying there, who had been disturbed in their sleep, and immediately thereafter the whimpering howls of several dogs that had felt a truncheon swept under their feet.

In small towns, in Indian villages, and in the remoter *fincas* little heed is given to the barking of dogs by day and far less by night. Of course, if all the dogs of the *finca* and the peon village had been present, their combined noise would have been so striking and unusual that perhaps the men in the *finca* would have realized that this barking warned of a genuinely serious danger. But because the dogs had been reduced by more than a half, and a goodly number of those remaining, intimidated by blows from stones and machetes, had crawled away and not joined in with the howling of the others, the barking and baying of the hounds aroused in no one in the *finca* the suspicion that anything unusual was brewing.

Now the leading files were only about fifty paces from the walls and gates. They were already on the path connecting the village and the *finca*, so that this route was cut both for the peons and for the people in the *finca*.

All the men, without awaiting any further command, firmly gripped their machetes or knives and raised the upper parts of their bodies in order to leap forward five paces at the first movement.

In long-drawn-out complaint, a coyote howled four times.

Glimmers became visible on the two flanks of the *finca* where the barns were, and also the houses of the major-domos and the *capataces*, the roofs of which were of dried palm leaves.

A second later a yellow-red flame shot out hissing and ran like a terrified lizard along the edge of an overhanging roof. Only a few more seconds and another corner blazed up garishly with a crackling roar.

It was extraordinary how nothing stirred, either in the patio or in the *finca* buildings, for at least fifteen seconds. Only the hounds which hitherto had been barking set up a terrified howling.

The muchachos were by now over the wall. Like driven cats they flitted in groups toward the rooms of the massive main building, which were all on the ground floor and whose doors, because of the heat, were standing ajar and not locked or bolted from within. But because General had assumed that all doors would be secured, he had detailed groups to climb onto the roof, tear off the tiles, and drop into the rooms through the ceiling, as the agility of the muchachos would make this a much quicker procedure and the element of surprise far more effective than breaking down the doors. For behind the doors would be standing the officers and *finqueros* with their revolvers in their hands. Now, however, the attack took place simultaneously from the roof and through the doors.

Before the groups who had to deal with the rooms had even reached the doors, not a man of those sleeping in the patio—soldiers, police, major-domos, and *capataces*—remained alive. The patio groups had slit their throats while the roof groups were still squatting on the buildings and prying off the tiles.

The clattering, falling, and smashing of the tiles were the first definite sounds to be heard. Everything that had hitherto taken place, including the killing of more than 120 men sleeping in the patio, had produced no more than suppressed grunting, quickly choked death rattles, a scream that died in a gurgle before it could take form, a scrape of machetes when their points struck sand or flagstones in the patio, and an occasional dull thump as when a block of wood is tumbled on a stone floor.

And now, some fifteen seconds later, there echoed across the patio the first human voices. It came from the house in which the major-domo lived with his family. "*Fuego!* Fire!" the voice shouted twice. Then it ceased.

In the great buildings of the *finca* there rang out the sharp crack of revolver shots within enclosed spaces. But wherever one, two, or three shots sounded, from the noise of those shots it was apparent that they were repeated at the most twice from the same weapon and that the next shot came from another room or a different corner.

It was remarkable that, even in the building, there was still no shouting, crying, or screaming. It was certainly not courage that prevented the brave officers of the Federals and *Rurales* and the equally warlike *finqueros* from yelling. Surprise had simply dried up their voices. And before they found time to utter a warning shout, their throats were already gaping too wide to be of any use in producing a sound.

The only screaming came from three female voices, which, however, could be heard from afar as they ebbed to a loud gurgle.

In the bright light of the crackling palm roofs, Professor was visible crouching high on the cornice of the main building.

He was the first to speak, and he spoke so loudly that it was audible over the whole patio and beyond the walls, probably as far as the village of the peons.

Shaking his fists, rising up to his full height, and giving his voice all the strength of which it was capable, he yelled, "In terror and brutality the dictatorship was born! With terror, brutality, and whips it kept itself in power! In brutality, terror, and the slaughter of millions of men it will be destroyed! In streams of scarlet blood the golden age of falsehood will drown! *Viva la revolución del proletariado! Tierra y Libertad!*"

The muchachos, suddenly awakening as from a trance, brandished their knives and machetes in the air and screamed the answer: "*Viva la revolución! Abajo los tiranos! Tierra y Libertad para todos, sin amos y sin capataces! Viva nuestra rebelión! Viva la rebelión de los indios!*"

And it happened in the course of the revolution that an attack like that on the Santa Cecilia *finca* was repeated not once, not ten times, but many thousands of times throughout the whole land, until at last nothing was left to recall that golden age except for the ruins of once-flourishing domains, and the smashed and now rusting machines in a hundred factories, and a population diminished by almost three million. The golden age of the dictatorship had been able to produce an unheard-of increase in productivity. But in doing that it had forgotten the human being and the individual, and it had also forgotten that each and every thing can be made into a product, with one single exception—the brain and the soul of a man.

When day broke and the victors began to search the *finca*, they came upon that piece of ground where their executed comrades lay with their shattered heads and mangled bodies.

"We will bury them, our poor *compañeros*," said Andreu, "and we'll bury them in the peons' cemetery."

"That would be an insult to them," replied General.

"General's right," said Professor. "We can do them no greater honor than to leave them here where we found them. Here they bled. Here they spat their last revolutionary cries into the faces of those uniformed animals. Here they shall remain. We will only cover their heads with mounds of earth and then build a fence of stones around their last resting places. And when God passes along here on Judgment Day to summon them, He will find them just as they were buried by the tyrants. Then God will know what to think of the accusations of those caballeros who are now being picked by the vultures, and who was in the right in this struggle between the rulers and the ruled."

"We are always in the right!" shouted Celso. "We are always in the right because we're rebels. Rebels are always right. For no one, whether Indian or *ladino*, is entitled to stop another's mouth; our mouths aren't given us only to eat with, like pigs and goats, but also to speak with, and to speak what we wish, whether it pleases the scientists and aristocrats or not."

"Celso," said Andreu to him softly when he had finished his speech, "that's what Modesta told you yesterday. You didn't think that up for yourself."

"And why shouldn't she have told me that? She's just as clever and learned as you. She can read well, and she can write, too. But you needn't tell all the world here that Modesta said that to me. I'm now in charge of a machine gun and mustn't let people notice that I'm just as stupid as I was before.

Besides, I can tell you I'm a great deal better at handling that buzzer than I am with a pencil."

"And it's far more use, Celso. For I don't believe it will always be as quick and simple as it was last night."

"Nor do I," said General, who approached and entrusted Andreu with drawing up a list of all available weapons, ammunition, and provisions.

"Professor has looked through all the orders, telegrams, and reports that the colonel of the Federals and the major of the *Rurales* received," continued General. "It's possible that a whole regiment is already on the march between Balun Canan and Achlumal to reinforce the garrisons in the northern district. They'll be coming our way. And we won't get out of *their* way. We march ahead!"

For a week the army remained at this rich, once so beautiful and regal *finca*.

On the day of their departure Professor divided the estate lands among the peons who, just like their forefathers, had worked this great domain with their sweat, their blood, and their tears for more than three hundred years.

When the army was on the march toward Achlumal and was no more than five miles away from the *finca*, all the buildings that had been spared during the attack now went up in flames. The peons remained in their huts, as before. They had no desire to live like lords.

8

   The little market town of Achlumal contained at
         the moment only twenty soldiers, because the greater
part of the garrison, which normally numbered sixty men, had
been sent to reinforce the contingent now providing meals
for vultures at Santa Cecilia.

The town, however, boasted a local police force consisting
of a commissioner and six men who went about barefoot and
carried as weapons a machete and a muzzle loader.

Besides these there was the *presidente municipal*, or mayor,
who had a revolver; the tax inspector, the civil judge, the post-
master, and the town clerk, who all wore revolvers as symbols
of their dignity and also to inspire respect. Without their revolvers at their hips they looked like any other ordinary citizen, and no one would know that they had some say in affairs
here. In addition, the majority of the shopkeepers and independent artisans had revolvers, which, even if they were badly
rusted and the ammunition did not always fit, at least gave the
impression of being deadly weapons. And that is quite sufficient to put the fear of God into one's fellow creatures, despite
the fact that one otherwise looks like a section supervisor in a
warehouse or a film clown with a black toothbrush mustache
under a runny nose.

General could have assaulted and taken Achlumal in exactly
the same way as he had Santa Cecilia. Yet he intentionally
tried another form of attack.

He sent thirty muchachos, all armed with their machetes, to

the market at Achlumal, just as if they were small peasants who had come to buy. Every Indian carries his machete with him everywhere. It would attract attention if he came without his machete.

The Federal soldiers, under the command of a lieutenant, were quartered in the town hall, in a room which served them as a guardroom and which, like all the other rooms in the one-story building, was situated on the ground floor with its door giving onto the portico. And like all the other rooms in the *cabildo*, this one, too, had no second door in the back and no windows, either.

Around the portico there squatted, as usual, a large number of Indians, partly for the sake of sitting in the shade and partly because they had some sort of business to transact with the civic administration or another of the government offices housed in the building. At night, traveling merchants and wandering Indians slept in the portico of the *cabildo*.

A soldier paced up and down in front of the door of the guardroom with his rifle at the slope, because a soldier must do something to show the taxpayers that their money is not being poured out in vain. The corporal, minus his tunic and with his shirtsleeves rolled up, sat at a minute table in the guardroom, surrounded by forms and documents, and chewed absent-mindedly at a pencil. The lieutenant was not present. Probably he was in a *cantina* in the plaza getting drunk, or else in search of a bed companion for the night. Two soldiers lay on mats in the guardroom and snored. Since the corporal could not perpetually chew at his pencil, he added another occupation to his duties in order not to appear totally inactive. When one of the sleeping soldiers snored too loudly, he stood up and kicked the man in the posterior until he turned over and ceased snoring. Then the corporal returned once more to the table and resumed the chewing of his pencil.

The remaining soldiers squatted on the portico, their tunics and shirts unbuttoned from top to bottom. A few were playing cards. One was picking his teeth. Another was reading a fable which caused him so much difficulty that he scratched his head incessantly and then licked his fingernails.

It was so peaceful that one could hear the flies buzzing. At intervals, from this house or that, a child howled, thus deepening the atmosphere of comfortable domestic bliss. The citizens of the town were recuperating from their labors and swinging in hammocks or squirming on hard beds. Now and then a girl or a woman hurried into a shop to purchase something needed at home. And the woman serving in the shop would waddle lazily out from her corner, half-drowsy and half-angry, and search in the drawer for the centavos change for the customer who had bought three centavos' worth of salt. It was scorching hot at this hour, and every honest citizen regarded it as a sin against God and an offense against morality and custom to work at this time or to carry on business or to walk about the streets.

The muchachos acted so swiftly and surely that when they entered the guardroom, the corporal had only time to look up and for a quarter of a second to be amazed at the impertinence of Indians coming running into the guardroom without first reporting to the sentry outside. But the sentry, as well as the other soldiers squatting in the portico, had been simultaneously hauled into the guardroom in such a manner that, had anyone witnessed it from the plaza, he would have thought it was the soldiers who had seized the muchachos and were dragging them in for interrogation by the corporal. In fact, the soldiers were no longer alive. Before the corporal had even realized this, he had joined them in the ranks of the departed. The soldiers who were sleeping stretched out on the floor suddenly ceased to snore. They emitted a noise similar to that of the last gush of water running out through the drain of a bathtub.

The next moment the soldiers were undressed, the muchachos put on their uniforms, and a sentry was calmly marching up and down in front of the guardroom with a rifle at the slope. At this instant the lieutenant came rolling along to hear the corporal's report of any incidents that might have taken place while he had been in the bar with various generous citizens, sampling for hours on end the different kinds of old *comitecos*.

Swaying slightly at the hips, he came up to the sentry and said, "You'll never as long as you live learn how to shoulder arms properly." Then he gave him a slap across the face and said, stumbling over his words, "I'll have a word with the corporal about you. He'll teach you to carry your gun like a broomstick, and you'll practice that till your shoulder swells up to your chin. Then someday you'll learn how a soldier holds his butt. Why the hell do I have to have such a lousy, filthy garrison in this lousy, filthy place, where at every step one skids twice in the dirt, having to deal with swinish Indians who think they're soldiers."

He went up to the open door of the guardroom and shouted, "Hey, Corporal, come out of there and take a look at this sentry." He took half a step forward and leaned with outstretched arm against the doorpost. Then, as if he were revolving about the doorpost in order to get into the room without letting go with his hand, he vanished inside. All that could be heard was a sound like the fall of a heavy sack and the dragging of that sack over a paved floor. This dragging caused the heels of his leather shoes to make a squeaking noise on the flagstones.

A few minutes later the muchachos were swarming into Achlumal from all directions. Then in that little town a howl of terror went up that would have roused the deepest sleeper.

There arose a wild, confused turmoil in the half-dozen streets and on the plaza. Women screamed, children cried, men cursed, dogs barked. There was shooting in the town hall. All the officials and employees of the municipality now paid dearly for the honor of carrying revolvers. For the muchachos had been too quick and too adroit for their opponents.

Everything found in the government offices—such as registers, documents, lists, books, papers, and regulations—was piled in heaps and burned. The prison, which was situated in the patio of the town hall and which, like all prisons of the State, was occupied solely by Indian peons and Indian peasants, all practically starving, had already been broken open. The prisoners, who felt no bond of sympathy with anything that smacked of the law, had but one impulse: they must now at last commit the crime for which they had lain in jail for weeks or even months. In many cases their offense had been insolence toward the authorities or to *finqueros*, and such insolence was always termed mutiny, rebellion, refusal to work. These released prisoners knew much quicker than the muchachos exactly where to find those with whom they had an account to settle—officials, citizens, and denouncers. They were the ones who now did in the town what neither General nor a single one of the muchachos would have dreamed of doing. Their fury and their desire for revenge knew no bounds. Wherever they broke into a house, not a man, woman, or child remained alive. Although they stole nothing, except for a blanket, a machete, or a shotgun, they left the house only when everything within had been completely destroyed, smashed, slashed, and cut to pieces. And then they lit any candles they found in the house and placed them against the piled-up wreckage of furniture, against the wooden walls, against the doors, and in cupboards and chests.

It was not very long before the town, the most important little market center in the area, was burning in a dozen different places. No one bothered about the fires. The rebels were masters of the town. But they had no thought of remaining masters there. Seeing greater tasks in front of them, what did they worry about the well-being of a town that had never done a thing for them? Wherever they came across a town that possessed a town hall and a prison, they knew that it was a stronghold of the dictator. Even the schools were only for the sons of the *ladinos*. And if children of the Indian inhabitants of the town, the proletariat, living in crumbling daub huts on the fringes of the town, were sometimes admitted to the schools, they were the children whom the teacher took pleasure in whipping, for the fathers of the *ladino* children turned up at the school with revolvers and had conversations with any teacher who had so far forgotten himself as to lay a hand on *their* children. Proletarians raise no objection to their children being beaten at school: therefore, not only are their children beaten but the fathers also when they fall into the clutches of the police.

On the plaza there was a shop in every house; that was why

the place had become a market where the whole population lived by trading and bartering with the Indians of the region. Even the numerous small artisans in the town, besides their occupations as carpenter, builder, or smith, owned a shop as well, which guaranteed them a small but certain income—more, generally, than did their proper trade. Admittedly, the majority of the shops were so tiny that it must have been difficult to find space in them for more than ten pesos' worth of goods.

When the muchachos broke into the town and the citizens realized what was happening, they immediately shut their shops. Or, rather, they attempted to shut their shops. The majority did not have time enough for this and preferred to run or to hide.

The shops that had been shut were quickly broken open by the first kick or thrust with a rifle butt. For if a shop is no bigger than will hold a hundred pesos' worth of goods, the proprietor can hardly be expected to fortify it with a heavy, iron bound door and good locks that would cost him at least two or three thousand pesos. The security of the shops was in direct ratio to the value of the goods in them. Unknown people who arrived here were always suspect and could not take a step without being watched. Thus thieves came into the town only when the *feria*, the great sacred festival, was being held. And since stealing was rare under normal conditions, there was no reason to indulge in heavy expenditure for the protection of the miserable array of goods.

Every shop was cleared out. But the muchachos took only what they needed for their onward march. It was not that they plundered less because they did not wish to thieve; they simply knew they would have to carry everything on their backs. None carried more than was necessary for his own existence. None cared whether they were called thieves, plunderers, looters, or vandals. In this respect they had no sense of honor. Their ambition was to win the rebellion and depose the dictatorship. Once that had come about, there would be time to think of other forms of satisfaction.

Although each took only what he needed, in the end the bourgeois were naturally right when they asserted, "Achlumal was so thoroughly plundered that not a grain of salt was left, not one stone upon another, and not a sheet upon the beds." Rebels must live, if they want to win a rebellion; and if they cannot find any leaders of industry or bank directors who will lend them money for their revolution, then they must make the revolution pay for itself, one way or another. But rebellions must be if the world is to progress. A lake that has no water flowing through it or is not fiercely agitated by storms soon begins to stink, and finally becomes a swamp.

General ordered the signal for advance to be given. It was three hours before sunset.

"We could spend the night in this place," suggested Colonel.

"Certainly we could," retorted General. "But we won't. I've got a feeling in my stomach, or perhaps my bones, that there's a battalion on the march against us—or even a division. You've seen today how easy it is to take a whole town. If we stay here when it's not really necessary, we'll just be sitting coolly and quietly in a trap. I'm for the open country or the bush; we'll have more space there. Besides, there's no more to be said about it. I say we're going to march, and everybody who's still got legs will march. Get ready!" he shouted across the plaza in a resonant bellow.

An hour after the muchachos had left Achlumal, the town slowly began to come to life. The inhabitants came creeping out of their hiding places in the patios and back gardens of their houses. A good number of them had hidden under and behind the numerous altars in the cathedral. For some reason, not one of the muchachos had entered the cathedral to see what it looked like from inside. It wasn't shyness or superstition; it was simply that not one of them believed that he would find anything in the cathedral that would be of the slightest use to him for the onward march. The most important item of all was weapons, and they didn't think the vestry would conceal weapons. All the weapons to be expected in the town had been captured. They had only hunted out the citizens in order to be sure of getting the last rusty pistol or shot-gun. As soon as they came near a man who was carrying a re-volver, the quarry made haste to throw it down. Every citizen felt that the non-possession of a weapon ensured the safety of his skin.

Although the muchachos had old scores to settle which the inhabitants richly deserved to pay, it turned out, when a count was taken, that the losses were no greater than was usually the case when smallpox invaded the town. Of course, all the sol-diers and the majority of the officials in the town hall had fallen for the honor of their Caudillo, as was subsequently re-ported in the newspapers.

The respectable citizenesses returned to their houses, and with the surviving pots and pans and the remains of their rice, corn, and dried meat began to prepare the evening meal.

While the women were thus occupied, the men were stand-ing about the plaza, telling each other how bravely they had dealt with the rebels and how they had once again shown them how far superior a *ladino* was to a dirty Indian.

The cleverer among the citizens, however, wasted no time with such boasting, which profited nothing. They hastened to divide rapidly among themselves the now vacant civic posts, before the rest of the people had had time to recover from their adventures and to discuss the question of holding office or even of holding emergency elections. Finally, one of the men in the groups that were standing about the plaza declaim-ing their heroic sagas, said, "*Caramba, vecinos*, we've now got to think about new officials for the jobs; I believe, *compañeros*, I've always shown that I have a righteous character and that I'm by no means disinclined, in these difficult times through which the fatherland is passing, to shoulder the burden of being mayor of Achlumal."

"We'll discuss that in a moment, Don Aurelio," replied Don Jesus Maria. "I am sure that you would scarcely seriously deny that I possess that sense of honesty, that proper feeling for justice to qualify me for the post of chief magistrate."

"Of course, of course, Don Chucho," responded Don Aurelio hastily, immediately sensing that in Don Jesus Maria, at all events, he had already found an influential citizen who was on his side.

"Caballeros!" said Don Pablo, coming up with half-a-dozen others to the chattering groups. "May I present our new civic officials and our new federal authorities? I myself, obeying at last the urgent persuasion of our most eminent citizens, have assumed the heavy duties of municipal president. We are convinced, caballeros, that in view of the prevailing circumstances you will raise no objections, for we are counting on your patriotism and on your benevolent support as good citizens."

"Of course, of course, Don Pablo," said Don Aurelio sourly. "We, my friend Don Jesus Maria and I, have nothing to object. I thought that I perhaps—"

"We thought of you, too, Don Aurelio," interrupted Don Pablo hurriedly, "and also of Don Jesus Maria. But we realized that you, with your tobacco-purchasing, and Don Jesus with his pig-trading were too heavily occupied at the present time for us to expect you to neglect your excellent businesses in order to serve the community and the country."

What mean spite that man displays in comparing my poor business with the fat perquisites of a mayor, thought Don Aurelio furiously. But aloud he said, "I am convinced, Don Pablo, that our town could find no better president than yourself."

"*Muchas gracias*, Don Aurelio. A thousand thanks for your kind opinion of me," replied Don Pablo. He walked over to Don Aurelio and embraced him. "I wish I had more friends as upright as you, Don Aurelio. Come over to my house for a while this evening, and bring Don Chucho with you. I've still got a few bottles of good old *comiteco* tucked away that those pestilential swine didn't find."

"Do you not think that these thieves and bandits may come back here again?" asked Don Emilio, the new mayor.

"Don't worry, my dear mayor. There'll be no rebels returning here so long as I'm municipal president. That I can assure you. I have already sent two muchachos to Balun Canan and two to Jovel to report to the military authorities and to describe the route those scabby curs have taken. There'll be a thorough clean-up during the next few days. This damned mutiny will be nipped in the bud. We've always been too lenient with those scoundrels. I've always said that insolent peons and loud-mouthed *campesinos* should not be put in jail, but hanged immediately, as soon as they open their stinking mouths and start talking about getting no justice here."

9

 On the flat land between Achlumal and Balun Canan the army of the rebels lay encamped. There were several reasons that made General delay the march on Balun Canan.

Balun Canan was no small market center like Achlumal, nor a little town like Hucutsin. With more than ten thousand inhabitants, it was among the most important centers in a state that contained only six towns with over five thousand inhabitants.

There was also a strong garrison.

Simply to attack the town, as the muchachos had done with Achlumal, would have been impracticable; even if this had been attempted, it would have resulted in the total destruction of the rebel army. Not one of the muchachos doubted that.

General pondered anxiously over plans that might enable him to conquer and wipe out the opposing troops without being compelled to attack the town so long as it was occupied by the garrison. If he wanted to advance on the capital of the state, he dared not leave these troops at Balun Canan in his rear, especially since the troops he would encounter in the capital city were far more numerous and better equipped than those that lay at Balun Canan.

"Can I help you?" asked Modesta, coming up to Celso. Celso was occupied with his machine gun, oiling it, cleaning it, and examining it with endless patience for loose screws and sand.

"Of course you can help me, muchacha," answered Celso. "Go over to that fire and fry some pig fat so that I can grease and oil this properly. Hell! while we were in Achlumal I should have gotten myself a can of olive oil from a shop. Do you know, Modesta, that olive oil, Spanish olive oil, is the best thing you can have for oiling a machine gun when you haven't got the proper oil handy?"

Modesta produced a thick bundle of rags, which she laid on the ground. "These are the best things for polishing such a wonderful weapon," she said, smiling.

"Where did you get those rags, Modesta? They look just like silk."

"They are silk, Celso. They're my silk dress that you gave me from the shop in the *monterías*. But what need have I of a silk dress now that we're at war? It's far better to use the silk for cleaning your machine gun." As she said this, she had already begun to polish the brass bits, which soon shone so that one could see one's own reflection in them.

"But get me the pig's fat first. Then you can go on with your polishing," said Celso.

"I can get that," said little Pedrito, who had come up with Modesta.

"All right, *chamaquito*." Celso grinned good-humoredly. "You can fetch it just as well as Modesta. And then I'll show you how one oils a machine gun properly and according to the rules. Because once we get into a fight, there's no time for oiling or cleaning, and if the thing jams just at the wrong moment, then the soldiers will be on us and it will be goodbye to my beautiful machine gun. If you ever want to become a proper machine gunner, then remember this: the important thing is always to be ready a day before the enemy, and always to be on the battlefield two hours before those mercenaries arrive."

"I'll remember that, *mi comandante*," answered Pedrito and saluted. Then he ran off to find a container in which to carry the hot hog's fat.

Modesta, somewhat pensive, kneaded the silk rags in her hands in order to make them even softer than they already were. Attentively she watched every movement of Celso's hands as he removed the screws and with a sliver of wood scratched the sand and dust out of the cavities, grooves, and crannies, screwed the gun together again, peered through the sights, then swung the barrel to left and right and squinted through that, too, as he rejoiced over the polished fittings.

When Modesta had watched him for a while, she sighed deeply and then said softly and shyly, "Celso, do you know what I'd like better than anything else in the world?"

"What, muchacha?" he asked without looking up from his gun.

"You told me you would teach me how a gun like that works and how one fires it on those mercenaries and ear-choppers."

Celso stood up and looked at her. "I do believe, Modesta, that you really could be a good and useful soldier with my machine gun if you paid attention to what I taught you. Do you know, girl, I haven't been able to sleep well for nights? Always wondering what would happen if I got hit. Who'd take over my machine gun, I'd like to know? All the other men have their own jobs and duties. Ambrosio and Eulodio, my two half-sections, aren't worth a torn sack, I must admit. They don't run away. They'd never run away, whoever attacked them. But if this gun stopped working because something was wrong with the machine, they wouldn't know what to do and they'd take to their machetes, which they can handle devilish well, but this beautiful gun stays out of action when we're perhaps needing it more desperately than the pure air we breathe. I've explained it to them a hundred times. But these asses can't learn. They can't even aim it. They let loose with it and think the bullets will fly of their own accord just where they want them to, mowing down the *Rurales*. General's got the same concern. We're all worrying ourselves to death because not a man knows how to handle an automatic he captures. But you could learn, Modesta, I know that for certain. You're clever. I could trust you with the gun if we needed it in a battle and I got a stopper in my guts. And why not? You could be just as good a soldier as I. I'll teach you everything I know. And I'm sure you'll be one of the best machine gunners in the rebel army."

Modesta looked at him and said softly, "You're such a good fellow, Celso. And I think I must kiss you because you *are* such a good muchacho, with a good heart. Really you are, Celso. I've been wanting to tell you that for a long time. And now I can because you're going to let me work with you and your beautiful machine gun."

Modesta had scarcely begun to polish the gun anew and even more energetically when Colonel came stumbling up. "My God, I thought I had a few machine gunners I could use against the enemy. And what the hell was I thinking of?"

Celso and Modesta both looked up aghast.

"No need to get scared, you young fools." Colonel laughed. "You've done no damage yet. An efficient soldier always keeps his gun in good condition and so brightly polished that he never needs a mirror. *In barracks*. And in peacetime, mind you. But now we're at war. Rub muck over all that polished brass and let it crust there—that's my advice. Then tie twigs with plenty of leaves on them around the gun as soon as you know the enemy's near. Of course, you mustn't let mud get into the barrel or into the chamber or breech, causing the gun to jam. But if it shines as it's shining now, my God! it can be seen a hundred miles away, and no need of a telescope either. Smear some paint on it, or grease it and then sprinkle it with ashes. That's the proper thing in wartime. When those damned swine attack, that'll have to spray them like a hose, but they mustn't see where the spray's coming from. Now do you understand the point, Celso?"

"You're right, Colonel. I didn't think of that."

"How could you? No one had told you about it. But from now on, you know. It's good advice."

"Now are you sorry about your silk dress?" asked Celso, after Colonel had stumped off.

"Not a bit," answered Modesta. "In any case, it was always in the way. I was ashamed of having it. It looked just like one of the dresses of those rich *ladino* women. What do I need a silk dress for? After all, we're rebels."

"Where have you been with that hot fat?" Celso shouted as he saw Pedrito come tearing along, carrying a little jug carefully in both hands.

"Here you are, Celso. The pig had to be slaughtered first," bellowed Pedrito as loudly as he could. But this retort distracted his attention from the stony ground. He tripped and fell headlong, smashed the jug, and the fat ran over the earth.

"And there lies Pedro and his brew in the mud," roared Celso, laughing and going over to the boy. "Run back to the fire right away and get some more fat."

"There's no more there," said the boy, and began to howl.

"Why no more?" asked Celso. "A pig has more fat than just that little jug full."

"Yes," sobbed the boy, "but when I said what you wanted the fat for, all the muchachos came up with their rifles and revolvers and wanted to grease and oil them, and in a flash it was all gone."

Celso bent down to the broken fragments of the jug and began, with Modesta's help, carefully to scrape up the top layer of fat that had not been in contact with the soil and to pile it on one of the pieces of pottery.

It was night. General walked up to one of the outer fires that served as assembly points for the forward sentries. Beside the fire lay two muchachos, squalling and singing.

"Stand up!" commanded General.

"You can't order us about, see?" said one of them, while the other made a clumsy effort to rise.

"What are you standing up for? Lie down!" said the first.

Several of the muchachos accompanying General sprang forward and hoisted up the two sentries with a fierce, unmerciful grip, standing them on their feet.

"What's your name?" General asked the first.

"Go to hell!" was the reply.

"A good name for you," retorted General. "Just the place you'll soon be going to."

"And you?" General asked the second.

"Davila. Angelo Davila."

"Where did you get the brandy you've been drinking?"

"Back there, from the little ranchito. From a poor peon, just like us," said Angelo Davila.

"I posted you—and four others—here on sentry duty because you have rifles."

"They're *our* guns," said the first, shouting. "We won them and we can do what we want with them."

"Where are they then? The rifles, I mean," asked General calmly.

"General," said Angelo, "General, you don't imagine that the peon in the ranchito can *give* us brandy. He's as poor as we are."

"Not quite as poor as you are," General informed him. Then he turned to the muchachos who were holding the couple upright. "Let them go. They're fools."

The muchachos stepped back, and the two men swayed from side to side without actually falling to the ground. General shot twice. "Throw them into the fire," he said to the muchachos. "Poke them in with your feet and shovel the fire over them."

After that he ordered four muchachos to go over to the ranchito and give the peon a peso, which he produced from his pocket, and to bring back the rifles.

Then he went on to another outpost where forward sentries were on guard. He went alone. The muchachos who had remained by the fire to carry out General's orders heard four more shots.

"Those out there," said General, when he returned, "we'll leave to the coyotes and the vultures. And besides," he added, looking at the muchachos, "anyone who thinks that we're marching about these parts for pleasure is mistaken. Every man must understand that by now. Either we've embarked on a rebellion or we're taking a walk. And if we've decided it's a rebellion, then it's a rebellion and not a holiday excursion. Right—or wrong?"

"Right, General," answered Professor. "Right in what you

say, and right in what you did. Anyone who doesn't expect
and understand this has brought nothing here and therefore
has nothing to expect here. We don't need him and are better
without him. Shouting *viva* won't win us any revolution. We
can do without those loudmouths, but not without rebels who
know why they *are* rebels."

General sent out other muchachos as forward sentries.

Late in the afternoon of the following day four peons came
into the camp. A sentry led them before Professor so that he
could hear what they wanted to say.

"What brings you here?" he inquired. And he asked in such
a tone and manner as if similar visits occurred ten times daily.

In fact, peons or other Indians never came into the camp
unless they stumbled upon it on their way elsewhere. And
even in these cases, such folk hastened away from the camp
quickly, as soon as they saw the first sentry. After four
hundred years of injustice, the Indian had become so mistrustful that he assented to everything with his lips, but in his mind
believed nothing and trusted no one, especially those who
came saying they were his friends or would like to be.

Therefore it was understandable that Professor studied these
visitors attentively, without, of course, letting them notice it.

One of the peons spoke up, "There was so much talk in the
fincas about you people from the *monterías*, that you want to
free everyone and give them land and soil, freedom, and inde-
pendence when you win. If that's really true, we've come to
talk to your chief so that he can come to our *finca* and free us
too, for we're very much enslaved!"

The way this man spoke convinced Professor that something
was not quite right. He noticed that the speaker was at pains
to make mistakes in his Spanish, as peons do unconsciously and
involuntarily, since they are more accustomed to their own Indian language than to Spanish. Professor was particularly
struck by the phrase "we're very much enslaved," which was
remarkable and odd. The peons, like all the Indians, did not
express their unhappy social and evil economic state in such
words. From their youth they had been accustomed to work-

ing as long as a spark of strength remained within them. Cash payment they never saw, and they never spoke of being enslaved or exploited; only at most that they were too poor to be able to pay their debts to their employers, and therefore unable to leave the *finca* and settle somewhere on an unoccupied patch of ground and live as independent settlers.

"Our chief's not here at the moment, muchachos," answered Professor in a casual voice. "He's training the men out on the plain where you heard those shots. We've got machine guns, too."

The spokesman of the visiting peons made an astonished face. But when he grew conscious of the fact that Professor was observing him closely, his expression immediately resolved itself into one of simplicity, submissiveness, and humility. This change in expression confirmed Professor in his opinion that all was not aboveboard with these visitors. Nevertheless, he could not imagine what the men wanted.

Now Colonel approached, having just finished his training session and wishing to collect a new squad. He looked at the four men, rolled a cigarette, but said nothing.

"What *finca* do you come from?" asked Professor.

"Las Margaritas."

"Who is your master?"

"Our master?"

"Yes, your master."

"Well, our master, yes, our master is Don Fernando, he's our master."

"What's his surname?"

"Sosa. Don Fernando Sosa."

"Then you've come here to guide us to your *finca* so that we can divide up the estate among you peons?"

"That's it, *jefecito*. That's why we've come here. And that's what we wanted to talk to your chief about."

"Well, just sit down by the fire," said Professor, with a grin now, which half-resembled that of the housewife who, faced with an unexpected visitor plainly intending to stay to supper, knows that, it being washday, she has only a leftover meal in the house, and half-reminded one of Satan's grin when he stands at the door as the latest convoy arrives and sees among them half-a-dozen Methodist preachers and a dozen desiccated nuns. "Yes, just sit down here by the fire. Of course, you're hungry after that long journey. The muchachos will give you some frijoles, tortillas, and coffee. As good—and as bad—as we make 'em."

Professor wandered over to a group of fellows whom Andreu was teaching to read and write. "Andrucho," he said quietly, "just come over to the staff fire. I think we've got *chinches*, bugs, in the camp."

"What do you mean, *chinches*, Professor?"

"Do you know where the *finca* Las Margaritas is?"

"Roughly. When I was still working with the *carretas* we had many loads for Don Susano at Las Margaritas."

"I see. Don Susano is the *finquero* of Las Margaritas? I thought he was called Don Fernando Sosa."

"Why should he be called Don Fernando when his name is Don Susano?"

"That's what I wondered. Do you know the Las Margaritas *finca*?"

"I've never been there. We took the loads for Las Margaritas only as far as Balun Canan, because the way to Las Margaritas is so narrow and bad that no *carretas* can drive along it. The *finca* sent their men to Balun Canan to fetch the stuff from there on muleback. It's probably six or eight leagues distant from Balun Canan."

"What language do the peons speak at Las Margaritas?"

"They speak Tojolabal and Spanish. Of course, among themselves and in their homes they speak only Tojolabal."

"You're sure that all the peons living on Las Margaritas, even if they speak and understand Spanish, understand Tojolabal as well?"

"All without exception. Even Don Susano knows a good bit of Tojolabal, and the major-domo and the *capataces* speak it as well as the peons. They're all from the district, born and brought up there. The major-domo is a natural son of Don Susano whom he had by a Tojolabal girl. She's had other children by him—by Don Susano, I mean. And although he's been married to Doña Paulina from Balun Canan for more than twenty years and has had nine or ten children by her, he spends the afternoon of every other day with his old flame. He built her a lovely little house and gave her some land and she has two dozen piglets every Christmas as a present. But he never gives her money."

"All right. I don't want to know all that."

"And you understand there's not a soul in Las Margaritas who doesn't understand Tojolabal."

"That's what I wanted to know. Four strange birds have arrived here. I'm not quite sure who sent them, whether it was the governor or the *finqueros* or the *Rurales* or the Federals. Come along with me and have a look at them and talk to them in Tojolabal."

"I don't know much Tojolabal. I'm a Tseltal. But I can manage enough to find out whether they're peons from Las Margaritas."

Professor and Andreu strolled casually over to the fire where the four men sat busily eating, while a dozen muchachos squatted around, some chatting with them, some smoking and talking among themselves.

In the army there were more than thirty or forty Tojolabal Indians, some of them possibly even muchachos who had been sold into the *monterías* by the owner of Las Margaritas or who had fled from that *finca*. But there would have been difficulties in searching them out, and in all likelihood they would not have easily understood what Professor wanted of them. In any case, Andreu was the best person to examine the four visitors.

Andreu walked casually up to the fire and rolled himself a cigar. Then he bent down to the embers and drew forth a glowing stick. Without looking at the four men, he said loudly in Tojolabal, "You've run away from your *finca*, haven't you?"

The four men calmly continued eating and threw a casual word here and there to the muchachos who were talking Spanish with them.

Now Andreu, straightening up and taking a draw at his

cigar, turned and directly addressed the one of the four who was nearest to him. Again he spoke in Tojolabal, "Have you still that old muleteer who always got drunk in Balun Canan whenever he was fetching his loads?"

The man now realized that he was being addressed and had to answer. He became embarrassed and scowled as if he were considering. Then he squinted shyly up to see if Professor was listening. Professor was standing apart and talking to a muchacho, but lost not a word or gesture of the speaker.

At last the spokesman of the four visitors replied. He said, with a crooked laugh, "We've come a very long way, *amigos*, that's true." He said this in Spanish and attempted to sound the vowels deep in his throat, as Indians generally do in their own language.

"Yes. I believe that," said Andreu in reply, this time in good Spanish. "I can very well believe that. That's why I asked. It must have been a very long way."

Andreu bent down again and once more lit his cigar. It was burning perfectly well, but he wanted to look more closely at something that he had already noticed in this man. He drew fiercely at his cigar and then walked leisurely over to Professor.

"Do they speak Tojolabal?" asked Professor.

"Tell me something. Have you ever seen a poor peon who's had his teeth filled with gold?"

"Had his teeth filled with gold? Never."

"But I have. And apart from that, they don't understand a word of Tojolabal."

Professor detailed three muchachos to watch the four visitors, but to watch them in such a way that they shouldn't notice it; and if they were to get up, they should be allowed to do so, but the watchers must on no account let them out of their sight and at all cost must stop them from leaving the camp.

Now it was dark. All the fires in the camp were glowing.

General came up to the staff fire, slowly and wearily. All day long, supported by Colonel, Matias, Celso, Fidel, and

other knowledgeable officers, he had been training the muchachos in maneuvering and shooting, running about with
them like a raw recruit himself—down-up, down-up, he had
practiced with them until he could scarcely get up himself.
Then he had taught them how to advance in open formation,
how best to take cover in lying down; taught them to avoid
getting sand in the barrels or chambers of their rifles when on
the ground or crouching; taught them to shoot from a squatting or prone position, and shown them how to scrape hollows
quickly in soft ground where they could lie and offer less of a
target. Everything that he could remember, that he had ever
learned and taught as a sergeant, he now taught the muchachos. The material that he had at his disposal was twenty
times inferior to what he had had to deal with when his battalion took in new recruits. If the muchachos had not shown
good will and an overwhelming enthusiasm for the next battle,
he might well have despaired at the meager results his training
produced.

So it was not to be wondered at that he now came up to the
fire like a washed-out rag.

"And so that's their chief, their general," said one of the
four visitors softly to his neighbor when they gathered from
the greetings and inquiries of the muchachos that this weary,
sagging, stumbling, dirty, unkempt fellow who approached
was the leader of the rebellion.

"Give him a slap in the face and he'd fall flat in the mud,"
whispered the one sitting next to him. "We could drive off
this lousy, dirty pack with a few cudgels. Don't know why
the old man makes such a fuss, wanting to send out three battalions. I'd thrash them with one company, the swine."

"Curse you," said the other softly, scarcely opening his lips
and forcing the words through his teeth. "Why don't you shut
your bloody trap? See how that fellow's already looking over
here and watching us." It was Professor, who kept glancing at
the four, wondering who they might be and what purpose
they had in coming.

Then Colonel said, turning to the muchachos who belonged

to the staff, "Let's go over to the fire where Celso's muchacha is cooking. They've got a pig there. The food looks pretty meager here."

"Where did the pig come from?" Professor asked Celso, who was walking beside him.

"It's not a pig. It's an antelope. I was in the bush with Modesta and let her blaze off ten rounds with the machine gun so she could learn to aim. And then the antelope came running across our path and Modesta fired and at the second shot it fell. Both shots hit the mark."

"Then I'll promote her to corporal tomorrow," said General, with a tired laugh in his voice. "And you, Colonel, can learn something from the muchacha. You let off twenty rounds at a tree, as I saw myself this afternoon, and just one bullet hit its fat trunk."

"You must take the distance into consideration," replied Colonel. "The antelope was so near you could have caught it by the tail with one hand."

"That's what you think, Colonel." Celso laughed. "Catch it with your hand? I'd like to see you do that. Catch it with your hand! It was at least two hundred paces away."

"Did you measure off the two hundred paces?" asked Colonel.

"I didn't need to. I ought to know what two hundred paces are."

While they squatted by Modesta's fire and ate roasted antelope with a tortilla and fresh green leaves plucked at the edge of the bush, Professor said, "We could have eaten at our fire, too. But then we'd have had to send away those four men because we wanted to talk. I preferred to leave them sitting there, so that they shouldn't realize that we know what sort of peons they are."

General made no answer to this. But as he ate and made desperate efforts not to fall asleep, numerous muchachos came up to him and whispered reports quietly into his ear and received orders from him, equally quietly whispered.

His officers paid no attention to what he was arranging and

how he was preparing his plans. Now and again he asked
something of Colonel or Professor or Andreu or Matias, and
the answers he received he seemed to incorporate into the orders with which he dispatched the muchachos.

Then he got Matias to roll him a cigar, and lit it. After he
had drawn at it a few times without speaking, his weariness
seemed to abate. He gave the impression of having half-slept
and rested and restored himself as he ate. He, like most of his
advisers around the fire, was not squatting on the ground as
was usually the case; instead, they were sitting on sawed-off
treetrunks that lay around and were later destined for bigger
fires, which should give the camp a cozier and jollier appearance and keep all the muchachos happy.

On the staff fire there now blazed up a mighty stack of
wood that was the signal for lighting all the other great fires
and for ending the day with singing, music, dancing, and general festivity.

Once more another muchacho approached and brought
him a whispered report. General stood up and beckoned to all
the others to follow him.

They went over to the staff fire, where they also sat down
on treetrunks.

"So you four worms are still here," he said to the visitors,
who seemed to be enjoying themselves at the huge fire, or at
least to be trying to give such an impression.

"Yes, *jefecito*, we're still here," answered the man with the
gold-filled teeth. "But with your permission, we'd like to be on our
way now. We've a long journey to go."

"What were you paid for the journey, *hombres?*" asked
General dryly.

At this all four paled slightly. However, the speaker quickly
collected himself and said, "No one paid us, *jefecito*. We're
poor peons and only want to know when you're coming to
our *finca* to deliver us from slavery and servitude."

As the phrase "deliver us from slavery" was uttered, Professor grinned and looked at General's face to see how he would
take this expression.

"You're poor peons from Las Margaritas, are you?" asked General, perhaps a shade more dryly than before.

"Yes, *jefecito, a sus muy amables órdenes!*"

"You," said General, his voice completely altering and all tiredness disappearing from his face, "you are First Lieutenant Ruben Bailleres, third company, sixty-seventh battalion, Yalanchen garrison. Who your three friends are I don't yet know, but I shall by tomorrow evening."

The four men tried to moisten their lips, without apparent success, for though they worked their jaws, their saliva seemed to have dried up.

Professor's eyes goggled, and he stared at General helplessly. The other muchachos were no less taken aback than the four visitors.

Three or four minutes passed before the lieutenant spoke. "It's all a mistake, *jefecito*. We're poor peons from Las Margaritas, and that's really, absolutely true."

"Do you swear by the Sacred Virgin?"

"Yes, *jefecito, por la Madre Santísima.*"

"You weren't invited here."

"I know, but we wanted to learn the truth."

"What truth?"

"That you're going to give us, the peons, land and liberty."

"The peons, yes. But to the officers of the Federals and *Rurales* and all other uniformed skunks and crawlers we're going to give something else. Perhaps you'd now like to see our armories as well?"

"No, *jefecito*. We'd like to go home now, to our families."

"All of us, all we muchachos, have for years been wanting to return to our huts and to our families, and we haven't been able to. So you, too, will have to wait an hour."

General beckoned five muchachos to him and spoke softly to them. The men squatting by the fire caught only the last sentence which he shouted after the muchachos, "Find a strong sack and then come back here."

The four visitors stood up and made as if to leave.

At this moment, however, the muchachos came running back, waving an empty sack.

"Follow the muchachos and have a look at our armory first before you go home again to Las Margaritas," said General to the four. He stressed Las Margaritas with an ironical smile.

When the four visitors had gone about ten steps and were beginning to vanish in the darkness, General called out, "No. You, Lieutenant, stay here a moment longer. Your three companions will find more than enough to see."

After this neither he nor the other men about the fire paid any further attention to the lieutenant, who with convulsive, jerking gestures stared out into the night in the direction where the muchachos had gone with his three companions. There was a great fire in that direction, but he nevertheless seemed not to see whatever he wanted to see.

No more than ten minutes had passed before the muchachos returned without the three visitors. They threw a sack onto the ground in front of them. The sack was tied at the mouth with strips of bast. It was wet and covered with filth, as if it had been dragged through slimy mud.

General gave two muchachos a sign. In one jump they were on the lieutenant. And when they leaped away from him again, blood ran over his face and down the sides of his head. He had uttered not a sound, attempting only to defend himself. His nose had been sliced off down to the bone and both ears cut in half along their length.

"The muchachos should have slit your lips, too, for your infamous lies when you called upon the Holy Virgin to help you in lying. But I need your lips, Lieutenant Ruben Bailleres. You have a message to carry from me to your commanding officer, Don Petronio Bringas. And in order that I shall know you when I meet you again and ask you whether you have reported to your general everything I shall tell you, I had to have your nose cut short. In the future they will now call you *Chato*. A very nice name, too. And why not?"

The lieutenant said nothing. With his sleeve he wiped off the blood that ran into his mouth and down his neck. He uttered not a sound of pain. But General knew, or could well imagine, that the lieutenant at this moment was oblivious to all pain and thinking only of the hour when he would have General as a prisoner, squatting opposite him just as he was now. Even if it was doubtful that he would ever capture General, the thought of it nevertheless did him an uncommon amount of good.

"I could, of course, have you hanged, Lieutenant," continued General, "but I have important messages to send to Don Petronio. And you are the best messenger that I can send. Your horses are at the ranchito La Primavera. You can be back with your battalion by eight or nine o'clock tomorrow morning. That's why I'm giving you this sack here. In the sack is the breakfast I am sending to your chief, in gratitude for his having thought of me in sending three officers and a sergeant here to inquire after my well-being. Or was the fourth one of you a lieutenant as well? But then the other three wouldn't have had a groom."

General drew a jug of coffee from the fire and filled up his little beaker, which he clasped in both hands as though trying to warm them. Several times he twirled the beaker in his hands; then, when it had cooled a little, he drained it in one gulp.

More and more muchachos had come up to the staff fire. They crowded closely around so as not to miss a word of General's message to the divisional commander of the Federal Army.

"Don Petronio has taken up position with two battalions of infantry, a cavalry regiment, and a machine-gun section immediately beyond La Peña Alta, where he is lying hidden and waiting for me to slip into his clutches in the long gorge there. Tell him I shall not do him this favor, because I would never fall into a trap so clumsily devised."

The lieutenant stared at General as though he saw a ghost rising up behind him.

"He would like to lure me to Las Margaritas in order to take me in the flank as well. It's not convenient for me to do that. I shall expect him here, now that you know our position. That lecherous old goat wouldn't be afraid of such filthy, stinking swine as we are? What a miserable, lousy son of an ulcerated bitch your commander is, if he only dares to attack us in a swampy gorge! If he's a first-class soldier who's earned his medals, then let the son of a whore come here and leather our asses for us. And don't you forget to tell him what I think of him."

These insults provoked the lieutenant to such a pitch of rage that he completely forgot where he was. He leaped up and in one bound confronted General.

General had sprung up simultaneously. None of the muchachos interfered. That may have been because it had happened so quickly, or else because they believed it was part of the prearranged plan.

The lieutenant lashed out with his fist. But before the blow could reach General's face, the latter had struck with all his strength at the lieutenant's chin. The lieutenant stumbled backward and fell approximately at the same place where he had been squatting.

"Pity you didn't have your revolver with you. That's what you're thinking now, isn't it?" asked General. "You're not the first officer I've hit in the jaw. That's why I'm now general of the muchachos, who aren't cowardly wretches such as let themselves be hit in the face without defending themselves. What I think of your chief, you know now. And if your commander isn't here within four days to have himself slaughtered by us lousy, filthy Indian swine, then he won't find me here any more. For I shall march in a wide detour around Balun Canan and make for Shimojol. That's a nice, rich little town too, where we'll have plenty of fun. Then on to Huninquibal, and after that I'll take Yalanchen, then Tsobtajal, then Acayan, then Nihich, and finally Socton. And after that the attack on Tullum, where we'll visit the governor, provided he hasn't departed to attend a wedding. Perhaps we may change our plans. But I'm only telling you all this so that you know that I've no need to go to La Peña Alta, where the trap's been laid. That's all you have to tell your chief. And if you forget a word, we'll get you again and the other half of your ears will come off. And don't forget to repeat to your commanding officer what I said."

General again drained his beaker and shook out the dregs.

"Who's got a fat cigar ready for me?" he asked, looking around. "So that you won't lose your way, I'm sending two of our muchachos with you as far as the ranchito where your horses are waiting."

The lieutenant stood up. "Where are my companions?" he asked.

"They're looking at our armory. First they looked at our treasures from above, now they're examining them from below. Probably they'll stay here forever. None of us invited them. Tomorrow morning at breakfast you can tell your commander: either he comes with a battalion to fetch them or else he lets us make our detour. And before you go, don't forget to say thanks for the frijoles, the tortillas, and the coffee. You've been very well entertained here. Or haven't you?"

Without answering the lieutenant wheeled about and followed the two muchachos who were to set him on his way.

Scarcely had the three men vanished into the night than the muchachos around the fire began to talk excitedly. "But, *hombre*, General, how did you know all that? Is it true that the Federals are waiting for us behind the rocks? How did you know who the four were?"

"That was easy enough," replied General, lighting his cigar and filling his beaker again with hot coffee. "Much easier than you might think. I didn't do anything wonderful. It just fell into my lap. Some peons really did come into the camp today. Three. Not from Las Margaritas. From another *finca*. But they were genuine peons, not spies. In a minute I knew they were genuine peons. And that's why you didn't see them. They never came into the camp, not right here in the middle. They lay out there in the bush, well beyond our outer patrols. For three or four hours they remained hidden in the bush until they were sure I was the one they were looking for. I was out at training exercises in the bush. When I was alone for a moment and the muchachos had run on ahead, I heard someone call softly, '*Oye*, listen, brother. We want to talk with you.' I let the muchachos go on running and went deeper into the bush with the peons. They came to warn me about the approach of the troops and to tell me about the ambush we are supposed to fall into for the pleasure of the Federals. They also knew about the four disguised officers."

Colonel laughed loudly. "Of course, anyone can lay his plans when he has such good informants."

"But they might not have come to you," suggested General, grinning and looking sideways at him.

"Why shouldn't they have just as readily come to me?"

"You don't inspire as much confidence as I do. What most excited me was not the valuable news they brought me. No. What rejoiced my heart was the fact that for the first time during our revolution, peons had come to us voluntarily and given us unexpected; but therefore all the more welcome, help. That's a sure sign that the revolution is now slowly beginning to make an impression, even in the minds of these intimidated peons. Once the hundreds of thousands of peons come over to us, once they begin to rebel on their *fincas* entirely of their own accord, then the victory of the revolution is assured, even if the struggle goes on for another two or three years."

"I couldn't have put that better by one single word, General," said Professor, with a long yawn. He stood up, sought out his mat and blanket, and crept behind a bush to pass the night there.

"I still don't understand much about making war," said Matias at last, when no one else showed any inclination to speak, "but I think, General, that you've made a bad mistake."

"What sort of a mistake do you mean?" asked General, who had half fallen asleep, but still remained squatting by the fire and puffing at his cigar. He asked in a manner that suggested he expected no answer, as though the question had escaped him purely mechanically.

"You needn't have told the lieutenant what your plans were."

"A mistake? I made a mistake? Oh well, why shouldn't I make a mistake now and again when so many mistakes are made by us, and even more by those damned swine lying in ambush beyond La Peña Alta? I had to tell him something so that he now won't discover what we *are* going to do. Had I said nothing to him about his plans, which I knew, he would have had nothing to worry about and would simply have marched against us. But now he won't be certain what to do. And what will that old fat sucker do? He'll send one battalion in one direction, and another in another, because he can't be sure where we might bob up. And the poor peons who came here so bravely to tell me everything, if they can't account satisfactorily for where they've been today, they'll probably be buried up to their necks and trampled to death. I hope they'll have enough gray matter in their heads to know what to say. They could have gone after a strayed cow. God, muchachos, I'm tired."

A second later the muchachos heard him snoring. Fidel stood up, fetched a blanket, covered him with it, and then pushed a saddle under his head. Contentedly General stretched out his legs. Several bare toes peeped out, for his boots, which had once belonged to a captain, were too tight for him, and he had had to slit the sides and also cut some holes to give his toes room.

The muchachos hastily raked the fire farther back, for General had pushed his boots, still encrusted with dried mud, into the fire and the leather had begun to smolder.

10

Don Petronio Bringas, divisional general and officer in command of the army that had been dispatched by the government to annihilate the rebels, sat at breakfast. It was a breakfast worthy of a general, although it was provided in the main house of a small rancho where the general had established his headquarters. The longer these headquarters lingered at the rancho, the thinner and more haggard in the face grew the unfortunate man to whom the rancho belonged. Of course, the general was no bandit chief. He was a genuine general of the Federal troops. He paid half a peso for each meal. That was what was paid by every traveler, every merchant traveling along that road and seeking and receiving lodging for a night in the rancho. There were no hotels along those lonely tracks; a traveler stayed the night at whatever rancho his road led him to by the late afternoon, for he stopped as soon as he was told he could not reach the next rancho in less than three hours, knowing that it would be pitch dark within an hour.

Every traveler is content with what the ranchero's wife provides for him and is grateful for any special concession, even for a rickety bed. But, of course, a ranchero cannot treat an army general like that. What was set before the general at each meal was worth at least four pesos. The ranchero dared not ask more than the customary price, for fear of arousing the general's anger and ill will and of falling into disfavor with all the little dictators who controlled his destiny. If the general had been alone, the situation would have been just tolerable, and the ranchero could tell himself that one has to make some sacrifices for the good of the fatherland. But from the general there depended a long tail of officers, men, and orderlies, who all helped to eat the ranchero out of house and home, all paying half a peso for a meal, and all being fed in a style which, so the poor man believed, generals, majors, and lieutenants were accustomed to.

The general and his other officers were bored because the cursed rebels seemed reluctant to advance into the gorge selected for their massacre. And therefore every day the rancho was visited by women from the garrison town, ordered by the general and his officers. The ranchero and his family passed their nights squeezed together in a corner of the portico, so that the visitors might have the best rooms and everything else besides. The twenty or thirty attendants, who also formed part of the tail, could not afford to pay half a peso; they paid only fifteen centavos. But not one might get up from the table hungry. Yet all this, painful though it was, was not the greatest sorrow of the ranchero, who was informed fifteen times a day how lucky he was to be able to amass a fortune by having the army quartered on him. Hens, pigs, calves, and whole sacks of corn vanished, and the girls of the rancho went around with yellowish-gray marks on their faces and told the mistress they were sure they had caught something.

So one can very well understand why, fourteen times a day, the ranchero prayed, "Oh, dear God in Heaven above, please make the rebels at last advance so that they can be killed and the whole horrible business here be over and I can have my own ranch back again, even if it is nothing but ruins."

The general, meanwhile, was in no hurry to attack the rebels. He received active-service pay as long as he was in the field. Once the rebels had been defeated, he would have to return to his garrison, and the active-service pay and the rich meals for half a peso each would cease.

It was ten o'clock in the morning when he lowered himself, comfortable, good-humored, ponderous, and powerful, into the crude chair the ranchero proffered him with a *"Ya listo, mi general,"* thereby indicating that everything was ready and the maidservants were actually en route from the kitchen with their dishes. The general sharpened a knife against his fork, smacking his fat lips, and said, "Ah, Don Rosendo, what have we delectable for breakfast today? I hope something specially good. Dammit, out here in the country I'm eternally hungry and could spend all the day and half the night just eating."

The ranchero drew in a painful, whistling breath and said, "Chicken broth, General, fried rice with red chilies and tomatoes, eggs *à la* Ranchera, roast cockerel, suckling pig, barbecue with drunk sauce—I mean of course, *barbacoa con salsa borracha*—then purée of papayas, and coffee."

"Is that all, Don Rosendo?" asked the general with an expression of disappointment. "No *mole poblano de guajolote* today?"

"*Siento muchísimo*, I'm extremely sorry, General," replied the sorely tried man with a shrug of his shoulders. "The turkeys still remaining are too young to be killed yet. The three dozen plump, full-grown ones that I had—well, you know, General, where they've gone."

"But my dear Don Rosendo, on a fine ranch such as you've got, these birds just grow wild and breed like mad. You must simply lay some more eggs."

"Who, me?"

"Don't you think I'd do the same for you, Don Rosendo? But with the best will you couldn't ask that of me!" The general was so pleased at his joke that he burst out in uproarious laughter and continued to laugh, until the other officers came into the room to join him at table.

"Gentlemen," he called to them, making another effort to burst with laughter. "Gentlemen! No! You won't believe it possible, but Rosendo has asked me to lay eggs for him. What do you say to that?" With both fists—a knife in one, a fork in the other—he banged on the table to lend greater musical force to his bovine roars.

"What sort of eggs does he want you to lay, General?" asked Captain Segu, with an innocent expression. Only his expression was innocent, not his question. He wished to stimulate his superior's pleasure still further.

The general could have kissed the captain for giving him an opportunity to renew and intensify his laughter. "Did you all hear that, gentlemen? What Captain Segu asked me? Did you hear, gentlemen?" He could scarcely get the words out between his bursts of merriment. "Captain Segu asked what sort of eggs I should lay."

The captain kept a straight face, not betraying by the twitch of an eyebrow that he understood the joke. That evoked still further laughter from the general, to see the captain standing there and looking so innocent. With his fork he now pointed at the captain and looked around at the laughing officers on all sides, to incite them to follow the direction of his fork. "Captain Segu asked me what sort of eggs I should lay. Gentlemen, gentlemen, what sort of eggs should I lay?"

The captain now changed his expression. He grasped his chair by the arms and drew it toward him preparatory to sitting down at the table. At the same time he looked around, astonished and questioning, as if he could in no wise understand what all the laughter was about. He sat down slowly and said now in an irritable voice, "Damnation, gentlemen, it's nothing to laugh at when I ask what sort of eggs should be laid: there are all sorts of eggs a general can sit on." It was not so much his answer as the offended and peevish tone in which he said it that intensified the effect of his apparent innocence at failing to understand a silly joke, which made the general laugh so much that he swallowed his broth the wrong way. He recovered, pointed at the captain with his spoon, and roared as he choked with laughter, "Captain Segu, you ought to be an undertaker, not an officer, making a sour face like that when everyone else is happy and laughing."

"Excuse me, sir, I am an undertaker," said the captain stolidly.

"Eh?" snapped the general. "You? An undertaking business? Where? Never heard of it."

"But, sir, is that so difficult to understand?" His expression remained impassive as he added dryly: "We are all undertakers here. Why else do you think we carry revolvers at our sides and the men out there have rifles and machine guns?"

"In other words, Captain, you're saying that I'm an egg-laying undertaker?" Once more the general bellowed with laughter. All the other officers joined in, a few out of politeness, the majority, however, because, like their general, they considered this conversation to be the wittiest and most intelligent they had heard for a long time.

When the laughter diminished somewhat, the captain found an opportunity to reply. "Those are not my words, General, they are yours. I must ask you to excuse me."

"*Hombre*," said the general, "you are really the dullest, most humorless and ungenial fellow that I've ever come across in my life. The man hasn't a spark of humor in him. You're a wet blanket. But that won't stop us investigating, with due regard and relish for its toothsomeness, this beautiful little suckling pig, which the equally beautiful maidens are now bringing in and setting before us. Hey, Lieutenant Cosio, push my beloved *comiteco* bottle across to me; I must baptize the crisp skin of this suckling with a swig of alcohol to sterilize it from microbes and bacilli! And talking of that, Captain Segu, what's your view of microbes?"

"It depends what sort of microbes you mean, General." The captain had speared a morsel of meat on his fork and twiddled it around several times, pensively staring at it, before he pushed it into his mouth. When he had finally swallowed it and the general had certainly long ceased to think of his question, the captain said, "What sort of microbes do you mean, sir? It's a matter of who's putting the question. Perhaps all of us who are sitting here and eating pork are nothing else but microbes, and probably the pigs regard us as their microbes. Let's ask them what their world looks like, seen through their eyes. Every parasite feels itself the most important object in the universe, while at the same time it regards the beings to which it owes its life as created for no other purpose than to serve as nourishment for it."

The general, fully occupied with his mighty hunk of roast meat, was unable to follow the discourse that far. He had gotten no further than the first sentence. With the last fragments still in his mouth, he gave vent once more to his bellowing laugh. "First I lay eggs for Don Rosendo. And you ask me what sort of eggs I lay. Then you turn me into an egg-laying undertaker. And now into a microbe. And you treat your commanding officer like that, Captain? I must seriously ask Lieutenant Ochoa later to investigate whether this microbe isn't a matter for a court-martial. But first, Captain Segu, let's down another good glassful of *comiteco* to deal with these millions of microbes that we've been swallowing during the last ten minutes. I know from long experience that my microbes are expert at distinguishing between a worthless, poisonous glass of cheap brandy and such a fine *comiteco* as we have before us now. And in this matter my microbes never make a mistake. Ha, and here comes the barbecue, to be greeted with cheers and jubilation. I say, Don Rosendo, the sauce could have been drunker; not enough fresh green chilies. Not sharp enough. Hand me that little plate of viriginal peas. *Muchas gracias!*"

The general looked up.

In the open doorway stood a human figure that at first he failed to recognize.

The room in which the officers were eating had no windows. All the light came through the door, which therefore always stood open. The general was sitting facing the door. The bright daylight was in his eyes. Therefore, he could easily see that someone was standing in the doorway, but could not immediately recognize the face. He perceived only that the man had an ordinary red handkerchief wound around his face, as if he were suffering from a toothache. Behind the man there now appeared an Indian, carrying a muddy sack on his back, and this sack he now let fall with a thud on the portico.

"What is it?" asked the general.

"Lieutenant Ruben Bailleres at your command, General, reporting back from reconnaissance and night patrol."

"Come in, Lieutenant Bailleres, come in. We're just having breakfast. Hey! Don Rosendo. Bring a chair for Lieutenant Bailleres."

The lieutenant now came into the room.

"What's happened to your face? Your nose shot off? Good God!" The general evidently found it funny and laughed. "Easier to kiss without your nose, Lieutenant. Was anyhow much too long." At this he once more fell into guffaws of laughter. "What do you say, gentlemen? Aren't we all of the opinion that our friend Bailleres's nose was far too long for kissing in the old and well-tried military manner?"

The officers did not laugh, but out of politeness drew their faces into sour grins.

The laughter of his commanding officer threw the lieutenant into a blinding rage that at first he did not show, maintaining his composure.

Meanwhile, an Indian boy brought in a chair, and the lieutenant sat down. A maidservant laid a place for him and gave him a plate.

In the little rancho where the lieutenant and his companions had left their horses, he had been provided with two young men to accompany him on his way back and to bring the other horses and the sack he was to deliver to the general for breakfast. One of these two Indian lads—the one that had brought the sack—cowered on the portico and waited to be summoned. The other unsaddled the horses in the patio and handed them over to the soldiers.

"Listen, Lieutenant;" the general addressed the new arrival, "at this hour of the day it's no longer so cold that you have to go around with that snot rag wound around your face like an old granny. Or have you got a toothache? Speak up, man, what's the matter?"

On the way the lieutenant had washed off the blood and the encrusted dirt in a brook. The stump of his nose had ceased to bleed. At the little rancho he had cleaned the stump with *aguardiente*, and the wound was now dry, though hideous enough.

The officer hesitated a few seconds; then he began to fumble under his chin to untie the knots of the red-flowered handkerchief. It had been his intention to tear off the handkerchief with a rapid gesture, as answer to the general's remarks, which he found to be both insulting and stupid. However, the handkerchief stuck fast to both ears, and when the lieutenant tugged at it, it caused him agony.

"Please, campañeros," he said, "would you mind handing me that bottle?"

An officer who sat next to him said, "You certainly need a drink. You look pale enough." He poured him out a tumblerful of spirits.

The lieutenant swallowed it in four great, gurgling gulps. Then he picked up the bottle and poured the contents over his scalp.

"Hey, hey, you!" exclaimed the general. "I thought you'd been baptized long ago. And now, wasting this precious *comiteco*. It's an unheard-of luxury out here in the wilds, where it's so difficult to get the stuff and where—a-ah, *hombre*, what's *that?*"

The lieutenant, when he felt that the brandy had sufficiently moistened and unstuck the cloth at his ears, had torn the handkerchief off with one brave jerk. Immediately the blood began to pour down his neck again. Thrusting forward his head at the general, he shouted, "That's why I had my face bound up, General. How do you like it?"

"Shot off too?"

"Nothing was shot off. All cut off. By those savages, those animals."

"Lieutenant Bailleres, you are not going to tell me that I sent you out there on reconnaissance? Certainly not. You suggested it yourself. And I let you go. Where are the two lieutenants and the N.C.O. you took with you?"

"The savages kept them there."

"As hostages?"

"That I don't know, General. Nothing was said to me about that. I was led out of their camp to carry a message which that filthy swine who calls himself General wanted to send to you."

"What does that criminal look like? A Chamula?"

"No, General. He is not a Chamula. But he's an Indian. How he can be their general, I can't understand. He hobbles

about like a lame dog. Can hardly stand upright. Don't know
how he can even grip a rifle barrel. No one respects him.
They all address him as an equal. Eats like the rest of the gang
with his fingers. Sleeps on a mat like the other swine. We can
finish off that collection of animals in three hours. All scum."

"That's no news to us, Lieutenant. I'd expected more."
The general began a gurgling laugh. "You've certainly lost
your beauty, Lieutenant. And they were such lovely little ears.
And it seems to me that that miserable general, who hobbles
about like a lame dog, certainly had little enough respect for
you. Perhaps he wasn't quite so stupid as you thought him to
be when you suggested disguising yourselves as peons in order
to spy out their disposition, numbers, armaments, and plans.
He saw through your disguise. And the next time you want to
get yourself up in fancy dress, you'll have to cover your
whole head; a mask in front of your face won't be much good
to you. How can anyone be such a fool as to let a pack of robbers cut off his ears?"

The lieutenant had certainly not expected pity, either from
his commanding officer or from his comrades. He would have
rejected it had anyone attempted to pity him, and he would
have asserted that a soldier must make sacrifices since he *is* a
soldier. But that no one acclaimed him as a hero, as a brave officer who had ventured into the camp of the enemy and had
suffered pain and humiliation to earn himself a name in his
battalion—that infuriated him. It was true that the general
had not ordered him to make a reconnaissance. He had volun-
teered in order to be able to boast among his comrades, not because it was a vital duty. The general attached little or no importance to intelligence concerning the rebels. He did not take
the revolutionaries seriously from a military point of view, and
in many respects had regarded it as unworthy of his rank and
position when he, the almighty general, had been sent out to
deal with a gang of verminous peons. In his view, that could
have been dealt with by a major with half a battalion. But
someone in the War Ministry had ordained that he should
attack the rebels with so and so many troops, and he had to
obey the order. If three young officers had a yearning for ad-

venture because they found it too boring to hang about in the dust and dirt, waiting for the rebels, that was their affair. He had given them his permission because they had asked for it. That their adventure had turned out disastrously for them was no concern of his. So why shouldn't he now have the pleasure of teasing the lieutenant, of twitting him on his appearance, just as he would have twitted a young officer involved in an unhappy love affair?

Lieutenant Bailleres, however, thought differently of the matter. And because his due recognition was denied him, he now thought that he, too, would have some fun, and this time at the expense of the general, who sat gobbling his gross breakfast with much gusto and noise and clattering, and who was more intent on the exact additions of salt, pepper, chilies, and tomato sauce than on the sufferings and injured pride of his lieutenant.

"The so-called general gave me a message to bring to you, General," said the Lieutenant, as soon as he had finished his broth.

"This message will be a really funny one, gentlemen, and nonsensical as well. A message to *me* from lousy peons! Well, out with it, Lieutenant." The general laughed loudly, choked and coughed.

"The message is not exactly respectful, General."

"I didn't ask you that, Lieutenant Bailleres. But I hope that at least it's funny." The general looked around at his officers and grinned. "Gentlemen, now we shall have some entertainment."

"Most certainly, General. But don't hold me responsible. I'm only repeating to you what I was told. Your mother is an old whore."

"What's that? What do you mean by this, Lieutenant Bailleres?"

"You wanted to hear what the general of those stinking Indians had to say to you."

"That's different. All right. Get on with it."

"And he wishes you to be told that he is going to slice you and all your army to ribbons and that he will have the pleasure of personally cutting off your nose, ears, and certain other appendages. He will not do you the favor of letting his men be massacred by you in the gorge near La Peña Alta, but instead he will take a wide detour around you and burn down all the large *fincas* and towns in your rear, and hang their inhabitants from the nearest trees and there let them hang in the hope that you will be degraded with dishonor by the War Ministry for laziness and for having your trousers too full to be able to attack him. And if you have a spark of courage and wish to show yourself a proper man and soldier, you will advance against him where he is waiting for you. But you are only an old broken-down, randy goat who doesn't dare go out against lousy rebels and who only thinks of his stomach and his pay. You are a hundred times lousier and more oversexed than the filthiest and stupidest of his muchachos, who have guts enough to deal with you, your whole army, and all those who wear uniforms and trot around with revolvers, rifles, and machine guns, and who can whip you with merely a few rotten cudgels, and who, without even the help of broken machetes, will throw the whole lot of you onto the muck heap to be eaten by ulcerated dogs and old swine. And you're of no use for anything except whoring and raping, and you're only soldiers because, if you couldn't wear a uniform, not one of you would be able to earn a crust of bread or a moldy tortilla by honest work. And you, General, are the greatest, stupidest, laziest, greediest scum that's to be found upon earth; in your head you have nothing but a bladder full of lukewarm water; if anyone knocked against your shinbone it would snap like a worm-eaten twig because you're riddled with disease. And, what's more, you're not really a general, but only have that rank today because your wife and all your daughters have gone to bed with all the people who have anything to say in the matter. And if your mother didn't whore about all over the place, assisted by her daughters, you wouldn't be even a sergeant, you'd be a mule driver. Forgive me, General, but you wanted to hear the message. And as a subordinate officer I had to obey your order, sir, and, as always, I am at your service and owe you my deepest respect. And now I have something to hand over to you which that louse-general sent you for your breakfast."

Neither the general nor any of the other officers, either those sitting at the table or those that had come in afterward and were now standing about, had interrupted the lieutenant. They let him talk himself out, as if he were a madman who could not be held responsible for what he said. But now that he had finished, they all realized that the lieutenant had not spoken for himself, but that, in actual fact, he had only repeated what the rebel general had told him to say. A single one of these epithets would have brought the lieutenant before a court-martial, and the whole speech would certainly have cost him at least 250 years in the military prison at Santiago. Quite apart from all this, the expressions he had used were such as an officer could scarcely have thought up himself, even if he had tried to. These were the reasons why neither the general nor the other officers had interrupted the lieutenant with a single word.

Both the general and the officers had ceased to eat as soon as the first significant words had been uttered. First the general turned purple in the face, then pale, then purple again. The officers, particularly the younger ones, turned pale and remained pale. Every man in the room expected the general to draw his revolver and shoot the lieutenant. But for the same reason that the lieutenant had been left uninterrupted, not a man made a movement to shoot him or strike him in the face. The lieutenant had delivered his speech without a second's hesitation. His fury gave him courage to deliver his message without excusing himself with a single interpolated apology. He reserved this for his conclusion. In the mood he was in, weary from a long ride through the night, humiliated by his disgrace, and weak from loss of blood and pain, it would have been a matter of indifference to him if the general had shot him. He would have taken it as a favor.

The speech was followed by a silence of several seconds, which seemed like minutes to all those present. No one knew what to say or do in order to relax the oppressive tension.

Then, however, this silence was sharply broken by the loud

shout of Lieutenant Bailleres: "Hi, Chamaco, bring in the sack you had at your pommel."

The youth had squatted on the portico, waiting for someone to give him something to eat. Now he took up the sack beside him and carried it into the large room where the officers were assembled.

"Here, General," said Lieutenant Bailleres, "is the present which that mangy hound of a bandit captain sent you."

"A present? For me? From that swine?" The general had not yet quite recovered from the flood of shameless, obscene insults that had swept over him. "Throw the present onto the dung heap. What sort of a present can that scum of an insolent, godless Indian send to me? Probably a stolen ham that he's poisoned. Put the sack on the dung heap, Chamaco."

The lad from the rancho picked up the sack again. But when he was already over the threshold and walking along the portico, the general was seized with curiosity to know what was in the sack. At the same time he thought the contents of the sack might yield some clue to the plans of the rebel leader. "Lieutenant Bailleres, do you know what is in the sack?"

"No, General. I must honestly confess that on my wretched ride back, my mind was occupied with other things than looking to see what it might contain. Besides, sir, I didn't feel justified in opening a closed sack, the contents of which had been sent to you or belong to you."

"Quite right, Lieutenant Bailleres. Thank you."

He beckoned to one of the junior officers: "Call that boy with the sack back again."

The lad returned and let the sack fall on the hard-packed clay floor of the room. All present stared at the sack is if they would guess what it contained. It might really be poisoned ham, or coconuts or pumpkins. Perhaps—and this thought occurred to all simultaneously—perhaps it was bombs that would explode the moment they rolled out of the sack.

A captain gave expression to this thought: "Sir, we should be careful. It appears to be bombs."

"Don't be so senseless, Captain. If it were bombs, the boy with the sack would never be here."

The officers laughed, and the captain made a face.

"Come on. Untie the sack, Chamaco," the general commanded the lad.

The youth squatted down beside the sack and took the knots between his teeth in order to loosen them, so tightly were they tied. This took too long for Lieutenant Ochoa. He seized a knife from the table and with one stroke sliced through the bast thongs.

"Shake out the sack, Chamaco," said the general, rising from his chair to get a better view across the table.

The boy took the sack by its bottom corners, heaved it up, and out tumbled the severed heads of Lieutenant Bailleres's three companions.

"They'll pay bitterly for this, those savages, those barbaric murderers!" yelled the general, when he had recovered from the shock. "And my holy mother, *mi santa madre,* my own mother—for him to speak her name with his filthy mouth, and sully it! I'll tear the skin off him alive, slowly and day after day, dragging him behind an ass. Those beasts, those wild animals. What have I always said and advocated, gentlemen? I repeat it, and will continue to repeat it until at last the government listens to me: exterminate all the Indians, destroy them mercilessly like the most poisonous creatures we have in the country. And as long as we haven't swept everything that's Indian from the face of the earth, so long will there be neither peace nor rest in this beautiful land. To sully my beloved mother, this filth, this lousy, ragged, stinking native! And here, our comrade, Lieutenant Bailleres, threatened with his life, and three of our comrades slaughtered in a bestial manner. What did the mangy hound have to say to me? I can't thrash him where he's waiting for me? He—waiting for me? He, a lousy swine of a rebel waiting for me? Such a worm, such a shooter of dog filth, and he says to me that I'm hiding from him and won't come out of my hole to tear the hide off him. Gentlemen, with one single battalion I shall deal with that muck heap. And what's more, gentlemen, you can all spit in my face if I don't utterly destroy that whole verminous gang within three days. But to that dog of a stinking Indian I won't grant the privilege of being beaten to death with cudgels like all the other riffraff. I'll bring him back myself, his syphilitic bones strung tight together, dragging him behind an old, lame mule. Colonel Viaña, you will take over command of the troops remaining here during my absence."

11

  The general wasted no time in finishing his breakfast properly. He decided that the punitive battalion was to be ready to march off at four o'clock.

While he was giving his orders, he interrupted himself twice every three minutes to intone his slogan: "To sully my holy mother, that vermin, that animal, that shooter of dog filth, to sully my holy mother."

After his orders had all been relayed and the troops were getting ready for departure, Colonel Viaña considered it advisable to waft a cooling breeze over the general. "With your permission, General, if I may presume to take the liberty, I would advise ordering out at least two battalions and a machine-gun section. We don't know how strong the rebels may be."

"My dear Colonel," replied the general, "don't, please, make yourself ridiculous. Originally I wanted to send only half a battalion against that mutinous pack. That would have been more than sufficient. But my chief ordered out almost a whole brigade—the devil knows why; perhaps it puts another five thousand pesos in his pocket or something—and as his subordinate I have to obey and lead a brigade into the field. I'd be ashamed to the end of my life and never be able to look a decent officer in the face again if I were to set out with a brigade against a gaggle of dirty Indian vagabonds. All right. I've brought the brigade as far as this, in obedience to higher orders, as a defense for Balun Canan. But that doesn't mean that

I've got to take a brigade with me to collect the scalps of that mongrel pack."

"You are my commanding general, sir, and I am bound to obey you. But I'd still like to make the suggestion that you take at least half a regiment of cavalry with you."

"Well, just to calm you, Colonel Coldfeet—all right; I'll take some cavalry with me, seventy men. Give Captain Ampudia the necessary orders. He's the drunkest. It'll cheer him up a bit."

"*A sus órdenes, mi general.*"

The colonel saluted and left.

The general then summoned Lieutenant Bailleres. "How are you feeling, Lieutenant? Ready for action?"

"Tired, sir. But I beg permission to take part in the expedition."

"You shall, Lieutenant. You've got a personal debt to settle with those savages. And I wouldn't like to do you out of it. You'll be very valuable to me. You know the terrain there and roughly their dispositions. You will lead the first company, Lieutenant."

"Thank you, *mi general.*"

"We'll camp for the night on the way. Then you'll be able to get a good sleep. In your opinion, could our troops be on their playground about the middle of tomorrow afternoon?"

"Without doubt, sir. And that seems to me the best time for our attack, because at that hour no one there expects an attack. In the afternoon they're out hunting, and those that aren't hunting or training are sleeping. So far as I could discover, they're not counting on any attack out there, but nearer the cliffs, where we're waiting for them. If there is to be an attack from our side, they are convinced that it will happen either early in the morning or shortly after nightfall when they think that we shall assume that they'll all be tired, squatting by their fires, dancing, sleeping, eating, and lying with their women. That's all I could gather from their conversations, sir."

"We'll whip them all right. To sully my holy mother with their filthy, stinking tongues, those swinish animals of Indians! To drag my holy mother in the muck—!"

At three o'clock the general saw that the time had arrived to occupy himself with another sustaining meal. While he ate, he complained of the burdensome duties of a commanding general, which had prevented him that morning from enjoying his breakfast in peace and finishing it with his customary pleasure. The repast this time was not embellished by the general's witty remarks. It was dealt with more seriously. Not that the general and the officers who sat with him at the table bothered to take this opportunity to discuss plans of the campaign. No, the seriousness of the forthcoming drubbing that he was proposing to administer to the rebels found its expression in the general's beginning every second sentence that he uttered, in the midst of chewing and swallowing, with: "I'll thrash these lousy swine who've sullied my holy mother with their stinking tongues; first surround them all, then club them down, then bury them up to their necks, and then each company will march over them, followed by the cavalry. It was excellent advice of yours, Colonel Viaña, that I should take some cavalry with me. I should have missed galloping those swine's heads into the earth." Then something else occurred to him: "Actually, I must confess, gentlemen, that I am ashamed to have to march against such filthy curs. A sergeant could do it. Am I not right, gentlemen?"

"In every way, General."

Shortly after four o'clock the punitive expedition moved off. Before seven they had reached a rancho where the general ordered camp to be pitched for the night, in order to continue the march on the morrow full of fresh energy. It was not advisable to march farther through the night, for it was possible that the rebels might evade the army by slinking around them.

Lieutenant Bailleres, however, stated that he did not believe the rebels would march on a direct route toward Balun Canan, because they knew that they would thus run into the arms of the Federals, and they had as little reason for involving themselves in a night battle as had the army.

The general twisted his mouth in a sarcastic grin, so as to convey the triviality of the whole thing to the few officers whom he had taken with him merely in order to let them par-

take in a little pleasure. It was purely a matter of pleasure, for
the slaughter of a pack of rebels can never earn laurels, or even
medals, for an honorable soldier. And through his twisted lips
he said, "Battle? I hear nothing but battle, Lieutenant Bailleres.
Battle! You mustn't speak of a battle with those ragged bandits. One doesn't do battle with mutineers, with rebels, with
strikers. One thrashes them and hangs them, or else buries
them alive to save the rope and the hangman's trouble. Battle!
When I hear that from an officer, it makes me feel sick enough
to vomit. But let's have a drink before the filthy supper that
will be served to us here. Miserable ranch. Eat nothing here
but beans, tortillas, and chilies. Don't know the meaning of
coffee; and boil up some sort of vegetable they pick from trees
and call the brew tea. And that's what they name a rancho
here. The Devil knows, that old nut-cracker on his throne up
there doesn't worry a damn that in this godforsaken wilderness
a general who's been sent out against lousy Indians has to suffer from fleas and not a soft cushion under his behind, and getting up in the morning with aching bones. *Dios mío*, let's get
this whipping over with and back to garrison, where a man
has some peace and his own proper bed. Don't you agree, gentlemen?"

"Absolutely right, General," answered Captain Ampudia in
the name of the younger officers, who nodded dutifully.

The troop camped in the patio of the rancho. The officers
were in a room in the owner's house. This was a miserable
daubed structure that was already beginning to lean askew and
that had only two rooms. The kitchen was in the yard, in a
hut built with thin stakes and a palm-leaf roof.

The patio itself was surrounded by a wall made out of
rough stones. About fifty paces beyond this wall lay the
wretched palm huts in which lived the three Indian families
who worked as peons on the rancho. The horses of the troop
were in a meadow where, with their forelegs hobbled, they
had to forage for their food. The ranchero received five centavos grazing money for each horse, just as he got twenty centavos for each man. All in accordance with regulations and in

accordance with the receipt he had to sign. How much he actually received in hard cash depended on how much the paymaster was short in his funds. However, the ranchero knew his fatherland and also knew the habits of all petty dictators whom the great dictator has to keep satisfied. For that reason the ranchero did not bother about how many men and horses his meager rancho had to fatten. To have to worry about it or even to have written it all down in his little notebook would merely have given him a headache, without making him a single peso the richer. No one looked at the billeting voucher that was handed to him. It was stuck up on an old nail until the nail rusted through, or the paper disintegrated or was eaten up by cucurachas. Only a six-year-old child would have taken the voucher to the garrison paymaster for cashing. Everyone over six years of age knew that the voucher would be continually disputed until the ranchero had meantime grown so furious that he would tear up the paper before the eyes of the paymaster and throw the scraps at his feet. For what is the point of a dictatorship if there are no perquisites?

The gate in the stone wall surrounding the patio consisted of six stout poles that were rammed crosswise between two posts set in the ground and that the boy, when he brought the cows home in th evening, dragged out in order that the cattle could spend the night in the patio, where they would be better protected against jaguars.

Now there stood before this gate a sentry with fixed bayonet, who marched up and down, and when he saw anyone approach, he took his rifle in both hands and shouted, "*Quién vive?*" If the challenged answered, "*Amigo!*" he was allowed to pass. Should he, on the other hand, answer, "Enemy!" he would immediately have been shot.

It was not necessary to post any other sentries. One doesn't post sentries against rebels. That would mean recognizing them as soldiers. Besides, it was superfluous to tire out a lot of men, and thereby make them unfit for the next day's hard march, by curtailing their night's rest with patrolling and sentry duty. The infantry slept in the open patio. Outside the patio, near the huts of the peons, slept the mounted troops. All the men lay in the open, fully clothed, near their weapons.

At sunset the general had sent out three reconnaissance patrols in different directions, all of whom returned with the report that they had not seen so much as a lame mule, not to mention a man. Indian peasants who chanced to pass the rancho were stopped and asked for information, but all avowed that they had seen no rebels, although they had indeed heard that far away there was a horde of bandits who were robbing, plundering, and stealing all the cattle.

"Then there's no doubt, gentlemen, that these stink-hogs are still hanging around where Lieutenant Bailleres visited them. It's a pity they haven't come nearer and saved us at least half that long march there. There must be a good seven or eight hours' march facing us tomorrow." The general yawned, poured a generous measure down his throat, filled his glass again, and pushed the bottle on.

Two more bottles were brought.

The general was playing dominoes with three officers. Ever since the ranchero had produced the dominoes, he had thought better of the man and regarded him as a civilized being; for men lacking in culture and intelligence have no conception of the mental effort which a domino player has to exert in order to deduce what spots are still out and which of his opponents has them lined up before him. It is a game worthy only of great strategists and similar masterminds. Half-wits occupy themselves with chess. But what is chess? One doesn't have to guess, to deduce; all the pieces are standing in full view; one can see what the opponent has and observe exactly what he does. A game for schoolboys and idiots! But dominoes! The general knew very well why he regarded dominoes as the most intelligent game ever invented by man.

When one of the officers preferred to make a fourth at a game of cards, the general invited his host, the ranchero, to join their dominoes.

"Forgive me, Don Facundo, for having been mistaken in you," he said with a friendly smile as the ranchero sat down opposite him. "I just assumed that you were merely the usual stupid, petty landowner, of whom we have such numbers in this state, who only think of cows and nothing else. I'm delighted to find a pleasant exception in you, a man of intelligence and talents. *Salud!* Your health, Don Facundo. Well, and now let's see what I have here." With a mighty pounce of his fist, the general slammed his piece on the table and matched a five with a five, as if nobody else on earth could have laid a five against another five. When he had accomplished this feat, he clapped his hands, rubbed them fiercely, and looked with greedy eyes at the pieces on the table to see what the next player would add. As soon as the piece was in place and he found that at both ends a six was awaiting its mate, he felt justified in downing another glass in reward.

It was eleven o'clock when he decided that it was at last time for him to rest and thus give the other officers the chance of retiring for the night.

By midnight the land on which the rancho stood shook with snores. Indeed, the sentry at the gate could not long resist so much snoring. He leaned comfortably against one of the posts and let his rifle with its fixed bayonet slip down between his legs. Even supposing, he thought as he nodded drowsily, the captain were to come with a relief sentry and find me asleep, he'll only slap me twice in the chops and give me another two hours' duty. A few slaps more or less won't make me a sergeant with better pay, and there's thousands of times I haven't dozed on duty, and still I'm not a captain, so what's the use of standing here and looking stupid when all the world's snoring and I alone have to stay awake? What lovely plump, fat legs Gabina has. It's bound to be at least another six days before we get back and I can swing her around in a dance. And Don Teodulo always has a good band when he gives a dance, and he ladles out damned good *comiteco*. Hell, my eyes are burning as if they were full of sand. Yes, the music at Don Teodulo's—there's nothing like it. It's good. And Gabina, with her fat, meaty, bulging calves. And tomorrow, to have to stride out all day like madmen. *Dios mío!* If only in God's wide world there'd sometime be an end to a soldier's life, when one could peacefully lie on one's mat if one wanted and never be hit in the face by an officer without being able to hit back three times at his crooked face. God knows, I'm tired as an old sow.

At these words he wriggled himself into a more comfortable position, pressed his back against the post, and drew his head down between his shoulders in order to feel a little warmer.

12

   No one, whether officer or soldier, was able to say
precisely whether he had been sleeping for only fifteen minutes or for four hours. No one remembered exactly
whether it was one o'clock in the morning or four o'clock.
However, it was cold and windy, and from this anyone who
knew the country concluded it must be nearer four o'clock
than one. And, astonishingly, no one, not even an officer,
thought of simply looking at his watch to find out what the
time was. Each man feared to light a match or turn on a flash-
light, for each man feared that he would betray his whereabouts and so lose his life. The attention of all was so riveted
on other things that it would have seemed absurd to know what
hour of the night it was. For if the darkness could not turn to
broad daylight within the next twenty seconds, it was already
a matter of total indifference whether the time were one
o'clock at night or four o'clock in the morning.

An extraordinary thing happened. Everyone sleeping in the
rancho woke up. All at almost the same moment, all as if
roused by a voice they had not heard but yet thought they
had heard.

The first definite noise that they were all aware of was the
sudden barking of the dogs, which increased. The dogs, as
usual, barked the whole night through, and incessantly. They
barked at the numerous mules and horses that hobbled around;
they barked at the large number of sleeping soldiers; and they
barked one against the other, the dogs of the rancho and the

peons on the one side, and the dogs that accompanied and were tolerated by the troops on the other side.

Therefore, no one heeded the barking of the dogs. Only when the noise grew stronger and swelled into a definite, powerful, furious chorus did everyone in the rancho know that something unusual was happening.

But each man, officer and private, remained where he was, merely sitting up sleepily and noticing that a lot of horses had broken into the patio and were careering about in wild fright. At the same time the sleepy observers saw shadowy figures running back and forth, apparently rounding up the horses and driving them out of the patio. These figures came close to the sleepers, stumbled over them, fell on them, got up with a brief curse, and ran on again, driving the horses together.

The horses roaming about the patio and disturbing the sleepers had lost the hobbles on their forelegs. This was how they had succeeded in coming so far into the patio, either out of fear of a hungry jaguar lurking in the meadows, or else having been attracted by the sacks of corn stacked up in readiness for feeding the animals in the morning.

Here and there were to be heard the oaths and curses of the men who had been startled from their sleep and had been trodden on by one of their comrades who had to leave the patio and go outside the wall to attend to his own private needs and now, because of the inky darkness, could not see where he was stepping.

In less than five minutes the strange noises, the cursing and swearing of the men, the nervous stamping of the horses died away as suddenly as they had started. The dogs again changed the note of their barking and now uttered only their customary nocturnal plaint. A few men who had stood up, without leaving their places, dropped to the ground again, still half asleep, and slept on.

Within ten minutes the whole camp was snoring louder and more contentedly than before.

When the bugle reverberated across the rancho, all began to stretch, all yawned so widely they threatened to swallow themselves, then all scratched themselves on head, back, chest, and legs as if they had one too many skins on their bodies. And the first words that everyone, soldier or officer, spoke to his neighbor, were "*Dios!* Did I dream it in the night, or did hell really break loose here for a while?" Whereupon his neighbor replied, "Then I didn't dream it, if you heard it, too. There must have been half a hundred jaguars out on the plain, which hunted all the horses and sent them trampling over my stomach."

And the general said to the captain, who sat on the neighboring bunk, yawning and scratching himself, "I'll teach that cavalry sergeant a lesson for not looking after the horses better. Hey, God's damnation, where's my gun? I wasn't so drunk that I don't know where I put my belt with my revolver. I remember clearly I hung it over the end of the bed so as to have it handy."

The general searched right, searched left, searched under his bunk, searched along the wooden pegs on the plaster wall, fumbled all around his stomach, and then said, with a look of amazement, "Well, where the Devil did I sling my artillery last night? Tell me, Captain, was I really so drunk that I didn't know what I was doing?"

"Of course not, sir. I had the impression that you were as sober as a monkey before Mass."

"Whether a monkey is always sober before Mass, I beg leave to doubt," replied the general, standing up and peering down his legs in the hope of finding that his revolver was dangling between them. "But monkey or no monkey at Mass, my gun's gone—that's one thing I do know."

"Perhaps your servant's taken it to clean," said a lieutenant.

"Then he seems to have collected all our revolvers for cleaning," said another officer, who for the last few minutes had been hunting, with the help of a flickering candle, under the mat, in his boots, and beneath his pile of clothes.

Outside the house, in the wide patio, there was the usual teeming confusion of men who have just wakened. It was still pitch dark, but at several places in the patio small fires were now burning, which gave some illumination to the courtyard.

"You, Claudio!" came a loud voice from out of the swarm. "Have you seen my damned gun? The Devil knows where it's gone."

"Don't ask me, you fool; for the last half hour I've been doing nothing but look for my own pea shooter. And I can't find the bayonet, either."

A sergeant roared out angrily across the mob, "Which of you lumps of dirt has knocked off the pile of rifles? There's not a sign of the bloody things."

The confusion grew.

Simultaneously, from all corners of the patio, came always the same furious cry: "Which son of a whore has taken my rifle?" And again: "Where's my gun, damn you all?" And from another corner: "I swear that when I catch the bastard that hid my rifle, I'll knock his teeth down his throat. To hell with the whole lot of you, where's my damned gun gone? It was right by my side the whole night like a frigid woman, and now its vanished."

The bugler blew fall-in for morning parade. There was a gray tinge of dawn in the sky. When a count was taken, it appeared that 130 rifles, eight officers' revolvers, two machine guns, four boxes of machine-gun ammunition, 150 loaded bandoliers, an indeterminate number of bayonets, knives, and small hatchets, and about thirty sacks of corn were missing. When the cavalry began to ride on to parade, the riders slid from side to side on their horses, and the horses, becoming frightened, ran wild. It appeared that all the saddle girths had been cut three quarters through so that they would break as soon as a horse began to gallop or became unruly.

"What sort of a half-baked gang of soldiers d'you think you are?" screamed the general. "Has such a thing ever happened before in the army? Letting your weapons be snatched away from under you? I'll have the lot of you given three months' punishment drill till you sweat blood from every pore. And a man that's lost his machine gun will get an extra ten days on top of that. I'll teach you what your equipment's worth, you scum. Every man who's lost his rifle will cut himself a cudgel, and with cudgels only we shall now attack those Indian swine who stole your weapons from under you. Otherwise, by God, I'll have the whole lot of you shot here on the spot. Dismissed for breakfast!"

"And as for you, gentlemen," said the general, as his officers sat down for breakfast. "I perceive that you, too, have no revolvers. What have you to say in excuse?"

The officers who very well knew that not only they, but also their commanding general, had lost all their revolvers without a trace, said nothing at first. They merely tried to smile at their general with a conspiratorial twinkle. The general, however, responded with a sour grimace that excluded all further familiarity.

A lieutenant who seemed quickly to have interpreted that sour and forbidding expression looked at the general's right hip and with a wink incited his comrades to follow the direction of his glance.

At the general's right hip hung a regulation .45 army revolver. They all had the impression that the general had hitherto carried not an army revolver, but a regulation automatic. However, each thought that he must have been mistaken and that the general, for this expedition against the rebels, had exchanged his automatic for a revolver without any of them having hitherto noticed it.

Of course it was easy enough for the general to deliver a stern reprimand to anyone who had had his gun stolen during the night. Immediately after he had searched for a few seconds and been unable to find his own automatic, and when he remembered the disturbance during the night, he had had the glimmering of an idea of what might have happened. Without searching further, he had hurried out of the room and gone to the door of the second room in the house, where the ranchero and his family slept. On the previous evening he had noticed that the ranchero possessed a nearly new heavy .45. And for a sum that he forthwith paid in cash, sufficient indeed to buy the ranchero two new revolvers and still leave something over for a few boxes of ammunition, the general secured for himself this revolver with the stipulation that the ranchero give his word of honor to betray nothing of the transaction.

"I ask again, gentlemen, what have you to say in excuse?" The general repeated his question with all the bitterness that he felt at having had such a trick played on him by the rebels. What, however, fanned this bitterness to a blaze of anger was not the actual theft of the weapons, but the fact that these filthy, verminous Indians had thus dared to attack himself and his own Federal troops, the pride of the nation, that they had shown so little respect for the flag that had been raised in the patio; and that they had cut this flag into small tatters and smeared it with the customary fresh excrement.

The next-senior officer stood up, saluted, and said, "With your permission, sir, I wish to state for my comrades and myself that we have nothing to say in mitigation."

The general looked sharply and menacingly at his youngest lieutenant. "You, Lieutenant Manero, you were on camp duty last night."

"Correct, sir. I was on camp duty."

"We will deal with that, Lieutenant Manero, later."

"*A sus órdenes, mi general!*"

The general nodded.

At this moment the maids brought in plates of sliced papayas for the breakfast fruit.

The general, who was the first to be served, gazed at his plate with a vacant expression as though oblivious of it. He nodded again. Then he reached mechanically for spoon and fork, cut off a piece of the juicy fruit, and pushed it into his mouth, which he opened uncommonly wide as if wishing to insert a piece that was three times the size.

As he gently pulped the fruit between his gums and his arched tongue, in order to savor its full deliciousness, he nodded once more. When he had emptied his plate and had to wait a few minutes before the eggs were brought in, he said, looking at each of the officers in turn, "According to immemorial military custom and precept, which admittedly has never been incorporated in military regulations, I should now be under the obligation of taking an honorable farewell of this world by sending a well-placed bullet through my head."

A loud protest from the officers followed, as was indeed their duty vis-à-vis a superior. "We're not at war, sir." "That's just a stupid old tradition." "We're modern soldiers, General." "That's moldy old superstition."

Lieutenant Manero particularly distinguished himself with a resounding and energetic: "I, sir—I alone am to blame. I am the one who should take my farewell. I've failed in my duty. I beg your permission to make an honorable end."

"What a man! What a figure of an officer! He would go down forever in the history of the battalion as the officer who preferred death to dishonor. That was the material the officers of this glorious army were made of. So long as such a spirit prevailed among the officers, there was not the slightest danger of the nation's possible decline. Without workers and similar rogues who are always grumbling about hunger, always trying to undermine the government, a nation could very well flourish and bask in the well-earned respect of all other civilized people on earth; but without such officers as Lieutenant Manero, no nation could survive for a day.

That was immediately and properly recognized by all officers present, who burst out in a thrice-repeated "*Viva, Manero!*" while all, with the exception of the general, stood up.

The general interrupted this exaggerated ovation with a curt "Lieutenant Manero, I do not give my permission for any such childish nonsense. Understand? And what is more, as your commanding officer, I forbid you to use any weapons against yourself. This battalion is on active service. Suicide on active service is equivalent to desertion in the face of the enemy. Do you understand me, Lieutenant Manero?"

"*A sus órdenes, mi general.*" The lieutenant had stood up and now saluted his general.

It was an extremely honorable, unquestionable, and, from the military point of view, satisfactory solution of the situation. So far as logic was concerned, the impregnability of this solution left nothing to be desired. The general could not give an order that he himself was not willing to carry out. An order emanating from him applied to all under his command. He was part of this command. Suicide on active duty was shameless and dishonorable desertion. And a general commanding a detachment was the last person who should commit an act of desertion. Rifles could be replaced. Not so a general. That, too, had to be taken into consideration. So there was nothing for it but to finish breakfast with the customary enjoyment and without impairing digestion with thoughts of suicide.

When breakfast was over and even the toothpicks had been used up, there was no further excuse for sitting longer at the table.

The general called several soldiers to carry out the hard, rough benches on which the officers had been seated, and here on the portico he summoned all the officers and sergeants to a council of war.

"Sergeant Morones, how many rifles have we left?" he asked the senior sergeant whom he had entrusted with the counting of all remaining available weapons and ammunition.

In the general's opinion, there were enough to warrant proceeding with the projected advance. The muchachos, even if they possessed three times as many guns as the Federals, knew so little about handling these weapons that, as all the officers unanimously believed, one armed soldier could easily take on twenty armed rebels. These Indians, as he well knew and as all his officers knew, too, held the butt toward the enemy instead of against their own shoulders. Those of the insurgents, however, who knew enough to point the muzzle toward the enemy always gripped the butt between their knees, or rested it against their stomachs, or else laid the gun flat on the ground and squatted down to fire it in the hope that the bullet would go in the exact direction desired. Those ignorant Indians would be more at home with stones or arrows, for they believed that modern weapons fired at the selected target entirely of their own accord. That was clear as daylight, and every officer and sergeant had had personal experience from their numerous battles against strikers, insurrectionists, and rebellious Indian peasants. In this case it was no different, particularly since the fellow who called himself general of the rebels behaved and acted like an ignorant ape. In support of which view, there was the report of a reliable eyewitness, Lieutenant Bailleres.

The number of the rebels was also unknown. According to all reports, and taking into account those who had been killed in battle and executed, there could not now be many more than a hundred or 120 men at most, of whom a considerable number must be wounded and an equally large number incapable of handling a weapon or of being dangerous to regular soldiers.

Also, after the attack, the soldiers would recover their stolen weapons, and in addition to their own guns they would get the weapons that had been previously stolen or had otherwise fallen into the hands of the rebels, and thereafter the battalion could march back to headquarters with its honor vindicated.

Everything the general suggested at this officers' council of war was agreed to without demur, because it was militarily correct and, from the point of view of honor, unavoidable. "Honor always comes first, gentlemen!" repeated the general on every occasion when he did not know what else to say, what orders to give, or what to do to advance the discussion.

Sergeant Morones, who was attending the meeting together with the other sergeants, was a great favorite with the general, owing to his long service and experience. In fact, the general regarded the sergeant as virtually an officer, and he had long ago sent in his recommendation to the War Ministry that Sergeant Morones should be promoted to lieutenant and thus inducted into the officers' corps. This recommendation would certainly be approved.

In all matters Morones took far more liberties than the junior officers who had just come from the military academy and who were regarded as green, still wet behind the ears.

It was Sergeant Morones who now said, "May I have your permission to speak, sir?"

"Speak, Sergeant Morones. That's what we're here for, to discuss the situation and make suggestions. Of course, there's not much to discuss in this instance. We shall advance and thrash those worthless, impertinent vagabonds once and for all. The only reason why we are conferring at all is that we lack weapons and our ammunition is not by any means too plentiful. Well, what have you to say, Sergeant?"

"I think, sir, that there's something not quite right in this whole affair, if I may put it like that, sir."

"Well, what? What do you mean, Sergeant Morones?" The general spoke with abrupt harshness. He feared that Sergeant Morones might even be going to criticize his brilliant suggestions or, what was worse, have discovered a flaw in his plans. But he was also aware that the sergeant had been well trained, particularly as a soldier, and would be most careful not to suggest flaws in the plans of a superior officer.

In this respect young lieutenants were tactless and blundering. At times they even came forward with half-a-dozen bright ideas that they certainly had not learned at the cadet school, where instruction was still based on the campaigns of Caesar, Hannibal, and Alexander; the methods of Napoleon were regarded as modern. No, they had discovered their ultra-novel ideas in a book on modern French tactics that they had half understood, not digested at all, and then attempted to bring out in order to show off their brilliance at times when their commanding officer was working out plans for maneuvers and had ordered the young officers to do the same in order to enjoy their stupidity.

But the general's face lit up contentedly when the sergeant, almost like a pupil, asked quite innocently, "Why, sir, do you think the rebels did not murder all our men in the night? They crept among us so quietly and light-footedly to steal our weapons that they could easily have cut our throats as well. And because they didn't do that, sir, I thought there must be something not quite right here."

The general smiled. With this paternal smile still on his fat, rosy lips, he glanced along the row of officers. Then he nodded at the sergeant and said indulgently and patronizingly, "Sergeant Morones, your question and your observation do you credit. They show that you are an excellent soldier, able to think for yourself and weigh unusual occurrences such as last night's. However, the question is easily answered, Sergeant Morones."

The officers, none of whom had thought this remarkable behavior of the rebels worth mentioning, striking though it was, waited with expectant faces for their commanding officer's explanation. At this moment they realized the importance of the sergeant's remark. The general, however, entirely overlooked the point. His explanation was an example of the atrophied powers of thought of all those who occupy a public office or a position of responsibility under a dictatorship. Intelligent men are unable to hold any appointment for six months under such a regime.

"Quite simple, gentlemen. There's nothing simpler on earth than to explain the behavior of those swine. They knew very well that the death penalty is inflicted on anyone endangering the life of any person representing authority. That includes not only El Caudillo, but all officers, soldiers, and police forces. Even an attempt on the life of a man in authority, be it no more than a threat, is punishable with shooting or hanging. And that, gentlemen, is what these shameless rogues are afraid of. They know very well that stealing weapons in peacetime is punished like any other theft, with a few months in prison, nothing more. That is why not so much as a hair of our men was touched. These sons of bitches are yellow cowards, and they all behave just as one would expect of such riffraff. In the bright light of day, when God's sun is shining, they creep into their stinking holes. That is also the reason, and the only reason, why they have not marched against us and come to where we were willingly waiting for them in order to inflict on them their long deserved thrashing and then to hang them. They're brave enough with defenseless men, like Lieutenant Bailleres here and our three unfortunate comrades. But these louse-eaters lack the guts to meet an honest soldier openly in battle. That's clear to you, I hope, Sergeant Morones?"

"Yes, sir, thank you very much, it's quite clear to me now." The sergeant said this with all the respect due from a subordinate to such a high ranking officer. But his tone involuntarily betrayed the fact that he was no wiser than before and that he thought differently. As a dutiful and experienced soldier who, moreover, knew that his promotion to officer depended on always conceding one's superiors to be in the right, always being tactful toward higher-ups, and not concerning oneself with matters not expressly entrusted to one, he carefully avoided even mentioning any doubts that still lingered in his mind after his commanding officer had expounded his opinion.

13

 General's military training had been limited to the practical knowledge that can be dinned into any ordinary soldier in the army by means of a great many kicks, knocks, and bawlings-out in the course of a year. The arcane mysteries of higher strategy remained closed to him, for he had had no prospect of rising higher in the army than, at best, to the rank of sergeant, and as sergeant he would have had no responsibilities other than to see that the men in his platoon were dragged out of their bunks at the appointed time and lined up at the appointed place.

The general, on the contrary, being the son of an old and respected family of half-Spanish, half-French ancestry, had attended the military academy with success, and there he had learned everything that army commanders from the Babylonians to Wellington had done, said, taught, planned, and recommended. Through this training he was gradually set apart from the common race of men and had climbed a fair number of steps nearer to the gods. This transformation from a mere mortal to one of the highest representatives of God on earth began on the first day of his entry to the military academy and proceeded precisely toward its apotheosis, according to long-established rules.

The first of these rules was that he had to use a new and totally different manner of speaking, and the inflections of his speech had to be so altered that, as soon as he had merely unlatched his jaw, every common man would immediately recognize that he was the incarnation of his country's honor and had been singled out by God to add one or more chapters to the triumphant and glorious history of the army.

The preparation for such a sublime task naturally necessitated exertion, sacrifice, patience, and hard work.

During the first few weeks after their entry into the military academy, the cadets who aspired someday to become generals had to parade at midnight, in the rooms of the older cadets, clad only in a nightshirt and carrying a lighted candle in one hand and, by displaying the object in question, to demonstrate how far they had progressed in the science of polishing an army boot.

At lunch, when a glorious haunch of luscious roast meat was brought in and the anticipation of devouring it made their mouths water, a senior cadet would order them, in turn, to define what sand is.

To an embryo general, sand is not what a mere civilian believes sand to be. Under a dictatorship things are not made so simple for a future army leader.

To a dutiful, patriotic, keen, studious, aspiring, lousy cadet in his first year, sand is something entirely different. He must learn to appreciate, even in his tender youth, that to a cadet sand is a substance composed of varying quantities of minute geological formations, partly granular and partly crystalline in structure, but also in some cases manifesting itself in all possible and conceivable known and unknown geometrical shapes, originating, to deduce from its visibly apparent characteristics, in the erosion or continuous influence of atmospheric conditions upon the rocklike constituents of the terrestrial surface, consisting of loosely associated masses that, when spread out on a parade ground and suitably leveled, serves the unique but vital purpose of providing a surface on which a group of green, undeveloped, semi-equipped, badly polished, half-witted cadets always arrive late, fall in raggedly, practice marching, and, in a manner contrary to all regulations and always in the wrong direction, do section drill and at the same time learn to carry out some further manifestations of physical-motor reflexes with the ultimate object of finally beginning to realize that the legs of a lousy cadet are not to be used for the purpose of wiping his own nose or that of a cadet of a senior year, who always and at all times is to be regarded as his superior, but for pressing the knees firmly back, pulling in the stomach, pushing out the chest, and at the same time not standing there like a pregnant cow, and keeping the hands aligned with the outer —not the inner, for that might cause difficulties—seams of the trousers, and in observing traditional and customary forms, such as the last joint of the little finger must barely touch the military material of which the trousers are tailored, while the palm of the hand arches outward so that, seen from the front, a half-grown mouse of the common sort, *muridae* in scientific language, can be concealed inside, and the outstretched forefinger must be in light contact with the aforementioned and more fully described material without, however, directly touching it, while at the same time care must be taken by means of delicate intuition to ensure that both elbows are slightly crooked without appearing affected, and held not nearer, and also not farther, from the belt than permits the gentle passage between elbow and belt of the flat of the hand of an otherwise normally grown cadet officer, without necessitating any particular muscular and mental effort—that is, in correct and regulation military language: sand.

To have to repeat this every single day except Sunday, while a most appetizing plate of food is lying in front of one, was a little joke inflicted by the older cadets upon the neophytes until the young generals-to-be could rattle off the whole sentence without a mistake and without hesitation at such speed that it was finished before the mess waiters cleared away the appetizing plateful to make room for the ensuing dessert.

In the course of time, the general himself became a senior cadet and now practiced on the newcomers exactly what had been inflicted upon him, the mental powers of these future army chiefs not sufficing to invent anything new in this field or to appreciate how idiotically they were shaping their own lives.

War against the hereditary enemy did not come, because the hereditary enemy knew how to get more out of the country by peaceful trading than he had ever been able to by war. In actual fact, no such thing as a hereditary enemy existed. The expression was only used now and again in order to prevent the taxpayers' interest in the necessity for a strong defense program from waning. It was the hereditary enemy from whom all the heavy ordnance, machine guns, revolvers, bayonets, military equipment had to be bought, because at home the munitions industry was not sufficiently developed to be able itself to produce these desirable weapons and armaments.

As captain, major, and colonel, he had at times had opportunities of testing the effectiveness and brilliance of the strategies of Hannibal, Alexander, Attila, and Napoleon against striking textile workers, refractory miners, and rebellious Indian peasants. It was proved, in all these campaigns, that the fundamentals of strategy and tactics as applied successfully by Hannibal and Napoleon were still wholly valid and that there was no reason to bother one's head with new theories.

The general would have considered it demeaning to have used against the rebel leader the same or similar tactics as he had employed in maneuvers against generals of his own caliber—soldiers by profession, as he called them. Against rebels he proceeded not as a general but as the head of a police detachment sent out to capture escaped criminals.

The first thing that he planned to do, as soon as he had the rebels encircled, was to demand the unconditional surrender of their leaders and the handing over of all weapons within half an hour. As soon as that had happened, he would have the leaders hanged. From the remaining rebel swine, he would then pick out every fifth man and have him hanged, too. The rest of the mutineers, men, women, and brats, he would sell to coffee plantations, *monterías*, and *fincas* to defray the costs of this punitive expedition.

An officer who has any consideration for his honor will never use against rebels any of the military measures in which he has been instructed and which can be effective only against organized military troops. The general would have felt himself unspeakably ridiculous had he regarded the rebel leader, even for a quarter of an hour, as a serious military opponent to be dealt with as a soldier. Rebels are not fought; rebels are simply hunted like hares, and the attack has to be organized like a sporting drive.

General, on the contrary, possessing no honor, knowing none of Napoleon's maxims, never thought for one minute of anything like a hunt. He took the general seriously enough. He took everything seriously: everything that, in his opinion, the general must have learned and everything that he must have discovered from experience during a long military career. Above all, he took the soldiers seriously, for he knew that they could shoot better and more accurately than the muchachos, that they were better drilled, better organized, and carried out more quickly and more skillfully the orders they were given.

And so, because he was never certain of a victory, because he was also not sure of winning the impending fight, he neglected none of those precautions he thought might help secure him the victory.

When they were about eight miles away from the rebel camp, the general ordered his soldiers to halt and make camp for the night.

He had decided not to attack immediately, as had been his original intention, but to wait until the next morning in order to carry out the hunt with greater thoroughness. The approach of night would have enabled too many of the quarry to escape into the bush or the mountains. But by postponing the attack until the morning, and with his troops well rested, he would have the whole day before him, and his sharpshooters would see to it that not a single one of these rebel hounds got away.

After a handsome tent had been set up for him and he had had a long discussion with the cook as to what he should have for supper and what he fancied for breakfast, he left it to the junior officers to see to the rest. That was what they were there for, the young sprigs, to relieve him from such subordinate work. He had the battle to fight: that's what a general was for. And because it was only a matter of hunting down filthy rebels and not of an organized, regular battle, he felt it his duty not to deprive the younger officers of the opportunity of displaying their abilities and of putting into practice for once all that they had learned at the military academy.

These officers, convinced of the importance of their task and fully conscious that, even though fighting against their compatriots, they were nevertheless serving the fatherland, went briskly to work.

They sent out three scouts to report on the rebels' position. After they had done that, they again assembled the soldiers, who were already cooking their supper, and made them parade for rifle inspection. This was done ostensibly for the sake of military preparedness. In fact, it was done so that the general should get the impression that his officers were actually doing something that mattered. It looked important. Whenever an officer, high or low, does not know what to do next, he parades his men for an inspection. There is always something to inspect, and there is no need to think of anything new. Even when, on occasion, an intelligent man becomes an officer and would probably be quite capable of devising genuinely new methods, he takes good care not to employ them or even to mention them to other officers. In order not to appear ridiculous or otherwise attract attention, which would be unfavorable for their career, they strive not to exceed the mean level of intelligence of their comrades. For that would be both tactless and unsporting. Throughout the entire military world, wherever it be, every hiatus, of whatever sort, can always be successfully filled by inspections and marching. In no other profession can mistakes, deficiencies, and negligence, and particularly lack of intelligence, be concealed so easily and by such simple means. The usefulness, not only of a good soldier, but, above all, of an officer, even of a general, is everywhere measured and judged according to how little he is capable of independent thought and how little he makes use of his own brain. Muddled thinking becomes a virtue under a dictatorship, but in a democracy it is simply regarded as laziness.

When the three scouts returned and came in to report, all the officers were sitting at dinner. The general, chewing with a full mouth and waving his knife, said, "Dismissed! You can tell me all that tomorrow when I've arranged for the trampling of those swine."

But this time he took one precaution. He summoned the duty officer and ordered him not to neglect the sentries; for these rogues and criminals might attempt to snatch another fifty rifles, and under the circumstances these could not be spared.

General, too, sent out scouts. He, however, listened attentively to what they had to report—so attentively and closely that he entirely forgot his supper. Celso then said, "What's your opinion, General? Couldn't we take the rest of their rifles, now that they're so near us?"

"We could indeed." General nodded. "And their general is certainly expecting it. And just because he does expect that of us, we won't do it. That's one reason. The other reason is that the soldiers couldn't then attack us. We need a healthy fight. To encourage the muchachos and for practice."

Then he had all his captains summoned, discussed the plan with them that he had thought out, and then gave his orders.

The general had determined to be back at his main camp late on the evening of the following day. That he would return victorious he never doubted for a moment, particularly since it was not a question of a victory but of a hunt. One doesn't speak of a victory at a shoot, only of the size of the bag.

And because the general wished to be in his base camp that evening, where he at least had a proper roof over his head and there was a bedstead instead of this miserably narrow camp bed whose side supports made bruises and holes in his fat body, he broke camp at an early hour, and by sunrise his troops were before the camp of the muchachos.

Together with his adjutant and his bugler he took up position on a small hill, while his soldiers, creeping through the underbrush and tall grass, skillfully encircled the enemy camp in such a manner that not a cat could have escaped.

Everything went as arranged. "Now, you can see what fools these miserable swine are, Lieutenant," he said to his adjutant. "They've neither posted sentries nor taken any other precautions. And the War Ministry expects me to take such rabble seriously. It's enough to make one laugh. Look, Lieutenant, you can see with your own eyes that the whole collection of bandits are intent only on guzzling. Another ten minutes, and we'll see them hop. They haven't even manned the machine gun they stole from us. One could snatch it from them with a lasso if one took the trouble."

The general's remarks were quite true. The muchachos were squatting around their fires. They were so engrossed in their cooking that they crouched there, bent over, and scarcely looked up. Now and again, and here and there, one would walk from one group to another to fetch something or to see what the others were doing. They all seemed to have their eyes still glued shut, so sleepy was the camp.

"How many men do you think there are, Lieutenant?" asked the general.

"Maybe a hundred, sir, or even a hundred and twenty or thirty. It's difficult to say."

"There might also be nearly two hundred?"

"Quite possible, sir. There are hollows in the ground, tall grass, bushes, hillocks, so that one can't see the the whole area. Dozens of them are certainly still asleep; I can see a lot of them lying around, still rolled up in their blankets and rags."

"I can see them, too, Lieutenant. I only want to make sure I've got the whole gang collected here, and that I won't have to make another expedition against them. This eternal scrambling about in the back of beyond and getting uneatable food in dirty ranchos does no good to my poor old bones. I don't mind confessing it. I could retire, but I need the money. I have too many expenses. And if I retire, what am I then? Nothing. A civilian, like any peddler going to the market in Balun Canan."

The general looked at his pocket watch. Then he took up his field glasses and studied the terrain. "There come the first signals from Lieutenant Manero. He's in position and ready. And over there's a flash from Sergeant Junco's mirror. He's taken up position, too. In five minutes the hunt starts."

The general lit a cigarette. He squatted on the ground. He had left his horse in the rear, at the foot of the hill, to avoid its being hit by any stray bullets. The hill was high enough for the general, even while squatting, to be able to survey the whole area.

"How stupidly those scoundrels are behaving," he said with a grin to his adjutant. "You can see that they haven't thought for a moment of putting a machine gun here, or even a lookout post. It would have been bad for us, and cost unnecessary casualties, if those bandits had thought of this hill."

He saw that several hundred yards to the right and left of the hill his troops were also taking up position. He had made them follow a detour, because here the ground was high and their approach could easily have been seen by the rebels. When he now received the signal that these troops, too, were ready and the circle thus fully closed, he drew his revolver and fired three shots into the air. These three shots were a signal to the troops for a general attack to begin. Simultaneously he ordered his bugler to sound the advance.

Scarcely had the shot and the bugler's notes rung out than a machine gun immediately began to pump bullets into the camp.

The assault had begun, and it was clear that there had been not a single mistake in the excellently organized disposition of the troops.

But now something extraordinary occurred—something that the general, in his long and glorious career as a soldier, had never seen before. It was something that not only provoked the general's amazement but also caused the first sign of confusion among his officers and men. In the beginning, this confusion was only manifested by a slight hesitation in the advance.

The general, holding his binoculars to his eyes, had expected, like all the other officers, that at the first burst from the machine gun the camp of the muchachos would spring to life as if struck by lightning. But the camp, as a whole, remained quiet. A few muchachos seemed to lean toward one another, and a few others, also obviously hit by bullets, fell over and lay motionless. Here and there one or two muchachos ran about doubled up, as if to rouse those who seemed to be asleep. Apart from these few flitting figures, not a movement was to be seen.

While the machine gun continued to chatter away, raking the camp in order to soften it up for the main attack, the soldiers with fixed bayonets, crouching low, slowly advanced on the camp from all sides, gradually tightening the ring.

The general ordered the bugler to sound the call for the cavalry to advance. The horse troops were half a mile in the rear, dismounted and hidden in the undergrowth, waiting for the general's signal to sweep around the area in a wide arc and thus prevent any of the rebels from escaping.

The riders mounted and at a gentle gallop proceeded to form an outer ring. Before this circle was completely closed, the infantry were already approaching the outskirts of the camp.

The general had anticipated that when the machine gun started, it would rouse the camp to a tumult. But since this did not happen, he assumed that it must be a ruse on the part of the muchachos, not with the intention of luring the soldiers into a trap, but in order to discover gaps through which they hoped to escape.

Now the infantry were even closer and must be plainly visible from the camp, while the encircling cavalry must also undoubtedly have been noticed by the rebels. But still the camp remained remarkably quiet, and the general grew uneasy. He stood up and studied the camp carefully through his glasses. As before, he saw here and there a man sink down, hit by bullets from the machine gun, which continued its incessant chatter and which had been ordered only to cease fire when the infantry were right up to the camp.

The adjutant, too, had his glasses up. Suddenly he said, "Sir! Do you see what I see? Or are my eyes deceiving me?"

"What?" asked the general, without lowering his glasses.

"Four men went up to that machine gun in the middle of the camp, and they've vanished. And now the machine gun has vanished, too, as if it had sunk into the earth."

The general swung his glasses to the spot where, five minutes before, he had seen his stolen machine gun. He had to admit that it was no longer there.

He searched the field with his glasses and saw that his men all around were now no more than fifty yards from the inner perimeter of the camp.

Behind them the cavalry had closed their own ring. The riders sat on their horses, rifles resting on the right knee, reins firmly grasped in the left hand, waiting for the vanquished rebels to start running. The infantry, obeying a bugle call and several whistles from their officers, halted for a second. Then they rose up from their crouching position, both hands tensely gripping their rifles with short bayonets mounted, and prepared to advance at the double. They remained in this attitude for about ten seconds. Then came another bugle call, more whistlings from all sides, and the soldiers stormed forward.

Scarcely had they started to run than from the center of the camp a machine gun opened up. It swept calmly and carefully around the whole ring. It was the machine gun that but a short while before had stood in the middle of the rebel camp, so weary and forlorn, and of which all that was visible now were the little thin puffs of smoke that burst from its circling muzzle.

The attacking troops stopped for two seconds. Then they continued their advance, although in not quite such a parade-ground fashion as hitherto. Here and there one stumbled and fell, apparently hit, but perhaps also stumbling intentionally in order to fall out of the front line. Ten seconds later it was clear to the stupidest soldier that their promenade was at an end and that they were faced with the gloomy prospect of ending their happy-go-lucky soldier's life with a mouthful of cold earth. That gives no pleasure to even the boldest soldier, all the less since he will be unable to hear the posthumous panegyrics showered upon him or to enjoy the fruits of them.

Even had they wished otherwise, the soldiers had no alternative but to go on and take the camp. For should they now turn about, they would be fired on all the more fiercely, and the result would be the same. Besides, the attacking troops would not have gotten far even if they escaped injury, for farther out stood the ranks of cavalry that would not have let them through, but would have driven them back again toward the camp.

The advance lost its beautiful precision and turned into a wild scamper in order to reach the camp quicker and thus avoid the machine gun, which was becoming seriously unpleasant and disorganizing all plans.

A respectful pace behind the general stood the staff bugler. The general remembered him and thought for a second of ordering him to give the cavalry the signal, not, as originally planned, to chase the fleeing rebels but to follow up the infantry in order to capture the camp more quickly. However, at the same time it occurred to the general that such an order would probably produce confusion, for he had given the cavalry commander, Captain Ampudia, the most explicit instructions that he was in no event to become involved in the fight, because the mounted troops would be absolutely necessary to ensure that not a man escaped.

The general drew fiercely and without pleasure at his cigarette. He became conscious that all was not as it should be. He felt that his plan was going wrong, if indeed it had not already done so. But he was unable to obtain an inkling as to what in reality was happening.

The advancing infantry were now close to the edge of the camp. And now the general thought he at last understood the rebels' plan. They plainly wanted to get the soldiers into the camp in order to slaughter them. That was the reason they had squatted apparently peacefully around their fires. They, as Indians, felt more certain of victory in a hand-to-hand fight, where they could use their knives and machetes instead of rifles with which they were not familiar. In which case only the cavalry could now turn the tide. He gave the bugler the order to sound the signal for the cavalry to attack. They started and began to gallop forward.

The front ranks of the infantry were now in the camp.

Through his glasses the general saw his men stabbing bravely with their bayonets at the muchachos and hurling them aside. But it was strange that the muchachos did not defend themselves, did not even get up and attempt to run away when the soldiers came storming at them. The muchachos fell over and did not move. Then the general noticed a disturbing confusion among the attackers. As they attempted to withdraw their bayonets from their victims, the bodies flew up in the air. They came to bits. Beneath the tattered rags and crumbling hats, dry straw was visible.

Since, apart from the twenty or twenty-five muchachos who had run about the camp to make the place seem alive and thus complete the deception, there was nobody else to attack, the soldiers, without waiting for any orders, stopped of their own accord and stood bewildered.

Some of the live muchachos had certainly been hit, and those of them who were wounded and unable to move were mercilessly spitted. But the majority of them managed to reach the pit from which the machine gun was still steadily rattling on.

The officers and sergeants whistled for the attack to be resumed and the original orders to be carried out in order to silence the machine gun at all costs. However, the fire from this gun swept so calmly and remorselessly over the ground that the nearer the soldiers drew, the greater were their losses.

Once more whistles rang out. The soldiers flung themselves on the ground so that, by creeping along on their bellies, they might now capture the machine gun with fewer casualties.

Scarcely, however, had the last whistle died away and the line of cavalry reached the outermost edge of the camp, than, from far outside, a rain of bullets began to pour into the camp from all directions. Simultaneously there sounded the sharp rat-a-tat of several other machine guns, similarly firing from far away, outside the ring of attackers.

And now followed a wild, inhuman babel of screams, shouts, and howls. And from the four corners of the landscape, swarming far across the plain, the horde of muchachos swept toward the camp.

The soldiers, who ten minutes before had still believed that they had surrounded all the rebels in their camp, were now, admittedly, in the middle of the camp they had captured.

But they were the ones who were surrounded.

The general turned to his bugler. He intended to order him to sound the retreat for all units and to leave it to the troops themselves to scramble out of the encirclement as best they could. From the vantage point of his hill, he could see several gaps through which the soldiers could succeed in escaping without suffering too heavy losses. But he did not know how and by what means to convey his knowledge to the officers other than by simply sounding a general retreat.

When he turned and saw no bugler, not even his adjutant, he turned to his left, and there stood two ragged muchachos, grinning impudently into his face.

The general reached rapidly for his revolver and found the holster empty. One of the muchachos held up the revolver and said, "Is this perhaps what you're looking for, General?"

The general paled slightly. However, he immediately pulled himself together, stretched out for the revolver, and snatched it back.

"You can have it back again for a few minutes," laughed the muchacho who had held the revolver. "It's not loaded and you can't do any damage with it."

The general felt hastily for his ammunition belt. But the belt, too, was gone; it had been cut through and removed.

That infuriated him and he shouted, "What are you lousy swine doing here? I suppose you belong to the rebels?"

"Yes," answered one with a loud laugh. "We do rather belong to the rebels. I'm only General. And this one here"—he pointed a thumb at his companion—"he's my captain."

The general looked around searchingly in all directions and then shouted in an overloud voice such as he was accustomed to use on the parade ground when something had infuriated him, "Where's my adjutant and my bugler?"

"Departed—with our assistance."

"Departed? Where?"

"We had no time to ask them," replied the captain. It was Santiago.

"Be off with you, you dirty, damned swine. I'll see to it that you're both shot long before we get back to Balun Canan." The general turned purple in the face.

"Of course," said General, grinning, paying not the least attention to the shouting and fury of the general. "You can have us all shot when you get back to Balun Canan. But for the time being, we've got you by the short hairs, and whether you ever get back to Balun Canan depends on who takes you. At the moment there's no one waiting to take you back."

From the moment the general realized he was in the power of the muchachos, he knew there was no hope for him. Even if by some miracle his troops could possibly succeed in reaching him and snatching him away, they would never get him alive. The dictatorship knew no mercy or pity toward those who opposed it. And no one who had ever served El Caudillo in any way or in any position could hope for mercy or pity when the rebels were the victors.

But he would have been ashamed for a thousand years after his death had he displayed any sign of fear in front of these despicable peons. This marked fearlessness did not, indeed, spring from personal courage. His courage had never been put to the test. He who is on the side of power does not need to be brave.

What still gave him a certain courage in this totally hopeless situation was simply the knowledge that nothing could alter his fate, irrespective of whether he showed fear or behaved bravely. It was all the same whether he begged for mercy and promised all his money, or whether he shouted at the victors and enraged them with insults. Even if he had offered his services and experience to the rebels, which in his case would have been highly improbable, they would not have been accepted, and such an offer would have made no difference to his ultimate fate. Therefore, since he saw no hope at all of altering his situation, he could very well afford to behave with dignity toward the rebels into whose hands he had fallen.

He spent a few seconds looking across at the camp, where not only his fate, but also that of his troops, and in many respects that of the whole state had already been decided. The soldiers who could still move had all thrown away their weapons in order to be able to flee the faster. But wherever they went, they faced the knives of the muchachos.

The rebels' machine gun was no longer firing at the retreating infantry, but was now directed at the disorganized cavalry, who had not had time to develop their attack properly. The soldiers belonging to the army machine-gun section abandoned their mules, since they found the laden animals hindered them in their flight. They left it to the beasts to follow them voluntarily. Several of the infantry caught the animals, who were running wildly, cut their loads off them, and jumped onto their backs in order to let slip no possibility of a chance of escaping alive.

"Santiago," called General to his captain, "take our guest, this beautifully uniformed general, over to our new camp. You know where. I want to talk to him. Later. I must get down there again. They're using too much ammunition. No point now. We must save it."

With that he ran down the hill, flung himself onto his horse, which he had left there before paying his respects to the general, and dashed across the battlefield.

In the pit, where the machine gun was now beginning to jam because its barrel was overheated, he found Colonel and his crew.

"I'm glad that thing's stopped of its own accord," he shouted down from his horse. "Let those few run off on their mules in peace. I need them for messengers to bring the news to the base camp. I only wish we had the rest of the brigade here, so that we could clear the way to Balun Canan."

Colonel, who had removed his shirt to give himself greater freedom of movement, now began to search for it. It had been trodden by the bare feet of his crew into the wet mud that had formed in the hole where the machine gun had been emplaced. "Give me your stinking shirt," he shouted to a muchacho who was passing the hole. Without waiting, he tore it over the muchacho's head, snatched up a stick, impaled the shirt on it, and waved it back and forth.

Immediately the clatter of the rifles died away in every quarter. The muchachos who were still chasing the fleeing soldiers sent a few extra shots after them and, when they did not fall, let them continue on their way.

General galloped up to his bugler and ordered him to sound the call to assemble.

About a hundred of the muchachos who now returned to the camp had not a stitch of clothing on their bodies—only a bandolier slung over their naked shoulders. Their knives or machetes were stuck into thongs knotted around their bare waists.

In the camp they searched for their trousers, shirts, hats, and sandals, out of which, on General's instructions, they had made straw-stuffed dummies the night before.

When they had collected their rags and supplemented missing articles of clothing from the dead and wounded soldiers, the battlefield was cleared up. Not one of the wounded or prisoners lived to see the afternoon. They spared the general till evening, since General wanted to speak with him.

The spoils in weapons were so rich that now not only were all the muchachos armed but the women and adolescents were also equipped with revolvers or rifles, and there still remained a surplus.

Professor advised burying all the extra weapons in the bush and leaving them there against the event of their perhaps losing some weapons in their next fight.

"Buried arms are worthless," retorted General to this. "Besides, the *finqueros* might find them, or the *Rurales* or the Federals or anyone else who would like to turn those weapons on us. I have better uses for them. In all the nearby *fincas* we shall visit, and in the towns and villages we shall capture, we'll now be on the lookout for strong, hefty fellows who'll join us, and then the extra guns will be of use."

"Good," said Professor to this. "Well thought out. There is only the question of whether these fellows won't run away from us or betray us and take the weapons with them."

"Don't worry about that, Professor. Once we've got on a bit farther, the lads and men in their thousands will be glad to be allowed to join us. They'll come and beg to be allowed to march with us. And once they've marched, the end of the revolution will come too soon for them, and hundreds will start other rebellions of their own accord. It will be much easier for us to get new soldiers and good soldiers than to get rid of them again when they are no longer needed and we want to live in peace."

"We'll see to it in good time that they'll all be glad to get home again," interrupted Andreu. "They'll march with us and fight with us until they're certain that the land that we've given them or that they've captured will never again be taken from them by the *finqueros*. Then they'll go home of their own accord. Who can they fight against when there's no one left to fight who's worth fighting? That's why I think General's right. Now's the time we need plenty of soldiers, and if they don't come to us voluntarily, we'll fetch them. How we get rid of them later, we can discuss when we control the country. Don't you think that I myself have reasons enough to go home right now? Reasons enough, I can tell you. And most of you would also rather be at home than going on wading about in the mud out here and slaughtering soldiers. But you all know as well as I that if we go home now, when the revolution has just begun, in six months' time or sooner we shall be in the same or even a more wretched state than before, and it may be a very long while before we can get a revolution going for a second time."

"The more we say that to ourselves, Andrucho, the better for all of us." Professor groaned as he said this. He had two wounds in his shoulderblade and Fidel was probing in the wounds with a knife in an attempt to dig out the bullet that had lodged there. The other shot had gone right through. "The better for all of us and for all working people, I repeat. Don't stop too soon, and don't listen to the chatter of those who talk about peace between brothers and crimes against the people. Empty, meaningless words. There'll only be peace between brothers, and war between brothers will only cease, when stability is restored in the country and justice is free and anyone can say what he has on his mind whether it pleases others or not. To break off a revolution too soon is worse than never starting one. And that's why you're right, General. Let's get recruits where we can. If we don't get them, then the others will. I didn't think of that right away when I suggested that they might run off and take their weapons with them."

14

 It was in a semitropical pine wood that the rebels had set up their new camp. The site had already been selected several days before the battle in which the Federals suffered such an unexpected defeat. Women, children, wounded, and sick were moved to this camp as soon as General received news of the approach of the force to which had been allotted the task of disposing of the rebels once and for all. It was General's intention to create a sort of settlement at this spot, instead of the usual field camp. His plan was to make sorties from here, to attack *fincas* and divide their lands among the peons, to do battle with Federal troops and police wherever they were encountered, and if they were not, to lure them by adroit maneuvers and surprise attacks to small villages and *fincas* where he could successfully overpower them and thus steadily reduce their numbers. In a more permanent camp it would be easier for him to train raw recruits, to create an army with which he could advance against the capital of the state in order to occupy the government buildings and thus bring the whole state under the rule of the revolutionaries.

The country in which the camp lay consisted partly of forest, partly of plains, and partly of several acres of bush and scrub that could with little trouble be converted into arable land where corn, beans, and chilies could be grown. In five or six weeks the first harvest could be gathered.

The land belonged to one of the great *fincas* that two weeks previously had been occupied and divided up among the peons.

The camp area offered all that an army of Indians needed in order to live there for years, even for generations. A broad stream of pure water that never failed, even in the dry season, ran the length of the rebel's new encampment.

The place was excellently protected against attack. On three sides it was surrounded by rocky mountain spurs traversed by only four narrow, stony paths that were easy to guard and that twenty men could defend against the advance of half a brigade. The fourth side was bordered by level, swampy ground that at this time of year was totally impassable and during the dry season could be crossed only at a few places where the surface, being somewhat above the general level, dried out when there had been no rain for a long time. But these crossings were so few and so exposed that, like the mountain tracks, they could be so well guarded by a few men that a surprise attack was virtually impossible. However, should such an attack succeed, the whole army could hide effectively in the surrounding clefts, crannies, crevices, and hollows, all thickly overgrown with thorny, tropical bush, and it would have been extremely difficult to force them out, the more so since the rebels knew the terrain, and from their hideouts behind bushes and rocks could keep the attackers under as heavy a fire as if they were sitting in a strong fortress.

It was, of course, only natural that the muchachos, assured of a long stay here, should start to build light huts and shelters like those in the *monterías*.

Only six, at most ten, days would pass before this camp looked just like any other Indian village. Although there was no thought of it at present, it was nevertheless possible that the rebels might settle here permanently. If the revolution were successful in overthrowing the dictator, it might easily follow that a democratic regime following the dictatorship would give the rebels the property on which the settlement was built. A democratic government would be all the more willing to recognize such rights won during the revolution, because thereby the former rebels could best be prevented from turning into common bandits, as they might do if driven by force of necessity. The possibility of such or similar outcome to their rebellion had in fact occurred to Professor, General, Andreu, Colonel, Celso, and many others of the more intelligent muchachos, and to the women with the army; they had all thought about it for weeks and at times discussed it.

This new camp was about fifteen miles distant from the old one, the site of the battle.

The muchachos who were marching back to camp with the captured Federal general did not hasten on their way. The general was too fat and too clumsy to be able to run away from them. Every ten minutes he groaned and moaned and had to sit down to rest. Perhaps he exaggerated his clumsiness and weariness in the hope that a relief battalion might possibly have been sent after him and be close enough to turn defeat into victory and incidentally liberate the general. However, the general knew very well that such a hope was totally unfounded, for he himself had ordered his colonel to initiate no troop movements unless on express instructions from himself.

Another hope was that perhaps a few of his soldiers who had escaped might be wandering around here and, seeing their general in the hands of three muchachos taking him to their camp, would try to rescue him. This hope, too, evaporated the farther they progressed from the battlefield and the nearer they got to the new camp. In fact, his soldiers, themselves hunted and wildly seeking safety in headlong flight, could never have succeeded in rescuing him. For along the whole way—a wretched, swampy path newly hacked out of the bush—he saw groups of rebels either returning to the great main camp or going back to the battlefield, probably to stand guard there or to glean the area for any further weapons and ammunition.

The boundless rage the general had at first felt at being led away prisoner by these filthy Indians had gradually evaporated in the course of this laborious journey. He knew well enough, too, that it would do him no good to vent his anger on the muchachos. Had he refused to walk, they would certainly have beaten him. The very fact that they showed not a spark of respect toward him, a person of authority before whom these fellows would have fallen on their knees a few months before if they had met him, proved to the general more plainly even than the lost battle that the country was on the verge of an upheaval unparalleled since it had shaken off the tyranny of the Spanish crown.

At intervals he attempted to exchange a few words with the muchachos. He did this with the faint hope—the very faintest hope—that he might be able to bribe the fellows and offer them a substantial reward to take him by a roundabout way to his headquarters. But the very first attempt misfired. Either the muchachos did really understand no Spanish or else they understood it well enough and only pretended not to have understood what he was suggesting to them.

When he sat down on the way, to rest and light a cigarette, the muchachos also sat down at some distance from him and talked and laughed together without apparently paying any attention to him. As soon as he made a motion to go on, they, too, rose and marched along behind him.

Anyone meeting this little group would have thought that the general was on a walking tour and that the muchachos were retainers sent to accompany him so that he wouldn't lose his way.

In spite of the general's efforts to prolong the march for as long as possible, always in the fading hope that something might happen to extricate him from his plight, he eventually arrived at the new camp.

His escort, without having been ordered to, had cleverly led him by such devious ways and taken him zigzag across country to the camp that, even if he should happen to escape, he would scarcely have been able to find the camp again. The Indians, always mistrustful of those not of their own community, had acted like this out of pure instinct. They had behaved exactly as they would when bringing anyone else—a trader, for example—to one of their settlements, whether in the bush, in the jungle, or in the sierra, which for good reasons they wished to keep secret from the outer world, particularly from officials and other authorities.

When the general arrived, the whole camp was exclusively engaged in cooking supper. Supper that day had to make up for all the other meals the men had missed during the previous thirty-six hours, since the preparations for the battle had left no time for either men or women to think of eating, far less of cooking. Here and there, and at odd moments, one of them had swallowed a few mouthfuls of cold tortilla or pushed a handful of moldy frijoles into his mouth.

The camp was concentrating on cooking, washing, and similar matters associated with peaceful domestic existence, and they did it with such intentness and concentration that it seemed almost a passion.

There was nothing to suggest that these very men, in the morning of the same day, had fought a bitter battle in which they had suffered thirty dead and about fifty wounded, even though the battle had ended for them in a decisive victory.

Since no one in the camp was occupied with anything that could be regarded as preparations for a new fight, the general knew that no troops were on the way to rescue him. He had learned in the meantime one of the causes of his defeat. The spies of the rebels were ten times better and a hundred times more accurate and reliable than the intelligence service of his own division. He was no longer in any doubt that every peon on a *finca*, every wandering, apparently harmless and ignorant Indian, probably even every Federal soldier of Indian origin was active in the rebel spy service.

No one in the camp was curious enough to look closely at the general when he was brought in. No one bothered about the presence of this man whose curses had made a division of Federal troops tremble. Here in the rebel camp everyone would have laughed at him had this highly placed, deeply respected officer demanded that the lousy Indians show him proper respect and receive him with due humility.

He was led across to a campfire burning in the center, which was the general staff fire.

As he approached, he saw to his great astonishment Lieutenant Bailleres squatting there, eating tortillas and frijoles and drinking coffee with these verminous muchachos.

During the morning's battle, Lieutenant Bailleres had found

himself in the hands of a muchacho who was about to cut his throat when Andreu came by and recognized the lieutenant.

"Wait, boy!" he had called to the fellow. "Better stay with him. Tie him up tightly, and later bring him to the camp. General might make use of him again as his messenger. His weapons are yours, of course."

So, after the battleground had been cleared up, the lieutenant had been brought here as a prisoner. Lieutenant Bailleres and the Federal general were the only soldiers to survive the fight.

In his astonishment, the general did not know what to make of the lieutenant, seeing him squatting so calmly, so apparently calmly, at the fire and eating with the muchachos as though he belonged to them.

His first thought was that the lieutenant might have been responsible for the theft of their weapons on the preceding night and even for this morning's shameful defeat. It was possible that he was in league with the rebels and had intentionally given incorrect information about their strength, equipment, and whereabouts.

This suspicion, however, lasted only a few seconds. In face of the bloody bandages the lieutenant wore over his ears, and the blood-encrusted stump of his nose, such thoughts could not be entertained for a moment.

Looking again at the lieutenant, the general grew once more uncertain. It was possible that the lieutenant had not been abused in this way by the muchchos, but by some enraged ranchero or *finquero* whose daughter he had seduced. It was by no means rare for cuckolded husbands or fathers whose daughters had been basely dishonored to revenge themselves in such ways.

While the three heads, which the lieutenant had brought the general as a present, might really have been chopped off by the rebels, it was possible that the lieutenant had also blamed his own mutilations on the rebels in order not to have to confess that he owed them to an adventure with a woman and that he had not been in the rebel camp at all, but in the hands of a ranchero who had felt it his duty to avenge his honor.

"Welcome, General," said General, as the prisoner was led unceremoniously to the fire. "Sit down on one of the conference chairs you see lying around and make yourself quite at home."

"*Gracias*," said the general mechanically and from habit. But he immediately added harshly, "You'll pay for this bitterly, muchacho. I can tell you that now. You'll be quartered and then nailed up and drenched with paraffin."

"It's a pleasure, General, to know that—to know that today. Of course, those who are going to enjoy themselves with me in this way must first catch me. And that, General, will take quite a while, I think. In the meantime, we ourselves can enjoy that pleasure—and indeed with you, General. Your idea is by no means so bad as it seemed at first sight. What do you say, Lieutenant Bailleres?"

"It's nothing to do with me," said the latter, chewing away.

The general turned to his lieutenant. "*Buenas noches*, Lieutenant Bailleres."

The lieutenant made a brief movement instead of standing up, nodded his head, and replied, "*Muy buenas noches, mi general, gracias!*" Then he quickly bent his head and devoted himself again to his interrupted supper.

The general was plainly uneasy, seated on the low, wide seat the muchachos had proffered him. He shifted back and forth on his fat hams. Whenever he made a movement, it produced a sound as if his whole body were clad in dry, creaking leather. Whether this sound was caused by the new boots he was wearing or the very wide belt and the somewhat narrower shoulder straps, or whether he wore beneath his tunic a laced leather corset that disguised the mighty fullness of his stomach could not be precisely decided at first glance. At any rate, the impression the muchachos received was that the whole man, body, limbs, head, brain, heart, and intestines, was constructed of raw leather, freshly come from the saddler and as yet unseasoned.

On the long, hard march to the camp, he had become sufficiently hungry not to refuse the food that the muchachos now offered him and that was the same as they themselves were eating. He accepted the hot tortillas, the frijoles spiced with green chilies, the dried meat roasted on hot coals, and the boiling coffee, although it all came from the hands of filthy, stinking pigs whom, even in his wildest dreams, he never thought he would have to be so near to. He devoured his food with enjoyment, although he knew that this might very well be his last meal on earth. Nevertheless, he took care to behave so that to outward appearances one might think he was doing the muchachos a great honor by sitting at the same fire with them, exchanging chipped and cracked dishes with them, and now and again asking, half-subduedly, half-condescendingly, "May I have some salt, muchachos? Perhaps you could spare me another two or three tortillas? *Muchas gracias! Gracias!*"

The muchachos who were squatting around the great fire behaved as if there were no one present but themselves. They paid no attention to either the general or the lieutenant. They talked, laughed, smiled, told stories and jokes that were full of spirit; and they went so far that, without any regard for their guests, they discussed how at their next encounter with the Federals and *Rurales*, they would thrash them even more soundly than today, how they would hang all the *finqueros* and pass their wives and daughters from hand to hand, and finally how fiercely they yearned to get to Balun Canan and other big garrison towns in order to attack and occupy them for no other purpose than to straddle the wives, daughters, and concubines of the officers there.

It was quite possible that neither the general nor the lieutenant understood much of what was being said, for the muchachos spoke not in elegant Spanish but in such a smattering of the language as they had learned and were accustomed to using, and that was a corrupt form of Spanish without any grammatical rules, intermingled with words and phrases of three different Indian dialects. In any case, the two officers gave not the slightest indication that they were even listening to what was being said.

Suddenly the general said, half-turning to the lieutenant, "I'm pleased, Lieutenant Bailleres, to find you among the survivors." The faintly ironical tone in which the general spoke did not fail to make its intended impression on the lieutenant.

He bowed slightly and said, "The pleasure is entirely mine, General."

"You don't by any chance think, Lieutenant, that, at this moment of my life which I may still call mine, I could have sold myself to these filthy, colored, stinking swine?"

The lieutenant smiled in a way intended to convey to the general that the smile had only been pasted on the surface, concealing mockery behind. The general understood it well enough. He did not wait for an answer, but added, "I could far more easily expect that of you, Lieutenant, since I find you sitting here at the fire so well looked after by these creatures, and I notice you are even smoking a cigar."

The lieutenant nodded, smiled again, drew deeply on the fat cigar, and blew out the smoke. "This cigar is the last I shall smoke in my life, General. This cigar, although it is uncommonly long and thick, having been rolled by one of the muchachos here, has a different purpose from the cigarette you offered me just now. The last puff from the butt of this cigar signifies for me the trumpet signal for my departure from this world. You will certainly smoke more cigarettes in your life than I cigars."

"What do you mean by that, Lieutenant, the trumpet signal?"

At this moment, General, who had been away for a while, returned to the fire.

"The commander-in-chief who thrashed us will very soon explain the trumpet signal and thus save me the need of giving you an explanation, General," said the lieutenant.

General, although he must have heard these words, said nothing. But Colonel, who came up to the fire at the same time, looked at the lieutenant's cigar and said, "You are a good smoker, Lieutenant. And it occurs to me at this moment that our chief strongly advised you, the last time you visited us, never to allow yourself to be seen in our neighborhood again."

The general swung his head so sharply, first toward Colonel and then toward where the lieutenant was squatting, that it seemed as if he had suddenly been startled out of sleep. It was plain to read from his face that he had received a severe surprise. His fat mouth dropped and hung open for a while, as he stared again, first at Colonel, then at the lieutenant.

The lieutenant took another puff at his cigar, looked at it pensively as though trying to estimate how long it would last, stroked off the ash with his little finger, and then said, "Yes, I remember, muchacho. I was told not to repeat my visit to you. That's right."

"And so that there should be no mistake," continued Colonel, "as regards the identity of the person who was told by us that a return visit would be unwelcome, our chief thought it necessary to give that person a certificate of identity which, unfortunately, entailed the loss of two beautiful ears and the end of his nose."

"That was obviously done with the expectation," replied the lieutenant calmly, "that I might pay my second visit to your camp as a swineherd instead of a peon, and in order to be quite certain that it was I, you made me leave behind my ears and my nose."

"Correct." Colonel drank a gulp of hot coffee he had poured out of a tin can into an earthenware mug. "You weren't invited then, Lieutenant, and you were equally, and even more, uninvited today. Instead, you sent several hundred of your people here so that we might take from them their rifles, ammunition, and their precious lives. But that was not what you intended, of course. And in the event that we had received the thrashing and you had won the fight, what would you have done with us then?"

The lieutenant looked at his general and said, "We would have buried you all up to your necks and then marched our soldiers over your heads. Wasn't that so, General?"

"I never gave such an order, Lieutenant," replied the general, with a choke in his voice.

"That's true, General. On this occasion you never gave such an order. But we've always done that when dealing with rebels, mutineers, and refractory peons. Only highway robbers were treated differently. They were simply shot. But all these swine who gabble about freedom and justice, their heads were stamped to splinters so that nothing should survive of their miserable brains."

The general made a worried face. He said not a word. Just shrugged his shoulders.

"This time, of course," continued the lieutenant in a loud voice so that all around the fire should hear him, "this time, of course, General, you gave us different orders. You said that prisoners were to be dealt with leniently. None was to be killed. As many as possible were to be taken captive and brought to Balun Canan in order to be tried before a proper court, where each could defend himself in his own way and have a chance of convincing his judges that he joined the rebels against the government out of desperation and misery and not with treasonable intent."

The general nodded, as if he wished to confirm these words. However, he did not look at the lieutenant. It seemed that, under the influence of these beautiful lies, he had grown years younger than he had looked during the past two hours.

Celso shouted, "Do you hear that, muchachos? We were only to be taken prisoner, just a little matter of being made prisoners, and nothing else. How lovely this world is, how gentle and tender are the soldiers."

Laughter welled up. Professor called across the group, "Pity we didn't know that sooner, muchachos, then we would have marched toward the Federals, *Rurales*, and *finqueros* with bunches of flowers in our hands and our machetes wreathed with greenery; and instead of our rebel songs and marching choruses, we would have sung 'Praise to our almighty ruler, who reigns so wisely over us!' "

"Hey, General, why didn't you send the happy news to us by your envoy, Lieutenant Bailleres? Only don't imagine we'd have fallen for it. Not us. But it would have made a lovely impression on all who like to scratch their hair without disturbing the lice. We can invent our own beautiful speeches about peace and humanity. We don't need generals for that."

"It was well spoken, Lieutenant Bailleres," said General, now joining in. "But fine speeches won't help you now. It's too late for that. How far have you gotten with your cigar?

It'll last another ten minutes. You had been warned not to show yourself among us again. Is that true or not?"

"Don't address me so familiarly, you impertinent son of a whore."

General grinned at the insult. "You shouldn't get so excited about familiarity. *We've* always been addressed familiarly. And as far as you are concerned, Lieutenant Bailleres, in an hour's time even the worms will be familiar with you, and the sad thing about that is that you won't even be able to resent it."

He looked around, beckoned to a muchacho. "Bring me three Salvajes, Pablo."

The fellow ran off to fetch the men.

When the three natives whom he had sent for approached, General turned again to Lieutenant Bailleres. "I cannot let you go a second time, Lieutenant. It might cost us another thirty or even more of our muchachos. You had your chance from me, and you made ill use of it."

The lieutenant grew scarlet with rage. The crusted stump of his nose began to crack as he now opened wide his mouth to inject into his words all the contempt of which he was capable. In any other place and circumstances he would have looked clownish, with the bandages wound tightly over his head and under his chin. The bandages had become dirty, and wet filth had mingled with the blood that had soaked through the dressings and was now dried. On his head he had squeezed a service cap that, because of the bandages, looked far too small for him. His face was unshaven and also spattered with mud, some of which had dropped off, leaving grayish-white patches. But no one took any notice of the fact that, with his stump nose and his bandages, he looked like a sad Auguste from some seedy circus.

He bared his teeth wide and hideously. Then he burst out with a short laugh. And simultaneously with the laugh he yelled, "You abominable swine of a traitor and deserter, son of a pimp and a mangy bitch, you, you gave me a chance of which I made ill use? And I did because from you, you stinking swine of a rebel, I wouldn't accept anything, not even a chance to save my life, and that's why I made such use of my release as pleased me and not you, you dirty, lousy dog of an Indian."

"Traitor and deserter? I? Very well spoken, Lieutenant Bailleres. It is, so everyone says, the highest honor to serve in the army. It was an honor for me, too, when I joined it. But which of you, the officers, allowed me and my comrades to have any honor? I was beaten and kicked as a recruit, and even later, when I became corporal. And not only beaten, but spat at in the face. And not only that. When one of you officers felt in a bad mood or was blind drunk, then he made us crawl over the parade ground on our bellies or our knees, or clean out the latrines with a toothbrush, or the senior men were incited to attack the recruits on their mats at night and beat them mercilessly, and the next morning the victims had to pretend that they had fallen out of a window or down from the roof, where they had no reason to be. I tell you, Lieutenant Bailleres, the deserter who ran away from this hell, where every trace of honor was thrashed, tortured, and tongue-lashed out of him, and who deserted this army, had ten times more honor in his body than those whose backsides were bursting with abject fear and who carried on obediently without revolting. Such a deserter had a thousand times more honor than the officers and N.C.O.'s who strutted and reveled in their authority. I, a traitor? The real and mighty traitors are those who beat every feeling of honor out of their soldiers and so degraded them that at last they no longer knew what army they were serving in or to which country they should show their allegiance. Traitors are the ones who have so long bludgeoned the people, so long humiliated them, so long robbed them of their honest rights, that the people could finally bear it no longer and preferred to unleash a civil war rather than to suffer such indignity any longer. Those are the traitors, the true, actual, and only traitors, who create and cause rebellions and revolutions by their thirst for power, their greedy ambitions, their swindlings, betrayals, and murders. Perhaps in ten years' time, perhaps in fifty years, it will be said that we, the lousy, filthy Indian swine, rebels, mutineers, bandits, plunder-ers—and whatever else you call us—were the real saviors of this country. You don't understand that, Lieutenant Bailleres. And that's why you came here a second time although I warned you."

"What right have you crawling lice to warn me?" shouted the lieutenant angrily and threw the remains of his cigar into the fire. "You have no right to warn. I come and go as I please. Let me tell you that."

"I knew it already. That's why we marked you, so that you couldn't come back again to our camp, spying around dressed up in women's skirts or some such. You didn't come here today to serve your general or your government: I know that, too. You came this time to catch me, to catch me alive and to take revenge on me for your missing ears and your worm-eaten nose."

"Right, you swine," yelled the lieutenant, working himself up more and more into a frenzy. "I wanted to catch you alive. And my failure to do that will be the only pain I shall feel when I pay for my burned-out cigar. So that you may know what I would have done with you had I caught you, I'll tell you before it's too late and my mouth's stopped up. I would have had you stretched out full length on the ground and then I would have had a wooden stake driven through your stom-ach, slowly, inch by inch, and so nailed you firmly to the earth because you shout so long and so ardently about land and liberty. I would have had you pumped full of earth until you burst, and then you would have had the liberty to rot slowly."

"I already had an idea, Lieutenant, that that was almost pre-cisely what you would do," replied General, with a gurgling laugh. "And because I knew that, I didn't send for some of my ordinary muchachos; instead, I've got these Salvajes for our evening's amusement. These Salvajes are familiar with such lit-tle entertainments because they were once the performers. We've now nothing more to say to each other, Lieutenant."

"Certainly not, you mongrel."

General called to the Salvajes: "Have you understood the

sort of stroll to Hell this caballero has chosen for himself?"

"*Seguro*," answered the three muchachos simultaneously. "Of course, General, we heard every word. *Tierra y Libertad! Salud*, General!"

"*Tierra y Libertad*, muchachos," answered General.

One of the three men walked up to the lieutenant, jabbed him on the ribs with the handle of his machete, and told him, "Come on, my friend. I'm going to sing you a lullaby out there, outside the camp."

The lieutenant jumped up as if unwilling to be driven by these people. He turned to the general, who during the long conversation had remained squatting on his tree stump without contributing a word.

"Have you by any chance a decent drink in your hip flask, *mi general?*" asked the lieutenant.

The general drew out an elegant crystal flask, slim and slightly curved so that it could be carried comfortably in the pocket. It held about half a pint, and it was still full.

"Drink half of it, Lieutenant," said the general, as he handed him the flask. "Leave the rest for me. Probably I shall need a drink later, just as much as you do now."

The lieutenant held a finger against the flask so that he could measure the amount correctly. Then he took a long pull, lowered the flask, looked at his finger, and when he saw that another drink was due to him for his fair share, he took a second, smaller swallow.

"There, General, I think I've divided it fairly." He laughed with one side of his mouth as he handed the flask back.

The general screwed the cap on pensively. Then he looked up straight into General's face. "But, muchacho, you wouldn't really do anything so cruel with my lieutenant?"

"At first, admittedly, that wasn't my intention, General. But you heard, just as I and all of us here heard, what your lieutenant proposed to do with me had I fallen into his hands."

"That was only a soldier's joke," the general assured him.

"Then perhaps it was only a soldier's joke, too, when a number of our comrades fell into the hands of the *Rurales* a few weeks ago at the Santa Cecilia *finca*, and they were then buried up to their necks and galloped over until all their heads had been stamped into the ground. Excellent soldier's jokes, General."

The general shrugged his shoulders. "Brutalities happen in wartime. And we are at war with one another. But such cruelties are exceptional. I have never ordered such acts, and had I been at the *finca*, I would not have permitted such abuses."

"Lieutenant," said General, "have you any comment to make on the soldiers' jokes that your general has been telling us about?"

"Not to you, you son of a bitch," said the lieutenant and contorted his face into a hideous mask.

"I will now tell you something, Lieutenant. You're a brave fellow. That's what you certainly think. I'll make you a proposition. You needn't think I'm afraid of such a miserable specimen of a despicable spy as you are."

General drew a knife from a sheath on his belt. As he did this, he turned to the muchachos who stood around and said, "Give this spy and son of a stinking coyote a knife of the same length as mine."

One of the men drew a knife and looked at General as if he didn't know whether he had rightly understood or not.

"Give it to him." General made a gesture with his head.

The lieutenant took the knife uncertainly.

"Just so you don't think I have to attack defenseless men. Neither I, nor any of us here who have some say and authority. Come on, take your knife. I'll take mine, and whichever of us wins will do to the other what you intended to do to me had I fallen into your hands."

"Are you mad, General?" shouted one of the muchachos.

"Why mad, Sebio? I'm in a good humor. We mustn't let these mangy officers think that we're afraid of them in equal fight. In the barracks they open their mouths wide and behave as if they could swallow any one of us as soon as look at us, and kick anyone in the guts when he passes by. That's us, the soldiers, the defenseless ones, and if any of us gave one of *them* a crack on the jaw such as he deserved twenty times a day, he'd get shot."

General turned to the lieutenant and smiled at him. "Come, come, my little lamb—you, a dog of a lieutenant, and me a sergeant deserter. You have a knife like mine; and there's no one here who'll shoot me if I slap your chops. If you like, I'll do without my knife. I don't even need it against a wet rag of an officer like you." He hurled his knife behind him in a wide arc. "You can keep *your* knife." General grinned again. "You may use a knife, I'll use only my two fists, nothing else, and if you win you can depart unhindered, back to your snot-nosed horde and dragging me behind you on a lasso."

The lieutenant looked around him.

A huge crowd of muchachos had collected in the last few seconds to see the duel. For a brief moment he was quite prepared to accept the proffered challenge. But when General threw away his knife and made ready to fight him, who was graciously permitted to keep his knife, with bare hands and with the presumable intention of twisting his neck with those dirty, knotty hands, like an old hen for the pot, the lieutenant felt so insulted in the face of that crowd of grinning, laughing, and jeering muchachos that he had to refuse the fight. Only by refusing to deal with General on such unequal terms could he save the remnants of his honor and take them with him to the other side. For even if he should win, he could never have borne the indignity of having entered into an unequal hand-to-hand fight with a ragged, lousy, half-Indian rebel in order to save his own skin. All who heard of it would have attributed it to cowardice unworthy of an officer. No deeper humiliation could have been inflicted on him than that given by General in the simple gesture of flinging away his own knife and allowing him his. He could have scratched his face for fury at not having thrown away his own knife first and at having allowed General to anticipate him in this gesture. Without a knife, of course, he could never have won against the sturdy, work-hardened proletarian, not even if it came to bare fists. But his comrades would have spoken of a hero's death.

So nothing remained for him but to reply in a manner that he conceived to be alone worthy of an officer.

He took a step forward. Filled with rage, he stared at General for a moment, baring his teeth as if desirous of devouring him, then he lifted up his arm and with a violent movement flung his knife to the ground so that it dug in up to the haft. Then he spat, hawking up thickly from his throat and landing the gob on the ground immediately in front of his opponent's feet, and he screamed as he pointed at the spittle, "There, you filthy, stinking dog of the lousy litter of an Indian bitch, you lick that up! You don't seriously believe that an officer would fight with a dung-heap maggot like you! I'd give a creature like you half-a-dozen slaps, but I wouldn't fight with you, you dirty swine."

As he bellowed, the lieutenant grew purple in the face. Blood trickled out of the scabs on his wounds. But the impression that he had expected to make, revealing himself as a hero to his general and the surrounding crowd of muchachos, failed completely. He had hoped that, in the face of this torrent of insults, General would fall into an indescribable fury and strike him down, thus quickly ending this tragi-comedy.

But instead of the anticipated outburst of wrath, there ensued only a mocking laugh from all sides. General roared indeed, but not with anger, only with amusement. Such explosions he had already experienced only too often from officers, when he was a soldier and sergeant, for them to make the slightest impression upon him. In the present situation the lieutenant's insults could only seem ridiculous to those present, for to all who stood around and rightly appreciated the position, the bawling of the lieutenant, who was powerless in the circumstances, was nothing else than the panting, yapping, and gnashing of a helpless coyote who has been caught fast in a trap and now sees the hunter standing before him with a laughing face. And since these jungle workers were only too familiar with the panting, yapping, and gnashing of captured wild animals, the lieutenant's behavior seemed only uncommonly ridiculous because he reminded them of a trapped coyote.

The lieutenant, of course, could not know why his abuse and his behavior, which had been calculated to create an heroic impression, so utterly failed and merely evoked laughter that made him for a second feel like a comedian.

When the effect for which he had hoped and which was to sweeten his departure from the world not only was not achieved but manifested itself in a form he had never expected, not even believed possible, he was overcome for the first time since his capture by an immensely sad feeling of helplessness and loneliness. He looked at his commanding general with wide, bewildered eyes that begged for help. He hoped that in him he might at least find some understanding of what was happening here. He would have been glad had the general come over to him and embraced him in a friendly manner. But the general was just as helpless in the face of this situation as his lieutenant, for he, too, had expected an outburst of rage from General and his muchachos, and he was perhaps even more astonished at the unexpected result than the man who now sought moral support from him.

Although this situation lasted scarcely thirty seconds, it seemed to the lieutenant an eternity. His sadness deepened with every ensuing second, as he looked at the laughing and grinning faces of the muchachos. If he had been ten years younger, he would have cried for his mother, so desolate and helpless did he feel. For a few moments he forgot his surroundings and recalled, with the speed, clarity, and briefness of a flash of lightning, an episode in his life he thought to be the saddest he had ever experienced.

Before he had entered the military academy as a cadet, he knew a girl who at that time was barely thirteen years old. They were deeply in love with each other, and they plighted themselves to marry as soon as he became a lieutenant. They wrote to each other twice every week, and when he was on leave they spent every afternoon together. She was his goddess and his saint. They had sworn to be faithful even beyond the grave. However, when he was in the middle of his last year at the academy, he received a letter from her in which she begged his forgiveness: she had been married six weeks before. His first thought was to end his life with a lump of lead in his skull. But he only retired to his room. And when he thought it all over, what the girl had been to him and how she had sworn eternal faith to him a hundred times, even on one occasion in church, kneeling before the picture of a saint, he felt so desolate, so helpless, that he cried for hours on end. Later he told his comrades, who teased him about his swollen face, that he had had the foulest toothache any cadet could have.

This episode, which quite unexpectedly leaped to his memory, now obsessed his mind. That same sadness swept over him, the same feeling of desolation that had come when he had received the letter, and he felt the tears welling up inside him.

He would actually have begun to cry had he had ten seconds more to dwell upon that episode and shut out the world around him. But he was prevented from this by an exclamation.

"*Caray!*" shouted General, energetically propping his fists on his hips. "Look at him! I always knew that I had a miserable coward to deal with, and him wearing a uniform. At first he was afraid because I had a knife and he none; then he was afraid because I gave him a knife and threw mine away. And now he's afraid of being staked to the ground, as he was proposing to do with me. He's even scared of that, the worm. And that's why this uniformed crab spat at me and bleated so that I should work myself into a rage and carve him up quickly and spare him from being staked to the ground. That's your lieutenant! An officer in the glorious army! A coward, nothing else; and now I'm ashamed of having wanted to fight here with such a coward. An old lame woman in our army has more courage in one loose tooth than such a wet rag of an officer. But, by God, I'd rather eat dog flesh for supper tonight than run my decent knife into his miserable body."

A mocking burst of laughter from the muchachos followed.

The lieutenant had listened to this speech with a terror that deepened with every word. He shook his head as if he feared his brain were becoming confused. Half-aloud he said, "*O Dios mío*, how can you permit a man to be so deeply humiliated?"

Then he opened his mouth wide, to yell in answer to General's mocking speech that it was a misunderstanding; that he hadn't spat at General's feet to make him shoot him in fury, but that it was just the opposite—it was from fearlessness and bravery that he had insulted General so grossly.

But even before he said this, he realized that he would only make himself still more ridiculous were he to speak of a mis-understanding. It would appear idiotic if he asserted that he had spat at General to display his courage.

When General had finally ended his speech, the lieutenant was so pale and shrunken that it seemed as if the very words had already killed him. Again he looked at his general. This time not in search of moral support, but merely to see how he had taken this humiliating speech.

The general did not look at him, but stared, so the lieutenant thought, intentionally away. Then he knew that the speech had persuaded even the general that it was not bravery but fear that had made him attempt to arouse General's anger in order to gain himself a quick and painless end.

And now, at last, the lieutenant could no longer hold back his tears. He began to sob, pulled out a handkerchief and buried his face in it.

General had turned around and stepped back a few paces nearer the fire. He stood there, beckoned one of the Salvajes to him and said, "Just hang the worm, quickly and simply, and hurry with it."

The lieutenant hastily dried his eyes, went up to the general, and said, "*Mi general*, please believe me seriously when I tell you that I only shouted at that swine because I wanted to—" He said no more. He turned half around. To himself he said, What's the use? *I* know it, and that will comfort me to all eternity. Whether others know it, too, and whether I would even be capable of making it clear to anyone, will be absolutely unimportant in five minutes' time.

He drew himself up, stepped close to his commanding officer, looked him straight in the face, and said in clipped military tones, "Excuse me, sir, I wish to take indefinite leave. With your permission."

Thereupon he saluted: "*Mi general, a sus órdenes! Adiós, mi general!*"

The general held out his hand to him, drew him close, embraced him, let him go again, saluted likewise, and said, "*Adiós*, muchacho! *Adiós*, Lieutenant Bailleres. We will meet again in a few hours. *Hasta la vista!*"

A faint smile crinkled the lieutenant's lips, but he saluted once more.

Then he turned quickly around. Without hesitating or waiting for a command, he walked rapidly ahead of the men who were to lead him away, one of whom slipped a muddy lasso noose over his head.

A few moments later there was heard a shout from one of the men: "No, Lieutenant, not there. Here—more this way! Here, here! Your feet are touching the ground!"

15

 The general squatted and seemed to have lost all interest in his surroundings. Automatically he drew a cigarette from his heavy gold case and lit it with a glowing ember.

Gradually the other muchachos belonging to the staff also crouched by the fire again, while the remainder withdrew to their own groups.

Then a fellow called Agapito came up, stood there, and looked first at the general and then at General, as if sizing up the two for a boxing match.

Finally he said, "General, you know you could wear that uniform. Then you'd look very smart, and everyone would know right away that you were our general. I think the uniform would suit you well. You're both about the same height. Only you're as thin as a pole and the great army leader whom we have here is fattened up like an old sow." Suddenly breaking off his quiet, humorous banter and changing his tone, he shouted at the general, "Up, quick, jump to it, my little fellow, and take off all your rags so that we can try them on here."

The general plucked up his courage and looked around at the speaker. He squirmed hesitantly and plainly did not know what to do, whether to obey this ragged Indian lout or not. Uncertainly he looked up at General and Professor, whom he recognized as the only authorities here, or at least was compelled to recognize them because he was left no other choice. But General, Professor, Celso, and the others were not to be disturbed in their conversation. They behaved as if none of them had heard what Agapito had said.

When the general made no movement to remove his tunic and was plainly waiting for General to say something, Agapito gave him such a hefty jab in the ribs with his naked foot that the general toppled over. "Didn't you hear what I said to you?" shouted Agapito. "Off with your rags, and be quick about it!"

The general now drew himself up, furious. "You swinish Indian, are you trying to give orders to a general? I'll have your hide off you for your impertinence."

"Don't talk hot air," answered Agapito, without being in the least deterred by the general's outburst of rage. With his powerful arms he wrenched the general into a standing position, beckoned closer some of the muchachos standing around, and a quarter of a minute later the general stood before the muchachos in a pair of extremely soiled green underpants, which reached down to his knees.

Now the muchachos who were chatting with General seemed to notice the incident. General looked at the pile of clothing. He went up to it, picked up each article, and appraised it as if wondering whether an old-clothes man would buy it.

"Will these tatters," he said at last, with a wealth of contempt, "these tatters with some shiny buttons and a gold eagle on the shoulders make a general?"

The muchachos laughed loudly and looked at the general, who, faced with so many scornful faces, had shrunk again into himself after having tried for a few seconds to behave with outraged dignity. He was shivering. He crept nearer to the fire and shriveled. It was not only the cool of a rainy evening which made him shiver so. It was much more the uncertainty of his fate that robbed him of his poise, and, more even than this, the discomfort inflicted on him by these fellows, that he, a prisoner, had to endure. He would ten times rather have stood up proudly and worthily, wearing his uniform and be shot, than, clad in only a pair of underpants that were also extremely dirty, be laughed at by these muchachos.

"Well, what are you now?" Professor asked him. "Squatting there, not even El Caudillo would take you for a general. And if you were to march up to your division in your present state, no one would even shout, 'Attention!' You'd have to come a bit closer for someone to recognize you, and then perhaps he'd say, 'Oh, *Dios mío*, there's our general. What on earth does he look like?' Without your uniform you look pitiful, General. That I must tell you. With you it's only the uniform that makes you a general, because if you were a real general, you wouldn't be standing here naked before us in all your insignificance. Instead, we'd be your prisoners and you'd have us all buried alive."

Arcadio nodded approvingly and said, "What Professor says is right. Here, look at our General, the one beloning to us. He hasn't got on a fine uniform like you; he hasn't got any uniform at all. The leather gaiters he's wearing are both right-legged because the left ones are either being worn by someone else, or they're still on the legs of two of your officers who aren't on their legs any more."

"No, Arcadio," General interrupted him, "that's not true. The two left ones were so ragged that I couldn't use them. That's why I have only the right ones."

"Of course you don't regard our general as a real one, do you?" asked Celso. "And you think he can't be a real general because he doesn't wear a beautiful uniform like you. But we don't need any uniforms. We don't need any flags or other muck, as you do to give you courage. We've got enough courage without drums and trumpets, and we always know our stations and where our battalion is. We don't even need stripes on our sleeves, or stars or eagles on our shoulders, to kill the Federals and *Rurales*. We know what we want. Every one of us knows what he wants. Your uniformed soldiers are like sheep running here and there when the shepherd pelts them with dung or when the dogs are at their heels."

"Well said," Professor intervened again. "Very well said, *manito*. That's the reason we shall win the revolution, even if the revolution lasts five or ten years, for we all know what we want, and your sheep don't know that, because you don't allow them to want anything or even to think for themselves. If you're shivering, General, just come nearer the fire. We won't eat you. At least not yet."

General bent down, picked up the general's tunic, held it on high, and called out, "Hey, muchachos, which of you wants a good jacket?"

A muchacho wearing an indescribably tattered and torn shirt and trousers full of holes cried, "I can use that jacket. It's goddamned cold at night when I'm on watch."

General flung it to him. The fellow picked up the tunic and immediately put it on. He buttoned it up and found it too large. "Doesn't matter." He laughed. "The next hacienda we take will produce enough food for me to eat myself so full that even this old goat's coat will fit me."

"Leave those eagles perching on the shoulders," shouted Celso to the muchacho. "None of us'll take you for a general!"

Professor laughed. "Yes, Esteban. Let the eagles squat there. They look pretty. When you get to Jovel one day and walk past the barracks, the guard will present arms. Then you can go into the barracks and have the whole regiment marching where you want, and then you'll bring them here with all their guns and ammunition. Not a soldier will look you in the face, so you needn't be afraid. They'll only look at your shoulder badges. When they see three stars there, or even an eagle, they'll lose all their senses and turn into machines. You have only to shout at the machine, and it'll rush off—into the middle of a lake if you let it get that far. Any fool can make the machine move if he sticks a few stars or an eagle on his shoulders. You obviously don't believe it, but it's true."

"And who'll have the trousers? They've got a leather seat," continued General, holding the trousers aloft for someone to claim.

"Give them to me," answered Cecilio. With one jerk he tugged off the rags he wore for trousers and pulled on the general's elegant pair. When he stood up and stroked the trousers to see how they fitted him, he said, "There's a piece missing. Where is it?"

The muchachos laughed. One shouted, "They're only long enough for a son of a whore like the general to wear. They're like that, so these gentlemen can unbutton them at the bottom."

And another said, "It's very necessary, you know, Cecilio, for these officers to be able to unbutton their trousers at the bottom. They always have to when they're sent against us rebels and we have rifles and machine guns. It's only when we've got nothing in our hands but machetes or clubs that they have the courage of a ravening lion."

The general did not know what to do. Everything, the jests, the mockery, were at his expense. So unworthy, so discredited was all his haughty dignity, so unimportant did he now seem to himself, that he was no longer able even to pity himself. Had he had his revolver handy he would have made a quick end to himself. When he thought of this, another idea occurred to him: that he wouldn't have shot himself, but would have fired at the muchachos up to the last bullet and taken good care that General received the first well-aimed shot. As his thoughts wandered, there suddenly occurred to him the idea of another way of escape, which he might perhaps attempt with success: simply to jump up and run away. Perhaps luck might have it that one of the muchachos would shoot after him and kill him, thus ending once and for all the humiliations and insults he had suffered and probably would have yet to suffer.

He raised himself to his knees and propped both hands on the ground to give himself a good start. But then he noticed that he was wearing only underpants and had no boots on, just stockings full of holes. In stockinged feet he could run over the rough ground only with the greatest difficulty, and he would have to hold up his pants with one hand to stop them from slipping down around his ankles. When he visualized this, he knew that in the attire he was wearing and under the circumstances in which he would have to run, he would make himself so indescribably ridiculous that, in contrast to it, his present humiliations seemed even tolerable, the more so since he hadn't called down this disgrace on himself, nor could he prevent it, whereas by running away he would simply be shaming and demeaning himself. So he remained sitting and waiting for his sentence of death, which, he knew, would be passed this very hour.

The muchachos who had taken the lieutenant away now returned and reported: "General, he is hanging."

"Good," replied General, "when he has hung there long enough, go and bring the lasso back to me. We need it now for our friend, the divisional general. We can't afford to use a new rope for every officer, and we haven't got the time to stone him to death. What do you think, General?"

"You might leave me the last slight shred of my honor by shooting me. You wouldn't need to waste more than one bullet on me." The general attempted to screw up a smile, but it slipped and remained wedged in a fold that ran from the left corner of his mouth to the farthest end of his lower jaw.

The muchacho who had received the general's trousers threw his own tattered pair over to the general's feet.

"I presume I may put these on?" asked the general.

"Of course," said Celso. "We're far too respectable. We don't allow anyone, not even a general, to run about forever in his dirty underpants. What would our women think? You might think we were still an immoral horde of wild Indians."

He turned and called across to a group, "Which of you has an old shirt to spare for our guest? You've got enough new shirts today brought by the soldiers out of pure love for us and for which we are duly grateful. Here, give me a shirt, even if it's only a rag. We gladly give the naked and the poor whatever we can spare."

A ragged yellow cotton shirt that stank of sweat flew over from somewhere. Celso picked it up. "There, now you've got a nice little shirt, General," said Celso, throwing the rags to him. "You mustn't think that we don't know how to treat guests who visit us, even if they are uninvited guests.

Then he shouted out again, "Has anyone a pair of old sandals he can't use any more? Give them here!"

An old pair came sailing through the air. They fell in front of the general, who was striving to pull the tattered shirt over his fat torso.

A muchacho pushed the sandals closer to the general with his foot. "Here are your riding boots, General, so you won't get any thorns in your dainty feet," he said, giving his voice a fawning whine. Then he immediately changed the tone and said roughly and half-shouting, "Nobody ever cared about us, whether we stepped on thorns or kicked against poisonous scorpions or tore our feet on sharp stones till they bled. But we're not so shameless as you think, General. We're very respectable people. We know what it is to have three-inch thorns run into one's foot till the points come out through the top."

"Now we might take a look at the camp and see what the muchachos are doing and what they have brewing in their pots for supper," said General, as he stood up.

All the muchachos belonging to the staff followed him.

When they had gone a little way, General turned around and called back, "Hey, General, you're coming with us, of course. Come on, come on, or we'll have to help you to your feet."

The general came, reluctantly enough at having to obey an order from these lousy swine, but he came nevertheless because, if he had not complied, he would certainly have been beaten. And he wished to avoid that.

The group wandered through the camp.

"We have a really fine camp here," said General casually.

"That's true," agreed the general. "This camp, skillfully defended and with a few trenches thrown out toward the plain, would not be easy to capture for a force that did not know the terrain and the disposition of the defenders. I could hold the camp with two battalions against a whole division—for months I should say."

"I'm glad to hear you confirm that, General." General nodded, obviously satisfied. "I picked out this site myself and chose it for our camp because we need to rest for a long time. Our strength has been reduced and we must also economize on ammunition. We're not so well off as all that. I can safely tell you this because you won't be able to make any use of it. For in about an hour's time, we shall finally have to push you over into eternity, sorry as we shall be to lose such a delightful guest as you, and so suddenly, too."

They went farther, in this direction and that. General pointed out to the general a machine-gun nest and let him see that ammunition was in fact not so plentiful—apparently, for the main dump of ammunition and extra weapons was well concealed.

"Have you any artillery in Balun Canan?" asked General, without look at his companion.

"Six guns. Light ones. Seventy-fives. And I may tell you that if we'd had only three of them here today, there wouldn't have been a trace of you left."

"Perhaps. Who knows? It's possible. I hope in any case that when your brigadier or your colonel comes next time to whip our tails, he won't bring just three but all six guns with him. Otherwise I shall take it very badly. You can write to him if you like. I'll give you a piece of paper. We could well do with those guns. And a few gunners as well, who could show us how to handle the things. I'm sure they must be guns that can be dismantled and loaded onto mules."

"They certainly can," replied the general. "But don't worry your head about whether they can be transported or not, muchacho. If I weren't such a sorry prisoner here, I'd give you my word that you'd see those guns all right. But only the muzzles, naturally."

"Naturally." General laughed. "It's a pity we can't change all that any more. You've seen too much here. You know the camp too well. Of course, I could lay it all out again. Or I could advance on you from a different direction. Really, when I think of it, General, I could almost be misled into letting you go free. No, no. Don't persuade me. It's a fact that I'd like to make a present of you to the glorious army of El Caudillo. A

sort of return gift, you know, for all the beautiful rifles, revolvers, and machine guns that you gave me in such a friendly
way. I'm thinking really seriously of letting you escape, just as
you are. If only so that the next time you could bring all your
artillery with you and finally have things out with us. Between
ourselves, General, we're sick of it. Really sick of it. Sick of
the whole thing. The muchachos all want to go home. I, too,
want to be at home. So, if you'd bring the guns with you, it
wouldn't last long and we'd have a good reason for all running
away. Ammunition's short, as you've seen, too short for us to
be able to hold out long."

The general nodded several times. But it was plain that he
was only half-listening. In his thoughts he was working out a
plan. The plan, however, was muddled, for he had two plans
and he kept confusing one with the other. At one moment he
was thinking whether it wouldn't be still possible somehow or
other to escape. At the next, the soldier in him gave him no
peace. He contemplated plans of attack and surprise tactics for
overpowering the camp, provided he was ever given an opportunity of reaching his headquarters.

Finally, his wildly wandering thoughts were interrupted
brutally by General's suddenly saying, "Muchachos, bring him
back to the staff fire."

General had summoned the three muchachos who had
hanged the lieutenant.

They came to the great fire.

General took them aside and spoke to them for a considerable time. From the muchacho's gestures it was apparent that
General was assuring himself, by questions and answers, that
they had understood everything correctly.

They departed at last and after an interval returned to the
staff fire. One of them was carrying over his left shoulder a
lasso that was stiff with dried mud.

They stood there awhile, waiting for further orders.

When General saw them, he turned to his guest of honor
and said, "I see to my great regret, General, that you are now
of a mind to leave us and to follow your lieutenant, who is al-

ready far ahead of you. In many respects it's a pity that we
can't bother ourselves with you any longer. You see, little
man, in the long run playing about becomes boring. When we
surprised you on that little hill from which you were directing
the great battle, we should have spitted you right away with a
machete. But, you see, it happens so seldom that a real live
general visits us. And the way we are now, we're very anxious
to familiarize ourselves with aristocratic manners, and that we
can learn only from our aristocratic visitors. One fine day one
of us might perhaps become governor, and when the British
ambassador calls on him, he couldn't very well say, '*Ay, que
chingue tu madre, cabrón!*' Don't you agree, General?"

He swung around and shouted, "Hey, who's got our guest's
hip flask? You? Give it back to the gentleman."

The muchacho passed it to the general.

General laughed. "Say 'Thank you.' You'll need every
mouthful from that flask during the next half hour."

"For that I can truthfully say, '*Gracias.*' *Gracias.*"

"*No hay porque.* Don't mention it."

The general took a deep draught and slipped the flask into a
pocket of the ragged cotton trousers he was now wearing. The
trousers were so tight on him that they had already begun to
burst around his legs. At his stomach they gaped several inches
wide and they were held together only with the help of the
string, which the general had tightly knotted.

"Have you got cigarettes for your journey, General? Our
guests must never be allowed to say of us that we let them go
out into the barren wilderness without some little gifts of
friendship. Of course, what we smoke might not suit your pal-
ate."

He turned around again and shouted, "Hey, muchachos,
who's got our good general's gold cigarette case?"

The muchachos looked at one another. Then one called out,
"Here it is, General. Here in the pocket of the coat I'm wearing. I've only just felt what it is. And here's his beautiful
lighter. *Dios*, it's really beautiful. I can't get a spark out of it."

General opened the case, counted the cigarettes, and said,
holding it out to the general, "There's enough there for you,

General, for the next hour. After that, your lungs will be too constricted to need any more."

"*Gracias*," said the general again, taking the case.

General nodded now and grinned. "And that's all now, General. Many thanks for the visit. *Adiós, adiosito*. It was a pleasure to have made your acquaintance. *Adiós. Vaya bien!*"

The three muchachos who were to accompany him came up to the general.

The general walked a few steps ahead. Then he stopped, turned about, and yelled, "But you're still a lousy, filthy dog born on a muck heap by a stinking Indian bitch. I just wanted you to know exactly what I think of you before I'm turned off."

"And that's what he calls aristocratic courtesy," shouted General after him with a cheerful laugh. "We've fed him, we've clothed him, we've taken him for a stroll to help his digestion, we've presented him with a lovely crystal flask of the finest brandy, we've handed him a heavy gold cigarette case filled with imported cigarettes to help him on his way, and now he screams these filthy words at us in farewell. That's the politeness of generals. Not even a thank you for the tortillas and frijoles we gave him to save him from dying dreadfully of starvation. But that's how it is in the world, and we must be satisfied with it as we find it."

All this General bawled out in a fit of laughter. Now his voice changed, and he shouted after the fellows who were leading the general away, "Give the old wind bag five minutes to pray and settle his account. Take him far enough away so that he doesn't infect our camp. Tomorrow we'll know who stinks more, a dead general or an Indian rebel. Take him well away, at least six miles. Do you understand, muchachos?"

"*Seguro*, General, certainly," the muchachos called back and jabbed the general in the ribs to make him move faster.

When the muchachos and the general were now some way away and far enough from the camp, they stopped.

One of them said, "We're in no great hurry, are we, General? Why shouldn't we sit down here and roll a cigarette?"

"Would you like to try one of my cigarettes? They come from Egypt."

"Maybe. Perhaps they're good. But we like to smoke our own. *Gracias.*"

The general drew out his hip flask and took a very small sip. Then he rubbed his thumbs squeakingly against the flask and offered it to the muchacho who sat next to him. "Have a drink, muchacho," he said amiably. "There's plenty left in the flask for me."

"I'd rather not drink any, Señor General, because if our chief smells my breath and finds that I stink of brandy, he'll give me a crack on the jaw. Isn't that so, *compañeros?*"

"Much worse," answered one of the other two. "He'd just blast a bit of lead into our stomachs if we smelled of brandy."

The general caught the words "Señor General" immediately, for it was the first time he had heard them since his capture. They cheered him, just as a convict is cheered by the news that he is about to be released, because it has been finally established that he was unjustly condemned and will now receive a public and honorable acquittal.

"Your chief must certainly be a very strict tyrant not to allow a muchacho the smallest pleasure," said the general.

"He certainly is. Yet what can we do? We're in his power."

"But whatever do you expect to gain here, muchachos? He and Professor yell '*Tierra y Libertad!*' at you a hundred times a day. But if all the country's destroyed, where will you find the land?"

"That's true, Señor General. We never thought of that."

"And there's something else I can tell you, muchachos. At the moment, admittedly, you've got the advantage. But that won't last long, and soon whole brigades with three hundred machine guns and five hundred heavy artillery will be sent against you, and then not a tuft of your hair will survive. What will you do with your *Tierra y Libertad* when you're all dead?"

"Yes, what will we do then, *compañeros?*" asked one of his escorts. "The Señor General's quite right. But what can we do?"

"You're all three healthy, strapping fellows," went on the general. "I could make good use of you as soldiers, with full wartime pay. That means a lot of money. And when you've served for three or five years, you'd have so much cash that you could easily buy any rancho you fancied. Then you could live in peace and cultivate your land, and everything that you bought would be yours, and no one could take it away from you."

"The Señor General is really right, isn't he, *compañeros?* It's all just as he says. But what on earth can we do?"

"I'll tell you something, muchachos. What are your names, eh? Oh. Good. I'll remember your names. And now listen to me. Why do you have to hang me here? That's murder. And it's a great sin. You can ask any priest. And that won't take you to Heaven, only to Hell. Why do you all want to end in Hell, when Heaven waits open for you? I'm an old man and won't live much longer. You can see that. I'll tell you something. You take me to the nearest small rancho where I can borrow a horse and ride away and live in peace for the rest of my life. Then you go back to the camp and tell your chief that I've been well and properly hanged and that my tongue stuck half a yard out of my mouth. You must go back to the camp, otherwise it'll be suspicious and your chief will send some of his muchachos on horses after us. If not, I could have taken you with me right away, and by tomorrow you could have been soldiers."

The muchachos listened with deep attention.

"But it's better for you to go back and say that I've been hanged. Then your chief won't send anyone after me. And tomorrow or the day after tomorrow, you creep away and come to our headquarters. And then I'll give each of you a hundred pesos."

"A hundred pesos, Señor General?" asked the muchachos incredulously.

"A hundred silver pesos to each one of you. And if you like, you can become soldiers as well. But if you don't want to become soldiers, then you can take your hundred pesos and go home to your villages. I'll also write each of you a letter to the authorities in your community saying that you're good people and that no one must put you in prison because you rebelled. All the other rebels will be shot. But not you."

"What do you say to that?" one asked the others.

And each one replied, "I'm for it."

But the sharpest of the three said, "Señor General, perhaps it would be better if you gave us a paper now so that we can be really sure of getting the hundred pesos."

"Of course, of course," answered the general. "It's only right I should give you a chit. But I haven't any paper. And no pencil. I left that all in my coat and trousers. All I was able to save were my cigarettes and my flask. Don't you trust a general, muchachos?"

"We've been so often betrayed by all sorts of people, generals or not generals," said one, "that we can't trust anyone any more. But we'll do it this time, Señor General."

"And you won't regret it, muchachos." The general got up and added, "Well, let's be on our way, so it won't get too late. It's dark already."

"Don't worry, Señor General, we know the way, even at night. We've been on sentry duty out here."

They marched on for about a quarter of an hour. The path was bad, alternatingly stony, swampy, and densely covered with undergrowth.

Slowly the moon rose, became visible, lighting the way, and then vanished behind tattered black clouds, only to reappear a few minutes later and then to disappear again.

The general groaned. His gait was stumbling and weary. He had been on his feet since three o'clock that morning. What he had suffered on this endless, decisive day, quite apart from the lost battle, would have robbed even a younger man at the close of such a day of all the strength of his legs.

The path now opened up into a clearing.

The general spotted a large stone, went up to it, sat down on it, breathing heavily, and said, "Muchachos, I don't believe I can go any farther. I shall have to spend the night here."

"Then our chief will surely come along and get you early in the morning, Señor General," said one of the men.

"That may be. That may very well be. But what can I do?" He wiped his face and forehead with the dirty sleeve of the ragged shirt he was wearing.

He lit another cigarette.

The half-moon had appeared again for a few minutes.

The general, puffing at his cigarette, looked around, first to one side, then to the other. Wherever he looked, he saw black bush. Only the clearing was open and bright, with light patches of low grass tufts and with dark patches caused by the shadows of these same besomlike tussocks of grass.

In the far distance, in the direction of Balun Canan, the headquarters of his division, there flickered now and again a flash of summer lightning over the black night sky.

Headquarters of the division, thought the general. How lovely and comfortable to be there now. To be sitting in the mess, a battery of bottles of good beer on one side, playing dominoes with Major Fernandez or with Captain Munguia. Captain Munguia, damn it, not worth a dog's turd as a soldier, not worth a damn as a gentleman. But in desperation one could call him over for a game of dominoes. Always comes. The toady.

The general took a deep pull at his cigarette. It glowed, gleaming whitely.

"*Dios mío,*" he exclaimed in a loud voice, and convulsively he shot up from the stone on which he had been sitting. He flung the cigarette away.

"Holy Mother of God, *Madre Santísima!* I never thought of that! Curse and blast it, I never thought of that!" He said this loudly, his voice filled with indescribable horror.

Without meaning to do so, he sank back again upon the stone. He let his gaze sweep across the black wall of the bush, to right, to left, to left, to right, steadily and incessantly, as if his head were moving of its own accord. Then he bowed his body up and down.

Suddenly and with a decisive jerk he ceased these movements and gave vent to a short, hard laugh.

"So that's it, that's what he intended to do to me. Just that. I'd never have believed it of him, never have believed that he'd have been capable of devising anything so treacherous. *Gracias, O Dios mío*, that I realized it in time!"

As if lifted of a burden, he breathed deeply. He took out a fresh cigarette and puffed several clouds of smoke in front of him.

The muchachos showed neither by word nor gesture that they had the slightest interest in whether the general was having convulsions or whether he had been assailed by a sudden, irresistible urge to caper in the clearing like a faun in the moonlight.

As if he had entirely forgotten the muchachos, who now lay stretched out on the ground, though at no very great distance from him, the general began to speak loudly to himself and in a manner he was accustomed to use before a gathering of officers, to whom he had to make a given situation clear.

As he spoke, he puffed steadily at his cigarette.

"What in the hell can I say when I get back to headquarters? They'll all stand around and stare at me. I come quite alone. Quite alone I return, hale and healthy, without a scratch on me. Not having lost a pound in weight. And there I come, dressed like a bedraggled, verminous Indian. I come back without my battalion. Not an officer comes back. Not a sergeant. All dead. Twenty wounded cavalrymen come back, and a few infantry clinging to saddleless mules. But I—I, general of the division, come back weaponless, in rags, without a cut on my face, as healthy and fresh as if from some peace-time maneuvers. That's what he's devised for me. That's why he sent me away with these men whom he ordered to allow themselves to be bribed by me. They? Let themselves be bribed? The ones who hanged Lieutenant Bailleres, and who know that I know it and have witnessed it? They wouldn't let themselves be bribed!"

He turned to the muchachos. "Hey you, will you tell me something if I promise you that in half an hour's time I shall no longer be alive?"

"We might, Señor General," said one of them, without getting up.

"I noticed that your chief talked to you for a long time, talked to you alone, before he sent you off."

"He did."

"He told you to let me go free. Didn't he?"

"Those were our orders. And you, Señor General, can do what you like. Whether you're dead or not in half an hour doesn't worry us. We'll tell our chief that we were pleased to let you know what orders he had given us. He even told us that we could tell you before we let you go."

The general began to brood. Automatically he lit another cigarette. Then he took a deep pull from his flask.

"The nearer a man is to his end, the better he understands the world and the people in it, and he sees the inwardness of all that happens. Who was it said that? I read it somewhere. So he wanted me to get back safe and sound to headquarters. And there I could have told a strange story of how I had escaped from their clutches. And you stand there now, gentlemen, looking at me incredulously. Do you think I'm lying, I, a divisional general? Why are you looking at me like that, Colonel Arizmendi? Because I'm standing alone before you? Because no other officer escaped. Only I? Because only a handful of bleeding, desperate, half-mad men escaped, no one else, while I, the divisional general, am standing hale and hearty before you? Of course, I had to leave behind uniform, money, watch, rings, revolver. Had to dress myself like a ragged Indian in order to get here with a whole skin and in safety. Listen to me, Major Maldonado, damn you! What are you thinking of? Attention! Why are you screwing your eyes up? Can't you look your general in the face any more? What? What have you been swallowing to make you look at me with one eye closed and those twisted lips as if you're trying to grin? Pay attention, gentlemen! You couldn't possibly think—Yes, gentlemen, what is it? You really, actually believe that I gave those filthy Indian swine my money and my uniform and my revolver in order to buy myself free? I, the general of the Petronio Bringas Division? I? *Gracias, caba-lleros. Adiós, camaradas y amigos!*"

The general started up. He stood and shouted at the black wall of the bush, shrilly and yet more shrilly: "*Adiós! Adiós, caballeros! Adiós! Adiós!*"

A hundred times he must have yelled this. He grew hoarse and finally was scarcely able to open his mouth. He snatched at his throat, as though to compel it to obey him. Now he fell into sobbing and soft laughter. Then he came to himself. He collapsed onto the stone and breathed deeply with wide-open mouth.

He felt for another cigarette.

The muchachos were still lying on the ground near him. One offered him his lighter.

When he returned it, he laughed at the muchachos. "I'm drunk, muchachos, drunk, drunk, drunk, that's what I am. Oh, so horribly drunk." He took his flask, set it to his lips, and let the liquid gurgle into him until only a few dregs remained.

He held the flask up against the moonlight. Staring at what was left, he unscrewed the gold stopper again and poured the last drops into his mouth and shook the flask, still holding it at his lips, back and forth, until he had licked out the very last drain.

"Over there, in that corner, muchachos, do you see that beautiful tree? It's a wonderful tree. Seen from here, it looks like a cedar. But whether it's cedar, mahogany, or ebony doesn't matter. Muchacho, give me that rope you're carrying over your shoulder."

He tested the rope in his hands. "The stuff's damned hard and scratchy. A miserable rope. But strong. It's got a knot and a noose already. All the better. Anyhow, I couldn't make a good knot like this one that slips so beautifully and smoothly backward and forward."

He faltered, as he slid the rope back and forth through the loop. "This isn't by any chance the same lasso that scratched my Lieutenant Bailleres's neck this evening, muchachos?"

"The same one, General," said one of the muchachos, with-out displaying any particular interest.

"Then this lasso's had some practice?" The general gave vent to a hacking laugh.

"It's had practice," said the muchacho, as indifferently as before.

"Muchachos," said the general now, abandoning his ironical tone and becoming serious, "I can't give you anything. What clothes I'm wearing are filthy, verminous rags, so torn that even your *compañeros* wouldn't have them and threw them away. I can't give you the flask and the cigarette case because you'll take those things anyway and won't leave them behind. Which is right and proper. All that I can give you are my sincerely meant thanks, given in advance, for something I want you to do. I have never said 'Please' to an Indian. I say to you: please, muchachos, please, when I have breathed my last breath, cut my face away from my skull so that no one finding me will ever know who I am. Will you do that, muchachos?"

"We could certainly do that, Señor General. It wouldn't be any special trouble to us. Nothing very special. In the *monterías* we had to hang living beasts who through some oversight of God's had been given human faces."

"*Mil gracias*, muchachos, for this small favor. Tell your chief he can come here tomorrow morning and kiss my foot, before breakfast."

"We'll tell him that, Señor General."

"Good. In five minutes—or shall we say, ten minutes—come across. Over to that tree. And now once more, many thanks in advance, muchachos."

"*No hay porque, Señor General*. Don't mention it. Farewell, and a good journey. Hurry. Ten minutes, you said. We'll wait that long."

The general was already on his way, swinging the rope in his left hand.

He swayed somewhat as he walked, probably as a result of the hefty libations from his flask. Now and again he stumbled over the wiry grass hummocks.

When he reached the selected corner of the little clearing,

the limpid light of the moon shone full on that wall of the bush.

He crossed himself. Bowed his head. Crossed himself again. Pulled at a cord hanging around his neck and drew out a black square of material embroidered with a cross. He took it in both hands and kissed it.

He crossed himself again.

Then he tested the lasso, letting it slip through his hands, looked upward into the tracery of the tree, and with a decisive swing threw the rope over a branch that extended far out from the trunk into the clearing.

The muchachos glanced indifferently across. One of them said, "I hope he's picked a good strong branch that won't break off. He's as heavy as an old, fat ox. Seems to be holding, the branch. Give us your tobacco."

It was about a quarter of an hour later. In the meantime the three muchachos had gone over to the big tree.

One now came back into the clearing. He squatted and began to wipe his machete dry on a tuft of grass. As he did this, he looked up at the sky. Then he called out, "There's an almighty thunderstorm over at Balun Canan. It's coming this way."

One of the two still over at the tree shouted across, "Say, shall we give him the rope, or what do you think?"

"We don't give anything away," the muchacho who was drying his machete called back to the other two. "It's a fine, useful lasso. Didn't even break with a fat lump hanging on the end of it. Can often be used again, that lasso. Besides, General will make a stinking row if we don't bring the lasso back. You know how he can be sometimes. He'd send us back here to fetch the lasso. It looks as if that damned storm is coming in our direction, and I don't want to have to travel this filthy way again."

"You're right, manito. We'd better bring the lasso back."

"Hey!" the fellow who was in the clearing shouted to his companions under the tree. "Don't talk so much. Let him down now and untie him. He's long stopped gurgling. Hurry up. I'm as hungry as a lame coyote."

16

    Five weeks had passed. It might have been even
seven, eight, or ten. No one bothered to count the
days and weeks. But that it couldn't possibly have been fewer
than five weeks was apparent to the muchachos from the
standing corn in the fields, where the harvest was already well
advanced.

The camp, with its numerous huts, shanties, and lean-tos
which had been built during the past few weeks, had taken on
the peaceful, half-sleepy, half-dreaming air of a typical Indian
village.

Everything necessary to found and maintain a community
was there—forest, open country with good grazing, fruitful
bush land, a broad, never-failing stream of clear, cool water.
The people had corn, beans, and chilies in sufficiency, and a
new harvest was already ripening. They possessed horses,
mules, donkeys, cows, oxen, bullocks, goats, sheep, and even
pigs. Whatever was lacking would be provided by the *fincas*
of the region, either voluntarily or with a little persuasion
from the muchachos' rifles.

Small detachments were always out on foraging expeditions.
They surprised military posts and patrols of the *Rurales*. Now
and again there was a scuffle with armed *finqueros* and their
underlings who had banded together in defense groups to rid
the region of rebels and bandits.

The *finqueros* were convinced that it was only a matter of a
small stray gang of mutinous Indians who had survived after

battles with the Federal troops and who were now wandering about and plundering. Similar petty gangs were always roving around in the Republic, even in the years of the dictator's most relentless rule, when no one dared even to think of rebellion.

Evidently the military authorities in the state were of the same opinion as the *finqueros:* that only insignificant bands, not more than three or four, were infesting the region, and that it was not necessary merely on account of these few dozen bandits to muster large numbers of Federal troops, which would add to the country's costs. The *finqueros* by themselves would deal with these gangs within a few weeks, just as they had done over the last four hundred years.

That was how General, Professor, Celso, and other muchachos interpreted the situation, particularly since, for weeks, not a battalion, not even a company, had marched against them.

"Come here and see what sort of a bird I've caught," said Eladio, bringing into the camp an intelligent-looking *ladino* who was fairly well dressed, but who plainly had not shaved for days.

The man was leading his horse by the reins. Behind him followed a half-grown Indian boy, also leading a horse, while in the other hand he held a rope attached to a mule that was laden with packs and two very shabby leather suitcases.

The new arrival looked around on all sides, but showed no signs of fear. His expression and his gestures said, "Everything will be all right here, and if not, then there's nothing I can do about it."

The visitor was surrounded by a swarm of yapping, barking dogs from the camp, which made it difficult for him to follow Eladio at the speed he was walking.

They came to a great open hall that had a roof partly of palm, partly of long grass, which had been erected in the middle of the camp. This spacious building served as town hall, council chamber, armory, and, temporarily, as a school for grownups and children.

"Professor, these seem to me a couple of fine birds that I've brought you here," went on Eladio. "They didn't come on the direct road, where we've got our guards. They rode past there. But I thought it would be a good thing for you to have a look at the pair of them. I think they're trying to spy here."

"Don't talk nonsense, muchacho," said the *ladino*, laughing. "Me spy here? I've other things to worry about. Believe me. And if you don't believe me, I don't care. With a wretched life like mine, one can only be heartily glad if someone takes it away. A spy? Me? Don't be ridiculous."

He laughed again. Then he said, "I'd rather you gave me something to eat and drink. Since yesterday noon I haven't seen a cake of fresh cow dung, much less a moldy tortilla. That's life, *amigos*. Life, dear God! Give me something decent to eat and you can hang me for all I care, if that's what you want. Only don't hang me on an empty stomach. That would be cruel of you, and you all look so peaceful."

Professor was sitting in the hall with Andreu, both occupied with a book that had recently arrived from a *finca* that had been visited. They joined in with the laughter of the *ladino*, enjoying his salty humor.

There were several other muchachos in the hall, for the hall was never empty, neither during the day and far less at night, when it served as a dormitory for some twenty and often thirty men.

Professor called over to the muchacho sitting nearest to him and told him to fetch from the "camp mother" a good meal for the *ladino*.

"That's what I call friendship, *amigos*," said the *ladino*. "To feed a hungry man in the wilderness is a pious enough deed to make the angels in Heaven blow their trumpets, and even St. Peter will inscribe it to your credit. I'll see to that when I meet him and get a look at his key. I've always worried about that key, whether it's big or small, of iron or silver, whether he's got it hanging by a string or on a golden chain around his neck. And as far as you're concerned, muchachos, I don't care whether you're bandits or murderers or peaceful peasants so long as you give me something to eat."

"I'd very much like to know what this man is, talking only

of hunger and eating and nothing else," said Andreu softly to Professor.

In Professor's eyes a sudden understanding blazed up. He laughed and said, "Oh, I know now what you are. You're no *ladino*. You're no trader."

"Of course not," said the man, "I never said I was, either."

"You're a schoolteacher. And what's worse a village schoolteacher."

"Only a colleague could have guessed that right. It's true. *Profesor rural ambulante*. A traveling village teacher. Every two months I get sent to a different village because the salary the village pays for the school is always enough only for two months. And the last four weeks of those two months are very hard times, and I must be thankful in the second month to get even the half of what I was promised. And then I receive a letter from the Department of Education in which they write me the name of the next village I have to go to. That's sometimes three or four days' journey away—the next village I'm being sent to. And for traveling expenses the Department gives me six reales, quite irrespective of whether my next post is only one day's journey or seven days or eight along these miserable, damnable tracks. Always just six reales. And from that I'm supposed to feed myself, pay for the horse that I hire, pay for the boy who accompanies me and brings the horse back and on top of that the hire of a horse for the boy, who obviously can't walk all the way in this heat; and then there's the hire for the mule that carries my miserable rags and my few books and exercise books, and after that there's the corn for the horses. I'd like the head of the department to show me how to pay for all that out of six reales."

"I know it all," Professor interrupted him.

"You're a professor, too?"

"Was, friend and colleague, was. First in our capital, at a secondary school with an adequate salary. Then down to a primary. Then to a smaller town. Then again to a smaller town, and again to a still smaller town, until finally I landed in the villages."

"But why did that happen? If you start well in a secondary

school, you can easily stick there or else move up to a preparatory and perhaps even as far as a director's job."

"Maybe, *amigo*. That's quite possible. If one keeps one's mouth shut. But I can't keep my mouth shut, and I'll never learn to. That's why I'm here. I certainly won't get any salary here, but I feel at home. What's all that salary worth if you don't feel happy? And if I daren't open my mouth and say what I think, then a hundred pesos' salary wouldn't pay for what I'm losing, piecemeal, in my heart and my soul. A man's neither a beast nor a puppet. I'm still a man. And I can be a man here. We can all be men here. And we'll remain so. And we'll defend it to our last drop of blood against El Caudillo and against that bloody, accursed dictatorship."

Meantime, a plate of food had been brought to the hall. From the way the new arrival devoured and gobbled it to the last crumb and licked every fingertip, the muchachos realized, better than from all his words, that this man had spoken the truth.

His muchacho, too, filled his stomach, which seemed to be as empty as that of the ambulant rural professor.

When the teacher had eaten and sighed with deep satisfaction, he said, "My name is Villalva, Gabino Villalva, at your service. My grateful thanks for the meal."

"And what shall we do with him now, Professor?" asked Eladio, who had brought in the half-starved teacher. "Is he a spy or not? If not, then I'll go back to my sentry post."

"I'll deal with him, Eladio, and you can go back to your post. At all events, it was right of you to have brought him here. One never knows who and what anyone is that comes creeping past our camp."

"So that's it, *amigos*," said the teacher. "You, too, have your troubles with the bandit gangs that are swarming about here and reducing all the *finqueros* to desperation. You're right. Be careful. They're an evil crowd who roam about day and night and give no one any rest. I see you've got a few dozen rifles hanging around. That's necessary in times like these."

General had come in and heard the last few words. "Times

are bad. You're right there, *hombre*. And all the worse since one doesn't know who are the real bandits in the land."

"Well spoken, *amigo*. That's right," said the teacher, turning toward General, who had now come nearer and sat down with the group. "Well spoken. In these times, one never knows who's ruling and who's ruled."

"That's why we say, '*Que muera El Caudillo! Abajo la dictadura!*'" intervened Andreu.

The teacher looked at him. Then he looked at all the others who sat around and watched him leisurely drink his coffee, sip by sip and pensively as if he'd never before drunk such good coffee.

His glance finally rested questioningly on Andreu. "Why do you say 'Death to the Leader! Down with Dictatorship!'? That's what I'd like to know."

"Because we're not free and can't live freely as long as the dictatorship muzzles and oppresses the people," said one of the muchachos.

"What leader and what dictatorship do you mean?" asked the teacher, astonished.

"Every child in the land knows who we mean," said Andreu. "There's no need for you to act so stupid and innocent. You can speak freely here, absolutely freely. There are no informers or police spies here."

Professor, with a mistrustful look in his eyes, said to the teacher, "Now I'd really like to know what to make of you. First you talk one way and then you talk another. What's the truth about you?"

"Have I landed on the moon, or in Africa, or in the middle of China, or where?" asked the teacher, looking at each in turn with a stare of incomprehension.

"Of course we mean El Caudillo, the leader and ruler, Don Prudencio Dominguez. Who else?" called out one of the muchachos.

"I certainly would never have guessed that *amigos*," retorted the teacher. "If you mean the Don Prudencio Dominguez who exploited this country for the last thirty or God knows how many years, you're very much behind the times; it was eight months ago that he abdicated because he couldn't hang on any longer. He's now in London; that's a town in France."

"England," interrupted Professor.

"England, Spain, or Holland, for all I care. Anyhow, he's gone away."

Andreu turned to Professor and said softly, "Many months ago? Then he couldn't have been in power any more when we left the *monterías*."

"So it seems, boy. What a joke!" he said, as if to himself.

"What a heavenly joke!" he now exclaimed aloud and shouted with laughter.

"Joke?" said the teacher. "There's not much to joke about nowadays, not anywhere in this country."

"Who's in power now?" asked Professor.

"That's what I'd very much like to know," replied the teacher. "That's what everyone in the country would like to know, poor and rich, capitalists and workers."

"But there must be a government," interposed General.

"A? *A* government?" The teacher made a wry grimace. "There are now five thousand governments. Five thousand politicians are shouting and yelling, and each one has his own government. There's not *a* parliament; there are ten, twenty, forty, all at the same time. Each state hasn't got *one* governor, but seven or eight, simultaneously."

"Isn't there a party to which the people could rally in order to set up a popularly elected government?"

"There are parties, too. Countless parties. Constitutionalists, Institutionalists, Revisionists, Reformists, Re-electionists, Anti-reelectionists, Laborites, Communists, Communalists, Imperialists, Anti-imperialists, Indo-Americanists, Agrarians, Dominguezists, Separatists, Regionalists, Continentalists, Unionists, and about two hundred more ists. It's impossible to remember the names. Every day new ones crop up, and every day there vanish some that yesterday had the most followers."

"And the army? What's the army doing, then?" asked General.

"In the army not a general knows who's in command, whose orders to obey and whose not. Every general, colonel, and major receives twenty different telegrams a day giving orders, and he doesn't know which one to follow. So he simply sits where he is with his men and draws his pay, no matter who's providing it. Besides, there are now about ten thousand generals who gave themselves the title overnight and then went off with their men. Most of these generals have no more than twenty men under their command. And all these ten thousand generals are at one another's throats, each one claiming to support a different party and the next day fighting the party on whose side he was yesterday."

"Then that is really all that El Caudillo, in nearly forty years of merciless dictatorship, achieved?" exclaimed Professor, jumping up and flinging up his arms as he was wont to do when he switched from an ordinary conversation to a harangue addressed to all. "That's what the dictatorship achieved. That's exactly what everyone who had any understanding of humankind prophesied a hundred times, proclaimed, wrote, printed, and thundered forth, and, for that, was martyred and slaughtered like a sick dog. Chaos. That's what he achieved, that idiot of a dictator, that madman of a leader. He has created chaos. Who are these who have now arisen and are rending the people in all directions? They are the very people who were born under his dictatorship, who were educated under his dictatorship, who grew up under his dictatorship, who were thundered into silence under his dictatorship, who, under his dictatorship, had no rights and no opportunities to think for themselves, to educate themselves in political thought. That's why they're now all shouting. And everyone who shouts is shouting his own tune because he doesn't know any other and doesn't hear any other and can't learn any other. That's just as natural as it is for a stream to run down the mountain and not up."

The hall had filled with men and women, crowding closely together to give all a chance to hear what Professor was saying. The majority, indeed, did not entirely understand what Professor was talking about, because they had not heard the beginning.

"And that's the bitter end of the dictatorship, a disgrace our country will suffer under for a hundred years to come. I have spoken, muchachos."

"Bravo, Professor!" echoed from all sides. "*Abajo la dictadura! Tierra y Libertad!*"

The teacher, plainly inured to such speeches through newspapers, brochures, leaflets, manifestoes, and programs that now flooded the country, so much so that they had now begun to bore him, continued to sip calmly at his coffee and rolled a cigarette from some tobacco a muchacho had offered him.

Professor sat down and said to the teacher, "This is really great news that you bring us. We've been so far out of touch that we couldn't know what was happening in the world."

"Maybe. Only it's not clear to me why all of you here shout so wildly about *Tierra y Libertad*. You've got all the *tierra* you need, and as far as freedom's concerned, it seems to me you've got more freedom here than anywhere else, much more freedom than even I have. In truth, I have no freedom. I'm a slave. A school slave. The head of the department orders where I'm to go, and I have to go there, and if I don't go then I have even less to eat than I do now. And what I get to eat now never fills me, with the exception, of course, of today," he added, with a grin. "I've never been so deliciously and gloriously full in my life. Today and here, for the first time. For that I must indeed say '*Gracias*,' and it comes from my heart. No, really, it comes from my stomach."

He fidgeted around uncertainly on his low seat. "*Bueno*, I think I've just enough time to get to the next ranchito before nightfall. So I must now be on my way, with your permission. Bitter as it is to my soul, I cannot longer impose my scrawny cadaver on your hospitality."

Looking around, he beckoned to the Indian boy who was accompanying him, gesturing to him to bring the horses and replace the packs on the mules.

Professor gazed at him pensively, as if hoping to discover from his face his character and future plans. Plainly satisfied with his scrutiny, he glanced across questioningly at General, Celso, Andreu, and Colonel. Apparently his look was answered in the sense he had expected.

At the same moment that the teacher stood up to depart, Professor prodded him gently on the shoulder. The teacher sat down again.

"Tell me, Gabino Villalva, *profesor rural ambulante*, why don't you stay here with us? Permanently, I mean. We could well do with a second teacher. One for the older children and one for the small ones—and Andreu will help, too. Of course, the salary will sometimes be lacking. That depends on how much hard cash the *finqueros* have at home. But, salary or no salary, I promise you that as long as you're with us, you'll always have a full stomach."

"If that's so, friend and colleague, what do I want with salary? A salary has never filled my belly. Of course I'll stay here. But what's the name of this village?"

"Solipaz," answered Professor.

"Sun and peace. A wonderful name for a village. But, in God's name, who are you actually?"

Professor bent close to the teacher's ear and whispered a word into it. Aloud he said, with an open laugh, "Don't repeat it, even if you're asked. We speak it only in special, very special circumstances. And since we now know, officially know, that the dictator has fallen, what we were has changed to what we now are, officially are, no matter what kind of government finally occupies the palace."

"So that's it. I might almost have guessed it. But times being as they are at present, it's difficult to guess right. Of course I shall now stay here. This is what I've wanted since I was eight years old. And I had to be thirty-seven before I could find you."

He stood up. Drew himself up. Held his clenched fist on high and shouted in greeting, "Muchachos, *Tierra y Libertad!*"

And the muchachos answered with one voice: "*Tierra y Libertad!*"